THE WEAVER

THE VRIX #1

TIFFANY ROBERTS

THE WEAVER

From the moment he first saw her, he knew their heartsthreads were interwoven.

Rekosh had little interest in taking a mate—at least not until he met Ahmya. Small, delicate, and human, she is so unlike his kind. She is a vibrant flower flourishing amidst strangling vines. And he recognizes in her a deep, indomitable determination, inspiring curiosity, and fiery passion. She awakens fierce protective instincts in him and rouses a craving like he's never experienced. He wants nothing more than to declare his feelings for her.

Yet with every breath comes a new obstacle, a new danger, threatening to take Ahmya away from him forever. As they are forced to fight for survival in a hostile jungle, it seems the gods themselves are intent on keeping the two apart.

So Rekosh will weave his own fate.

Ahmya is the mate of his hearts, and she will be his, no matter what he must do to gain her affection. He will claim her, shield her, love her, and entwine their souls so thoroughly that they will never be severed.

Check the author's website for detailed content warnings.

Even as the world unravels around us, we'll always remain bound.

To our readers: thank you for your patience, understanding, love, and support. It means everything to us.
And thank you for dreaming of fucking spider monsters. This spin-off wouldn't be possible without your undying love of our vrix.

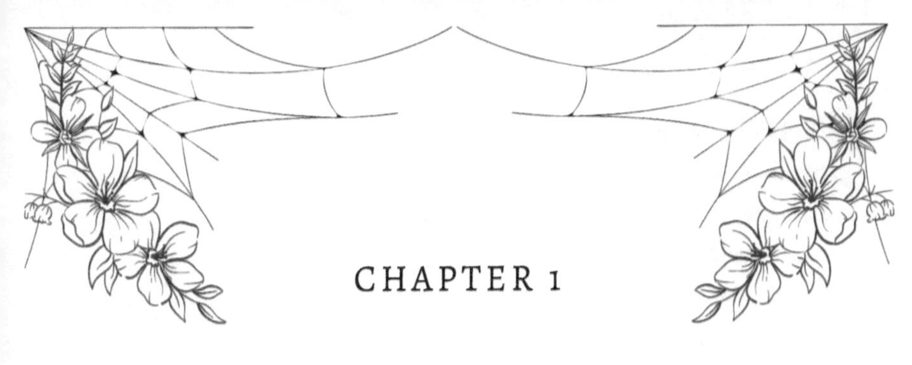

CHAPTER 1

GOLDFLAME TUNNEL BUZZED with activity as Rekosh strode along it. Vrix both male and female, young, old, and everything in between talked, worked, and played. The goldworkers' forges at the far end of the tunnel spread warmth even from this distance, bathing the rough-hewn stone in an orange glow that made the shadows deeper, darker, and colder, but those shadows held no menace. The clanging of tools and the hissing of flames and molten gold echoed off the walls, layering with the vrix voices to create a web of sound.

Certainly, there was no shortage of work to be done here. By decree of Queen Ahnset tes Ishuun'ani Ir'okari, all Takarahl would soon gleam with hints of gold, a display of its dwellers' indomitable spirits. In accordance with that order, The Queen's Fang—the female warriors serving as the city's elite guards— had relinquished many of their heavy, impractical gold adorn- ments, providing abundant material for the goldworkers to refashion.

Ahnset sought to elevate Takarahl as a whole. The practice of enriching only those closest to the city's ruler had died along with the former queen, Zurvashi.

Under Ahnset's leadership, Takarahl was almost unrecognizable. Rekosh knew the tunnels themselves were the same, but the light seemed brighter, the air fresher, and the stone more welcoming than ever.

The silk hanging over the entrances of the dens Rekosh passed rippled with Takarahl's gentle airflow. Like the stone around them, the cloths were dingy and soot-stained, far removed from the vibrant colors they had once been. But at least they were whole.

That struck Rekosh as fitting. Bitter, yet fitting.

A group of females sat in an alcove ahead, painting clay pots. Such sights made Rekosh's spirit swell with joy and pride. He and his friends had not left Takarahl with the intention of changing it forever, but it was undeniably different now.

"...not what I have heard," a female was saying as Rekosh neared them.

"You cannot accept all that Jiras says as truth," replied one of her companions, whose hair hung in a mass of thin braids.

"But he has been told that *her* followers remain in Takarahl. They hide in the burial chambers, in chambers deep and long forgotten."

"And how would anyone know, if the chambers are long forgotten?" demanded the female with the braids. "How would her followers have known to hide there at all?"

Despite his eagerness to finish what he'd come here to do, Rekosh slowed his pace, drawing the hide-wrapped bundle in his lower right hand closer to his body. Many such rumors whispered amongst Takarahl's dwellers had only the most tenuous connection to the truth, but that made them no less valuable. Knowing what other vrix believed was often as important as knowing what was true.

"I do not know," said the first female, "but Jiras said no living vrix has ventured so deep since Queen Takari herself walked the city."

A third female huffed, setting down her pot. Yellow paint stained her big hands. "Only spiritstriders delve so deep, and we should beg the Eight to ensure that those pale things are never roused from the depths."

"There are not truly spiritstriders beneath Takarahl, are there?" the second female asked. "Those were just stories our mothers and sires told to make us behave. Were they not?"

"I know nothing of spiritstriders or forgotten burial chambers," said the last of the group, a larger female with a dark brown hide and pale green eyes, "but I know Urshar, whose broodsister Ulkari was one of Zurvashi's Fangs. She claims her broodsister and the remnants of Zurvashi's followers are out in the Tangle, awaiting a chance to avenge their fallen queen."

Rekosh drew to a halt near the females, taking hold of the tattered end of a piece of silk hung on the tunnel wall. He lifted the frayed cloth as though examining the damage done to it.

But his attention remained on the females' conversation. Such rumors were not new. They'd been whispered in both Takarahl and Kaldarak, and warriors from both cities had been vigilant in the moon cycles since Zurvashi's fall. But Rekosh was far away from his tribe—from Ahmya—now. Even at his fastest, he'd be hard-pressed to reach Kaldarak in less than four days.

The distance between Rekosh and those he cared about while potential threats lingered in the jungle was, at best, distressing.

And he knew of the Fang who'd just been mentioned. Ulkari. He was sure he'd seen her in Zurvashi's army at Kaldarak when the old queen was slain…but he could not recall her fate.

"Queen Ahnset has remained in Takarahl all this time, helping us. Why would her enemies await her in the jungle if they mean to strike?" the first female asked.

"They are too few to attack Takarahl," replied the female with paint-stained hands.

"Is it not whispered that Ketahn crept into Zurvashi's private chambers unseen? He was but one," the female with braided hair said.

"But who else could have done so? None in her Claw could match Ketahn."

Rekosh released the silk and turned to face the females. "It is because Queen Ahnset did not slay Zurvashi."

Their eyes fell upon him, and he recognized the intrigued light in their gazes, the unmasked interest. The faint but enticing scent that wafted from them only added to it.

They desired him.

His human friends called such scents *pheromones*, which were meant to trigger reactions in other creatures. The pheromones exuded by female vrix could often stir arousal in males regardless of their true interest—even if the male despised the female.

And he already felt the first flickers of it even now, much to his irritation.

"So you truly believe Zurvashi was slain by one of those… strange creatures?" asked the female with braids.

"I know she was," he replied.

"How could you *know*?"

"He witnessed it with his own eight eyes," said the green-eyed female as she placed her pot aside. "I know you. You are called Rekosh, yes? The weaver?"

He bowed his head and spread his arms. "I am."

"You are Rekosh?" asked the first female, looking him over again with a glimmer in her red eyes. "You are even more attractive than the stories say."

The scent of the females' want intensified, flooding his senses and making heat skitter beneath the surface of his hide. Despite his disinterest, despite turning all his willpower against the effects, his hearts quickened, and his stem pulsed behind his slit. His claspers pressed subtly but firmly inward, keeping his slit closed.

This was not what he wanted, not at all. These females were not who he wanted.

"One of our greatest warriors," said the female with braids.

"And I have heard he is quite skilled with silk," the green-eyed female added with a trill as she drew herself straighter.

Though he did not regret listening to their conversation, speaking to these females had been a mistake. Rekosh hadn't had time to spare to begin with. He certainly couldn't waste any more of it.

And he had no interest in battling these accursed pheromones.

The female with paint on her hands slid a foreleg toward him.

Rekosh sauntered backward before she could touch him and sketched a bow. "Please, your words are far kinder than I deserve."

She chittered softly. "I recall my elder sister mentioning she used to speak with you from time to time. A handsome weaver from Moonfall... Do you—"

"Is it true you are a friend to the queen?" asked the first female, drawing a glare from the one who'd been speaking.

He'd encountered such interest often enough, and his manner of speaking typically didn't deter it. Now that he'd taken part in Zurvashi's downfall, many females would see him as even more desirable a mate. But none of them had ever caught his eyes. No female had awoken that same weerest in him.

Not until he'd first glimpsed Ahmya, the small, soft, delicate creature who roused every protective instinct within him, whose scent stirred a consuming desire he'd never experienced, whose every touch made him crave more.

Ahmya, who was the mate of his hearts.

Ahmya, who he had not seen in nearly a moon cycle.

Forcing his mandibles to remain in a neutral position, he pressed both sets of forearms together, creating a vertical line, to signal his apology. "Forgive me, but I must go. There are important matters I must attend, and I have already delayed overlong."

The green-eyed female's mandibles sagged. "Must you go already?"

"I must. Perhaps I will return another day. I am sure there are a great many words we could share, many of them far more pleasant than talk of the dead queen."

"Will you offer me your word on that?"

He chittered and retreated a step. "That, I cannot offer. I will not make a vow I cannot keep."

Such as the vow I made to protect Ahmya from harm? The one I failed almost immediately afterward?

The females made disappointed hums as he turned and strode away, but he did not slow, did not glance back. Not even when one of them said, "I wonder if he is doing the queen's bidding."

"Perhaps," the green-eyed female replied. "But I believe he has kin here."

"He does? Who?"

Rekosh strode faster, putting enough distance between himself and the group to ensure that their voices were overpowered by the other sounds echoing along the wide corridor.

What little information he'd gathered still held some value. That made it worth his discomfort, did it not?

Would that I could say the same of what is to come.

Finally, he reached his destination. To most, it would've been just one of many dens along the tunnel with a dingy cloth hanging across the entryway, indistinguishable from the rest. But Rekosh dreaded this place.

Every step of this journey had strengthened his urge to turn around and leave. His limbs were taut, the fine hairs on his legs bristled, and his hearts thumped; escaping the females had not eased his tension. His body was reacting as though he were about to engage in battle.

What could he possibly hope to accomplish here apart from delaying his return to Kaldarak and his tribe?

Apart from delaying his reunion with Ahmya?

He raised the bundle and stroked his thumb across it. His greatest work was within. A creation crafted with such intense passion and artistry that it had nearly been enough to make him give thanks to the Eight.

But the gods had no hand in it. Ahmya had been his inspiration, his purpose. The dress was for her, because of her, and the only thing in all the world that surpassed its beauty was Ahmya herself.

"And still, it will not be enough," he rasped as he lowered the bundle.

There were causes worth fighting for, worth bleeding for, worth dying for. Battling Zurvashi had been worth all the risk and more. But coming to this den…it wasn't a cause, whether noble or otherwise. This wasn't a necessary fight. He didn't need to be here at all.

His mandibles twitched closer together as he shifted his rear legs back. Telok and Urkot awaited him, eager to depart. They all wished to reach Kaldarak before Ivy birthed her broodling, which would happen any day. He should not have kept them waiting this long.

As he began turning away, the silk curtain was swept aside from within the den. A vrix with dull red markings stood in the large opening—a male neither quite as tall nor as thin as Rekosh.

Forcing his mandibles to relax and willing his hearts to ease, Rekosh faced the elder vrix.

Raikarn's eyes widened. A tremor coursed through him from his headcrest down to the tips of his legs, and he drew in a shaky breath through his nostril slits.

Rekosh's fingers flexed. Despite the tunnel's sounds having not diminished, his world was silent and still until words emerged, unbidden, from his throat. "Greetings, sire."

Raikarn rushed forward, rising as he cupped the sides of Rekosh's face and tipped their headcrests together. "Thank the Broodmother, the Protector, thanks to all the Eight!"

His sire's voice was thinner than Rekosh remembered. And though there were old, familiar notes to his scent, they were overwhelmed by the lingering smells of unfamiliar vrix, smoke, and soot.

Rekosh could not decide how he felt about all of that—or whether it made him feel anything at all. He fought the urge to recoil from his sire's touch.

"When they whispered of what Ishuun's brood had done, that you had fled Takarahl with them, and that Zurvashi was hunting you..." A faint growl sounded in Raikarn's chest, more relieved than anything. "But you are alive. You are home."

"Alive, yes." Rekosh drew back, though his sire did not release his hold.

"Come. We need not speak out here amidst the noise." Raikarn all but dragged Rekosh into the den.

Rekosh didn't resist. It was cooler inside the den, and the tunnel's sounds were muted once the thick silk curtain fell into place behind him, but his tension and restlessness did not fade.

Raikarn released Rekosh and stepped back. The two vrix studied each other in the soft blue glow of the crystals on the walls.

"You look worn," said Raikarn, mandibles drooping.

Rekosh chittered. "And you look old, but I had not intended to make mention of it."

"I have spent moon cycles wondering whether you lived, and you jest?"

Anger stirred in Rekosh's gut, sour and hot. "Considering all I have endured alongside my friends, I would say I have more than earned the right to jest."

Huffing, Raikarn turned away. His shoulders sagged, and his movements were stiff as he stepped deeper into the den. "I cannot imagine, Rekosh. I cannot imagine what you have faced, just as I cannot imagine what your mother must have faced."

Rekosh's hearts constricted. He clamped his jaw shut and held his mandibles apart, if only barely.

"Nor can I understand why, even after all we suffered, you chose to face the Tangle, the thornskulls, and the ire of the queen..." Raikarn spun back toward Rekosh, suddenly seeming smaller and weaker, his hide duller. "But it matters not. Takarahl has a new queen, our lives are a little better with each day rather than a little worse, and you are home."

"Sire..." Rekosh shook his head. He wasn't sure what he wanted to say, what he should have said, not due to a lack of words, but an overabundance of them. Years of thoughts he wished he'd voiced fought to get out at once, so numerous and substantial that they formed a lump in his throat.

After taking so many risks, after overcoming so many dangers, this was too difficult for him?

"Your siblings will be thrilled to finally meet you," Raikarn continued. "All they have had are my old stories, and you were always the better spinner of tales, even as a broodling."

Your siblings.

Rekosh stilled his fingers before they could squeeze the bundle any tighter. He drew in a slow, steadying breath. "I am not certain that would be for the best."

Raikarn chittered gently and brought his forearms together in an apologetic gesture. "Forgive me, Rekosh. You have traveled far to return to Takarahl, if the stories are true, and you must be tired and hungry. We have meat stored. Eat with me." He skittered across the den to a shelf laden with clay pots and woven baskets.

Releasing a slow breath through his nose holes, Rekosh studied his surroundings. This was a brood den, spacious and lived in. Fluffed silk and woven blankets lay along one wall, where Raikarn slept along with his mate, Eshkhet, and their broodlings. How old were the little ones now? Five years? Six?

Small playthings carved from wood and stone or crafted with cloth and stuffing lay scattered about the chamber. Again, something clenched around Rekosh's hearts, and a long slumbering pain pierced his chest. The den of his youth had often looked like this, before...

No. Not now, not here.

"Where did she put it?" Raikarn muttered as he rummaged through the containers on the shelf.

Rekosh glanced down at the hide-wrapped bundle in his lower hands. "I have come for a purpose, sire."

"Of course you have," replied Raikarn distractedly. "The threads of fate were tangled, but they have finally led you back to where you belong."

Rekosh's mandibles nearly snapped together. He did not look away from the bundle, not immediately, and his mind's eye filled with the image of what it contained.

The dress he'd woven for Ahmya. The finest work he'd ever produced. When it came to this dress, the threads of fate hadn't been tangled at all. They'd been woven—delicately, intricately, masterfully. And they had guided his hands in this work.

"Oh, they have led me to where I belong. I finally know it," Rekosh said softly.

Raikarn opened a jar and angled it toward the nearest crystal, eyes narrowing as he peered inside. "We have had our disagreements, but I have ever known you would one day understand."

When Rekosh looked up, his gaze fell not upon his sire, but the wide stone slab carved into an alcove on the far wall. The tools and materials arranged atop it belonged to a goldworker. Adornments and pieces of jewelry in various states of completion lay there too, many of them displaying elaborate details and designs.

He could not help but notice that many of the tools on the right side were the same as the tools on the left, just larger. Sized for the hands of a female.

Sized for Eshkhet, the goldworker who Raikarn had taken as his mate ten years ago.

Nothing in this den hinted at the life Raikarn had left behind. Nothing in this den suggested that he'd once performed different work, that he'd had a different mate, that he'd been sire to a different brood. No needles and thread, no loom, no tools for sewing or weaving. No chunks of wood being slowly shaped into clubs or spear hafts by the hands of a seasoned warrior, no shards of blackrock to give those weapons their bite. Not a single one of the toys that had been the favorites of Rekosh's brood siblings held a place of honor upon the many shelves.

Not a single one of Rekosh's early attempts at adorning fabric were upon the wall, displayed with the pride a parent took in their broodling's efforts.

It was as though Rekosh's mother, Loshei, and his brood siblings had never existed.

As if Rekosh had never existed.

"I understand," Rekosh said.

I only hope that you will also understand, one day.

Rekosh carefully tucked the wrapped dress under his arm. He'd come here to show the work to his sire, but thinking there'd been even the slightest chance of it having a positive effect on Raikarn had been foolish. Nothing could ever be as it had been. His sire had found someone to live and work alongside, someone to fill the hole in his hearts in a way Rekosh never could have.

Raikarn covered a basket with a cloth and straightened, looking at Rekosh. "Perhaps we should await Eshkhet. She should return with the broodlings soon, and we may all eat together."

Harsh words stung like venom upon the tip of Rekosh's tongue, but he bit them back. "No, sire."

"No?" Raikarn tilted his head. "Have you anything else to do?"

"I have far to travel before sunfall."

"Far to travel?" The tips of Raikarn's legs scraped the floor as he stepped closer. "You have just arrived, Rekosh. If you still keep your den in Moonfall Tunnel, it is no harrowing journey to reach it."

"I den in Kaldarak. With my tribe."

Raikarn's mandibles spread, and the fine hairs on his legs rose. "Rekosh, this—"

"I have not come to argue, sire," Rekosh said firmly, drawing himself more fully upright. Rage and sorrow roiled within him. "Our threads have long been separated, and we have both been fools not to admit it. You have a place here. My place is elsewhere."

"You came to say that? To say… To say what, Rekosh? That you want nothing more to do with me, with your family?"

Rekosh hissed, mandibles sweeping wide open. "My family is in Kaldarak. Not here."

He emphasized that last word by stomping a leg on the floor.

Raikarn thumped his own chest with a fist. "You are my blood!"

"And is that meant to matter?" Rekosh demanded, striding toward his sire. "When I most needed you, when my world came undone, where were you?"

Raikarn met Rekosh head-on, their chests nearly bumping. "I never left you."

A harsh growl clawed out of Rekosh's throat. "But you did, sire. Here." He tapped a knuckle against Raikarn's chest, over his hearts.

"My world also came undone," Raikarn said through bared fangs.

"Yet instead of clinging to the kin remaining to you, you let your hearts and mind drift away."

"I never—"

"Spare me. I have no desire to hear your justifications." Clenching his jaw, Rekosh raked his gaze across the den, across all the evidence of the life, the family, his sire had made here. "I came to say goodbye. You have found joy and purpose again, and I will not stand in the way of it. Be content in knowing that I have found my own elsewhere and let that be the end of it."

Their gazes locked and held. Untold emotions swirled in Raikarn's eyes, which served as mirrors to the turmoil within Rekosh.

This was not what he'd wanted. Not what he'd hoped for.

But it was exactly what he should have expected, wasn't it?

"I know that light in your eyes, Rekosh," Raikarn said, voice broken and posture withering. "You will not be swayed. For all that I have done or did not do..."

Raikarn shuddered, mandibles twitching. When he reached up for Rekosh's face again, Rekosh did not pull away. Their headcrests touched gently, and Raikarn's fingers twitched on Rekosh's hide.

"I will not have us part with hatred, my son. I will not allow my pride to blind me to the wounds I have dealt you. I am sorry, Rekosh. For the pain I have caused you, for my failures, I am sorry. I pray you will find it in your hearts to forgive me. But if you do not...know that I love you no less for it.

"May their eightfold eyes look upon you favorably, Rekosh.

My hearts swell with pride in you, and your mother's spirit sings with it."

A tremor coursed through Rekosh. He squeezed his eyes shut, as though the darkness behind his eyelids could somehow banish his tumultuous feelings. As though it could calm the storm raging within him.

"Be well, sire," Rekosh rasped before pulling away. He did not look back as he strode out of the den, though he felt Raikarn's gaze upon his back until he'd passed through the entryway.

He offered no attention to the vrix he passed as he stalked along Goldflame Tunnel—not to their appearances, their postures, or their conversations. For most of his life, he'd been fascinated by gossip and rumors, by sifting through the endless information that flowed through Takarahl as surely as the air currents, but he had no interest in doing so now.

His place was not here in Takarahl. Perhaps it hadn't been for much longer than he cared to admit.

His place, his home, was in Kaldarak. He needed only claim it. He needed only find the boldness to declare himself.

To claim Ahmya as his.

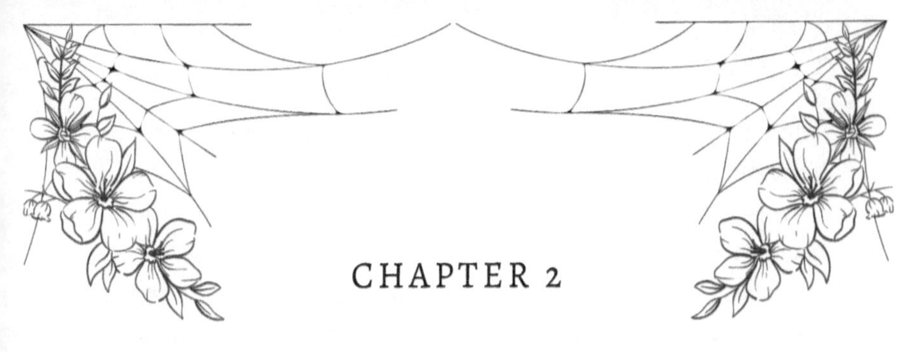

CHAPTER 2

THE DEN OF SPIRITS had long been a sacred place to the vrix of Takarahl. It was said that the spirits of their ancestors resided within the glowing blue crystals that dominated the cavern, instilling it with the wisdom and strength of untold generations. Supposedly, the power and influence of the gods could be felt most purely here.

Rekosh felt none of that as he crossed the massive chamber.

Sunlight streamed down through a gap in the ceiling high overhead and struck the crystals below, reflecting countless times to fill the space with brilliant, scintillating light. Where there were no crystals on the walls, intricate carvings from ages past covered the stone, depicting stories of Takarahl's history back to the time of the city's founder, Queen Takari.

Rekosh had always found beauty here, though it had never moved him to pray or offer sincere thanks to the gods.

But it did feel different now. It was cleaner, brighter. Calmer.

It helped that the immense statue Zurvashi had been building to immortalize herself in stone had been torn down.

That material was being used to create new sculptures honoring the true heroes of Takarahl.

It was another way in which the former queen's shadow had been lifted off the city.

Several vrix were present. Some were studying the carvings, others were paying reverence to the Eight, and a few were basking in the sunlight.

Rekosh set his attention on the tiered stone dais at the center of the cavern. His friends awaited him there.

Urkot reclined on the edge of the lowest tier, all three hands braced on the stone surface. The reflected light from the crystals heightened the contrast between his blue markings and his black hide, and made the big scar on his left side, where his lower arm had been completely torn off, stand out more than usual.

Telok stood nearby, leaning his shoulder against a carved pillar with his arms folded across his chest save one, in which he held his barbed spear. During Zurvashi's reign, weapons of any sort had been forbidden within the Den of Spirits save those carried by her Fangs and Claws. The edict had stemmed from the fear Zurvashi had carried in her hearts—a fear that the vrix she ruled would rise against her.

Ahnset had lifted that rule, encouraging trust rather than fear.

Unsurprisingly, Telok, ever the alert hunter, had found one of the few places in the cavern where the shadows were unbroken, leaving his green eyes and markings to glow faintly in the relative darkness.

A supply-laden bag was slung over his shoulder, and a pair of similar bags, each with a spear, lay beside Urkot on the dais. One set was his, the other Rekosh's.

Telok's mandibles twitched with clear agitation when his eyes fell upon Rekosh.

Bringing his forearms flat together, side-by-side, in apology, Rekosh hurried across the last few segments to reach his friends. "I lost my way navigating the tunnels."

Telok scoffed.

Urkot thumped a leg on the floor. "I feared you had pricked your finger sewing and scurried off to the spiritspeakers for aid."

"You should have run a thread to mark your path," Telok said in his rough, raspy voice.

"Amusing as always, my friends." Rekosh extended his forelegs, brushing one against Telok's leg, the other against Urkot's. The fine hairs on his legs picked up his friends' familiar scents—one tinged with jungle, the other with stone. "Yet I cannot help but wonder if I should have delayed longer."

"Why?" Urkot asked with a grunt. "Eager to have Telok thrash you and drag you out of Takarahl by your hair?"

Rekosh chittered and grasped his bag, dragging it to the edge of the dais. "No. Because it would have granted you both more time to come up with insults that had some bite."

"I will gladly show you some bite, Rekosh, if you take any longer," replied Telok with a snap of his mandible fangs.

Opening his bag, Rekosh reached inside and shifted its contents to make room. "For so skilled a hunter, you certainly lack patience."

Telok huffed. "I have patience aplenty. I simply refuse to spare any more of it for you."

"Then I fear our journey may feel eightfold longer to you." Rekosh carefully tucked the bundled dress into his bag.

Urkot dipped his chin toward it. "Did you show him?"

"That is why I went to his den, Urkot."

"That does not answer my question, Rekosh."

With a chitter, Telok tapped the end of his spear on the floor. "You are caught there, weaver."

"You will need far tighter a net to capture me, my friends." Rekosh closed the bag and secured the tie. Though he didn't intend to say anything more, the words came out anyway. "But no. He... The opportunity did not arise."

Urkot sighed and bumped a hind leg against Rekosh's hindquarters. "Hid away working on it for days, and you could not even show it to your sire?"

Mandibles twitching, Rekosh snatched up his bag and slung it over his head and shoulder. "You are wrong, stoneskull."

"In what way, needlelegs?"

"It is not for him, and I was not hidden away while I worked on it."

"I entered your den eight times in the last few days, and Telok"—Urkot tilted his head toward their friend—"said he did so six more, yet not once did you notice our presence."

"Indeed," Telok said flatly.

"I knew of your presence," Rekosh replied. "I simply chose to keep my focus upon my work."

Based on the way the others looked at him, they didn't believe his claim any more than he did. They knew he'd been utterly lost in the task...and so did he.

"Have you even had a meal since you began?" Urkot asked.

Rekosh let out a heavy breath, turning a palm upward. "I have eaten enough. Such was my focus that I did not feel the need to eat more."

Urkot pushed himself upright and slid down from the dais. "So, you starved yourself and hid in your den. You could well have done that back in Kaldarak."

"I do not have all my tools in Kaldarak."

Telok restlessly scraped the tip of a leg on the floor. "You have every tool you could possibly need there."

With a low growl, Rekosh gestured to his bag. "This is the finest piece of weaving ever to come from Takarahl. It has no equal. Not here, not there. It could not be crafted with any tools but my own. And once I give it to Ahmya, all shall know that both her beauty and her mate are unrivaled."

Urkot chittered. "You are not her mate."

"Yet," Rekosh corrected.

"And you are not unrivaled," added Telok.

Rekosh drew himself taller, squaring his shoulders. "Name my better at the loom."

Mandibles rising in what the humans called a smile, Urkot said, "Ketahn is your equal, at least."

"Ketahn is years out of practice, not that practice would make a difference. It is an insult that any of you even give thought to the possibility that he is my equal."

Telok clicked his fangs. "I do not believe he would agree."

Rekosh huffed. "Because his pride outweighs his honesty."

"He is also your equal in his unwavering focus on this rivalry you two have rekindled," Urkot said.

"Focus is not the word you mean, Urkot," said Telok. "It is obsession."

Bracing his hands on his sides, Rekosh glared at Telok. "No, it is *passion*. Perhaps you will find some of your own one day."

"I am still willing to bite, Rekosh."

"Ah, but you will not." Rekosh lifted his mandibles. "A wound would only delay us further."

"I will refrain not because it would delay us, but because your agonized whining along the way would plunge me into madness."

Urkot crossed his forearms in a sign of the eight—an incomplete gesture, given his missing arm. "Eight shield us from that. We would not survive the journey."

"Yet if we rely upon Telok to speak with us, we would instead die of boredom," said Rekosh.

With a dismissive wave of a hand, the hunter said, "It would be less painful."

"When have any of us been deterred by pain, Telok?"

"Apart from right now?"

"You truly intend to offer the dress to Ahmya when we return?" asked Urkot, the seriousness in his tone breaking through Rekosh's amusement.

"I do."

Again, Urkot chittered, a mirthful light dancing in his blue eyes.

"What is that for, stoneskull? What amuses you?" Rekosh demanded.

"The thought of little Ahmya clad in your silk, so fine and fancy, but with those large black foot coverings all the humans wear."

"*Boots*," Rekosh hissed in English. "They are called boots."

"Yes, those. *Doots*. Always covered in mud. Your silk will look radiant compared to them."

Rekosh's mandibles fell. The jest was clear in Urkot's voice, but he was not wrong. Boots were sturdy foot coverings that had protected the humans' soft feet from countless hazards on the journey through the harsh wilderness between Takarahl and Kaldarak. They were useful.

But they were not elegant, graceful, or flattering. They would stand in complete contrast to the dress Rekosh had made.

And in Ahmya's case, they were overlarge. How many times during their travels had a boot slipped right off one of her dainty feet? If he was going to give her the dress, she needed appropriate footwear to accompany it—appropriate both in function and appearance.

"You have shattered his spirit, Urkot," said Telok. "He had not considered her feet."

With narrowed eyes, Rekosh let out a huff and snapped his fangs. "If you are through throwing barbs, let us depart. My hearts are glad for this journey. We will reunite with our tribe, and I will claim my mate and put to rest any questions of who is the better weaver. Even Ketahn will not be able to deny that my skill is greater."

"That depends upon what skill you speak of, Rekosh," said a female in a deep, warm voice from behind him.

He chittered, mandibles lifting a little higher, and turned to face the newcomer. "Skills, my queen. There are several in which I am your brother's better."

Ahnset, queen of Takarahl, drew to a halt not two segments away from Rekosh and the others. She, along with her brood-brothers, Ketahn and Ishkal—the latter of whom had fallen during Zurvashi's war—were Rekosh, Urkot, and Telok's oldest friends.

Though it had been moon cycles since last she'd donned the gold, leather, and beads the Queen's Fang used to wear, it was still strange to see her without such adornments.

She wore a loose, white silk garment that covered her chest and hung down past her waist, secured with a blue sash around her middle. The humans had referred to it as a *tunic*. It seemed the perfect blend of simplicity, humility, and elegance for one such as Ahnset.

Prime Fang Korahla, consort to the Queen, stood beside Ahnset. Bowing her head, she tapped her knuckle to her head-crest in respect and greeting to Rekosh, Urkot, and Telok. She too had divested herself of the trappings that had once been associated with her position in favor of a tunic similar to Ahnset's. She still carried a war spear, its haft tucked in the crook of a lower arm with its head directed down.

The only gold either female wore was in the form of matching gold bands—one around Ahnset's right mandible, the other around Korahla's left.

"Shall I guess at some?" Ahnset asked with a chitter, her purple eyes narrowing in amusement.

"I would not dare impose by asking you to do so." Rekosh bowed his head and touched a knuckle to his headcrest.

Ahnset slid a foreleg forward, touching it gently to Rekosh's. "You know I do not wish for such formalities between us."

"He cannot help himself," said Urkot, bowing slightly before extending his foreleg to brush against the queen's. "The fluffed silk in his head takes up all the space, so the words simply tumble from his mouth."

Telok pushed himself away from the pillar against which he'd been leaning, offering a similar greeting to the queen. "She knows, Urkot."

"Yes. Ahnset is keenly aware," said Korahla.

"This is a greater honor than we deserve," said Rekosh, taking a step back. "The queen of Takarahl herself here to see us off."

"So you are leaving, then." Ahnset's mandibles sagged. "Foolish as it was, I hoped you might change your minds. There remains so much to be done here."

"We are needed in Kaldarak," said Telok. "Diego said Ivy will birth her broodling soon."

Urkot hummed thoughtfully. "We mean to be there to do all we can to aid them."

"Would that I could be there myself," she replied, voice low and raw.

"We understand, Ahnset," Rekosh said. "I know Ketahn would have you there were it possible, but your responsibility is to Takarahl. And between yourself and Korahla, this city is well cared for. The two of you are more than capable of doing what must be done."

Ahnset turned her head, glancing toward the statues deeper within the cavern. The tallest were the eight stone pillars standing in a circle, each inlaid with eight gemstones—representations of the gods of the vrix, the Eight. At their center was the founding queen, Takari. The new statues were being carved around the base of that monument.

Rekosh knew which of those statues Ahnset was staring at,

knew it by the wistful light in her eyes. He followed her gaze with his own.

A couple of the newest statues were unlike any others in Takarahl, and they stood side-by-side. Two arms, two legs, two eyes. No mandibles, hindquarters, or headcrests. Humans. When Rekosh and his companions had arrived in the city two eightdays ago, the faces of those statues had been featureless, but now they truly resembled the beings they were meant to depict.

The first was the female who'd been dubbed the Once-Queen, whose rein had been the shortest but most impactful in Takarahl's history. Ivy Foster. She who had slain Zurvashi, she who had freed the vrix of this city. She stood with a spear in hand, legs apart, her stance powerful despite her odd shape.

Beside her was the sweet, sickly human who'd been slaughtered by Zurvashi in this very chamber. Ella. She stood tall now, free from the ravages of her illness. Free from the horrors she'd faced here. Hers was the statue Ahnset stared at now.

While Rekosh had worked at the loom, Urkot had spent his time here, shaping those stone faces, correcting the stone bodies, instilling life into the statues. Ahnset had requested his aid in the task not because the stoneshapers of Takarahl lacked the necessary skill, but because none of them had ever seen a human.

Even after that tragic night, the number of vrix in Takarahl who had seen a human could be counted on four hands.

And that was not likely to change any time soon. There'd been talk of bringing some humans to Takarahl during this visit, but though Zurvashi's remaining supporters were few, there was no way to guess how the other vrix would react to seeing the strange little beings.

The first and only human to enter Takarahl had been Ella, and the end she'd met here…

A pang struck Rekosh's chest. Even now, with Zurvashi

gone, no one had fully escaped the effects of her cruelty. Her spirit still haunted the darkest corridors of Takarahl. It would be a long while before she was truly banished, but Ahnset was working hard to accomplish it, and she had already stridden far along that path.

"Would that I could agree, Rekosh," Ahnset said softly.

Korahla shifted closer to her, pressing a leg against Ahnset's hindquarters. "Do not speak so, my queen."

"That you doubt and yet stride onward is exactly why you are Takarahl's best hope," said Telok.

Ahnset let out a heavy breath. "I want Ella's death to have meaning. That is the only way I know to honor her. The only way I know to show how sorry I am, and to claw some good out of Zurvashi's horrid legacy."

Rekosh studied the human statues. It was strange to see them depicted this way—so large and solid, so stiff and unmoving. So silent.

"Ella's spirit is here with you, Ahnset," Urkot said gently. "She knows."

"Such is my hope. I will work to ensure Takarahl will become a place where she would have felt welcomed and safe. It will become a place for everyone."

The hard light in Korahla's green eyes—the light of a veteran warrior protecting her queen—softened as she watched Ahnset. "And you will succeed, my heartsthread."

Ahnset's mandibles rose as she turned toward her mate and leaned close. The females gently touched their headcrests, and their eyes fluttered shut.

The weight of Rekosh's bag was suddenly greater. He had not yet made such a connection, had not yet secured those ties with Ahmya. He had not yet claimed his mate. Now, the dress in his bag seemed more like the tangled threads of fate his sire had mentioned—every moment of his life caught in a jumble, impossibly heavy, impossible to unravel.

When the females separated, Ahnset faced Rekosh and the others. She looked them each in their eyes, finally settling her attention on Rekosh. "I have asked Telok to serve as Prime Claw and Urkot as the queen's stoneshaper. They have refused."

To either side of Rekosh, his friends bowed, gesturing apologetically.

Ahnset waved for them to rise. "I expected nothing different. And though I know you will refuse my request as well, I must ask you, Rekosh."

"I do not believe myself the best choice for either Prime Claw or queen's stoneshaper, Ahnset," Rekosh said.

She chittered and extended her foreleg, playfully bumping Rekosh's. "I would have you as my advisor, Rekosh. You have ever been aware of what the vrix of this city think and feel, and your web of whispers would be of great aid in righting Zurvashi's wrongs."

The weight of fate still dragged down on him. He did not know what those threads would lead him through, but he did know where they would take him in the end—back to Kaldarak.

Back to Ahmya.

"You honor me with such a request," Rekosh said softly, touching a knuckle to his headcrest, "but you are correct, Ahnset. I must refuse. My place is no longer in Takarahl."

"I know, Rekosh. These tunnels will be too quiet without you."

"While Kaldarak will be far too noisy," said Telok.

"I will miss the noise." Ahnset spread her arms, beckoning Rekosh, Urkot, and Telok closer with her hands. When they drew together, she wrapped all four of her big arms around the males in what the humans called a hug. "You are as much my brothers as Ketahn, though we do not share blood."

She tipped her forehead forward, and all three males touched their headcrests to hers.

"And you, our sister," Telok rasped.

"Keep yourselves safe," Ahnset said, her voice rumbling into Rekosh. "Keep our tribe safe. I command it as your queen."

"And we will obey as your brothers," replied Rekosh. "I weave my words into a bond, Ahnset."

"As do I," echoed Urkot and Telok.

"Good." Ahnset relaxed her embrace and straightened, releasing a soft trill as she looked down at the males. "Now go, before I decide to command you to remain."

"May their eightfold eyes watch over you, Ahnset," Urkot said, making his incomplete sign of the Eight.

Ahnset crossed her arms in the same gesture. "And you, my friends. My brothers."

As Urkot and Telok withdrew, the former collecting his bag and the spears from the dais, Rekosh leaned closer to Ahnset, lowering his voice. "A final whisper before we depart."

At Ahnset's gesture, Korahla also moved close, eyes intent upon Rekosh.

"There are fresh rumors of Zurvashi's followers hiding in the burial chambers," he said.

"We have searched the burial chambers thoroughly, and Archspeaker Valkai and her spiritspeakers remain vigilant," said Korahla, "but we will look again."

"There are also whispers of her followers in the Tangle," he continued, "as we have long suspected. These are said to come from Urshar, the broodsister of a former Fang called Ulkari. She claims Ulkari is in the Tangle with other followers of Zurvashi."

Korahla hummed, the sound low and troubled. "I know of her. We will determine if Urshar speaks from knowledge or speculation."

"Thank you, Rekosh," said Ahnset. After a final brush of forelegs and a lingering meeting of their eyes, she pulled away.

Rekosh accepted his spear from Urkot, and the three males set out.

The first time Rekosh had left Takarahl for more than a few days had been to fight in Zurvashi's war against Kaldarak. He'd been young, eager to experience adventure and glory with his friends. Eager to see the depths of the Tangle with his own eyes after hearing stories of its beauty and perils for years.

The second time had been when he'd joined Ketahn at the pit. When he'd given up his ties to this city to help his oldest, closest friend. He'd been more cautious then, but he'd not been able to deny his excitement despite the vast unknown stretching out before him—and the fury of the former queen blazing at his back.

This time was different. He was leaving not with a vague sense of his destination, but full knowledge of it. He knew exactly where he was going and exactly what he would do when he arrived there. This was no adventure into the unknown...at least not in the way his prior journeys had been.

He glanced around the Den of Spirits again, absorbing the serenity it had gained by being purged of Zurvashi's taint, admiring the brilliance of the crystals. Perhaps his ancestors did dwell here in spirit, but Rekosh's future was beyond Takarahl.

It awaited him in Kaldarak.

"Tell Ketahn I will visit soon," Ahnset called, her powerful voice echoing through the cavern.

"We shall," Rekosh replied over his shoulder.

"Ahnset," Korahla intoned.

"Soon, Korahla. Takarahl endured without a queen before. Surely it can survive an eightday or two without its queen again, especially if you are here to oversee it."

Korahla growled, and the end of her spear clacked on the floor. "I will not be here to oversee it, Ahnset. The city will survive an eightday without its queen, but *I* cannot survive without you again."

Rekosh's chest tightened, and his hearts stuttered.

He was not going to waste another moment. He'd waited

long enough, had delayed long enough. When he returned to Kaldarak, he would make the foot coverings to finish his mating gift, and the instant the final stitch was in place, he would present the garments to Ahmya.

He would claim his mate before all, and he would not spend another day apart from her.

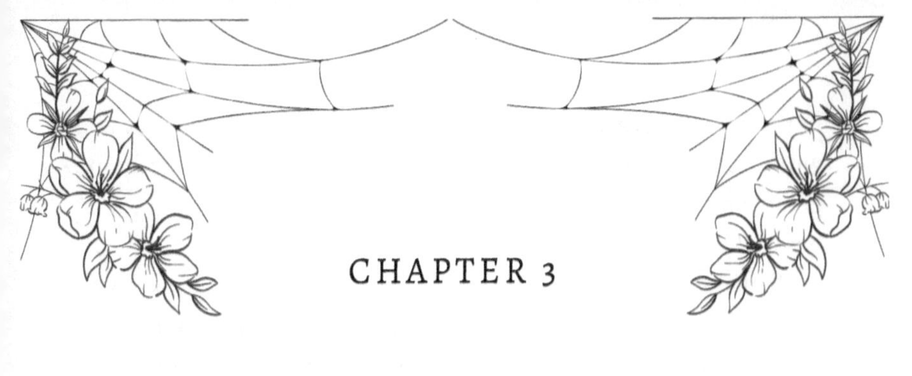

CHAPTER 3

WITH HELD BREATH, Rekosh pressed the tip of the bone needle into the silk. His whole world was silent and still but for his fingers and that needle. This was the moment. After more than an eightday of toil in Takarahl and three days more work here in Kaldarak, his vision was finally about to be complete.

The needle pierced the fabric. He pinched it between forefinger and thumb and drew it fully through. His hearts thumped as he carefully pulled the fine thread taut, tied it off, and trimmed the excess with a small blackrock knife.

Rekosh slowly released his breath through his nose holes. Somehow, that only made his chest tighter. His fingers ached and his hands trembled as he set the needle and thread aside. Angling the tiny foot covering, he studied the lacy embellishments he'd just finished attaching around its opening.

His mandibles rose. The white silk was strong and durable, and the bottom of each covering was reinforced with thick, supple leather. Pleasing to the eye and capable—just like Ahmya.

He slid his fingers further into the shoe and spread them. It was snug just where it should have been. Rekosh could only hope that his measurements were correct. He'd had only guesswork and the memory of how his hands fit on Ahmya's body to go by, and his opportunities to touch her had been limited even before his return to Takarahl.

Setting the foot covering beside its companion, he took hold of the dress and lifted it. The sunlight coming in through the window of his den struck the garment, setting off hints of color in the undyed silk.

The material was so finely woven that it was sheer, making its intricately stitched adornments stand out. Flower and leaf patterns ran across the silk, placed with consideration as to what part of Ahmya's body they would cover—like those tender mounds of flesh humans called *breasts*. The flecks of white crystal he'd sewn into the patterns caught the light and set the garment aglow as he turned it.

The dress was lovely, and, at a glance, exceedingly delicate. But much like the female he'd made it for, the garment was far tougher than appearances suggested.

He hadn't been boasting when he'd told his friends that this was his finest work. Neither Takarahl nor Kaldarak had ever seen its like, and it was the perfect gift for an alluring little creature whose kind was also unlike anything the vrix had ever seen.

"No more waiting," he said.

From the instant he'd first seen her, Rekosh had been drawn to Ahmya. Her appearance had intrigued him—small and lithe, with soft, pale skin. She was different from his kind, his opposite in many ways, and he found such beauty in it. Such beauty in her strange, rolling brown eyes, which glittered in the sunlight, in the silken shimmer of her black hair, in the malleability of her lips when they curled into a smile or fell in a frown. In the light, lyrical sound of her laughter and the soothing gentleness of her voice.

His want for her, his *need*, had grown day by day, and it was becoming increasingly difficult to control his instincts. Everything inside him demanded he wrap her in his silk and claim her as his mate.

And his recent visit to Takarahl had only further proven to him that the time had come.

Zurvashi was gone, Ahnset ruled Takarahl, the humans had settled in Kaldarak, and peace had been made between the two vrix cities.

Rekosh would wait not a moment longer to claim his little flower.

Mindful of the decorative stitching, he folded the dress and laid it on a large piece of cloth. Folding the cloth over the dress, he plucked up the tiny foot coverings and set them atop it before wrapping the items into a neat, snug bundle.

In his mind's eye, he saw his long, claw-tipped fingers sliding those foot coverings onto Ahmya's feet, saw her remove her human clothing to reveal the soft, smooth flesh beneath before she pulled on the dress, saw the sheer silk—*his* silk—caress her skin, and—

No. I will not imagine. I will see it myself with all eight eyes and both hearts.

With his lower arms, Rekosh clutched the bundle to his abdomen and rose fully, stepping back from the table. He brushed aside the many-colored pieces of silk and bundles of dried flowers—the latter of which had all been gifts from Ahmya—hanging from the ceiling as he strode to the doorway. The scents of those flowers, though faded, filled his nose. As sweet as they were, they could not compare to the only fragrance he longed to have in his den.

Ahmya's fragrance.

Soon.

The dress would demonstrate his skill, declare his intentions, and convey his feelings, his want, his passion and dedication. It would speak all the words he'd not yet dared to say.

Sweeping open the heavy cloth hanging across the doorway, Rekosh stepped outside.

Warm, pleasant air flowed over his hide, redolent of growing plants, roasting food, and mist from the nearby waterfall. Though he and his companions had lived here for only a few moon cycles, he'd greatly missed its air while he'd been away.

Towering trees with lush leaves surrounded him, their trunks stretching both above and below. Kaldarak's buildings stood upon platforms built around the tree trunks and atop the thickest boughs, their walls and roofs crafted of interwoven wood, leaves, and silk. A network of bridges connected the platforms in a weblike pattern.

When the shadowstalker vrix of Takarahl had made war on the thornskulls seven years ago, they'd often spoken of striding to Kaldarak and burning it to ash. But by the time they'd reached this side of the mire that separated the territories of the two cities, Rekosh and his friends had all but lost their drive to do so. Their eyes had been opened. The lives of their companions, their friends, had been thrown away for the queen's greed.

Zurvashi had begun the war to seize the areas where mender root grew in abundance—not because of the root's healing properties, but because it could be used to make her favorite shade of purple dye. It didn't matter that the thornskulls had freely traded the roots with the shadowstalkers. The queen had decided that she needed to seize those grounds and hoard the root for herself.

Urkot had lost an arm, Rekosh, Ketahn, and Telok had collected countless scars, and Ishkal, Ketahn's broodbrother—along with so many other shadowstalkers—had died, all so Zurvashi could hang purple silk from her belt.

Having obtained what she'd wanted, Zurvashi had grown disinterested in making war on the thornskulls, and had withdrawn her army before they could march on Kaldarak. Rekosh doubted that she'd known how many of her warriors had lost their will to fight, doubted she'd known how many of them had been ready to abandon her cause and go home.

But that knowledge wouldn't have made a difference. The queen had only ever taken her own feelings into account.

He never would've imagined he'd see this place, much less that he and his companions would live here in peace and friendship with the very vrix they had so brutally battled years before. Yet he already felt more at home in Kaldarak than he had in Takarahl for a long, long time.

Rekosh navigated Kaldarak with ease. By now, he could've gone from his den to Ahmya's even with his eyes shrouded, moving only by touch and memory. How many times had he made this trek? How many times had he watched over the female he yearned to make his, speaking every word but those his hearts urged him to share?

Though he greeted the thornskulls he passed as he traveled, he did not stop to make conversation as he normally would have.

No whispers on the web today. No gossip, no rumors, no amusing stories. Each step was faster than his last, carrying him with increasing speed toward his destination.

Toward his destiny.

During his visit to Takarahl, he'd been painfully aware of the threads of fate, which had been pulled taut despite remaining tangled. But as he and his friends had made their return, he'd sensed those threads winding together in harmony. They'd formed a rope infinitely stronger than any individual thread.

A tether leading him directly back to Ahmya.

The arrival of Rekosh and his tribe had led to an expansion of this city. Skilled thornskull crafters had built three new platforms on one of the massive trees, connecting them to the rest with bridges made of thickly woven silk cord. Sturdy steps linked the platforms to one another, making them easy for the humans to travel between.

The lowest, widest platform held the two largest structures. One was a place where the humans could gather to share meals and words—a place to *hang out*, as they said. Beside it was the den shared by Will and Diego, which was nearly thrice the size of the other human dens. That size was necessitated by its dual purposes as both a living space for a mated pair and a place of healing, where they tended to humans and vrix alike.

The highest tier held Cole's den, which stood out thanks to the large wooden deck he'd built around it. Between the deck's low railing with its carved posts and the chairs and table he'd fashioned to occupy it, nothing else in Kaldarak looked quite the same.

But it was the middle platform that always caught Rekosh's attention, with its three small dens—Callie's on the left, Lacey's in the middle, and Ahmya's on the right, where the platform flared out and grew more spacious.

His hearts thumped as he looked toward her den. She was outside, standing with her back to Rekosh and strands of her long black hair fluttering in the breeze. Only her head and shoulders were visible from his vantage.

He quickened his pace, bounding across the rope bridge to reach the human platforms with the gift tucked securely against his abdomen.

Rekosh had gone an entire moon cycle without seeing or speaking to her, and much longer without declaring the claim he'd felt in his hearts for so long.

He raced across the lower platform and up the stairs to the next. He didn't even glance at Callie and Lacey's dens as he passed them, keeping his eyes forward in anticipation of the moment when the platform's gentle curve would bring Ahmya back into view.

Words tumbled through his mind, forming a hundred things he could say to her, a hundred ways to make his claim. But which were the right words? Which would truly express his yearning, his adoration?

Could he even properly express his feelings in her language?

Then his gaze settled upon her, and his heartsthread thrummed, casting aside all his doubts.

His *vi'keishi*—his little flower—who shone as brightly as the sun.

She was facing her den, arms crossed over her chest, with one hip cocked and her lips curled in amusement.

Rekosh's mandibles twitched upward in a smile, but they fell when his gaze ran over her body. Rather than a blue jumpsuit or the white shirt and shorts she and the other humans normally wore, she was dressed in bright pink silk—one piece wrapped around her chest, revealing her stomach, another tied around her waist and hanging to her knees.

He clenched his fingers, pressing his claws against his palms, and only barely held back a growl. He longed to tear that silk from her body not because it was inferior, which it certainly was, but because it wasn't *his*. She deserved to wear only the finest silk.

She was meant to wear only *Rekosh's* silk.

Ahmya laughed. The light, musical sound chased away Rekosh's tension, soothed his spirit, and tugged directly on his heartsthread, beckoning him to her a little quicker.

Calm yourself, Rekosh. Patience. She is yours to claim, and she will never again wear anyone's silk but yours.

As he neared Ahmya's den, movement from the left caught his attention. Rekosh stilled.

Cole was kneeling in front of the window, holding the ends of a silk rope that was looped around a halved log. A second rope was tied off around the other end of the log, suspending it from a framework of thick branches that jutted out from the top of the window.

"This good?" Cole asked in English.

"A little higher," Ahmya said.

"You said that last time, and then it ended up being too high!"

Last time? How often had Cole visited Ahmya during Rekosh's absence? What else had the male human done for her?

She laughed again. "Not my fault you yanked it too hard."

Cole snickered. "No such thing as yanking it too hard."

"Oh, you're so gross."

Rekosh tilted his head. He knew their words, but Ahmya's tone implied deeper meaning, which humans always seemed to weave into their language.

And from what he had observed, they seemed most fond of using unrelated words to suggest—

"I'm just a man with basic human needs. It's not like I'm asking anyone else to yank it for me. Unless you want to—"

Face reddening, Ahmya jabbed a finger at the male. "Stop right there! It's never going to happen, Cole."

To suggest *mating*.

Though Rekosh did not fully understand, the humans were able to twist seemingly any word in their language to imply something sexual. Based on their tones—and Ahmya's reaction —that was exactly what Cole was doing now.

Heat flared in Rekosh's chest and skittered outward beneath his hide. Squeezing his fists, he closed the distance between himself and the humans.

"Aw, come on," Cole continued. "I can't hel—"

"I will yank it," Rekosh growled.

Both humans started, with Ahmya drawing in a sharp breath, and Cole uttering a curse as he fumbled to keep hold of the small log.

"Shit, man!" Cole jerked his face toward Rekosh. "You scared the hell out of me."

"Rekosh!" Ahmya exclaimed with a bright smile, flashing her flat, white teeth. "Did you just get back?"

"No," Rekosh replied as gently as he could manage, extending a foreleg to brush along Ahmya's bare calf. Her alluring scent teased him.

But neither the sweetness of her scent nor the softness of her skin quenched the fire inside him. His fingers squeezed the bundled gift, his mandibles twitched closer together, and his hide bristled. Tension coursed through his limbs. Though he longed for nothing more than to hoist Ahmya against his chest and carry her to his den, Rekosh glared at Cole.

The tufts of fur over Cole's eyes, his eyebrows, knitted together. "Uh…hi?"

"Did you hear my words, human?" Rekosh extended his upper hands, splaying his fingers before hooking his claws. "I will yank it."

Cole shuddered and let out an unsteady laugh. "Going to go out on a limb and guess that you don't even know what *it* is."

Rekosh strode closer to Cole, ignoring the rumbling in his chest. The human laid the halved log on the platform and pushed himself to his feet.

"I know it cannot be yanked too hard," Rekosh said.

Cole's laughter was more confident this time. "So what is it then, man?"

"Show me. Then we will learn if you speak true."

Shaking his head, Cole ran his fingers through his yellow hair. "Rekosh, it was a joke about—"

"The rope," Ahmya said hurriedly as she stepped up beside Rekosh, her cheeks bright red.

Mandibles drooping, Rekosh gazed at her. "The rope?"

She nodded and pointed at the wooden framework. "He was just joking about the rope he's using to hang the *planturr*."

"Sure I was," Cole said with a chuckle, rubbing the short hairs on his jaw.

Rekosh looked from Ahmya to the halved log. It had been hollowed out to form a basin with a few small holes through the bottom. "I know plant, but what is *planturr*?"

Cole crouched and lifted the log, laying it across his thighs. "It's for growing plants. Toss in some dirt and bury your seeds. These"—he pointed to the holes—"are for *draynidge*. I got the idea when I found a natural hollow inside a log I split, and I figured Ahmya might like it."

She smiled. "I love it. It was really thoughtful of you, Cole. Thank you."

The hairs upon Rekosh's legs rose.

This planter was a gift—a handcrafted gift, from a male to a female. Paired with their talk of *yanking it*, which Rekosh knew was not about rope, this could only be interpreted in one way.

Cole was attempting to claim Ahmya.

He was challenging Rekosh.

Cole grinned. "No problem. I've got nothing but free time and wood out here, so I can make more if you want."

Growling, Rekosh gnashed his mandibles. "She does not need your wood, human."

The male stood, tucking the planter under his arm. "That one's so easy I'm not even going to say anything, out of respect for Ahmya. And because you're clearly in a bad mood. You have a spool of thread unravel in your bag on the way home or something?"

"Did you stuff your head with wood dusts?"

"You mean sawdust?"

"It cannot be seen between your ears."

"Not what sawdust means, man. Maybe take a moment to chill?"

Rekosh snapped his fangs. His hearts pounded, forcing prickly heat into his limbs.

A challenge was something to face head-on. A challenger was someone to be crushed. The only claim that would be made upon Ahmya was Rekosh's, and he would refute any other with fury and ferocity.

"Is everything okay, Rekosh?" Ahmya asked. Though she didn't touch him, she moved close enough to Rekosh that he felt disturbed air flow across his hide, and his fine hairs absorbed her scent.

He drew in more of that fragrance through his nose holes and turned his head toward her. Concern dwelled in the crease between her brows, in the depths of her brown eyes, in her subtle frown.

I am not going to battle a human. I am not going to harm a member of my tribe.

"What is not okay will be in a small time," Rekosh replied. "Soon."

"Aaaanyway…" Cole rocked back on his heels before shifting the planter into his hands. "Going to go ahead and finish this up if that's okay with you, Rekosh?"

"I will help." Rekosh snatched the planter out of Cole's hands and held it up to the window, ignoring the other male's protest. He looked at Ahmya over his shoulder. "Here?"

"Thanks," Cole muttered.

Grinning, Ahmya stepped back to observe. She lifted her hands. "Just a little higher."

Rekosh eased the planter up, moving it barely a threadspan at a time.

"There!" Ahmya called, thrusting her palms out. "Perfect."

Chittering, Rekosh raised his mandibles in a smile and turned it toward Cole.

"Just keep it still, you *smuhg bassterd*," Cole grumbled as he looped the ropes into place.

Though Rekosh held his arms utterly still, his eyes moved freely, following Cole's fingers. "Your knot is ungood."

Cole glared at Rekosh and tugged the knot tighter. "Ungood isn't a word."

Rekosh barely suppressed a growl. Why did the humans' language have to be so unnecessarily complicated, so inconsistent? "I have seen broodlings make knots better than this."

"Yeah, well you're more than welcome to—"

"Hold." Rekosh shifted the log toward Cole, who grasped it with a blank expression on his face. Rekosh's hands worked without need for thought, tying off the rope with an elegant but strong knot before untying and resecuring the other rope to match.

When he was done, Rekosh stepped back. Cole did the same, releasing the planter to let it hang. The log swayed gently, almost imperceptibly, in the breeze.

The human male braced his hands on his hips. "Looks pretty damn good."

Ahmya ran her fingers along the top of the log. "Thank you. I can't wait to grow something inside it."

Tilting his head, Rekosh regarded the planter. His knots were the finest part; nothing else about it bore any elegance or refinement. Now that Rekosh was back, Cole's attempted claim was meaningless. There was no competition here.

"Thank you for helping, Cole," said Rekosh. "Safe journey to your den."

"Wow. Did you just tell me to fuck off?" Cole folded his arms over his chest, the corner of his mouth lifting in an amused half smile.

"Not *fuck*," Rekosh growled, pointing toward Cole's den. "Go."

"Easy guys," Ahmya said, placing herself between them. "We're all friends, right?"

Rekosh clenched his jaw and folded his arms across his chest. It took a surprising effort to keep from clacking his mandible fangs at Cole.

Cole brushed his hands off on his pants. "I'm totally cool, Ahmya."

She looked at Rekosh again. "Are you sure you're okay? Did something happen?"

Cole's smile stretched across the rest of his mouth. "Pretty sure it has more to do with what *hasn't* happened."

By that mirthful light in his eyes and the teasing tone of his voice, Cole's implication was apparent.

Rekosh wasn't sure whether to be angry that Cole was implying mating again or angry that he was right.

"Lighten up, man." Cole patted Rekosh's shoulder.

Rekosh glanced at the human's hand. "You are right, it is about what has not happened. I have not yet dropped you from Kaldarak. I am curious what would happen."

Narrowing his eyes, Cole tilted his head. "Human go *spuhlat*, is what would happen. Look, I'm used to a friendly death threat from Ketahn and Telok every now and then, but it's not usually your thing. So"—Cole lifted his hands, palms toward Rekosh, and took a step back—"I'll just leave you to it. We'll talk when your, uh…balls aren't so blue."

"Cole!" Ahmya gasped.

"Oh, that's right. They're not blue, they're red. Same color as your face right now, Ahmya."

"Oh my God," she groaned, covering her face with her hands. Her next words were muffled. "Just go, please. Before I push you over the side myself."

Laughing, Cole walked away, turning after a few steps to say, "Maybe if you two finally figure your shit out, you can throw me over together. It could be your first *dayt*."

Chest rumbling, Rekosh advanced toward Cole. Though the human was retreating, Rekosh's instincts remained on alert, and they insisted this was a challenge even if he knew at heart that Cole was only teasing. "If I throw him now, will you tell me what his words mean, Ahmya?"

She lowered her hands and glanced up at Rekosh, offering him a smile, but she didn't hold his gaze. In fact, she seemed to look everywhere but at him. "So…you've been back for a little while then?"

He released a long, slow breath as he studied her. The bundle clutched in his lower hands felt so much heavier in that moment, its weight only increasing as that internal fire shifted from rage to something softer but no less intense.

"Three days," Rekosh said. "I was… I had much to attend." He brought his upper forearms together. "Forgive me. I should have come to you more soon."

Finally, Ahmya tipped her head back and met his gaze. "It's okay. You don't need to apologize, Rekosh. It's just when I saw that Urkot and Telok were back, I wondered if you had stayed in Takarahl since you were nowhere to be seen."

His mandibles rose. Strange how naturally that expression came to him. It was not so profound a look on a vrix face, perhaps, but when humans smiled, when Ahmya smiled, their features were transformed.

And he'd gone much too long since he'd last seen her smile.

Since he'd last seen her smile at *him*.

"I could not stay. My place is here, my tribe is here." Rekosh stared into her eyes. Their warm brown was so expressive, so deep and inviting. "You are here."

Ahmya's eyes flared. She tucked a loose strand of hair behind her ear with a strained laugh as she dropped her gaze. "Well, where else would I be?"

A thoughtful trill sounded in Rekosh's throat. "You were to be in Xolea, and I was to be in Takarahl. But we are here now. Together."

She peeked up at him. "Don't you…don't you miss Takarahl? You lived there your whole life."

"Do you miss Earth?" he asked gently.

Ahmya drew in a slow, deep breath, and again looked at her surroundings. "Sometimes. There are some things I miss." She met his gaze, and her smile returned, this time softer, warmer. "But not enough to want to go back. I love it here."

Rekosh curled his fingers tight to keep from reaching for her. "I feel the same about Takarahl. It is more good—better—here, where I can see the sky and sun. Where I can see...flowers."

Though her cheeks retained their pink stain, Ahmya did not look away from him this time, and Rekosh did not miss the flicker of delight in her eyes.

"But don't you have family there who will miss you?" she asked.

Rekosh's hearts stuttered, and something coiled tight around them. "Only Ahnset."

"We all miss her." Ahmya folded her hands against her belly. "But...I'm glad you made it back safely."

His chest swelled, flooding with warmth.

My female is happy to see me.

His eyes dipped to follow her hands. A trail of small pink scars ran across her stomach, disappearing beneath the silk of her skirt; marks of his failure to shield her from danger.

That warmth faded as quickly as it had come.

Had Ivy been any slower to react, Ahmya would've been killed by a firevine. The plant's tendril would've wrapped around her slender throat, piercing her flesh with its venomous thorns, and taken her from Rekosh right before his eyes.

Had I been faster, I could have spared them both from harm. Had I been more observant...

Never again.

He extended one of his upper arms and took her hand, guiding it away from her belly before curling his fingers closed around it. Her hand was so small within his own.

Rekosh drew her closer. "Ahmya, I must share words with you."

"Words? What...what kind of words?" She chuckled nervously. "Aren't we sharing words right now?"

With her hand in his, he felt her faintly trembling, and almost swore he could feel the fluttering beat of her heart. His hearts thumped faster in response. He raised the bundled dress a little higher, but he did not yet offer it to her. "Words from my heartsthread, *kir'ani vi'keishi*. Words—"

"*Diego!*" a vrix shouted in a deep, booming voice.

Rekosh's fine hairs rose, and his head snapped toward Ketahn's distressed call. Ahmya withdrew her hand from his and turned to look as well.

Ketahn was racing across a rope bridge, moving toward the human platforms, with Ivy clutched in his arms. Rekosh had never seen anyone traverse Kaldarak with such speed; even the wild swaying of the bridge beneath Ketahn's legs did not slow him.

"What's wrong?" Ahmya asked. "Is it the baby?"

"I do not know," Rekosh replied.

It had to be the broodling finally coming. Because if it was something else, if Ivy was ill or injured, or...

When Ketahn reached the solid platform beneath Rekosh and Ahmya, his legs carried him even faster. He called for Diego again before barging into the human healer's den. Muffled voices rose from inside the den, but Rekosh could not understand their words.

"What's going on?" Cole called from his deck above.

Callie ran across the platform, stopping beside Rekosh. "Was that Ketahn yelling?"

"I think it's the baby," Ahmya said. "Diego said it could be any day now."

"Already?" Cole asked as he briskly moved down the steps from his platform.

Will rushed out of the den below. The dark-brown-skinned male was dressed only in pants, and his chest and shoulders heaved with his rapid breaths.

Cole leaned over the edge of the platform. "Will! What's going on?"

Will looked up. "Baby's coming. We need all the cloth you guys can spare."

"On it!" Callie said, running toward her den.

Ahmya and Cole also hurried to their dens, leaving Rekosh alone.

At least until Lacey emerged from her den, brows drawn together. She looked at Rekosh. "Why's everyone yelling?"

"Ivy's broodling is coming."

Her green eyes widened. "For real? *Holee* shit!"

When the other humans returned, Rekosh accompanied them to the lower platform, where Will took the cloth they'd gathered before going back into his den. There were others arriving now—curious and concerned thornskulls who'd heard Ketahn's shouts.

Rekosh bade one of them inform Telok and Urkot, while sending another to report to Kaldarak's *daiya*—their queen—Nalaki, and her mate Garahk.

The humans stood a few segments away from the entrance of Diego and Will's den, from which muffled voices and cries could be heard.

"Isn't this too soon?" Lacey asked.

"The vrix said their eggs take four months to hatch," Callie replied. "And from what Ivy said, it's been about that long since she thinks she got pregnant."

"Yeah, but it's nine months for humans," said Cole. "Shouldn't it be like...six and a half for this? Meet in the middle?"

"The days here are longer than on Earth," Ahmya said. "So it's technically been longer."

Callie sighed and shook her head, her long, thick, curly black hair swaying. "And that's not how any of this works anyway, Cole."

Lacey crossed her arms over her chest. "All of this is unknown for us."

Ahmya pressed her fists against her chin as she cast a worried look toward the den. "Do you think she'll...she'll be okay?"

"I don't know," Callie said solemnly. "But I guess we'll find out if humans and vrix are truly compatible."

Mandibles sagging, Rekosh studied Ahmya. There was a glimmer of fear in her eyes. The humans had explained that there were risks for them in birthing young without a *hozpitul*, that they faced inherent dangers. Would Ahmya be hesitant to mother a brood because of that?

Humans were small to begin with, and Ahmya was smallest of all. Would her body be able to endure the ordeal?

That uncertainty sent a shiver across Rekosh's hide. He only barely resisted the urge to reach for her, wrap his arms around her, and draw her against his body, to shelter her in his embrace. Instead, he tucked the bundled dress beneath his arm, accepting that the moment had passed.

For the first time in a long, long while, he was tempted to pray. He was tempted to beg the Eight to see Ivy and her broodling through this, to keep them safe and unharmed. Because Ivy was part of his tribe. Ivy was his friend, his family, the mate of a vrix who was Rekosh's brother in all but blood.

And if she did not survive this, if humans could not birth vrix broodlings, it would mean Rekosh could not claim his Ahmya...because he would not risk her life.

But if all went well, if Ivy and Ketahn's broodling was birthed without complication, it would mean...

Everything.

It would mean that despite all their differences, vrix and

humans were destined for each other. That they were meant to be.

He clenched his fists.

"Ivy and her broodling will be fine," Rekosh said, meeting Ahmya's gaze as she looked up at him. "She is strong. Ketahn is strong. Their little one will be strong too."

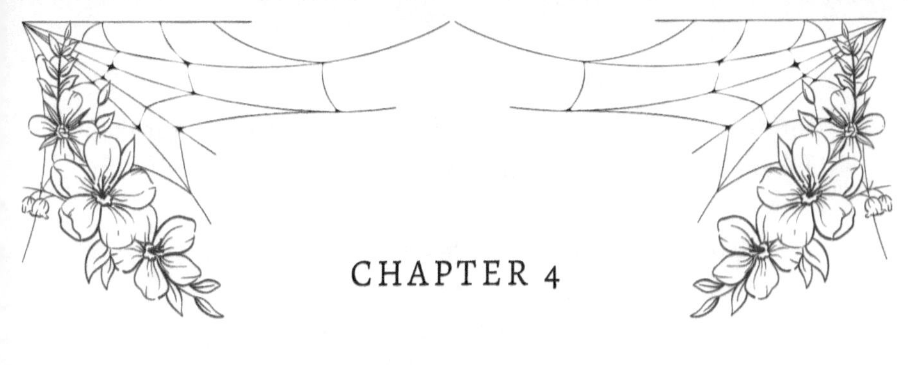

CHAPTER 4

AHMYA SAT atop her pallet with her legs crossed and a blanket on her lap, running a wooden comb through her hair. A soft morning breeze blew in through the open window, carrying the scents of the jungle—moist earth, potent vegetation, and fragrant flowers.

Every day was surreal to Ahmya. She woke up each morning upon a bed of fluffed silk and cloth, in a home high above the ground on a ginormous tree, in a village where she lived alongside spider-like aliens, and wondered to herself if she was dreaming. How could any of this be real?

When she'd left Earth aboard the *Somnium*, ready to start a new life on Xolea, she'd certainly never imagined anything like this. Humans had never made contact with other intelligent lifeforms, had never found evidence that such beings even existed. And yet, here Ahmya was, one of seven survivors out of the thousands who had been on the *Somnium*, living in the jungle with the vrix.

The vrix, who humans could procreate with.

Even after everything, after all the wondrous, terrifying things Ahmya had seen since awakening on this unfamiliar world, that was the most staggering discovery by far. Not that humans could mate with the vrix, but that they could *breed* with them.

Such a thing shouldn't have been possible. Humans and vrix were so different from each other.

Diego guessed it was due to the injections the colonists had been given before departure. They'd been told all those shots were supposed to build their immune systems, amplify their resistance to toxins and diseases, and help their bodies adapt to their new world.

Apparently, the injections also allowed human bodies to adapt to alien sperm.

Setting the comb on the small wooden table beside her bed, Ahmya drew in a deep breath and slowly released it. She was going to see Ivy this morning. Despite the screams and cries having continued well into the night on the day Ivy had gone into labor, she and the baby had thankfully survived and were perfectly healthy. Exhausted, but healthy. It had been an immense relief for everyone.

They'd already lost one friend. They hadn't wanted to lose another.

The next day, Callie, Lacey, and Cole had waited until the evening to visit Ivy, giving her and the baby—Akalahn—time to rest. Ahmya hadn't joined them. There'd been an anxiousness within her, roiling and overwhelming, that had bordered on panic throughout the day. She still wasn't sure where it had come from or why it had stricken her so suddenly...

You know why, Ahmya.

It's because you're next.

"I'm not." She flipped the blanket off her legs and pushed herself to her feet.

You are, and you know it.

"Stop it. I'm not...I'm not having spider babies."

Ahmya had to admit that the thought petrified her. She'd

always been afraid of spiders, and she was still creeped out by any and all insects and arachnids. Though the vrix were definitely not spiders, she could not ignore their many, many arachnoid traits. She'd grown comfortable around them over time, but to have sex with one?

You mean to have sex with Rekosh?

She glared, cross-eyed, at the voice in her head. "No more from you."

You know you're curious. You have been ever since you heard Ketahn and Ivy mating. All Ivy's pleasure-filled cries, Ketahn's guttural grunts and growls—

"Ugh. Shut up." She shook her head as though it could silence that pesky inner voice and the sounds that were so entrenched in her memory.

Plucking a couple green, serrated leaves from the *xal'keishahl* —the spiceblossom—growing from a clay pot on the table, she slipped them into her mouth. The leaves' cinnamon-like flavor burst across her tongue as she angrily chewed. The leaves' texture, while not exactly pleasant, worked well for cleaning teeth.

"There's nothing wrong with being a little curious," she muttered.

She was a virgin, but she wasn't ignorant. Ahmya knew what happened when people had sex, knew that it could feel good— though she'd never experienced anything other than self-pleasure. And considering Cole was the only human male available...

Ahmya straightened, tugging down the hem of her silk skirt. "No. Just...no."

Cole was handsome, and he'd changed a lot in the time she'd known him, having become a genuine friend to her since they'd left the *Somnium* three months ago. At heart, he was thoughtful and dependable. But he just wasn't her type, and she felt no attraction toward him. The only other single humans were

Callie and Lacey. They were both gorgeous, but Ahmya wasn't interested in either of them sexually.

That left her with two choices—die a virgin or mate with a vrix.

You know exactly which vrix.

She groaned and scrubbed her hands over her face. "Why am I thinking about all this now?"

Because Rekosh is back, and you know the truth.

Ahmya snapped off the spiceblossom's pink flower. "I'm done talking to you."

She walked toward the doorway, only to come to an abrupt halt. Her head tipped back as she stared up at the ceiling. "I've been spending way too much time alone with my thoughts."

And wasn't that how it had always been? When she was still living with her father, it had been hours in her room doing homework, broken only by silent, stifling family meals. She'd been alone when she finally moved out, and though she knew that wasn't the case here, it felt like it sometimes.

Especially for those first few days after Rekosh had departed a month ago.

Vrix had excellent senses of smell, and they apparently reacted...excitedly when humans were ovulating. Ivy had explained it to Ahmya, Lacey, and Callie. It was like when female vrix put out their pheromones, only stronger.

So when Ahmya ovulated for the first time since awakening, she'd been forced to spend several days cooped up in her little den, avoiding contact with all the vrix. She could only imagine what it would've been like had Rekosh been around when a male thornskull scented her during that time.

The peace between Rekosh's kind and the thornskulls might've been put into jeopardy.

To say it had been an unsettling experience would've been an understatement, but the worst part had been the quiet. Even though she'd still seen Lacey, Callie, and the other humans every day, something had been missing. Something that had become so natural a part of her days, that had become so natural a part of her life.

Not something. Someone.

Don't you dare, Ahmya. Don't you dare admit that...that you missed Rekosh being around. That it was too quiet without him. That...

"Okay, time to go!"

Proceeding to the door, she tugged on her boots, slung her backpack over her shoulders, and brushed aside the silk hanging to step outside. Bright rays of sunlight gleamed through the canopy above, casting dancing shadows of the leaves and branches swaying in the breeze. She walked along the platform toward the descending stairway. There was no sign of Callie or Lacey. This early, they were either sleeping or having breakfast in the lounge. Cole was always up with the dawn, either busy with one of his many projects or joining the thornskulls' hunts.

What was Rekosh doing? Was he resting, or was he awake? How would he spend his day?

Ha! See, still thinking of him.

Ahmya sighed. The last few months had been filled with labor as the humans worked alongside the vrix to help make a place for themselves here in Kaldarak. Most nights, she'd gone to bed exhausted, with every muscle in her body aching, and had passed out the instant she hit her pallet.

But there'd been other nights when she'd lain awake, longing for the days when it had just been their small tribe. When they'd all gathered around a fire beneath the stars and talked. Everything had been so much more intimate then, and they hadn't been so busy and scattered. Sure, they'd been running for their lives, but...Ahmya had enjoyed that time with her newfound family.

And during this last month, she'd missed Rekosh's presence.

She hadn't realized how bright her days had been when he'd shown up to work alongside her, watch over her, or talk to her —which he'd done often, as he was eager to learn English. He made her feel seen. Made her feel included. He didn't treat her like a burden or make her feel like she was in the way.

Then he was gone, and every day had been gloomier than the last.

Rekosh had been kind, supportive, protective. He was her friend.

You know that he wants to be more, Ahmya.

Her thoughts flashed back to two days ago, when Rekosh had come to speak with her after his month-long absence.

Words from my heartsthread, kir'ani vi'keishi.

My little flower.

Ahmya's heart thumped, and she pressed a hand to her chest. What had he been about to say? What had he been about to profess?

His unspoken words were an unknown that loomed as large and as intimidating as what she'd faced by boarding the *Somnium* to leave Earth.

But they weren't entirely unknown, were they? She had a pretty good idea of what he might've confessed, and if her guess was right, it only led to an entirely new set of uncertainties.

He...he wanted her as his mate.

Ahmya chewed on the inside of her bottom lip.

Was that so wrong? Was it so unappealing? Ivy was mated to Ketahn, and she was happy. Based on the sounds she made when the two had sex, she was *really* happy. But their relationship went well beyond sex. They loved each other, cared for each other, and it was evident in everything they did, even when they weren't together.

Could Ahmya find that same happiness with Rekosh? When she'd first seen the vrix, that answer had been a firm *heck no*, but in the time since...

Ahmya jogged down the stairs to the main platform.

In the time since, her heart fluttered with Rekosh's every crimson glance, her skin tingled with his every touch, and she ached and yearned for him in a way she had for no other.

Seeing him again had reminded her of all that, had made her body react, had made her crave. And last night, when Ahmya had given in to temptation and touched herself in the darkness of her den, it had been Rekosh she'd imagined as she stroked her clit. It had been his name, muffled in her bedding, that she'd cried as she came.

Cheeks flushing, Ahmya shoved that memory aside. "Ivy. I'm going to see Ivy and the new baby."

She crossed the rope bridge connecting the humans' platforms to the rest of Kaldarak and hurried toward Ketahn and Ivy's den, replying to the thornskulls who greeted her along the way in their own tongue, albeit a bit haltingly and likely mispronounced. But the natives of the tree village were used to the strange accents of the humans who'd become their tribemates, and they'd found ways around the lingering language barriers.

When she finally reached her destination, she found Telok standing on the platform outside the den, scanning Kaldarak with his bright green eyes, both sets of arms folded across his chest and abdomen. He turned his head toward Ahmya as she approached, mandibles ticking upward.

Ahmya smiled wide. "Good morning, Telok."

He dipped his chin in acknowledgement. Though he wasn't nearly the largest vrix she'd encountered, he might've been the most intimidating. With all those scars on his black and green hide, that piercing gaze, and a deep, rasping voice, he often seemed rather intense. But she'd seen how deeply he cared, and how quickly he'd come to the aid of the members of their tribe when there was trouble.

"Everything okay?" she asked.

"Yes."

"Why are you standing out here alone?"

Telok huffed and waved toward the rest of the village, replying in English, "All go here to see. I tell all go away. Ivy and Akalahn no rest with thornskulls seeing."

"Is it okay for me to see them if they're awake? I won't stay too long."

He closed his hand into a fist and raised his thumb in a gesture that Cole and Will had taught him. It was both strange and comical seeing him do it. "Awake now."

Ahmya grinned. "Thank you." She knocked on the intertwined branches of the doorframe. "It's Ahmya."

"Come in!" Ivy called.

Shifting aside the cloth door, Ahmya slipped inside the warm den. It had been given to Ivy and Ketahn when they'd first arrived in Kaldarak, and it was larger than those that had been built for the humans—a den for a mated pair.

There were spears standing next to the doorway, nets and coils of silk rope hanging on the wall, and built-in pockets and shelves containing all sorts of items, including tools, herbs, and small jars. Clay pots and woven baskets sat in one corner, and near them was a vrix-made furnace crafted from slabs of stone. The slabs formed a box that was open on one side, revealing a bowl with a low, blue-green flame burning within.

And beside the fire were Ketahn and Ivy, resting upon a mountain of fluffed silk. It would have put the biggest, comfiest bean bag to shame.

Looks like someone was busy.

As Ahmya stepped out of her boots, she wondered if making fluffed silk was an instinctual thing male vrix did in preparation for their broodlings. Kind of like what women would call nesting.

With the soft fur rug beneath her bare feet, she approached the couple.

Ivy reclined against Ketahn's chest, her golden hair woven into a braid which rested over one shoulder, and the big black and purple vrix sat behind her with his lower pair of arms around her middle. She cradled a blanket-wrapped bundle in her arms.

Ahmya stopped in the middle of the room. "I hope I'm not intruding."

"You are," Ketahn said.

Her eyes widened. "Oh."

Ivy chuckled and glanced up at her mate. "Hush. It's okay, Ahmya. Thanks to Telok, we were able to get some sleep without being interrupted by an unending stream of visitors."

"I can come back later if you'd prefer," Ahmya said. "I know it's kind of early."

"You're fine. We've been awake for a little while." Ivy beckoned Ahmya with a hand. "Come closer. You don't have to stand all the way over there." She grinned and patted Ketahn's arm. "Despite his threats to do so, Ketahn won't bite."

Ketahn snapped his mandible fangs together, and his violet eyes settled on Ahmya. "If I must bite to ensure you get rest, my heartsthread, I will do so."

Ahmya shuddered. She would not want to be caught between his fangs—or any other vrix's.

Except for Rekosh's?

Shut up, brain.

"He's being extra protective right now, but he won't hurt you, Ahmya," Ivy said.

"No bite, no eat," Ketahn said with a chitter. "No fun."

The women laughed.

He lowered his head and nuzzled Ivy's hair before looking back at Ahmya. "I will not hurt you. Come. See my pride, my hearts, my love. See our broodling."

Unable to shake her nervousness, Ahmya closed the distance between them. Her unease wasn't due to Ketahn. He'd definitely scared her in the beginning, but he'd since become family. She knew he wouldn't hurt her, knew his threats had been jokes. She'd seen firsthand just how selfless he was when it came to protecting Ivy, the other humans, and his friends—his tribe.

No, Ahmya's anxiousness was due entirely to the baby in Ivy's arms.

As Ahmya drew closer to Ivy, she noted the woman's paler than usual skin and the dark circles beneath her eyes. Ivy was clearly exhausted, but she still bore a glow of vitality, and was as beautiful as ever.

Ahmya smiled and lifted the pink spiceblossom, offering it to Ivy. "For you. It's not much, but there's not exactly an abundance of flowers up here for me to make a bouquet out of. This was the first to bloom."

"Aw, thank you," Ivy said as she accepted the flower by the stem, bringing the blossom to her nose.

"How...did it go?"

When Ivy lowered the flower, Ketahn gently took it from her. His big hands, tipped with black claws, delicately slid the stem into Ivy's hair behind her ear, tucking back the wayward blond strands.

"Truthfully? It was scary," she said, taking Ketahn's hand and lacing her fingers with his. "There were moments when I thought I couldn't do it. When I thought I...wouldn't make it. No matter how many times or how hard I pushed, the baby wouldn't come. I was just so exhausted, constantly in and out of consciousness, but the urge to push was as powerful as ever."

Ivy looked down at the bundle cradled on her arm and smiled. "When he finally came, it was such a relief. Then I saw him. He was so beautiful. And he's...he's perfect, Ahmya."

She looked up with a short laugh. "Tore me up something fierce though. Thankfully Diego patched me up quick, so yay for Earth science. But despite all that pain... It was worth it just to hold our son. To look into his eyes. I would do it all over again."

Ketahn growled and pulled her against him a little more snugly. "Not again, Ivy. You will not suffer that pain again."

Ivy rolled her eyes, released his hand, and reached up to pat the side of his face. "Unless you're willing to give up sex, it's bound to happen again."

His mandibles drooped. "I do not like these choices."

Ahmya chuckled.

Ivy grinned at him. "It's one or the other, spider man. Your choice. I know which one I choose."

"I choose for you to be safe, Ivy." His voice was raw and thick, and his face, though unable to change expressions, still managed to convey all that emotion and vulnerability. "You were in pain, and I could not help. Now you both are safe"—his eyes flicked to the baby—"and I will not risk you again."

Her gaze softened, and she stroked her thumb across his jaw. "Childbirth is natural, Ketahn. There will always be risks, will always be pain, but that can't stop us from living. Has it yet?"

Ketahn pressed his headcrest to Ivy's forehead and trilled, caressing her cheek.

Blushing, Ahmya turned her eyes away. She couldn't help but feel like an intruder during this intimate moment between the couple.

But she also felt a deep longing to share moments like this with someone. To experience the affection and adoration she'd only ever seen secondhand, to be the source of someone's strength, to be supported in her own weakness. To share comfort, companionship, and laughter. She longed to share her life with someone.

Longed to be *loved*.

Her chest constricted, and she pressed a palm over it as though that could ease the growing ache of loneliness.

"Ahmya?" Ivy asked.

Ahmya blinked and looked back at Ivy. "Sorry. I...kind of..."

"It's okay." Ivy lifted the baby. "I asked if you would like to hold him."

"Oh." Ahmya's heart quickened as she stared at the swathed baby. "Um..."

"He's pretty sound asleep after eating, so he won't fuss."

"Okay." Ahmya eased closer and held out her arms.

Ivy relinquished Akalahn into Ahmya's care, showing her how to hold the baby. He was both smaller and heavier than Ahmya had expected.

She looked down at his sleeping face, and her breath caught.

Though Akalahn had four eyes, currently closed, and a pair of small, fanged mandibles, his features were surprisingly human. His little nostrils flared with his exhalations, and his lips stuck out in a gentle pout that was both amusing and endearing. Instead of a headcrest, he had a full head of black and gold hair.

Ahmya brushed a finger over his cheek. His black skin was soft and smooth, but there was a toughness to it that made her wonder if it would harden into a thick hide like his father's.

He stirred, shifting his arms and causing the blanket to fall open, then yawned, revealing his baby fangs. As he settled, tucking all four of his arms against his chest, Ahmya smiled. His little hands—each with five fingers instead of the four typical of the vrix—curled into fists. Tiny black claws tipped those chubby fingers.

Since awakening on the crashed ship, Ahmya had felt like she'd been in a world of giants. But here was Akalahn, so small, so precious, so adorable. Far cuter than anything she had imagined.

The anxiousness swirling within her eased, though it didn't fade completely.

"He's beautiful," Ahmya said, gently rocking the baby.

"He is," Ivy replied. "I didn't know what to expect. I mean, we all thought I was going to lay eggs."

Ahmya chuckled. "Now we can all rest assured that there will be no egg laying."

We, Ahmya?

I'm not talking to you anymore.

Still, Ahmya couldn't help but picture a vrix baby of her own, one with red markings instead of purple.

"Coming in!" announced a familiar feminine voice. "Hope your boob isn't popped out. Not that I'd care."

The curtain door flipped open, brightening the den momentarily as Lacey swept inside, jabbing her thumb over her shoulder. "You got ole fuddy-duddy on guard duty?"

She was dressed in a Homeworld Initiative jumpsuit from the ship, but due to wear and tear, it'd been altered into a two-piece outfit consisting of shorts and a sleeveless top.

"I do not know that word, Lacey. But if it means he is failing his duty, it is the right word," Ketahn said with a rumble.

The curtain was moved aside again, and Telok poked his head through the opening, green eyes narrowed. *"Kess'ur ikar tes kir,* Ketahn?"

Did you speak of me, Ketahn?

Ketahn gnashed his mandibles. *"Kir'ur ikar tes kess."*

I did speak of you.

"Lacey *kota?"*

Ketahn nodded.

Telok stepped fully into the den and jabbed a long, clawed finger toward Lacey. *"Ah'ur ven'dak zeta. Kir'ur ikar ven'dak nek ursh, ova ah'ur lenaal ahn'ganok saal saavix ursh."*

He was speaking too quickly for Ahmya to understand everything, but the gist seemed to be that Lacey hadn't listened to him.

"Hey!" Lacey pointed at Telok. "It's rude to talk about people when they can't understand you."

"What *thuddy-duddy?*" Telok asked in harsh, accented English, glaring at Lacey.

She smirked at him. "It means you're boring, dull, no fun. Like you have a stick rammed up your spider butt." Lacey finished that sentence by swinging her fist like she was jabbing said stick up there herself.

He narrowed his eight eyes further, reducing them to faintly glowing green slits. "*Arvok ah'ur ikar,* Ketahn?"

What did she say, Ketahn?

Ivy covered her grin with a hand, but it didn't hide the mirth in her eyes.

"*Kess'al shon uniran ah'ani ikarahl,* Telok, *vux kess'al zeki ah,*" Ketahn replied.

Telok growled, casting his narrow-eyed glare at Ketahn before demonstrating another gesture he'd learned from Cole, Diego, and Will—lowering all but the middle finger on his hand.

"What did you say to him?" Lacey asked.

"Ketahn said he should learn your words so he can ask you himself," Ivy replied with a chuckle.

Lacey smiled sweetly at the black and green vrix. "Telok wouldn't like the words I have for him."

Telok stared at her, eyes dipping to her mouth. Something intensified in his gaze, a building heat not unlike that which Ahmya had so often seen in Ketahn's eyes when he looked upon Ivy.

Or Rekosh's eyes when he looks at me...

And yet Telok offered Lacey the same gesture he'd just made toward Ketahn, raising his long middle finger.

Ahmya's jaw dropped, and Ivy burst into laughter.

"Wow. I missed you too, smart ass. Anyway!" Lacey approached Ahmya and peered down at Akalahn, her expression softening as she brushed a finger along the bridge of his tiny nose. "I'm here to collect Ahmya. The thornskulls are ready to head out to gather supplies for the celebration."

"Celebration?" Ivy asked. "What are they celebrating?"

Lacey gave her a droll look. "Ivy, you just had a hybrid vrix baby. That's kind of a big deal."

"Garahk and Nalaki wanted to celebrate right away, but Diego convinced them to give you a few days to recover beforehand," Ahmya said. "He had to make them understand that giving birth is strenuous for humans and that you need time to rest and heal, so they want to use that time to go out and gather extra food."

"They're pretty much holding a village-wide feast in honor of you two and little Akalahn."

Ketahn growled, hugging Ivy closer to his chest even as his eyes fell on the infant in Ahmya's arms. "They may do as they like. My mate and broodling will remain here, resting in peace."

"Suck it up," Lacey said. "It's not every day that a half-human half-vrix baby is born. And Akalahn is the first."

Ivy cupped Ketahn's face and peered up at him. "This is our tribe now, and they're happy for us. It wouldn't hurt to join them."

He huffed through his nose, mandibles falling. "If it is your wish, my heartsthread. For a small time, we will join them."

She smiled.

Once more, Ahmya's heart squeezed in response to the open love passing between Ketahn and Ivy. She looked down at Akalahn and was startled to see four wide, luminous violet eyes staring up at her. "Oh!"

He didn't cry, didn't fuss or protest that it wasn't his mother holding him, he simply looked up at her curiously.

Ahmya smiled at him. "Hi there, little one."

"Perfect timing," Lacey said.

It was, but Ahmya suddenly found herself reluctant to give him up.

"And you're both going out with the thornskulls?" Ivy asked.

Ahmya shifted closer to Ivy and carefully returned Akalahn to his mother's arms. "We're gathering food and looking for herbs. I also wanted to take this chance to study more of the plants."

Lacey smiled. "Ahmya's itching to get back out in the jungle to explore."

She was. It wasn't often that she was able to venture outside of Kaldarak, especially as it was much too dangerous to go out alone.

"Is Callie joining you?" Ivy asked.

"Not this time," Ahmya said. "She's checking out a tunnel with Urkot and some thornskulls. I think she said its where they're mining limestone."

Ivy adjusted the baby in her arms, tucking the blanket more snuggly around him. "Just be careful out there."

Lacey snorted. "What could go wrong? Giant beasties, carnivorous plants, floods? Pfft. Been there, done that."

Ahmya's scars flared with echoes of pain at the memory of the firevine's thorns piercing her flesh. The encounter with that particular carnivorous plant had been so sudden, so startling, and so dangerous.

But it wasn't enough to stop her from exploring. It wasn't enough to make her love plants any less.

"Let's...take a pass on all that," Ahmya said with a soft laugh. "Going through it once was more than enough for me."

"Agreed," said Lacey and Ivy in unison.

"Now let's get going before they leave us puny humans behind." Lacey hooked her arm through Ahmya's and led her toward the entrance, sticking her tongue out at Telok as they passed him.

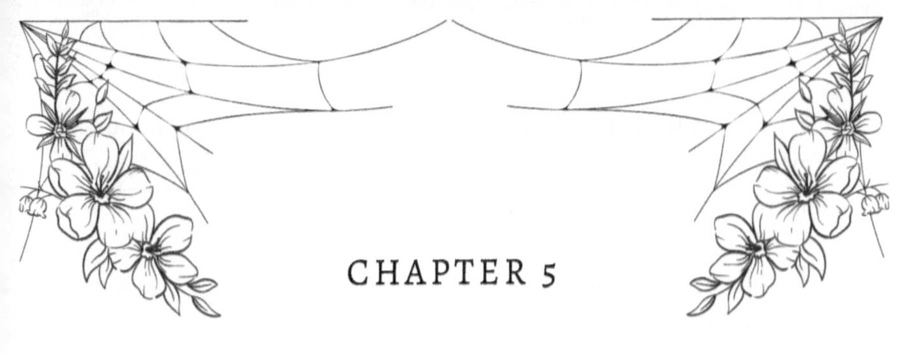

CHAPTER 5

"You two are like school children, teasing each other back and forth," Ahmya said as she and Lacey walked arm-in-arm across one of the busy platforms.

Many vrix in Kaldarak were outside their homes. Some chatted with one another, some went about their morning chores, and others lounged in the sun, all while younglings played, their chitters and trills as pleasant as any birdsong.

Lacey glanced at Ahmya from the corner of her eye. "Who?"

Ahmya laughed. "You know exactly who I'm talking about."

The red-haired woman wrinkled her freckled nose. "Telok can't stand to be around me, and the feeling is mutual. He's rude, broody, and impatient. He also acts as though I smell offensive anytime I'm around him, which isn't often as he seems to avoid me as much as possible. It was nice not feeling like I'm some nuisance while he was gone."

"Wow. I guess I hadn't realized he's been acting that way toward you."

"Except for Ketahn, Urkot, Rekosh, and Ahnset, he doesn't seem to care to make any friends. He tolerates Cole. Like for real? *Cole*? But he can't stand to even be near me?" Lacey brought Ahmya to a stop and lifted her arm high in the air, revealing the long, crude pink scar running along her inner bicep to her elbow. "So do I stink?"

Ahmya jerked back. "What?"

"Smell me. Do I stink?"

"You're serious?"

"You have no idea how self-conscious he's made me over this." Lacey moved closer. "Come on, Ahmya, get in here and take a sniff."

Ahmya laughed and shook her head before leaning toward Lacey's armpit. She sniffed. She didn't smell anything off-putting. All she could detect were the light floral notes from the homemade deodorant Lacey had concocted and traces of sweat, which was perfectly human.

Ahmya straightened. "You smell fine to me."

"See!" Lacey lowered her arm. "He's just mean."

"He's always been pretty stern. I wouldn't let him get to you." Ahmya looked ahead to the next platform to see a group of thornskulls near one of the main bridges leading out of Kaldarak. "We should hurry so we don't keep them waiting."

Lacey adjusted the strap of her backpack on her shoulder and stepped onto the bridge. "Yeah, you're right. Let's go be one with nature."

Ahmya chuckled and grasped the rope handrail. "Aren't we already that?"

"Ahmya!" Rekosh called from behind.

Her breath hitched. Stilling with one foot on the bridge, she turned to find him quickly striding toward her. Warmth suffused her, chasing away the slight morning chill, and her belly fluttered at the sight of him.

The thornskulls of Kaldarak were big, broadly built vrix. Ketahn, Rekosh, and the others from Takarahl were shadow-stalkers, whose bodies tended to be leaner and more graceful but no less powerful. Yet even amongst them, Rekosh was especially lithe and elegant. Of all the males, he was second only to Ketahn in height, and his limbs were long and svelte.

She'd heard the word spindly used to describe him, but to Ahmya, that implied a fragility that didn't fit him at all. His shoulders were broad, and lean, solid muscle flexed beneath his hide. She'd seen Rekosh fight. There was untold strength in him, and a ferocity that should have frightened her. Yet he'd shown her nothing but gentleness.

The rays of light breaking through the canopy made the unique crimson markings on his headcrest, wrists, and leg joints stand out and lit up the strands of red and white in his braided black hair. Back on Earth, that shade of red meant danger. It was the same color as the marking on a black widow's belly, which had been the first thing Ahmya had thought of when she'd met Rekosh.

But that color had come to mean so much more. It had become safety, comfort, and caring.

He stopped a few steps away from Ahmya, mandibles twitching. His eyes flicked from her to the thornskulls on the other side of the bridge. "You are going?"

Ahmya reached up and caught the strands of hair blowing across her face in the wind, tucking them behind her ear. "We're going to help gather food and look for herbs. I also want to explore a little more."

Rekosh's eyes widened, and a low, unhappy sound rumbled from his chest. "You are going only with them? No others?"

Both Lacey and Ahmya turned their heads toward the waiting thornskulls. Garahk was amongst them, leading the party, which was comprised of several male hunters.

Ahmya's brow creased. "Um…yeah?"

"Not enough to protect you, *vi'keishi*."

Her eyes widened, and that fluttering in her belly intensified.

Lacey chuckled. "How much trouble could Ahmya get into that fourteen beefy vrix wouldn't be enough protection?"

Rekosh blinked, tilting his head. "What is *beefee*?"

Lacey flexed her arms. "Big, strong, muscular."

He huffed. "I am strong."

"But you're not beefy."

Rekosh narrowed his crimson eyes. "I do not need to be *beefee* to protect Ahmya."

Lacey chuckled. "Well, if it'd make you feel better, you could join us. We could use a translator, anyway."

Rekosh straightened, mandibles rising in a vrix smile as he nodded. "Yes. I will come. Tell Garahk wait."

"To wait?" Ahmya asked.

Stepping backward, Rekosh waved toward his den. "I will get my things."

"Oh! Right."

He extended a foreleg and brushed it over her bare calf, making her skin tingle. "Wait for me, a small time."

Ahmya smiled. "I'll wait."

Even when Rekosh withdrew his leg, she could still feel his touch. Could still feel those soft, tiny hairs against her skin.

"*We'll* wait." Lacey gave the back knot of Ahmya's top a tug. "Come on."

The women continued across the bridge to join the thornskulls, who greeted them cheerfully in a mix of vrix and English. None of the thornskulls could carry on a conversation in the humans' language, but most of them had learned *hello*, and used it with genuine enthusiasm. The sense of community in this place, even with the existing language barriers, was unlike anything Ahmya had experienced before leaving Earth. The thornskulls were kind and helpful. They teased sometimes, but there was always a good-naturedness to their teasing.

"Ah, Lacey, *Ahnya*," Garahk said as the women approached him. Though Nalaki was essentially the queen of Kaldarak,

Garahk was looked upon as a leader in his own right. His compassion and understanding had likely been the only reason Ahmya and her companions had survived their journey to escape Queen Zurvashi. "We…go?"

Ahmya smiled. Garahk was big and stocky, with hard, spiky protrusions on his head and shoulders and black spots scattered across his pure white hide. Yet despite his intimidating appearance, his friendly demeanor and natural warmth always put her at ease. He spoke very little English, but he'd made efforts to learn, and that meant a lot to the humans.

"Rekosh'*ur ikar*, uh"—Ahmya waved her hands down toward the platform—"*akkan*. He asked us to wait for him."

"*Et rayathahl'al saavix?*" Garahk asked. "Rekosh go?"

Smile widening, Ahmya nodded. She grasped the strap of her backpack and lifted it off her shoulder. "He is getting his things."

"*Rekosh'al saavix saal tavit*," the thornskull announced to his companions, who responded with excitement.

Despite the thornskulls' dialect being a bit different from the shadowstalkers'—and thus being harder for her to follow— she understood his words.

Rekosh will come to hunt.

But she knew that wasn't quite right. He wasn't coming to hunt, he was coming to protect her.

Or maybe he is hunting, and I'm the prey?

That thought and its implications set her cheeks ablaze.

"You okay?" Lacey asked.

"Huh?" Ahmya barely resisted the urge to cover her cheeks with her hands. Instead, she grasped the other strap of her backpack and pulled them closer together, as though the bag were a shell in which she could hide. "Yeah, I'm fine."

"All right," Lacey replied skeptically. "You looked pretty red there for a second. I thought maybe the heat was getting to you…"

It is. Oh God, it is.

"Nope, all good." Ahmya rocked on her heels, fighting a new urge—this one to look back and seek out Rekosh. "Just excited to get out there, you know?"

"Me too. Nice as things are up here, it feels good to have my feet on the ground sometimes."

"It does. We've been kind of cooped up here for a while."

The thornskulls chatted amongst themselves as everyone awaited Rekosh, whose arrival was met with a chorus of cheers from the gathered hunters. It meant the wait was over. The excursion could begin.

Unsurprisingly, Rekosh walked directly to Ahmya. He had a bag of his own strapped across his back, and a spear with an obsidian head in hand. The sash across his chest, which usually held his sewing tools, seemed only to hold knives now, including one that was human-made, smaller than the rest but exceptionally sharp and durable. Ahmya had one just like it in her own bag, one of the few items still in her possession from the *Somnium*.

Rekosh gestured in apology to Ahmya and Garahk, bowing his head. He spoke first in English, and then repeated his words in vrix. "Please forgive the delay."

Garahk chittered, thumped a leg against Rekosh's, and replied with what Ahmya understood as essentially *glad to have you along*. When Rekosh's eyes met hers, their intensity triggered something inside her.

Lacey nudged Ahmya with an elbow. "The heat again, huh?"

"You are too hot?" Rekosh asked, leaning closer to Ahmya.

Ahmya shook her head and glared at her friend. "I'm all right, Rekosh. Really. Lacey is just teasing me."

He growled, gnashing his mandibles.

"Oh, come on!" Lacey pointed at Ahmya. "It's not like she never teases me."

Ahmya gaped at the other woman and pressed a hand to her own chest. "I would *never* do that."

Lacey rolled her eyes. "Of course, you wouldn't."

At Garahk's signal, the group set out. Ahmya, Lacey, and Rekosh hung back, allowing the thornskulls to pass.

"Maybe we should invite Telok along too," Ahmya suggested with a saccharine smile. "You know, to keep *you* out of trouble, Lacey."

"Low blow, Ahmya," replied Lacey with a laugh. "Low blow."

"I know those words, but I do not understand," Rekosh said. "Ahmya did not blow on you."

Chuckling, Ahmya shook her head. "Blow is another one of those words with more than one meaning. In this case, it means I hit her with my words."

"There's at least one other meaning I can think of…" Lacey grinned at Ahmya, waggling her eyebrows.

"We're not going there," Ahmya singsonged as they trailed after the thornskulls.

Rekosh hummed thoughtfully. "I have much to ask, humans."

Ahmya's body flushed hotter. "No, no, no. No need to ask about that."

"But Ahmya," Lacey said over her shoulder, "don't you want him to learn our ways?"

"What ways do you speak of?" Rekosh asked.

"Mating rituals, like blow jobs and—ouch! Ahmya! Did you seriously just pinch my ass?"

"And I'll do it again," Ahmya said. She gripped Lacey's backpack and pushed, steering the woman across the bridge. "Conversation over. Let's go! We have a jungle to explore."

Lacey snickered as they continued out of Kaldarak.

To Ahmya's relief, Rekosh didn't press for more information, but she knew that it was only a temporary reprieve. His silence meant he was thinking. He was always observant and unabashedly inquisitive, especially when it came to language. He wasn't going to forget. He was just waiting for a better time to ask again.

And Ahmya was *not* ready to explain what a blow job was.

Do you want to show him instead?

Shush!

But it made her to wonder… Did vrix even perform oral on each other?

Considering their sharp teeth and lack of lips, Ahmya was inclined to guess *no*, which meant Rekosh had likely never had a blow job, and she could be the first one to—

Stop!

But she couldn't stop herself from picturing it in her mind. Though she didn't know what his cock looked like, she imagined his long, clawed fingers tangling in her hair, imagined those crimson eyes blazing down at her before his head fell back in pleasure, imagined his lean, powerful muscles flexing beneath his dark hide. What sounds would he make? How would he react to her taking his cock into her mouth, teasing it with her tongue?

What would he taste like?

Ahmya's sex clenched. Her heart pounded fiercely, and her skin heated as the ache in her core sharpened. She gripped the straps of her backpack and released a quiet, shuddering breath, keeping her face forward. How could a little daydream cause such a visceral reaction in her?

Because you want him. Admit it.

Ahmya could feel Rekosh's presence behind her. Could feel his eyes on her.

This is going to be a long, long trip.

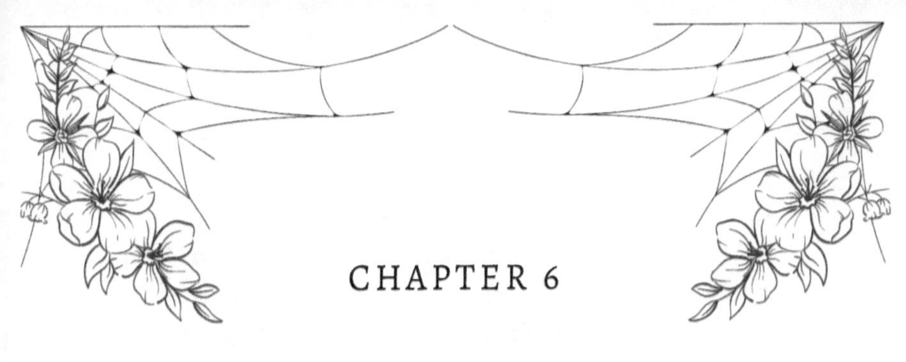

CHAPTER 6

HAVING RETURNED to Kaldarak only a few days ago, Rekosh had not intended to leave again so soon. Yet he was unsurprised by the eagerness that lightened his stride and carried him onward as Garahk led their group into the Tangle.

Because he strode alongside Ahmya.

He could feel her joy as clearly as he felt the breeze or the warm sunshine against his hide. Perhaps he should have chided her for looking upon the jungle with wonder rather than wariness, for not being appropriately solemn and alert, but how could he have done so?

The whole group was in a bright mood. The birth of Akalahn was the talk of Kaldarak, and the thornskulls were determined to celebrate with the fullness of their hearts, just as they had when Nalaki and Garahk's first brood hatched more than a moon cycle ago. The hunters were invigorated and excited, chatting freely and jesting often. Rekosh was given no shortage of words to translate between the human females and the vrix.

When he wasn't translating, he remained vigilant, studying their surroundings not only to watch for danger, but to learn the path—especially after they journeyed beyond familiar ground.

Once again, Rekosh was trekking into the unknown.

But his attention always found its way back to Ahmya. Often there was good reason for it—the rocky, uneven ground in this part of the jungle presented many obstacles to the humans, and Rekosh never hesitated to offer aid.

Any reason to touch Ahmya was too precious to ignore. The feel of her hand in his, of her soft, warm flesh against his rough hide, of her heartbeat fluttering beneath his fingertips on her wrist; it was all maddening, all blissful. And the way her cheeks pinkened almost every time he touched her only made him ache with longing and adoration.

Rekosh adjusted the strap of his bag. The movement of the yatin hide against his back was far more significant than it should've been.

He wasn't sure why he'd packed the silk dress and its matching foot coverings. It had been a compulsion as he'd rushed into his den to gather his belongings, an instinct that had driven him to wrap the gifts in a secure bundle of cloth and leather and tuck them away in his bag. He'd done so knowing full well the nature of this journey.

They were out here to hunt and forage for food for Kaldarak. When did he expect to have time to give the gifts to Ahmya? When did he expect to have the privacy to do so?

Rekosh didn't care who witnessed his declaration to her. He would've made it before every eye in Takarahl and Kaldarak alike; this group of rugged thornskull hunters would not deter him. He had no shame for his feelings for Ahmya.

But he didn't *want* onlookers.

No, when he presented his gifts and spoke the words that had for so long thrummed along his heartsthread, it would be for Ahmya alone. He would not have her distracted by anyone or anything else.

Only he would see her don his gift.

And then he would claim her.

His stem stirred at the very thought, and he clenched his jaw, swallowing a growl. He willed his claspers tighter against his pelvis to ensure his slit didn't bulge.

He'd never hungered for anything like he hungered for her. How would her body fit with his? How tight would her slit be around his stem, how deeply would her blunt claws rake his hide? What sounds would she make, what ways would she move?

Was her hunger as desperate and insatiable as his own?

He yearned to see fire in her eyes as their bodies moved in unison. Yearned to feel the blaze that threatened to consume him whenever he looked upon her echoed in her heart, in her core, radiating through her skin.

He yearned to taste her.

Rekosh's eyes moved to her now, and he watched as she and Lacey steadied each other to climb to the top of a small but steep incline.

Hints of muscle moved beneath the skin of Ahmya's bare legs, a subtle glimpse of her surprising strength and endurance. She was thinner than the other humans—*petite* was the word he'd heard them use—but he found limitless appeal in her form.

Of course, there remained the problem of her being dressed in another vrix's inferior silk. His lower hands twitched back toward his bag as a primal urge flared inside him, pushing him to tear that fabric off her here and now so he could replace it with his own.

"We are to watch, weaver," said one of the nearby thorn-skulls, a green-hided hunter named Okkor.

Rekosh clicked his mandibles. "I am watching."

Okkor chittered. "Watch for danger, not for *hyu-nanz*."

Rekosh waved him off with a huff and continued onward,

making more of an effort to keep his eyes moving, to remain alert.

The sun crept steadily higher, and the air warmed, though the occasional breezes that swept through the jungle bore the slightest chill. Thick clouds drifted across the blue patches of sky overhead. The Tangle was fragrant and alive, and Ahmya was here.

The unexpected journey, the thornskulls all around, the unfamiliar land…none of it mattered because he was with her.

At midday, they reached a lush, relatively level area full of all manner of plants, where Garahk called a halt.

"The Rootsinger has left her blessing here," Garahk said. "When the river swells, it makes this ground rich. All things grow fast. All things grow large and full of taste. It is true under sun and sky."

When Rekosh translated for the humans, they said there had been places like that on their world, where their people had taken advantage of the *furtle* dirt to grow many plants to eat. Vrix in both Kaldarak and Takarahl did grow some of their food, but they still relied upon foraging and hunting in the bountiful jungle.

Given the humans' efforts in Kaldarak thus far, Rekosh imagined that growing plants for food and other purposes would become far more commonplace in the moon cycles to come.

Garahk pressed his upper hands together and then spread them. "We will part. One *vekir* to stay and gather plants, one *vekir* to hunt. Our *shar'thai* will burn bright, and we will feast well in honor of the new broodling."

The thornskulls thumped the blunt ends of their spears on the ground in response, creating a brief, rhythmic noise, before splitting into two groups. Eight of them joined Garahk, while the remaining four joined Rekosh and the humans.

"Here will be our wild den, weaver," Garahk said to Rekosh.

"If our *vekir* does not return by next suncrest, go to Kaldarak. We will follow when we carry meat enough for all."

Bowing his head, Rekosh tapped a knuckle to his headcrest. "I will watch over ours, Garahk."

"You give many words, Rekosh. Yet the best are when you give words like a thornskull."

Rekosh chittered. "It is true under sun and sky."

The white thornskull trilled, extended a foreleg, and bumped it against Rekosh's. "You must join the hunt another day. I would witness your *shar'thai* by my own eyes, weaver."

"Another day, Garahk. I weave my words into a bond."

Chittering, Garahk turned and strode away. The others in his group followed. Soon, they were all out of sight, though their cheerful voices carried back to Rekosh for a bit longer.

"They will find nothing while their voices are so big," said Okkor, who was amongst the remaining thornskulls.

"Big voice, big *shar'thai*. Is it not so?" Rekosh asked.

A thoughtful hum rumbled from Okkor. "When giving war, yes."

"But for a hunt it is big voice, empty belly," added a yellow thornskull called Elharat.

"Ah, that is why the weaver does not hunt this day," said another thornskull. "His voice is too big."

Rekosh chittered along with the other vrix. "Not too big. Too tireless. Words fall out like rain from the sky, making a flood."

"A flood that will make ours pray for dry season to come early." Okkor sketched the sign of the Eight with his arms.

Mandibles lifting into a grin, Rekosh replied, "Perhaps I will make my voice big then, so the Eight cannot hear you."

Okkor thumped a foreleg against Rekosh's with a chitter. The thornskull's scent—stone and wood with the merest hint of the mire—was at once familiar and foreign. He and the other thornskulls set down the baskets and bags they'd brought and quickly set up a camp.

Lacey stepped up beside Rekosh. "This the spot?"

Rekosh nodded, but whatever words he might have offered vanished from his mind when Ahmya appeared on his other side.

She was so close that her presence alone made his hide tingle with warmth and his fine hairs rise. Whenever they were so near to each other, Rekosh faced a desperate struggle to keep himself from reaching for her, and now was no different. His bag seemed to tug down on his shoulder, its contents feeling eightfold heavier than before.

"Did Garahk say we were staying here tonight?" Ahmya asked as she and Lacey each collected a basket.

Rekosh's chest swelled. "You understand vrix words better each day, *vi'keishi.*"

She smiled at him. "You're learning English pretty fast yourself."

He trilled and sank into a bow, touching his knuckle to his headcrest. "I learn for you, Ahmya."

"Rekosh…" She ducked her head, making her hair fall to partially shield her face, and clutched the basket in front of her. "You don't have to do anything for me."

"It is a need"—he extended a hand, hooked her dangling hair with a finger, and gently tucked the strands behind her ear—"and a want."

Ahmya's dark gaze met his. As he straightened, he trailed his finger along her jaw to her chin, tipping her face up to keep their eyes locked. "No hiding. Not from me. Never from me."

Pink blossomed on her cheeks, but she did not look away. Instead, she licked her lips with her little tongue and curled her fingers around his wrist. Her skin was warm, and her hand trembled. "I don't want to."

She said those words so softly, so quietly, that Rekosh

wondered if he'd imagined them. His hearts quickened, thumping louder than her voice had been.

Lacey coughed loudly. "Should I, uh, leave you two alone, or should we…"

Ahmya sucked in a sharp breath, and her eyes flared wide. She jerked away from Rekosh and hurried toward the other human. "No. No, sorry. Lots of work to do, right?"

Rekosh's hand lingered in the air. More of that prickly warmth pulsed beneath his hide. His claspers pressed in around his slit as he battled the instinct to take hold of her, to prevent her escape.

To bind her.

He glared at Lacey as he loosely closed his fist and lowered his arm. "Yes. Much work."

Lacey offered him a crooked smile, mirth dancing in her eyes. "Oh, did I interrupt? I'm so sorry!"

"You're impossible," Ahmya muttered as she shifted her hold on her basket and turned away, walking deeper into the jungle.

With a huff, Rekosh waved Lacey away. "Telok should have come."

Expression blank, she lifted her hand, bending down all her fingers but the middle one. Then she followed Ahmya.

"Do you require aid, weaver?" Okkor called, catching Rekosh's attention. The thornskulls, having established their small, simple camp, had already begun spreading out to forage.

"Help giving words, it seems," said Elharat.

Rekosh clicked his fangs. "I have many, many words to give. Who would like to hear?"

Chittering, the thornskulls strode into the jungle, quickly vanishing amidst the foliage.

If only it had been that easy to get Lacey to run off.

Why was everything and everyone determined to prevent him from making his claim? Fate had brought him to Ahmya, and he would not allow fate to alter course now.

Growling, he snatched up a spare basket and hurried after the humans.

He caught up to them swiftly, and he was pleased to see Ahmya treading carefully, her head turning from side to side as she searched her surroundings.

Unlike you, you fool.

And yet he could not look away from her. He was fascinated by the sway of her hair as she walked, by those dark strands sweeping across the bare, tantalizing skin of her back. His fingers flexed with the desire, with the need, to touch her.

"You know what I'm thankful for?" Lacey asked.

Ahmya grazed her fingertip over a large, broad leaf, making dewdrops trickle down its smooth surface. "What?"

"That there seem to be no *tiks.*" Lacey turned and walked backward, sweeping her arms outward, dangling her basket from her forearm. "All this time we've spent in the jungle, and not a single *tik* delving its beady little head into my skin."

Ahmya shuddered. "Ugh. I can be thankful for that. They were bad in *kali fornyuh.* I remember hiking in the woods as a *teenayjur* and coming home with *three* of them on my legs. I don't remember ever screaming so loud in my life. My dad burst into my room with a gun thinking there was an *introodur* only to find me freaking out in my underwear."

"Oh God. I bet that was embarrassing."

"I didn't even care. But my dad could barely look at me. All I could think about was that I had bugs in my skin, and he just awkwardly covered his eyes before leaving and closing the door behind him."

Lacey laughed and faced forward.

"It's not funny!"

"It's not. Sorry. Well, maybe it is a little."

Ahmya glared at Lacey. "I found no humor in it. I still don't. I had bugs in my skin, Lacey. *Bugs.*"

Rekosh's eyes widened, his mandibles flared, and his attention dragged once more over her skin—that thin, delicate skin, easily broken, easily damaged. The last thing he'd seen break her skin had been the firevine…and it could've been deadly.

Chuckling, Lacey stopped next to a tree, crouched, and started collecting the goldcrest mushrooms growing near its base. "I agree, it's gross. I guess growing up in *mayn* and spending most of my time outdoors I was pretty used to *tiks*. Checking for them was routine."

"These *tiks*… They do harm to you?" Rekosh asked. "They must, to go into your skin."

Ahmya kicked at some foliage as she looked at the ground. "They carry *dizeezes* that can make people really sick, but we've developed medicines to cure them."

At first glance, what vrix would have believed that these small, odd looking creatures called humans were capable of so much? Far beyond their strength of will and capacity for learning, humans demonstrated astounding cleverness and innovation.

Their descriptions of their home world, Earth, were beyond Rekosh's imagination. They'd dwelt in structures taller than any tree in the Tangle, made entirely of metal and glass. They had traveled in things they called *karz*, *playnz*, and ships, which carried them all around their world and into the stars beyond.

Rekosh had seen enough of these human creations with his own eight eyes to believe even the wildest stories. He'd walked in their ship, had seen the pods that had kept them asleep but alive for one hundred and sixty-eight years. He'd witnessed their tools—a device that could instantly seal wounds, metal knives sharper than any blackrock blade, lights that shone without a flame. He himself had used human fire starters to ignite campfires with startling ease. And he'd watched Ivy use a gun, which had hurled fire into Zurvashi's face.

The lives they'd described leaving behind surpassed Rekosh's comprehension in many ways. But for all their advancements, for all their tools, these humans were here now. Without the human trappings, they were little different from the vrix—small creatures in a large world doing their best to survive.

He did not understand the lives the humans had led before, but he understood the humans. Their pain and sorrow, their contentment and joy. He understood that they had needs and wants, that they loved and hated, that they carried everything within their hearts. And that their will to push onward was just as strong and fierce as that of any vrix.

And he admired them for all of it. Admired all of them...but it was more with Ahmya. Much, much more. For even amongst these humans, she was different. She was special.

It was in the way she carried herself, in the way she spoke, in how quiet and unintrusive she so often behaved. In the way she observed through sharp eyes what others often missed. It was in her size, and in the way she didn't let it hold her back.

He recognized something in her that he'd experienced himself—a silent strength forged by being dismissed, by being underestimated, by being ignored. By being seen as the smallest and the weakest.

Her heart and spirit were so much larger than her body belied. While she often seemed to prefer not being seen by the others, Rekosh saw her. And he needed to make her his so he could remind her every day that she was strong, she was fierce, she was worthy. She was...loved.

The three of them continued their search, talking as they gathered what herbs, fruit, mushrooms, and roots they came across. Occasionally, the thornskulls called out from nearby, ensuring that the groups did not stray too far from each other.

Rekosh kept watch and helped when the females found things they could not reach. Each time Ahmya requested such aid, he had the urge to put his hands on her flaring hips and lift her off the ground so she could gather the jungle's bounty with her own hands. He didn't succumb to those urges; he would not have Lacey ruin such moments.

The Tangle was hot, but the day remained pleasant despite the increasing dampness in the air. His fine hairs sensed coming rain on the breeze. When Ahmya took a moment to catch her breath and wipe the sweat from her brow, Rekosh watched her, head tilted and mandibles twitching.

He'd been at her side through many of the hardships she'd faced since she'd awoken on the crashed ship. He'd seen her struggle and stumble, had seen her fall, had seen her shoulders sag and her lips turn down. He'd seen the sheen of tears in her eyes. But he'd never seen her give up, had never heard her complain.

When she stumbled, she righted herself. When she fell, she picked herself up. When the weight of despair crushed down on her, she clenched her jaw, drew in a deep breath, and lifted her head. If there was another step to be taken, Ahmya took it without fail.

The thornskulls spoke of *shar'thai*, the fiery spirit at the heart of every warrior. If *shar'thai* was real, Ahmya's was blindingly bright.

The other vrix might not have seen it, but Rekosh did.

Ahmya set her near-full basket on the ground, straightened, and reached back to gather her hair in her hands. Parting the strands into sections, she started weaving them into a braid.

Rekosh glanced toward Lacey, who was currently occupied with digging up some whiteroot from the jungle floor. A low trill sounded in his chest as he set down his basket.

He strode up behind Ahmya, steps silent, and gently covered her hands with his. "I will help, *vi'keishi*."

Ahmya started and turned her face slightly toward him to meet his gaze. Her lips curled into a smile as she slipped her hands out from beneath his, relinquishing her hair. "I'm sure your braid will hold up better than mine."

Lifting his mandibles, Rekosh chittered softly. He stood his spear in the ground beside himself. "Yes. You make good braids, I make the best."

Ahmya laughed and faced forward. "You do. Thank you, Rekosh."

"It is small thing." He slipped his claws into her hair and combed them through the strands. Her hair was soft and silken against his fingers, but it was thick and strong despite its seeming delicacy.

Just like Ahmya herself.

Though he knew they were out in the middle of the jungle, he went slowly, carefully combing out any snags and tangles, smoothing her locks, grazing her scalp with the tips of his claws. She tilted her head back toward him with a pleased sigh and a small, contented smile upon her lips, closing her eyes.

Heat stirred behind Rekosh's slit. He knew of kissing because of the humans—because of Ivy and Ketahn. Their lips were pliable, seemingly even softer than the rest of their skin, and he longed to feel hers against his hide. Longed to feel her kiss.

Longed to kiss her.

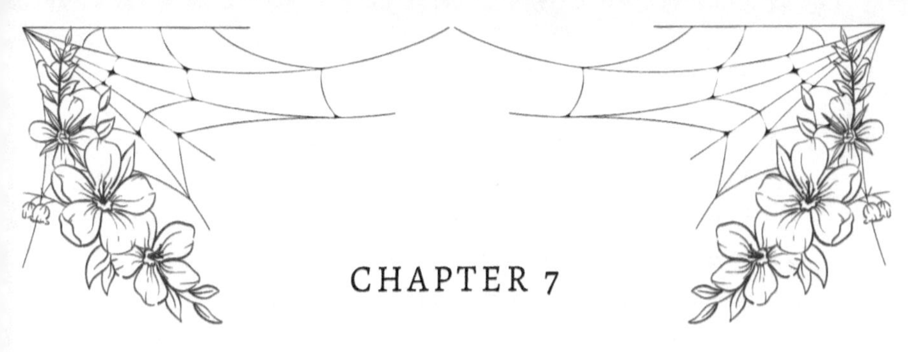

CHAPTER 7

TINGLES COURSED through Ahmya from her scalp all the way to her toes. Rekosh offering to braid her hair had been such a simple, kind gesture. Except his touch was anything but simple. He turned braiding her hair into a sensual act. It was soothing, intimate, and arousing. Heat kindled within her, building with every brush of his claws. And it took everything inside of Ahmya to remain still, to prevent a moan from slipping past her lips.

As he separated her hair into sections, his claws grazed the back of her neck. That hint of pleasure-pain sent a jolt through her nerves, making her nipples harden and her core clench. Ahmya drew in a sharp breath.

His fingers stilled, and he shifted closer. "Did I harm you, Ahmya?"

She opened her eyes to find him leaning beside her, his bright red eyes filled with concern.

"N-No," she said, voice breathier than she intended. "I'm fine."

He flattened a hand over her hair, smoothing it down. "You are sure?"

Ahmya smiled. "Just a graze. Didn't hurt at all."

The pad of Rekosh's thumb stroked the back of her neck with tantalizing delicacy. Ahmya shivered, and her skin prickled in awareness. Her lips parted with a shaky breath.

To have him touch me in such a way all over...

"Good," he rumbled.

He repositioned himself behind her and continued sectioning off her hair. Ahmya stared ahead, attempting to keep watch, to focus on anything other than the feel of his fingers working, but she couldn't help it when her lashes drooped. Though the heat within her didn't fade, there was something relaxing about having someone tending to her hair.

And that someone just happened to be a seven-foot-tall vrix who definitely knew how to use his hands.

A strong breeze swept around Ahmya, chilling her sweat-dampened skin and serving as a balm to the fire burning inside her. It carried all the scents of the jungle, earthy and sweet, and whispered of rain. It also flooded her senses with something more, something spicy and warm.

Rekosh.

Teak and amber with a hint of lavender.

Ahmya drew in a deep breath, allowing his scent to suffuse her. She wanted more of it.

Lacey chuckled. "I leave you two alone for a moment and you're playing salon?"

Ahmya opened her eyes with a start. Lacey stood several feet away with her hands on her hips.

Smiling sheepishly, Ahmya said, "You're just jealous you don't have someone braiding your hair."

"Maybe I am." Lacey twisted her hair up, lifting it off her neck, and fanned herself with a hand. "It's so humid that I'm thinking about chopping it all off."

"I've considered cutting mine too."

Rekosh raised a free hand, displaying his claws. "I will cut

Lacey's hair now. Very fast. But you must keep yours, Ahmya. It is too pretty to cut."

Lacey looked at Rekosh drolly. "Wow. Thanks. Rude." She dropped her hair and bent down, picking up her full basket. "Guess I'll take my ugly hair and go."

Ahmya gaped. "Your hair isn't ugly at all!"

"Not ugly," Rekosh agreed. "Telok likes your fire hair."

Rolling her eyes, Lacey said, "Seems to be the only thing he likes."

"So I did hear *hyu-nanz*," Okkor said in vrix, drawing Ahmya's attention toward him. The thornskull approached with an easy stride, his green hide blending well with the surrounding vegetation. He carried two baskets, each laden with fruits, vegetables, and mushrooms, including many round, white moonblossom fruits.

"Two full baskets?" Lacey remarked. "Someone's showing off."

Rekosh chittered and said in vrix, "The Tangle is bountiful today."

"It is true under cloud and leaf," Okkor replied. "But rain scent dances on the air, weaver. I return to our wild den to make ready for what may come."

A soft hum escaped Rekosh. "A wise choice."

Okkor continued past them, walking toward the camp. "Come soon, weaver. You may share words while we wait out the coming rain. Then we will know if your words fall faster than raindrops."

"It would take quite the storm to outmatch me, Okkor."

"Is he heading back to camp?" Lacey asked.

"Yes," Ahmya replied.

"Oh hey, wait up!" Lacey snatched up her basket and hurried after Okkor. Over her shoulder, she said, "I'm all full, so I'm going to go back with him."

Ahmya chuckled. "Okay. We'll probably do the same soon,

since my basket is almost full as well. See you there!"

"Good journey," Rekosh said, perhaps a little too pleasantly.

Balancing the basket on her hip precariously, Lacey raised her hand and waved.

Okkor slowed, waiting for Lacey to reach him, and chittered softly. "Stay close, *hyu-nan*."

She gave him a thumbs up, then spat a curse as her off-balance basket nearly tipped. Ahmya covered her mouth and watched as Lacey stumbled forward a few steps, somehow managing to keep anything from falling out of her basket

"All good," Lacey shouted once she'd recovered. She and Okkor were soon out of sight.

Rekosh's fingers moved as he finished the braid. He tied something around it, hesitated, and then stepped back. "Done, *vi'keishi*. Beautiful, as always."

Warmth flooded Ahmya's cheeks. As she turned toward him, she ran her hand over her hair and paused. "Oh my gosh. Rekosh..." She lifted her other hand and traced the design with her fingertips. "This is..."

The pattern he'd woven her hair into was so intricate, so elegant, that Ahmya couldn't believe he'd created it that quickly. When she reached the tail of the braid, she pulled it over her shoulder. The end was tied off with red silk, bright against her black hair.

Ahmya couldn't help but wonder if this was a small claim on his part—his color, his mark.

Rekosh trilled. "You are pleased?"

She looked up and smiled widely at him. "I wish I could see it."

His eyes softened. Easing closer, he lifted his lower arms and took her hands in his, curling his long, rough fingers around them. "There is something else I would have you see. Something I would give you."

Ahmya's breath hitched. She knew. Knew what he was going

to say, what he was going to confess. She'd had this same feeling when he'd come to her den the other day and taken her hands exactly like this.

Tiny drops of rain lighted upon her heated skin.

Ahmya tightened her fingers around Rekosh's and lowered her gaze, studying the rigid, armor-like sections of his torso. His hide darkened where raindrops landed.

She watched the water trickle over his hide and glisten in the fading sunlight. "You don't have to give me anything, Rekosh."

He caught her chin with the fingers of his upper hand and tipped her face up toward his. All eight eyes, bright red, intense, and piercing, looked down at her as though there was nothing else to see in the universe. "Ahmya... I said it is a need and a want. My gift, my words."

Ahmya's belly was aflutter. She'd known early on that Rekosh had taken an interest in her. It'd been clear from the moment he'd introduced himself in the pit—the way he'd bowed and curled a finger beneath hers, the careful but smooth way he'd attempted to pronounce her name.

She'd seen it every time he looked upon her, spoke to her, touched her. Rekosh cared for everyone in their little tribe, but he was most protective of her. Most...*possessive* of her.

Callie had told her what had happened while Ahmya had been unconscious after the firevine attack. Rekosh had been a mess. Pacing frantically, fidgeting, constantly turning his gaze back to Ahmya. Even with one of his arms dangling numb at his side from the firevine's paralytic venom, his only concern had been for her. When Diego had cut away Ahmya's clothing to treat her wounds, Rekosh had nearly fought him.

He'd refused to allow another male to tend her wounds, refused to let another male touch her.

That night, unable to fit inside the small cave in which the humans had sheltered, Rekosh had lain on the ground with his body exposed to the rain just to be near Ahmya.

Why had she fought so hard against what she knew deep down to be true? Why had she allowed her fear of the unknown, of what he was, to prevent her from seeing what was right before her eyes, to stop her from recognizing what lay within her own heart?

I want him too.

It didn't matter how large he was, how frightening he'd been at first. It didn't matter that he was of a different species. He was Rekosh.

He was kind and considerate, funny and witty. When things were at their bleakest, he was a spot of brightness. When danger loomed, he was the fiercest of protectors, throwing himself into danger to safeguard the people he cared about. She loved talking with him, learning from him, and teaching him in turn. She loved his curiosity and passion. And the way her body responded to him... A single brush of his fingers was all it took to make her crave more.

He was everything she'd yearned for.

The rain fell a little harder, a little faster. Rekosh's eyes narrowed in irritation, and a growl rolled in his chest. He tipped his head back and glared at the gloomy sky.

With a soft laugh, Ahmya brought their hands to her chest and pressed her face against the fingers holding her chin, gently rubbing them with her cheek.

Rekosh's gaze snapped back to her, eyes wide.

She softened her smile. "I would hear your words, Rekosh."

A shiver coursed through him, flowing directly into her from where they touched. It was followed by a low hum, the sound brimming with eagerness and anticipation. His mandibles rose in a vrix smile.

"Ah, *kir'ani vi'keishi...*" He stroked her jaw. Despite the thick, hard calluses on his fingers, his touch was gentle. But that gentleness still sent a pulse of warmth through her body.

Rekosh withdrew his hands, trailing his fingers over her skin as he did so—as though he were loath to break contact. She nearly swayed toward him to follow. Her next inhalation was shallow, shaky, strained.

So much roiled just beneath the surface. So much desire and emotion, so much that she'd held inside for far too long because of shame, fear, and uncertainty. It all threatened to burst out, here and now. Though she'd not admitted it to herself, Rekosh had awoken things within her, passions and yearnings, that she'd never experienced.

And all she had to do was embrace them.

Embrace *him*.

"For a big time, I have known, Ahmya." His words were careful, measured, as he grasped the strap of his bag and slid it around to his front. "My eyes saw you, my hearts felt you, and my soul sang for you."

She clasped her hands against her belly both to keep them from trembling and to keep herself from reaching for him. Her eyes dipped to watch his clever fingers take hold of the silk string that kept his bag closed.

"Ahmya, you are my—"

The brush rustled somewhere behind her.

The hairs on the back of her neck rose, and a fresh shiver stole through her, emanating from her spine in a cold wave.

Rekosh's chin ticked upward, and his fingers froze. Despite his lack of pupils, Ahmya knew he was looking past her. His mandibles spread wider.

"Shitfuck," he rasped.

"I'm guessing those aren't the words you've been wanting to share," Ahmya said, her voice coming out small, thin, and unsteady.

Distant thunder rolled across the sky, but she barely noticed it. Neither did she notice the sound of heavier, faster raindrops pattering on the surrounding vegetation. The only noise she truly registered was an ululating growl from behind her.

Against her better judgment, she turned her head to peek over her shoulder. Her stomach plummeted.

A beast stood in the open not thirty feet behind her. She glimpsed a sleek, narrow head, long limbs, dark blue fur and a full green mane. It was at least as large as a mountain lion.

And its predatory yellow eyes were fixed on her.

Great. Another wild animal that wants to eat me.

And here she was having broken one of Ketahn's golden rules—she was unarmed.

The creature burst into motion, muscles rippling beneath its short fur as it charged toward her.

Ahmya cried out, flinching away from the creature. She'd barely moved an inch when a pair of long, powerful arms banded around her and swept her off the ground.

Instinctively, she threw her arms around Rekosh's neck, clamped her thighs around his sides, and clung to him.

"I have you." His voice rumbled into her. It was strong enough, clear and steady enough, to overcome the deafening pounding of her heart and the thrumming fear radiating from her bones.

He swung his bag behind his back, snatched up his spear in his right hands, and twisted his torso, angling Ahmya away from the charging beast as he thrust his weapon.

She felt the impact jolt through him, and she heard the faint squelching of punctured flesh, the crunch of breaking bone, and a bestial whine. Something heavy crashed onto the ground before Rekosh. The beast thrashed, disturbing the detritus. Rekosh raised his forelegs, growled, and slammed them down.

The struggles ceased. Ahmya felt his muscles tense as he tore his spear free.

She released a shaky breath and eased her grip on Rekosh. "What was—"

"Hold," he commanded. "Tight."

Before she could even wonder why he'd tell her to do so, Rekosh broke into a run. The sudden movement jostled her. Ahmya dug her fingers into his hide as she clutched him—not that his arms would've let her fall.

She blinked raindrops from her eyes. Trees and plants whipped past on either side. Over Rekosh's shoulder, she saw the spot where they'd been foraging only moments ago growing increasingly distant in the deepening gloom, which meant their camp was growing increasingly distant.

Why were they moving away from camp? Away from the others?

Was Lacey okay? Had she and Okkor made it back safely?

A chill crept through Ahmya's veins, coiled in her chest, and constricted. The thought of her friend being harmed was far scarier than any danger this jungle could throw at her.

"Rekosh, we need to find the others!"

"No," he replied.

"But—"

A pulse of lightning illuminated the jungle. Multiple pairs of yellow eyes flashed in the surrounding shadows, all directed at Ahmya. That instant of light was enough for her to make out the dark, bestial forms attached to those eyes giving chase to Rekosh.

Every hair on Ahmya's body rose in alarm. She curled her fingers, pressing her nails even more firmly into his hide.

"Um, Rekosh..."

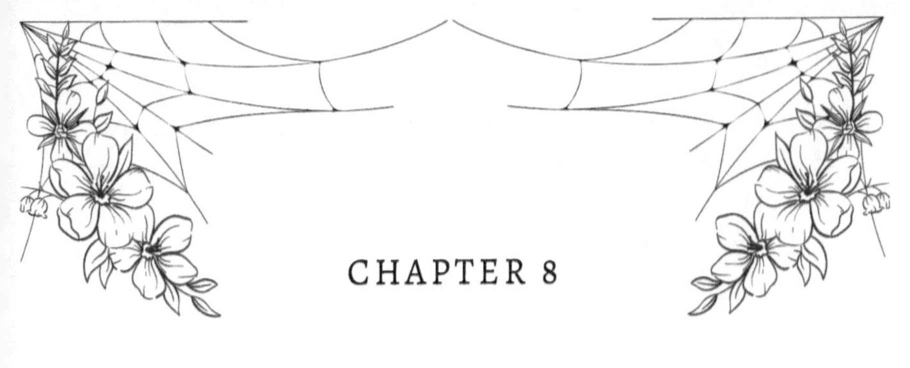

CHAPTER 8

"I KNOW." Rekosh squeezed the shaft of his spear and clutched Ahmya against him.

He'd known even before he'd heard the kuzahks rushing through the undergrowth behind him, had known the instant he'd seen the first one.

A kuzahk ahead meant a pack of them behind.

Hearts thumping so quickly that he could not discern their individual beats, Rekosh ran. He charged through vegetation, jumped over fallen logs, and scrambled along raised roots. With every segment he crossed, he sensed the kuzahks drawing nearer.

Crackling thunder echoed between the trees, making the air tremble. Huge, heavy raindrops pelted Rekosh's hide, each coming quicker than the last, each colder than the last. But they could not cool the fire within him, could not diminish his fear and fury.

Ahmya's breaths were rapid, and he felt her shaking, felt her heart racing.

His mandibles ticked, and his fangs ground together.

Instinct demanded he stop, turn, and fight, demanded he

destroy this threat to his mate. Yet it also demanded he run faster and carry Ahmya as far away from this danger as possible.

A kuzahk snarled to his left, just behind him.

Rekosh responded with a snarl of his own. He could see the creature at the corner of his vision. The slits at the end of its snout flared as it scented the air, and its fur glistened with moisture.

Rekosh kicked out with a hind leg, striking the beast's front shoulder. The kuzahk stumbled, falling back, only for another to dart around Rekosh from the right.

Without slowing, he leapt into the air, drawing his legs up tight. The beast's jaws snapped just beneath him. Rekosh came down heavily on the other side of the creature, pouring his momentum back into running.

The kuzahks yipped and howled behind him. Much too close behind him.

Ahmya is unharmed. She will remain unharmed. She will be safe.

He repeated those words again and again in his mind, and each repetition lent him a little more speed, a little more strength. But he knew in his hearts it would not be enough.

Vrix were fast. Kuzahks were faster.

More of the creatures entered the edges of his vision, keeping beyond his reach. They understood that they possessed the speed to surround him.

Rekosh pushed himself onward. He had no idea how many segments he'd traveled from their camp, from the spot they'd been foraging, from Kaldarak. No idea where he was. But only Ahmya mattered in that moment.

He scaled a low, rocky rise, and his eyes widened. Less than a body's length ahead, the ground fell away sharply into a ravine.

Everything within Rekosh seized. His hearts stilled, the breath locked in his lungs, even his blood refused to flow through his veins. He dug the ends of his legs into the ground and threw his weight backward.

"Oh God!" Ahmya's body tensed around him, her breaths coming quick and ragged.

One foreleg slid over the edge before Rekosh skidded to a halt. Stones, dirt, and leaves tumbled down into the raging waters of the river ten segments below.

He staggered back only a few steps before a kuzahk leapt in front of him. The creature's fangs caught on Ahmya's backpack, and it tugged backward, nearly pulling her from Rekosh's grasp.

Ahmya cried out, nails raking his hide as she struggled to hold on to him.

Fear fanned the flames of his anger. She was not going to be taken from him, and he was not going to lose her, not here, not now, not to this thing. He thrust his spear, striking the creature's hindquarters with a glancing blow that opened a gash. The kuzahk released its hold and hobbled away with a whimper.

Rekosh hugged Ahmya to his body again.

She stiffened. "Rekosh, look out!"

He turned his head to see a kuzahk on his left pounce.

Releasing his hold on Ahmya with his upper arm, he raised it, using his lower arm to shove her across his chest toward the right. The beast's jaws clamped on his raised forearm. Pain burst through the limb, swept away by rage as quickly as it had come. He swung his head down at the beast and pierced its skull with his mandibles. When he shook the dead kuzahk off his arm, he barely noticed the blood mingling with the rainwater on his hide.

The other creature before him recovered and lunged again —not for Rekosh, but for Ahmya. He braced his hand on her backside, lifting her higher. She made a startled sound and planted her palms on his shoulder to stabilize herself. The kuzahk's jaws clacked shut on empty air barely a finger's breadth from Ahmya.

Rekosh reared back and slammed his forelegs down on the beast. Its claws raked at him as he stomped again and again, mangling flesh and bone.

Ahmya was *his*. Nothing could have her. Nothing would harm her.

Another beast lunged from the side, the arc of its leap carrying it straight for Ahmya. Rekosh hammered an arm into the creature's side and heaved. The kuzahk's claws opened fresh wounds on his hide before it was flung into the air. It twisted and kicked but could not catch itself before falling over the edge of the ravine.

"Every time," Rekosh growled in vrix. "Every time we speak, something gets in the way. Something stops us."

He hissed and staggered forward when something heavy landed on his hindquarters. Hooked claws snagged his hide, latching the kuzahk on. Its hind legs scrabbled for purchase as it dragged itself up. Rekosh snarled.

"No!" Ahmya cried.

More of the beasts rushed in from the sides, swiping claws and biting at Rekosh's legs. He kicked and swung at them reflexively. All his thoughts, all his focus, went into keeping Ahmya out of their reach. But some part of his mind understood that he was moving dangerously closer to the edge.

The kuzahk on his hindquarters leapt higher, its claws sinking into his shoulder. Ahmya let out a cry and thrust herself away from the creature. Rekosh stumbled forward, desperately clutching at her as the beast's jaws gnashed beside his head.

He hooked an arm up around its neck, squeezing its throat down on his shoulder. The kuzahk dug its hind claws into his lower back, pushing against his hold. Rekosh spread his mandibles wide, and a deep, pained growl tore out of him.

Those claws were just below his bag. Just below his gift. His muscles bulged, increasing the pressure on the beast's throat, but its wet fur was allowing it to slip away.

Ahmya's face was pale, her eyes wide and full of fear, but her hand was steady as she tugged a blackrock knife free from his sash. With a growl of her own—and those flat human teeth bared—she raised the knife over her shoulder and slammed it down into the kuzahk's skull.

The creature twitched, briefly forcing its claws deeper, before it went limp.

Rekosh met Ahmya's gaze. Though her eyes remained fearful, there was something solid at their core, something unwavering.

My little flower...

He drew her close to his chest again. She wrapped herself around him, burying her face against his neck. Rekosh roared and hurled the dead beast over his shoulder, knocking back several of its pack.

Using the space he'd created, he swung his spear in a wide arc, forcing the creatures back farther as they avoided the bite of the bloody stone head.

His chest heaved with his strained breaths, and dull pain pulsed across his hide from his wounds, each of which radiated its own warmth.

There were at least five of the creatures still standing, many of them wounded—and most with Rekosh's blood glistening on their mouths and claws. They'd tasted blood now. They weren't likely to abandon their hunt, even after the losses suffered by their pack.

The kuzahks bunched their shoulders, bared their fangs, and crept forward.

Rekosh slid his hind legs back, seeking to maintain the distance between himself and the beasts. One leg slipped past the edge of the ridge. The other sank into ground softened by rain, skewing his balance.

A kuzahk darted forward.

Widening his stance, Rekosh met the beast with a thrust of his spear. The weapon plunged into the creature's throat.

Lightning arced across the gap in the trees overhead. Thunder shook the ground before the light had even faded.

Ahmya made a sound that Rekosh only felt as a faint vibration against his hide. Heat radiated from her skin, in stark contrast to the rain's chill.

The beast struggled at the end of Rekosh's spear, pawing at the ground to get closer. He shoved it down with a foreleg.

The world quaked, and the earth beneath his rear legs crumbled.

His insides lurched. He pushed off with his middle legs, but they found no purchase on the collapsing ground.

"*No,*" he rasped. "No, no, no!" Releasing the spear, he clawed at the dirt and stone before him with his free hands and forelegs. He was falling.

They were falling.

The side of the ravine rushed up before him. Mud, dirt, and stone melted away, flowing down the steep canyon wall like runoff from the storm. Ahmya screamed. Rekosh's claws raked through the debris, and his arms and legs scraped the ravine wall, but there was nothing of which to catch hold.

There was no way to stop the fall.

He wrapped all four arms around Ahmya, cocooning her, and kicked away from the side of the ravine.

"Rekosh," she said breathlessly.

Not how I hoped to hold her. Not how I hoped to hear her speak my name.

They fell for but a moment, yet that moment stretched on and on like a bolt of silk unraveling into a single thread. The roar of the wind mingled with the drumming of rain, with the hiss of water rushing below and the ragged whispers of shaking leaves and boughs, with the heavy splashes of stone and dirt plunging into the river. The pounding of his hearts lay beneath it all, setting a frantic rhythm.

Rekosh's back struck the water. Pain burst across his hide, concentrated more intensely on his numerous wounds. The churning river swallowed him, deafening him to all but its fierce flow, and its current snatched control from him. Rekosh tumbled and spun, his limbs striking unseen obstacles. When his left shoulders crashed into a large stone, the strength and pain of the impact forced his arms open.

Ahmya slipped from his grasp.

No!

Somehow, he fought his way to the surface. Somehow, Ahmya made it with him. He heard her suck in air even as he filled his lungs.

"Rekosh!" Ahmya called out. "I'm here!"

Turning, he glimpsed his mate through the water and hair clinging to his face. She was swimming toward him.

Then the river dragged Rekosh back under.

Blinded by the dark water, he fumbled for Ahmya. He felt her grabbing at him, and caught one of her hands, but his hold slipped as the water's punishing current threatened to tear them apart.

The river dipped, dropping Rekosh into a swirling section that spun him about violently. Ahmya's hand was ripped out of his grasp.

A cold unlike any Rekosh could ever have imagined flowed out from his chest, colliding with the thrumming heat of his panic to create a sickening storm.

Using all his limbs, he struggled to right himself, again forcing his head above the surface. The river's roar was so powerful that even the thunder was dull in comparison. Rekosh swept hair and water out of his eyes and searched for any sign of his little mate.

That inner cold deepened, penetrating his bones. Branches,

bark, and leaves floated atop the murky, frothing water, but where was Ahmya? He'd had her only a moment ago. He'd *had* her.

He called out her name. His voice scratched his throat as it came out, but neither that pain nor any other would match his agony if she was—

She is safe, he told himself.

Rekosh would accept nothing less.

Ahmya splashed up from the murk several segments ahead of him—first her head, that dark hair a tangled mess in her face, and then her arms, moving wildly to keep her upright.

Yet something was dragging her down.

She brought her hands in to clutch the straps of her bag, wrestling with them. The current dragged her under before she could free herself from them.

His hearts stuttered, and he fought to close the distance between them. "Ahmya!"

The backpack bobbed to the surface momentarily, no longer on Ahmya's back, before vanishing into the murky river.

A single word echoed inside Rekosh, instilled with impossibly volatile emotion.

Please.

Ahmya's head reemerged, and she gasped for air.

"Ahmya! Here!"

"Rekosh!"

He could barely make out her voice amidst the noise, and yet hearing it fought back some of the cold inside him.

She wiped her black tresses aside, revealing her fearful expression, and turned in place until she was facing him.

They swam toward each other, but the conflicting currents battering their bodies made it a trial to overcome even that short distance. He shifted his course over and over as the water shoved him in one direction and carried her in another, as it sped her along while trying to catch his legs and hindquarters in more of those swirling pools where currents converged. His hearts stopped each time the water pulled Ahmya under, only to resume beating when she came back up coughing.

The ravine walls sped by on either side, with rainwater pouring down them to feed the already swollen river. Branches shook in the wind high above the ridgelines against a dark gray sky.

But Rekosh could only focus on Ahmya. His little flower. The mate he'd yet to claim, the clever, courageous, determined, kind female who he so desired.

Who he so needed.

The threads of fate that had brought them together were tangled and knotted, spanning across the jungle, across worlds, across the stars. He would not allow them to be severed. He would weave those threads around himself and Ahmya, would fashion them into a cocoon. It would be their warmth, their shelter, their shield. Their unbreakable bond.

Drawing in a deep breath, he plunged forward, paddling with all his arms and legs.

The distance between them shrank, first a threadspan, then a hand's width, then segments at a time. When finally they were near enough, he thrust out a foreleg.

Ahmya grabbed hold of it immediately. Her hands slipped along his slick hide, but she clenched her jaw, turned away from the water splashing into her face, and clutched at his limb until she'd fully taken hold. The instant her arms were secure, Rekosh pulled her toward him.

She clambered into his arms and clung to him with her whole body once again, squeezing tight. Shivers wracked her, and her skin was far cooler than normal.

Rekosh embraced her, smoothing down her hair. "I have you, *vi'keishi.*"

"I know," she whispered raggedly. "I know."

They clung to each other as the river carried them onward

and the current spun them about, barely managing to keep their heads above the water. But Rekosh didn't care about that. He had her in his arms, and that was all that mattered. He could overcome anything else that was thrown at them so long as he had her.

He scanned the sides of the river, narrowing his eyes against the spray kicked up by the rain and churning waters. The ravine walls offered no apparent points of escape; they were steep, rocky, muddy, with signs of recent landslides everywhere.

Kicking his legs and swinging his arms, he fought the river's incessant downward pull. Fire sizzled through his limbs, igniting countless aches and stings from his wounds, many of which he hadn't realized he'd suffered.

And the current only gained speed.

Rekosh blinked water from his eyes and stared hard downstream.

Through the gloom and mist, he couldn't make out the river for much farther ahead. From his perspective, in fact, it seemed to stop abruptly after an upcoming calm patch.

And beyond it he could see...nothing.

"Shaper, unmake me," he rasped.

"Rekosh, wha—" Ahmya turned her head to follow his gaze with her own and stiffened. "That's...not what it looks like. Right?"

He was already drawing a thick silk strand from his spinnerets, passing it to his lower hands. "Looks like nothing. It is nothing."

"Yeah." Her lower lip trembled with her next inhalation, and she shifted her hips to accommodate him as he wound the strand around her waist. "Nothing."

Unable to look away from the water's edge, Rekosh tied the strand off around Ahmya before securing the other end around his own waist, leaving a bit of slack between them.

The closer they came to that edge, the faster the river carried them toward it, and the more tumultuous the waters grew.

He wrapped himself around her again. "Still have you."

"I know." She buried her face against his neck. "And I have you." Her breath was warm on his hide, and her fingers curled into his tousled hair as she tightened her hold on him. The bite of her little nails on his scalp was the sweetest sensation in the world.

Dark masses took shape beyond the water's edge—the tops of towering trees, thrashing in the storm, made indistinct by the rain and mist.

Rekosh's insides twisted, drawing tighter than any knot ever could. All the words he'd longed to say were caught within him, trapped, silenced.

His friends would've found that the most unbelievable part of this tale.

He tucked his chin over Ahmya's hair, curling more protectively around her. A few kicks of his legs turned him so he was facing away from the nothingness ahead.

The river carried them over the edge of the world.

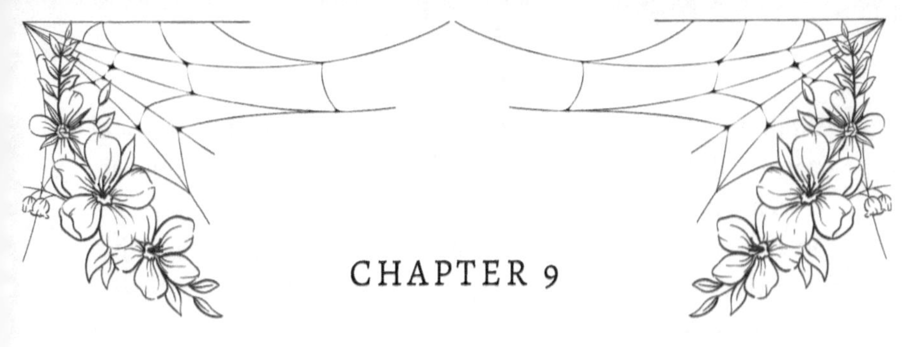

CHAPTER 9

FOR THE SECOND time that day, Rekosh's gut lurched, and he fell, now amidst a torrent of water rather than dirt and stone.

Foolish as it was, he couldn't help wondering if this was how flying felt. Was this the sensation Ahmya and the other humans experienced during their journey across the stars?

His back struck the water, which felt much more like solid ground than liquid, and his left foreleg slammed into something hard and unyielding. The bursts of pain jolted him, body and mind. All went black and silent, as though a spinewood fire had been snuffed out in one of Takarahl's deepest, darkest caverns. Despite all that pain, he felt...nothing. He was nothing.

No. Not nothing. Need to protect her...

My mate.

Sound and feeling rushed back. His chest burned from a lack of air, and the pressure within it was overwhelming. Churning water had closed in around him, the waterfall was forcing him down, down, down, and his arms...were empty.

His arms were *empty.*

No!

Fighting to right himself, he sought the silk tether. Everything was dark, tumultuous, murky, so much so that he could not see. But his grasping fingers found that line, and he pulled. It went taut. He tugged harder.

Rekosh found Ahmya on the other end, and he drew her into his arms.

But something wasn't right. Why did she not grasp him? Why was she so still, so limp?

Every oath he knew in vrix rattled through his head, accompanied by every human curse he'd been taught. He held Ahmya against his chest, ignoring the fire in his lungs and the pain radiating from every part of his body, and swam toward what he hoped was the surface.

Each beat of his hearts was harder and louder than the last, until they were all he could hear. More thoughts must've been raging through his mind, powerful emotions must've been thrumming in his chest, but he perceived none of them. He was aware only of Ahmya's unmoving form and the impossible expanse of water separating him from the air they both desperately needed.

He broke the surface with a ragged inhalation that felt like a thousand bone needles stabbing his throat and chest from within. Raising Ahmya's head above the waterline, he pushed toward the shore.

The instant his legs touched the bottom, he ran.

His left foreleg buckled when he put weight on it, breaking his stride. Agony pulsed along the limb, emanating from his bones. Rekosh growled, lifted the leg higher, and hobbled onward, water sloshing around him. Every step met a little less resistance from the increasingly shallow water.

Ahmya's head lolled on the crook of his elbow, and her dangling limbs bumped his hide as he moved.

Hungry mud grasped at his legs when he finally neared land. Rain fell relentlessly, creating countless ripples on the water's surface that were swept away by his passage.

As soon as he was out of the river, his legs folded, dropping him onto their joints in the mud. The pain in his left foreleg drew a breathless snarl from him, but it was quickly forgotten. He cradled Ahmya in his lower arms as he smoothed her wet hair out of her face.

Her skin had lost its color, and the usual pink tinge of her lips had been replaced by faint blue. When he cupped her cheek in his palm, it was cold, and she did not react to his touch.

"Ahmya," he rasped. "You must wake."

She did not open her eyes.

With the pad of his thumb, he eased her eyelid open. Her brown eye was dull, unfocused, nearly...lifeless. Lowering his head and battling back an onslaught of chilling thoughts, he took hold of her jaw and angled her face toward his.

No breath escaped her lips, no air flowed from her nose.

His fine hairs stood, and tension rippled across his hide. Shivers coursed through him that had nothing to do with the cold. Everything was unraveling—Rekosh, the world, the whole universe beyond. Every fiber of his mind and spirit fought to hold it all together. Fought to tie off those threads.

He slid his hand down her neck and settled it over her chest. *Please. Please...*

Her heart beat under his palm, a faint, weak *thump-thump* that echoed through him like a peal of thunder.

"Ahmya, please." He patted her cheek. "Please, *vi'keishi*."

Nothing.

Heat and cold raced through Rekosh in waves, shredding him from within with scorching, stinging thorns and frigid lashing tendrils that spared no part of him.

No, she will not—cannot—

All the anger and fear he'd felt during the kuzahks' attack returned eightfold. It was strong enough to rival the fury of the storm, intense enough to challenge the river's rage. But it had not been enough to protect her.

Rekosh lowered her legs onto the ground, braced a hand on the back of her neck, and shook her. His words came out in a jumble of English and vrix. "Ahmya, do not leave me. Wake! Breathe!"

But she would not move, would not rouse, would not breathe.

Again he peeled open one of her eyes. She did not look at him; she didn't look at anything.

"That fire in your heart must burn. Burn for me, Ahmya. You are mine, and I will not let you go."

Rekosh halted himself before he shook her again, and his limbs trembled with the exertion of that restraint. Any more force would only do her further harm.

He had woven too many death shrouds in his time. He would not weave another this day. Could not. Not for her.

He curled over her, shielding her from the rain, and drew her chest against his. Body shuddering, he whispered her name again. Whispered it with sorrow and guilt, with fury and longing, with desperation and need.

"Broodmother," he whispered, "Rootsinger, Protector... whichever of you may listen. Do not take her from me. I will not allow it. You cannot have her. She is mine and mine alone."

All existence pressed in around him. The raindrops, the air, the clouds, the moisture on his hide, the entire Tangle. The pain wracking him, dull but insistent, added to the weight. And his spirit was collapsing on itself as he did all he could to deny the possibility that... That she...

Ahmya coughed. It was a small sound, insignificant against the roaring of the waterfall and the storm, but it stilled and silenced everything within Rekosh. She jerked, and that cough built into a hoarse, wet hacking from the depths of her chest. Her entire body spasmed, and her fingers raked his hide. She twisted in his grasp, bent over his arm, and vomited water onto the muddy ground.

He gathered her hair and pulled it out of her face as she clutched at him and coughed up more water. She was shaking as fiercely as a lone leaf clinging to a branch through a raging storm, drawing in one ragged, rasping breath after another between wet coughs.

But she was moving. She was alive.

Despite everything they'd just endured, everything they'd just suffered, a tiny, relieved spark of warmth ignited in his chest. A flicker of happiness.

Even if everything else was shit, as the humans might've said, Rekosh and Ahmya were *alive*.

Rekosh gently rubbed her back. His voice was barely steady when he said, "Breathe, Ahmya. Take many breaths. I am here."

A sob burst from her. It was followed by another and another, broken by more wretched coughs. Helpless, Rekosh crooned softly and held her, continuing to run his hand up and down her back. The small bumps of her spine reminded him just how fragile his little human mate was.

Reminded him that he'd nearly lost her.

Again.

Rain continued falling upon them, mingling with Ahmya's tears. Would that he could've cried with her. Would that he could've produced even a single tear to fall alongside hers. Closing his eyes, he lowered his head and nuzzled the back of her neck.

She shook with her sobs, with the cold, with the strain of the ordeal she'd just survived. As much as Rekosh hated those tremors coursing through her, they were far better than the feel of her unmoving, lifeless body in his arms.

A soft, trembling touch upon the side of his face coaxed his eyes open.

"I'm...okay," Ahmya said quietly. "I'm okay."

He trilled and drew in a deep breath. Her scent was diminished by the rain, but it was still there, still sweet, still comforting, still Ahmya.

"You are not hurt?" he asked.

She laughed. The sound eased his hearts, even though it was interrupted by another bout of coughing.

"I hurt. A lot." She leaned her head against his jaw and cupped his face with her palm. Her words and breathing were short and shallow. "My chest feels like it's on fire and I feel so weak, but...but we're alive."

Rekosh glared out at the jungle, where leaves and branches whipped violently in the wind, where danger lurked in every shadow, where every moment presented new threats to everything he cared about.

The world around them lit up with a flash of lightning, which was followed swiftly by booming thunder.

"As we will remain." He pushed himself up. His left foreleg throbbed even without bearing any of his weight, and he could not count the other wounds now adding their aches to the agonizing maelstrom encompassing him.

But he could not rest, could not stop.

Not until they were safe.

Rekosh helped Ahmya stand. "We must find shelter."

Keeping hold of one of his hands, she slitted her eyes against the rain and nodded. "I guess we're lost?"

"No." He guided Ahmya closer, hooked his arms behind her, and lifted her off her feet, cradling her against him. "We know we are here. Just...not where here is."

"Which is another way of saying we're lost." Ahmya wrapped her arms around his neck, letting out another cough.

Rekosh's mandibles drooped, and a fresh shudder rippled across his hide. Though it didn't sound nearly as bad as it had before, her cough was unsettling, and she was still trembling. He needed to get her out of the rain. Needed to get her dry and warm.

"Yes. Lost, but alive." He lifted his mandibles in a smile. "We will find home, Ahmya."

Lightning arced across the sky again. Rekosh set into motion as rumbling thunder vibrated the ground beneath him.

He strode as swiftly as his stilted gait allowed, keeping his eyes in constant motion to watch for danger and scout out a shelter. The river lay behind him. To one side, rocky cliffs stretched onward; to the other side and ahead, the jungle loomed, as dense and dark as ever.

"Rekosh?"

"Yes?" He shifted his gaze to Ahmya.

Her features were strained with concern as she stared down. "What's wrong with your leg?"

He grunted, shifting his foreleg a little more to the side. "Small hurt. It will heal soon."

"But you can't walk on it!"

Rekosh chittered. "Urkot is good with three arms. I will walk with five legs. Still more than you, *vi'keishi*."

The concern remained in her eyes. "You can put me down. I can walk. I don't want you hurting."

"The hurt is small if I carry you, small if I do not." Rekosh cupped his hand over the back of her head and drew her closer, shielding her from the rain. "So I will carry *kir'ani vi'keishi*."

He continued onward, keeping close to the cliffside. They would have to find a way back up eventually to return to Kaldarak, but in this weather, the climb wouldn't have been safe for even the most capable vrix.

And Rekosh wasn't exactly in peak condition at the moment.

The silk strand still connecting him to Ahmya brushed against his hide as he moved. Its purpose had been served, but he could not bring himself to remove it yet. It was part of his physical connection to her, a tether that bound their bodies, that offered him some comfort, some security. Yet it was nothing compared to the other connection he felt with her.

His heartsthread had been interwoven with hers, bound tighter than he could ever have imagined possible. It was stronger than any thread, than any rope, than any wood, stone, or metal, and he would protect it—would protect her—with all his being.

But that dedication could not fend off the agony of his wounds. Each step came with fresh pain, and his limbs became stiffer, his aches deeper. An unfathomable weariness crept into his spirit, growing and growing. It was Ahmya who kept him going, Ahmya who kept him strong, who stoked the flame in his core.

The sky had darkened when he finally spotted a place to rest. His legs nearly gave out in relief. The rocky overhang wasn't ideal, but it would at least provide shelter from the wind and rain.

Rekosh hunched down under the stone ceiling. Cutting away the silk tether, he set Ahmya on her feet in the shelter, keeping his hands upon her until she gained her balance.

He could not help but find himself again bewildered by the human form. That they stood and walked on two legs remained so strange to him. So unlikely. Yet despite their seeming limitations, they were surprisingly agile. And in Ahmya's case, quite…graceful.

Ahmya took a wobbly step back.

Well, not graceful *now*…but neither was Rekosh currently.

She wrapped her arms around herself and looked around. Even in this gloom, her skin was far too pale, and there were dark circles beneath her eyes. Her lips retained a blue tint that he did not like.

"At least it's dry, right?" she asked with a small smile. When she turned her face back to Rekosh, her smile disappeared, and her eyes widened. "Oh Rekosh…"

Brow creasing, Ahmya closed the distance between them and brushed her fingers beneath the bite wounds on his arm. Tears gathered in her eyes.

Gently, Rekosh covered her cheek with his hand and wiped away an escaped tear with his thumb. "No crying. We must keep it dry in here, Ahmya."

She shook her head. "Even now you're trying to make me feel better when you're so wounded. Look at all of them. There are just so…so many."

"You will not like if I look more like Telok?"

"I don't care what you look like, Rekosh, only that you are *hurt*."

"Ah, *vi'keishi*." He bent lower, resting his headcrest against her forehead, and closed his eyes. The pain receded. There was only her, her scent and warmth, her concern for him. In vrix, he said, "I would gladly suffer eightfold the wounds to shield you from the slightest harm."

Ahmya cradled his jaw with her hand just beneath his mandibles and pressed her head more firmly against his. She sniffled. "I didn't entirely understand what you said, but…but I like it when you call me *vi'keishi*."

He trilled and rubbed his uninjured foreleg against her calf, just above her boot. Her skin was soft and smooth, but it still bore a chill, and her trembling had not yet subsided. The slight rasp in her breathing offered him no ease.

She pulled away from him far too soon, and her watery eyes met his. "We should get your wounds taken care of. I lost my bag in the river. Do you have anything in yours? Or…" Her lips curled into a smile. "We could use your butt silk?"

Rekosh huffed. "Why *butt silk*? It is just silk."

Ahmya chuckled, but it swiftly turned into a cough that she stifled with her arm.

Rekosh's mandibles fell. Not all wounds were apparent on

the surface, and she was clearly still suffering the effects of nearly drowning. "You must rest, Ahmya."

"I'll be okay," she said once the coughing subsided. "I'm okay. But you're still bleeding. Let me help you for once."

"For once? You always help, Ahmya." Rekosh lifted off his bag, then his sash, both of which were still dripping, and set them against the wall. The gift had been wrapped in both cloth and leather; it would be fine.

It had to be fine.

Mindful of his injured leg, he lowered himself to the floor of their shelter. With the immediate danger past, his wounds screamed, each one declaring itself the direst. Yet the most persistent pain, the deepest, was the throbbing ache in his left foreleg, which had taken on a sharpness that made it impossible to ignore.

He reached back to gather sticky silk from his spinnerets, letting out a low hiss at the discomfort caused by his movements.

Ahmya withdrew the metal knife from his sash, grasped the hem of her skirt, and cut the fabric, tearing two strips from it. Rekosh delighted in the damage done to silk spun by another vrix, but that pleasure died when he realized she had nothing else to wear.

Not that the short skirt would've kept her very warm, especially with it being soaked through.

Setting the knife on a large, flat rock, she stepped between his legs and leaned close, using the wet cloth to wipe away the blood from the puncture wounds on his arm. Her ministrations were tender, careful, as though she feared hurting him further. Warmth bloomed in Rekosh's chest.

His mate was tending to him.

It mattered not that he hadn't declared himself, that he hadn't yet claimed her. She was simply his.

Ahmya held her hand out to him, palm up.

He handed her a wad of his silk. She applied it to the deep bite marks, smoothing out the edges and making sure the sticky substance was firmly in place.

Her bottom lip quivered, and tears streamed down her cheeks. Rekosh's chest tightened. She wiped her face with the back of her hand and moved on to the next wounds, taking great care in cleaning them. Her hands trembled, her body shivered, and her breath shook, but she worked diligently, seeing to every injury she could find.

Rekosh handed her more silk as she required, but with each passing moment, his shame grew.

As much as he craved her touch and attention, he could not bear for her to continue like this. Ahmya was cold and exhausted, pushing her body beyond its limits. She needed rest and warmth.

The only thing he needed was for her to be all right.

Rekosh curled his fingers around her wrist. She looked at him. There was such sorrow in her eyes, but he much rather would've seen sorrow in them than the nothingness they'd held as she had lain limp in his arms.

He plucked the cloth from Ahmya's hand, pulled her closer, and drew her down in front of him, curling his uninjured foreleg on the ground beneath her. Wrapping his arms around her, he held her against his chest. "You must rest."

Ahmya tensed, placing a hand on his leg, and attempted to rise again. "Rekosh, your leg needs—"

Keeping his hold on her firm but gentle, Rekosh caught her chin and tipped her face back, forcing her gaze to meet his. "I will heal, Ahmya." He brushed his fingers along her jaw, following the delicate shell of her ear, until he reached her damp hair, through which he combed his claws, carefully working out any snags they encountered. "Vrix heal in a small time."

"You promise you'll be okay?" The tension was already leaving her body as she relaxed against him.

"Yes. We will be okay, *vi'keishi.*"

As he continued to comb his claws through her hair, Ahmya's lashes fluttered, and her eyes closed. She slumped against his chest, and though her breathing was still ragged, still shallow, it was steady and unbroken.

Rekosh leaned his shoulder against the cool, hard stone wall of their shelter. He felt impossibly heavy. Impossibly weary. She deserved fluffed silk to rest upon, a cushion to cradle her in her sleep, but he knew that such was beyond him now.

Getting this far would have to be enough.

My mate slumbers in my arms.

His mandibles ticked upward. Despite everything, he could find joy in something so small as this. For the first time, Ahmya was sleeping not merely near him, but with him. She was comfortable enough in his embrace to fall asleep.

It made no difference to him that she had simply succumbed to exhaustion.

She cares for me. She has shown it, and I have seen it with all eight eyes.

"Would that this day had gone differently, my little flower," he whispered in vrix.

The jungle flashed outside the shelter, but only a little of the lightning's harsh illumination reached inside, reflected in the moisture still clinging to Rekosh and Ahmya. Thunder crackled over the trees, vibrating in the stone, and the rain fell as hard as ever.

Rekosh rested his head against the rough wall, and his eyelids slowly fell. He did not know where they were, did not know how they would get back home, but he knew one thing without a single shred of doubt.

He would never be lost so long as he had Ahmya.

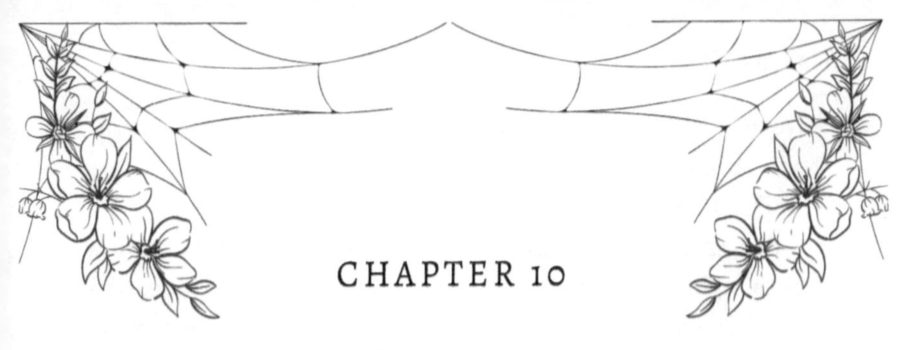

CHAPTER 10

Awareness came to Ahmya slowly as she woke, and pain came along with it.

She'd been in pain before. Trekking through the unforgiving jungle and swamp to escape a giant, bloodthirsty vrix queen hell-bent on killing Ahmya and her companions had introduced her to all sorts of discomfort and agony.

Nearly getting killed by a moving, carnivorous plant topped the list, and Ahmya still felt echoes of its fiery venom whenever she saw the scars it had left on her body.

This was a different kind of pain.

Her chest felt tight, like there was a great weight upon it, and she couldn't draw a deep enough breath to fill her lungs. Her throat was raw, and her head throbbed. Underlying that was a dull, deep-seated ache permeating her whole body.

I almost drowned.

How many times would she face death? How many times would she escape it?

Escape it? You were rescued, Ahmya. Every. Single. Time.

In every situation, Rekosh had been there to protect her, to save her. What would have happened if not for him? If he hadn't been nearby?

"Dead," she whispered, opening her eyes. "I'd be dead."

But in direct opposition to the pain—and the dark turn of her thoughts—was the soothing heat surrounding her. Rekosh's heat. His arms were wrapped around her, and one large palm covered her shoulder. This was where she always felt safe. Every time he carried her, every time he held her, the world wasn't as scary.

His ridged chest was beneath her cheek, and though his hide was hard, there was a suppleness to it, like leather. She rubbed her face against it and inhaled as deeply as she could manage. His warm, spicy scent flooded her senses.

But it was tainted.

Blood.

Carefully, Ahmya lifted her head, pulled back from Rekosh's chest, and looked up at him. He was leaning against the rough stone wall, head down, eyes closed, and mandibles limp. His hair had come undone from its usual neat braid. The long, tangled black tresses, threaded with strands of red and white, hung around his face and past his shoulders.

She'd never seen him so disheveled, so ragged. Not in all their time together.

Ahmya lifted a hand toward his face only to pause. Her fingers itched to touch him, to comb through his hair, to rid it of those tangles, but she didn't want to wake him. She ran her gaze over his body.

Wads of silk clung to the many cuts, scratches, and bite wounds she had treated, and dark bruises covered his black hide, which was splotched with mud and dried blood. Some of the worst bruising was on his left foreleg.

She could only hope he hadn't broken a bone. The way he'd been favoring it while walking yesterday had been alarming.

Seeing him so off-balance, limping, had been as unsettling as it was heartbreaking.

His injuries looked so much worse now that there was light enough to see all of them.

What did you expect? He fought off a whole pack of those things.

And they...they were trying to get to me.

She curled her fingers and withdrew her hand, clutching it against her chest. She'd known he was more hurt than he'd let on. She'd known, and she should've pressed him, should've forced him to let her tend to all his wounds. To let her comfort and care for him for once.

Vrix did heal quickly, but that was only a tiny comfort for Amhya. Her heart ached at all the suffering that had been inflicted upon him.

But if she'd learned anything since waking up in this alien world, it was that you had to keep moving no matter what. You couldn't stop and feel bad when you were out in the jungle. You had to act, had to...*do.*

There was something she could do for him while he rested. A simple task, but an important one, nonetheless.

Ahmya grasped Rekosh's wrist and carefully lifted his hand off her shoulder, lowering it to rest upon his leg. As she extracted herself from his arms, her eyes flicked toward his face again and again, watching for signs that he was waking. But he slept on.

While she was glad her movement wasn't disturbing him, it wasn't normal for him to sleep so deeply. He'd been through war, had survived in the wilds, and had woken, alert and ready to fight, at the slightest disturbances during their flight from Zurvashi. This just proved how exhausted he truly was now.

Extending her legs, she placed her feet on the ground, braced a hand on the rocky wall, and stood. Even with the wall for support, it took much more effort than she'd expected to get herself upright.

She cringed when her feet squished inside her wet boots. That was a sensation Ahmya hadn't missed during her time in Kaldarak. If not for the protection the thick soles provided, she'd have done away with them altogether.

And really, she should've been grateful they were still on her feet. It was a minor miracle that they hadn't been swept away in the river. Goodness knew they'd come off at every other opportunity during her travels.

But now that she was standing, there was another pressing matter making itself known to her.

Her bladder.

After retrieving the metal knife from the rock she'd set it upon, Ahmya moved to the edge of the rocky overhang and peered out. A light rain misted the jungle beneath an overcast sky. Her skin prickled as a chill breeze drifted past, making her aware that her clothes were still damp.

Leaves and branches swayed, rustled, and creaked, and alien creatures called in the distance.

Unease filled her. She'd lived in the Tangle for months, had witnessed its beauty and its dangers. She'd walked amongst these towering trees under bright, warm sunshine, had camped between shadowed trunks in the dark of night, had huddled in meager shelter through raging storms. She'd endured everything the jungle had thrown at her so far.

But she'd never been out here alone.

This is stupid, Ahmya.

But I...I want to do this. For Rekosh.

She glanced back at him. He hadn't moved, hadn't opened his eyes. He was exhausted and hurt.

"I won't go far," Ahmya said quietly. "I'll stay close."

She tightened her grip on the knife and walked forward.

Ahmya kept her eyes in constant motion, watching for any beasts, for the slightest sign of danger. If she saw anything at all, she wouldn't hesitate to call for Rekosh and run back to the overhang.

The ground sank beneath her feet as she walked. The mist coated her skin and hair, and she blinked as it beaded on her lashes. The scents of rain, vegetation, and earth were heavy in the air, but the smell of Rekosh's blood lingered in her memory.

He's only out here because of me.

That realization sent a shard of guilt straight through her heart, nearly bringing her to a halt. Ahmya let out a shuddering breath as she rubbed her chest.

But it was true. Rekosh had only joined the foraging party because she was going with them. He was always getting hurt because of her.

And right now, she needed to help him.

"He needs food, needs rest, needs strength. I can do this."

The discomfort in her pelvis increased with each step.

"Well, I can do this after I pee."

Ahmya came to a stop and searched for a spot to relieve herself where nothing would leap out of the undergrowth and bite her on the ass.

"Because that would be just my luck, wouldn't it?"

Once she'd emptied her bladder, using some wet leaves to clean herself, she continued on, making sure to keep track of where she was going in relation to their shelter. She hadn't traveled for long before she spotted a small copse of *sahn'hadurii* trees—bluevine trees.

Grinning, Ahmya pumped her arms in triumph. "Yes, yes, yes, yes!"

The trees were over eight feet tall, with thick, bulbous trunks reminiscent of pineapples in shape and texture. Long branches sprouted from the top of each trunk, all ending in dangling vines from which clusters of deep blue fruit hung.

She double checked to make sure there were no lurking beasties before jogging closer to the trees. Lifting one of the fruits from the vine, she used the knife to cut the stem. The rind was hard and lumpy, but she knew what was within. Simply thinking about the purple, raspberry flavored, jam-like fruit made her stomach growl.

Ahmya poked her belly. "You have to wait until we bring them back to Rekosh."

She cut away four more of the fruits, setting them on the ground at her feet. She'd just started on the fifth when she heard rustling behind her. Stilling her hands and her breathing, she turned her head to look over her shoulder as the sound moved closer.

She released the fruit and spun, brandishing her knife before her.

Sitting upon a mossy fallen branch was a small creature, hunched over and eating what appeared to be a large grub in its long-fingered grasp.

Ahmya blinked and tilted her head, lowering her arms slightly.

The plump creature had gray and black fur, a long, fluffy tail, and a narrow face with large, pointed ears and wide eyes. It couldn't have been much bigger than a raccoon. And…it was cute.

But it was also food. Meat. Something that would benefit Rekosh far more than a bunch of fruit.

Adjusting her grip on the knife, Ahmya crept forward.

The creature paused, glanced at her, and its tail, curled like a squirrel's, flicked.

She froze.

The creature resumed eating.

Ahmya wasn't sure if she should be offended or not. "Guess you don't consider me much of a threat, huh?"

The animal simply stared at her, unconcerned.

"Wow. Okay then. Just you wait until you're roasting over a fire."

Keeping her steps slow, Ahmya closed the distance between her and the creature until only a couple feet remained, and its back was mostly toward her. It had finished eating and was licking its long fingers before running them over its snout like a cat grooming itself.

Ahmya huffed. "Fine. Don't fear the big bad human that's going to eat you. Makes it easier for me."

Clutching the handle of the knife, she raised it, bending her knees in preparation to attack.

But she couldn't move.

The creature was right there. It was easy prey. It was food.

But she remained immobile.

Think of Rekosh, Ahmya. He needs this. He needs you.

She pressed her lips together, and her body tensed.

And still, she could not do it. Just the thought of plunging a knife into this creature, of making it bleed, made her sick to her stomach.

She'd done it before, when those vicious beasts were attacking her and Rekosh. Why was this so different?

Because this animal posed no threat. It was out here surviving, a small creature in a big jungle...

Like me.

Ahmya lowered her arm as tears filled her eyes. She couldn't do this. She wasn't a hunter, wasn't a survivalist. She was a florist who'd become an intergalactic colonist, and her primary role on Xolea would've been to give birth to a new generation. Meant to be nothing more than an incubator.

"Ahmya!"

She started, heart nearly leaping from her chest. The creature's ears perked, its posture stiffened, and its fur bristled.

Vegetation shook nearby. The little animal darted off into the undergrowth, moving far quicker than she would've expected. Her hand trembled around the knife grip. Whatever chance she'd had to procure meat for Rekosh was gone.

Useless. I'm...I'm useless.

Tears spilled down her cheeks, and the knife slipped from her grasp to land dully upon the ground.

"Ahmya," Rekosh rasped, rushing toward her. The rhythm of his gait was still wrong; he was still favoring that left foreleg.

That only drew more tears out of her.

"I woke, and you were not there." He stopped before her. His hide glistened with moisture, but the mud and blood from yesterday remained. He captured her face between two large hands and ducked his head close. "You are out alone. Why?"

All eight of his crimson eyes studied her. Though vrix faces were like hard, expressionless masks, their eyes conveyed so, so much. And in his, she saw his panic, his worry, his fear.

For her.

"I...I was trying to get food." Her throat strained with the effort of holding back everything she felt in that moment. Her despair, her incompetence, her worthlessness. Those emotions wound in her chest, coiling so tight that it was hard to breathe.

"I would have—" His eyes narrowed, and he canted his head. "What is wrong, *vi'keishi?*"

Ahmya couldn't hold back the flood any longer. Her words came out in a sobbing burst. "I wanted to get food for you! I wanted... I wanted to be the one to provide for you." She waved her hand in the direction the creature had fled. "But I-I couldn't do it. I couldn't kill it. It was right there, and I just stood here and did *nothing.*"

Her chest burned, and every breath was a struggle, but she couldn't stop crying. "You've done so much for me. *So much.* And all I've ever been is a burden."

"No. Not a burden." Rekosh pressed his headcrest to her forehead and stroked her cheeks with his thumbs, wrapping his lower arms around her waist and drawing her close. "*Never* a burden."

Closing her eyes, Ahmya flattened her hands on his chest.

His hide was warm, his hearts thrummed beneath her palms, and his scent enveloped her.

"I feel like that's all I've been. To everyone. To…to you." Her voice was small, quivering, and raw when she said, "I play with flowers. What purpose do I serve here?"

A low, unhappy rumble emanated from his chest.

"Ahmya…" Rekosh dropped a hand from her face, placing it over one of hers. "Your heart is…soft."

Ahmya's throat tightened as new tears seeped from her closed eyes. The world spun around her. Her breath shook as she again struggled to contain the emotion, to hold back another sob.

He'd just confirmed it. Had just reaffirmed her doubts, and—

Rekosh lifted his head, caught her chin, and guided her face up to his, his firm grip leaving no room for resistance. Ahmya opened her eyes, blinking away the moisture from her lashes.

There was fire in his crimson gaze, deep and bright, intense and consuming. "I do not have all the words, Ahmya, so you must listen. Listen much good."

She curled her fingers against his chest and nodded as much as his hold allowed.

"When you are tired, hungry, hurt, it is strength to do for your tribe before yourself. When danger is most big and you have much fear, it is strength to protect others. When death and pain are most easy to give, it is strength to give kindness instead.

"Do you know my words?" Those dexterous fingers caught the tears flowing down her cheeks, wiping them away, before tucking her hair behind her ears. "Soft is not weak. It is a different strength, strength inside. Your strength. And it is needed here. You are needed."

Ahmya turned her face into his hand, closed her eyes, and drew in a calmer breath. She'd needed so badly to hear those words from him. Though they didn't silence the whispers of her inadequacy, they helped.

Keeping hold of her hand, he stepped back, leading her along with his hands on her hips. "Come. I am cold in this rain."

She knew the truth. He wasn't really cold, he was just cushioning what little of her pride remained. And she couldn't help loving him for it. "Better get you warmed up then."

He chittered gently before bending to pick her up.

"The fruit!" Ahmya slipped out of his grasp and ran toward the bluevine fruit she'd piled on the jungle floor. She crouched to gather them on the crook of her arm. "I know it's not much, but…"

Rekosh scooped her up from behind, coaxing a startled cry from her. He cradled her against his chest, which vibrated with a long, appreciative hum. "*Sahn'hadurii uta.* You did much good, *vi'keishi.*"

Her lips rose in a small smile, and contentment danced in her heart, but both faded too soon. She brushed her fingers over the outer shell of one of the fruits and whispered, "I wish it was more."

He grunted, held her close, and started walking, plucking up the fallen knife as he passed it.

When they reached their shelter, Rekosh ducked beneath the overhang and set Ahmya on her feet. Her weariness came rushing back tenfold. She felt heavy all over, physically and emotionally, and a chill seemed to have taken permanent residence in her bones.

She stepped back from him to deposit the fruit on the ground, only to notice the bag resting against the stone wall. Ketahn and the vrix had drilled it into Ahmya and the other human survivors—keep your bag and your spear with you *always*. For Rekosh to have left his bag here when he'd come looking for her…

Frowning, she straightened and met his gaze again.

His mandibles drooped. "You are shaking, Ahmya."

Ahmya looked down and lifted the hem of her wet top, peeling it away from her belly. "It's like when we first left the *Somnium*. When it never seemed to stop raining and I could never get dry and warm."

Rekosh pinched the fabric of her top with his lower hand, squeezing out a bit of the moisture, which trickled down his fingers. Ahmya found herself staring at his hand. At those long, sharp claws, the slender but powerful fingers, the subtle play of tendons beneath his thick hide. She'd always been fascinated by his hands. So alien, so graceful, so deadly, yet so tender when they touched her.

She didn't realize he'd slipped his upper arms around her until she felt him untying the knot holding her top in place. The fabric loosened, and the sides dropped.

Ahmya gasped, slapping her hands to her chest to hold the material in place as she looked up at Rekosh with wide eyes. "What are you doing?"

He withdrew his hands, but kept them raised, fingers partly bent as though in uncertainty. "You must dry."

He was right, and she knew it. Keeping this soaked silk on would only ensure she remained cold and miserable.

But she'd never been fully naked in front of him before. She'd always had a blanket or some sort of covering to shield herself. Even after all these months, Ahmya hadn't cast aside her modesty—though at this point, she figured it was really just self-consciousness. Modesty wasn't really a thing in this new world. The vrix had never even heard of such a concept before the humans explained it to them.

She clutched at the silk. "We could build a fire?"

With another low, unhappy hum, he turned his head to glance out of their shelter, where that light rain continued. "Nothing dry to burn, Ahmya."

"Of course. You're right." Ahmya looked down. Though the

floor of their little shelter was mostly dry, it was comprised only of dirt, rocks, and thick, green vegetation. "If there was, we...we would have had a fire already."

He covered her hands with his lower pair. They were warm and gentle as he loosened her grip on the silk. "I will be your fire, Ahmya."

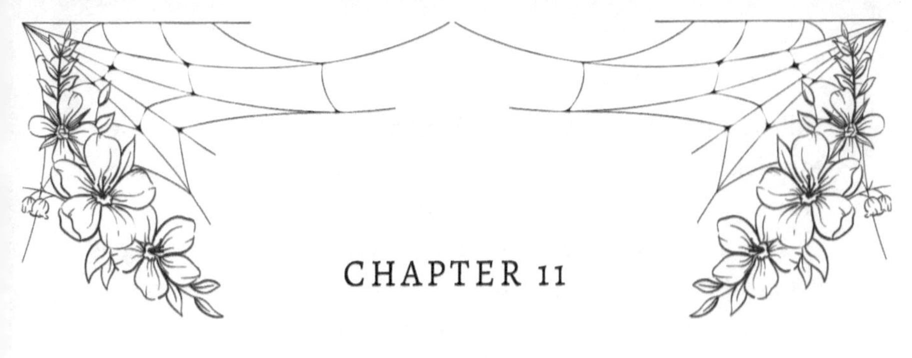

CHAPTER 11

A DIFFERENT SORT of warmth bloomed within Ahmya, deep in her core.

He...he couldn't have known the effect those words would have on her. Couldn't have known the deeper meaning they implied, couldn't have known how much she wanted them to come true.

As he guided her hands aside and pulled the silk away from her chest, baring her breasts, that warmth spread outward. Her wet skin prickled in the open air, and her nipples, already hard from the cold, tightened further into aching buds.

Rekosh had grown very still. She could feel him staring at her, could feel his eyes like a branding iron upon her skin. A shiver stole through Ahmya as his fingers flexed around hers. With a shuddering inhalation, she slowly tipped her head back and looked at him.

He *was* staring—at her breasts. His head was tilted to the side, and curiosity shone in those crimson eyes. But there was something more in them. Something wickedly dark and primal.

Hunger.

Arousal curled low in her belly. Though her skin warmed in

embarrassment, Ahmya didn't look away from him or attempt to shield herself as he draped her silk top over a nearby rock. He raised that hand back toward her.

Her heart quickened. She understood what he was doing as his hand inched nearer, and still, she made no attempt to stop him. Some part of her yearned for it—for his touch, for him—and maybe she'd silenced that part of herself for too long. Maybe she'd left it unfed for too long.

His fingers brushed along the side of her breast. Those whispers of callused heat were followed by the gentle stroke of his thumb across her nipple.

A startling, powerful jolt of pleasure swept through her. Ahmya flinched back with a gasp.

Heat unlike anything she'd ever felt pooled between her thighs, making her pussy pulse. What she felt was pure, unadulterated desire. Though Rekosh's touch had been light, her nipple throbbed.

Rekosh snatched his hands back with an uncertain trill, eyes going wide. "I hurt you?"

Ahmya crossed her arms over her chest, pressing firmly to alleviate the aching in her breasts, and shook her head. "N-no. You didn't hurt me. I'm okay."

"Okay," he echoed, mandibles twitching as he regarded her. "But you moved like I hurt you."

God, he was hurting her, but not in the way he thought.

"I...was just surprised." She squeezed her thighs together, wishing the sensation would go away and free her of this torment. How could something as simple as a thumb brushing her nipple instill her with such lust?

Because it was *him*.

Even when she touched herself, she never felt anything nearly as potent as that one little caress.

"You didn't hurt me," Ahmya said. "I promise. I'm just...just cold."

A low hum rumbled from him. He skimmed his knuckles over her cheek. "But your skin is red and warm."

A nervous laugh bubbled from her. "Humans don't usually feel comfortable being naked around others, remember?"

"Ah." He dipped his chin in a shallow nod. His lower hands settled on her hips, one catching the knot of her skirt and pulling it loose. "But you will feel better without wet silk, and I am not others. I am Rekosh."

Her heart thundered as he unwrapped the silk skirt from around her waist. He drew it away, and cold air blasted her fully naked body. She curled her fingers into her shoulders. Besides Ivy, Callie, Lacey, and Ahnset, she'd never stood naked before anyone who wasn't a medical professional.

But it was different with Rekosh. There was something thrilling about being vulnerable and exposed in front of him. Something thrilling in the way his crimson eyes moved over her body. She trembled, and the arousal in her core intensified.

Rekosh took in a slow, deep breath that tapered off into a barely audible growl. His claspers shifted, drawing tight against his slit, and Ahmya's blush blazed across her whole body, from head to toe.

He knows. He knows. Oh God, he knows.

Rekosh absently dropped her skirt beside her top. She could only watch as he spread his legs wider, forelegs moving to either side of her, and lowered himself.

"*Kir'ani vi'keishi.*" He trailed the back of a claw lightly along the line of tiny scars on her abdomen, making her flesh quiver. His hand continued downward to the scars on her thigh—the uppermost of which was *very* close to her pussy.

She held her breath, afraid to move, afraid to make a sound. Afraid to fan the flames raging within her, lest she be consumed by them.

The light from outside dimmed, and the rain fell harder.

Rekosh bent forward, catching himself with his lower hands

upon the ground as he moved his head close to her. Ahmya's eyes flared. His breath was warm against the chilled skin of her belly, but it could not compare to the heat of his stare.

It was all she could do not to squirm, not to drop a hand to her sex and clamp her thighs around it.

It was all she could do not to beg him to put *his* hand there.

The half-trill, half-growl he released vibrated in the air between them, making it that much harder for Ahmya to retain control. He slid an upper hand around her thigh, hooking it behind her knee, and lifted her leg.

"Rekosh!" She wobbled and threw her hands out, bracing them on his shoulders.

His other upper arm slipped around Ahmya, and his big hand settled upon her ass to steady her. Her wildly beating heart hammered in her chest.

Oh God, oh God, oh God.

With her leg up, and his face mere inches from her pussy, there was *nothing* to shield her from his view.

"I have you," Rekosh rasped, his breath tickling her pubic hair. He curled his fingers against her backside, pricking her skin with his claws. For what felt like an eternity, the two of them remained like that, with him so close to her, and Ahmya so close to giving in to her desires.

It would've been foolish to think Rekosh couldn't smell her arousal, especially with his face right there.

He dropped his hand from her ass. She felt the strain in his body. Felt it under her hands, saw it in the play of muscle beneath his hide, in the twitching of his mandibles and the fine hairs standing on his legs. It was in every hot, ragged breath teasing her sex.

Just before her body could scream at her to take action, Rekosh plucked off her boot. He set it aside, lowered her leg, and repeated the process for her other foot.

But when he was done, he did not release her. He smoothed

his upper hands up her legs and settled them on her hips, where his fingers flexed on her ass.

All eight of his bright red eyes were focused intently upon her pussy.

He pressed his headcrest against her belly.

Ahmya's breath hitched, and her eyes widened. She lifted her hands, uncertain of where to put them, of what to do or what to say. Uncertain of what *he* was doing.

Tightening his hold, Rekosh drew her closer and inhaled deeply. A shudder wracked him, rippling through his long, lean body from top to bottom. He bent his right foreleg behind her. She felt its soft, tiny hairs as his hide rasped against her calves.

Not long ago, Ahmya would've recoiled from such a touch. Spiders were creepy, unsettling things, alien to her in their own way. The sight of one had been enough to send her fleeing from a room, and the mere thought of coming into physical contact with a spider had made her flesh crawl.

But Rekosh was not a spider. And though his touch made her feel many things, none of them were even remotely close to disgust.

What she felt most fiercely was need.

Rekosh rubbed his face against her belly, back and forth, again and again, releasing a sound not unlike a deep, rolling purr that vibrated into Ahmya. She bit down hard on her bottom lip to lock in a moan.

Slowly, she lowered her hands to the top of his head, slipping her fingers into his damp, silky hair. As his purring continued, stimulating her from the outside in, her clit thrummed, and her breath came in shallow pants. His mandibles spread, their fangs teasingly grazing her outer thighs.

"Rekosh…" she whispered. "What… What are you…"

Her small breasts felt heavy, her nipples painfully tight, and the hollow pressure in her core expanded with every brush of his face against her skin. He wasn't just drawing in her scent—he was marking her with his own. His spicy aroma filled her nose, overcoming the fragrances of rain and earth.

There was something animalistic about this, something primal, and it spoke to a part of Ahmya that she'd never known existed. A long-sleeping part that had been roused by him, an instinctual answer to his scent, his touch, his intensity, his desire.

She delved her hands deeper into his hair, curling the strands around her fingers and squeezing as the pressure in her became nearly too much to bear.

Rekosh growled and slid his face lower. His claws bit into her ass as he tugged her impossibly closer and parted her thighs, his breath sweeping through the short hair on her mons.

And then something long, wet, and firm dragged over the folds of her pussy and her clit.

The sensation was so strange, so overwhelming, so startling, so *pleasurable*, that Ahmya cried out and shoved away from Rekosh.

He jolted back, and she stumbled, catching herself on the wall with her hair falling around her face. Body trembling and breath ragged, she clutched her chest. Her lungs ached to draw in more air.

The stone was frigid and unyielding at her back, but it did nothing to cool the inferno within her. Even the pain of rocks digging into the soles of her feet and the sting from Rekosh's claws and fangs having scratched her didn't assuage the yearning in her core.

But the strongest sensation of all was the lingering feel of his tongue having licked her sex.

Ahmya squeezed her thighs together.

He licked me.

She curled fingers, pressing her nails into her chest.

He licked me.

Her clit throbbed with the memory of his tongue's feel, aching with desire for more.

Rekosh licked my pussy.

Ahmya flattened a palm on her lower belly and pressed down. It did nothing to alleviate the discomfort.

Something scraped on the ground. Ahmya ran her fingers through her hair, combing it from her face, and peered at Rekosh.

He'd shifted farther back from her, toward the edge of the overhang. His long black, white, and red locks hung about his shoulders, and there was a distant, frenzied light in his eyes. Harsh breaths had his chest and shoulders heaving. His lower hands, one atop the other, were covering his pelvis—covering his slit. He shook his head, and the motion rippled through his entire body.

"I… I will return. Small time. Soon." He brought his upper forearms together with a shallow bow, half the vrix gesture of apology, and strode out of the shelter.

Ahmya pushed away from the wall to follow. "Rekosh, wait!"

He paused and halted her with a thrust of his hand. "Stay."

"Where are you going?"

"I will not go far." He turned his head, and four of his bright red eyes locked with hers. "Stay, Ahmya."

Brow furrowing, she crossed her arms over her chest. Her urge to obey his command warred with her need to follow him. In the end, she nodded.

Silently, she watched as he disappeared amidst the greenery. Cold swept through her to replace the heat that had suffused her only moments ago. The rain fell steadily, and runoff from the overhang splashed upon the ground at her feet.

"What happened?"

What happened? He licked your pussy and you shoved away from him like you were repulsed. That's what happened.

But she hadn't been repulsed at all. Shocked, but not repulsed.

Does he know that?

Ahmya chewed on the inside of her bottom lip as she searched the jungle for any sign of Rekosh. He was nowhere to be seen. But he was close. She knew he was, trusted he was. He would not leave her alone.

Would you have let him continue?

The answer came without hesitation. *Yes.*

She would have. If Rekosh had pursued her, had pulled her to him once again and told her to spread her legs, she would have done so willingly. Wantonly.

Heat washed over her. Ahmya forced herself to turn away and glanced around their suddenly very lonely shelter. Her clothing lay draped over rocks, torn, bloodstained strips of her skirt lay on the ground, the bluevine fruit sat forgotten in a pile, and Rekosh's sash and bag rested against the far wall.

Ahmya stared at that bag.

A guilty pang struck her gut at having lost her own bag to the river, though she knew keeping it on would've made it impossible to keep her head above water.

She couldn't stand here and do nothing, couldn't just sit and wait, wondering where Rekosh had gone.

Wondering why he had gone…

And once again, he'd left without his bag, without the supplies that could mean the difference between life and death out here in the jungle. Her only consolation in that regard was that he'd said he would remain close by.

Make yourself useful.

Walking to the bag, she crouched and reached for the string, untying the knot before throwing back the flap and tugging it open. Everything was wet. Had they only been contending with rain, the yatin hide bag would've kept its contents dry. But being fully submerged in a raging river had ensured nothing was spared.

She removed the items from inside and laid them out to dry. A couple of blankets, a waterskin, a hatchet with an obsidian head, several small bundles wrapped in waxy leaves, various scraps of silk and leather, several wooden spools of tightly wound thread, and a small jar of what Ahmya assumed was the oil the vrix used on their hides. Despite the trials they'd faced, much of it had been packed surprisingly neatly.

There were a few tools, mostly made of bone, that she'd seen him use to make ropes and nets and to punch holes in cloth or leather, along with several needles in a small case. Though all of it had taken on that damp, musty smell of being left wet for just a little too long, Rekosh's scent remained present—a hint of spice and allure.

Ahmya lifted one of the little cloths to her face and inhaled. It was likely silk he'd produced himself, woven by his hands, and it bore his unmistakable fragrance. A fragrance that had come to mean so much to her. That comforted her, soothed her, excited her.

At the very bottom of the bag, beneath everything else, was a leather bundle. She couldn't tell what was inside, but it was wrapped so tightly and securely that she doubted any moisture had worked its way in.

He'd been holding something in his hands when he'd visited her the other day, bundled in cloth rather than leather but of similar size and shape. Could this be whatever he'd meant to give her?

As curious as she was, she wouldn't violate his privacy by opening the bundle. Its contents seemed to be protected from the water, and that was all that mattered right now.

Ahmya spread his bag out and stood, once more scanning the jungle.

There was still no sign of Rekosh.

Grabbing one of his knives, she found a spot where the ground was cushioned by vegetation and sat, drawing her legs close to her chest and wrapping her arms around them.

He's close. He won't leave me here alone.

She rested her chin upon her knees and stared into the jungle.

There was nothing to do but wait.

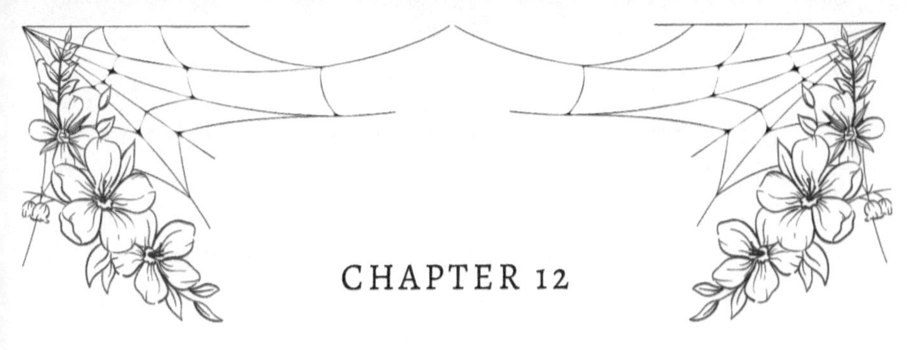

CHAPTER 12

THE FIRE at Rekosh's core only intensified with each step away from Ahmya, with each cold drop of rain splashing upon his hide, with each thump of his hearts. He could not escape that heat, and it would not diminish.

His stem throbbed, trapped beneath the palm he'd clasped over it. The ache behind his parted slit was a deep-seated torment that made his mind hazy with need.

Growling, he staggered to a halt and pressed harder on his stem. A shudder swept through him, forcing his fine hairs up, and water sprayed as he let out a harsh exhalation. Every pain he'd collected yesterday was more pronounced now, but none of it could overcome the heat.

He'd never felt anything like this. He'd never been so consumed by desire, so driven by lust. And he'd never had his stem suddenly...*force* its way out.

Every instinct demanded he go back to Ahmya. Go back and claim her the only way that mattered—by binding her and thrusting into her wet, warm slit, by leaving his marks upon her, outside and in. His limbs thrummed and his hide itched with want to return.

The red haze at the edges of his vision spread, and his hearts quickened.

"No!" he snarled, shaking his head.

Though he'd never experienced it, he knew what this was. The mating frenzy. His instincts were trying to seize control, threatening to drive him to a bestial claiming of his mate. Rekosh finally understood.

But he would not let the frenzy overcome him. He would not relinquish control, not if it meant endangering his little flower.

Bad enough that she'd been twice injured under his protection. To even think that he might harm her himself—

No. He could not do so. Would not.

His stem pulsated as though in disagreement. Rekosh curled his fingers around his shaft and squeezed, hissing through his fangs. That grip exacerbated the ache in his core. He shut his eyes, bowed his head, and breathed. The rain fell in an erratic rhythm all around, contrasting the steady but blistering pace of his hearts.

No female had ever affected him this way. The scents of female vrix could be maddening when they were swept up in lust, and Rekosh had felt the stirrings those pheromones had caused, but he'd never been swayed by them. He'd never been tempted to succumb.

One inhalation of Ahmya's fragrance had nearly plunged him into a mating frenzy. One taste of her nectar and he'd nearly lost himself. Had she not shoved away from him, he undoubtedly would have.

Rekosh filled his lungs with jungle air. Rain and damp ground overpowered most other smells, but he still scented her on his hide, still tasted her.

And damn his tongue, but he yearned for more.

A growl rumbled in his chest as another shudder coursed

through him. Her slit had been so hot, so wet, so…delicious. That one taste hadn't been enough. It would *never* be enough.

Rekosh shook himself again, shedding water from his hide, and took another breath, then another, and another.

"I must be her shield," he said. "Her protector. Her guide. Her safety comes before all else."

Though he knew those words were right, they were not easily enacted. He wanted her with every thread of his being. Yet in this jungle, which already overflowed with danger, his want was another threat to her. A serious threat.

Finally, his stem eased. Slowly, it receded, pulsing with each heartbeat until it had retreated fully into his slit. He did not withdraw his hands immediately, keeping them in place as the ache blossomed, its petals forcing open a gaping hollow in his chest shaped just like his little flower.

Only Ahmya could fill that chasm.

She leapt away from me…

Yet Ahmya had not initially pulled away; she'd held him closer. Her fingers had been tangled in his hair, her voice had been breathy, and her scent had been laden with desire of her own. It had enveloped him, had seduced him, more potent than the pheromones any female vrix could have produced.

She'd wanted him.

Tentatively, he lifted his lower hands. His claspers drew snugly on either side of his slit, forcing it closed. His stem did not stir.

He clenched his fists as a ragged, relieved breath escaped him. He needed to focus. Needed to be not the axe hacking through the undergrowth in broad swaths, but the spear, pointed and direct. Not the hammer, but the needle. Precise, controlled, exact.

She was his. That would not change. She was his purpose, his meaning, his heartsthread. And standing out here alone was of no service to her.

Rekosh opened his eyes.

The rain persisted, leaving the air cool and misty, and the Tangle seemed peaceful. He knew that serenity was but a mask, a thin veil obscuring the danger and chaos beneath, but that did not stop him from appreciating the relative quiet.

Turning around, he set off toward the shelter. He swayed with each stride, his gait still disrupted by his injured foreleg. The bone was not broken; he knew that much, though he could not guess the depth of the damage otherwise. A healer like Diego would have the right words to describe the injury.

As long as he kept weight off the limb, it pained him far less than the many wounds he'd suffered from the kuzahks. His healing hide was tight and itchy, and it burned whenever stretched by his movements.

Pain is not new.

No, it was not. He'd endured no small amount of it as a broodling, and much more during Zurvashi's war. But Ahmya... Ahmya was his joy. No pain inflicted upon him would ever change that.

He spied her through a gap in the greenery before she noticed him, and he couldn't help but study her. She sat upon the soft vegetation on the shelter's floor, still bare skinned, looking so small and slight. Yet he did not miss the way her eyes roved, sweeping back and forth across her surroundings. Nor did he miss the knife she held flat across her slender legs.

His mate was competent and capable, much more so than she believed.

That emptiness within him filled with something bright and warm—pride and admiration.

As he neared the shelter, he made sure to brush his legs against a plant, rustling its leaves.

Her face snapped toward him, eyes rounding as she raised the knife in a trembling fist. When Ahmya saw him, her tension faded, and she lowered her arm, setting down the weapon.

Rekosh lifted his mandibles and crossed the last few segments separating them. Just outside the overhang, he pressed his forearms together and offered a low bow.

"Please forgive me, *vi'keishi*. My threads were...coming undone."

Her brow furrowed. "Are you okay?"

Straightening, Rekosh nodded. With her before his eyes again, those desires stirred anew, but they'd lost their ferocity and overwhelming urgency. At least for now. "Are you?"

"I am. I was just worried about you." She beckoned him with a hand. "Come out of the rain, Rekosh."

He hunched down and entered the shelter, moving through the runoff falling from overhead. Shaking his head, he brushed the excess water from his hide with all four hands.

His hearts stuttered as he beheld the items laid out within the space—the contents of his bag. Had she seen it? Had she discovered his mating gift? Heat swelled within him again, wholly different from the heat of earlier, skittering under his hide and speeding his pulse.

Rekosh's gaze fell upon the leather bundle, still exactly as he'd bound it.

No. She has not seen.

Every time he'd been about to present his gift, to declare himself to her, fate had intervened. And now, when they were alone, when he finally had Ahmya to himself, he could not do it.

It would've been so easy to speak the words, to give her the dress. To at last see her clad in *his* silk.

But he knew that doing so would be to surrender whatever control he'd managed to wrest from himself. Seeing his silk caressing her lithe little body would shatter his tenuous restraint on the instincts he'd only just quieted, and he would succumb to them. He would mate her. There would be no resistance, no denial. Some part of him longed for that.

Yet he could not, would not, submit. He wouldn't risk harming his Ahmya.

He would wait just a little longer.

The heat fled him in a slow, barely controlled breath.

"I took everything out of your bag so it can dry," Ahmya said as she stepped around him from behind. "I...hope that's okay?"

Rekosh turned his face toward her. She stood beside him with her long black hair hanging over her shoulders, covering her small breasts, and her hands fidgeting against her belly. Even her tiny toes, so strange and yet so delightful, wiggled on the ground.

Perhaps he should've felt shame for failing to tend to his belongings, but he could only feel pride in her.

His mandibles twitched up into a smile. "Yes. It is good, Ahmya. You did what I should have done."

"You were exhausted and injured." Frowning, she gestured toward his left foreleg. "You're still injured."

"Small hurt," he said with a chitter. "Could have been more bad."

"But you can't walk on it, Rekosh."

Ahmya bent down and picked up one of her silk coverings, but not before Rekosh noticed the subtle quivering of her bottom lip and the tears gathering in her eyes. She stepped closer, maneuvering between his left legs, and draped the damp silk over the top of his hindquarters, wiping the water from his hide.

A soft trill rose from his throat. He'd never been tended to like this by anyone, not since he was a broodling, but to have Ahmya doing this for him...

It was what mates would do for one another. A simple, intimate way for them to serve each other. To show their care.

"You're hurt because of me," she said, voice quiet and spiritless. "Those beasts attacked because of me."

Rekosh twisted toward her, catching her chin in one hand

and forcing her to look at him. Her eyes glimmered, and the tears that had been welling in them had spilled down her cheeks. He did not care to see her cry. It made everything in him feel tight and unsettled, made the whole world feel wrong.

He emitted a distressed buzz.

"Not because of you, Ahmya. Because they were hungry. Because we were alone. Because I did not see good." He slid the back of a knuckle up her cheek, wiping away one of those escaped tears. "And we fell because of me."

Ahmya shook her head as she clutched the silk to her chest. Releasing it with one hand, she circled her fingers around his wrist, drawing his hand down. "You were protecting me." She touched his forearm, below the silk-packed bite marks. "All of your wounds came from protecting me."

He leaned his head closer to hers. Her scent filled his nose holes, and the echoes of her taste lingered on his tongue, but he did not allow himself to submit to either. "And I will carry the scars with joy. Wear them like the best silk."

He looked down and lightly brushed a finger from his lower hand over one of the pink scars on her belly, making her skin quiver. "Because my scars mean you will not have more."

"Rekosh…" Ahmya took his upper hand in hers and raised it, pressing her face against his palm. Nuzzling it, she released a shaky breath. "I don't want to be the cause of you getting hurt all the time."

Her skin was soft, warm, and smooth, and Rekosh reveled in its feel. He yearned to run his hands over more of it, to feel her muscles flex and relax, to learn every bit of her body by touch.

"You are not," he said. "I am friends with Ketahn, Urkot, and Telok. Most of my hurt is because of them. And needles."

A laugh burst from her. Rekosh had always been intrigued by the sounds humans made, but the sound of Ahmya's laughter? It flowed straight to his heartsthread, dancing along it with warmth and pleasure that permeated his soul.

"I'm sure you prick your fingers with needles often." She turned her face and pressed her lips to the pad of his thumb.

Everything inside Rekosh stilled.

A kiss.

It was not the sort of kiss he'd seen Ivy and Ketahn share, but he knew what the press of a human's lips meant. Knew it was a simple but powerful gesture—as intimate as vrix touching headcrests, if not more so.

And it was like a breeze over the embers in his core, rousing them back into flames.

Ahmya's eyes flared, and her cheeks pinkened. Releasing him, she brought the silk cloth up to his shoulder and resumed drying him. "I just don't like seeing you hurt and hate that I can't do anything to stop it."

A storm swirled inside Rekosh as the effects of that kiss clashed with the guilt and vulnerability in her voice. His claspers pressed tighter around his slit, and his mandibles ticked down. "You did help, Ahmya. One kuzahk died because of you. It would have made much more hurt."

More tears gathered in her eyes. She clamped her lips together before stepping in front of him and running the silk down his chest. Though she did not reply, he knew what she was thinking. Words she'd previously spoken sounded from his memory.

And all I've ever been is a burden.

His chest ached for her, and that ache rippled along his heartsthread.

"Ah, *kir'ani vi'keishi.*" He cupped the back of her head with an upper hand and flattened a lower hand over hers, locking it in place against his chest.

She tipped her face up, and her dark brown eyes met his.

He knew the rawness in her gaze. Understood the emotions in its depths, the doubt. "When I was a broodling, I was small," he said. "More small than my brothers and sisters. Other vrix were not kind. They said I was...a stick, weak and easy to break. And they hurt me. With words, with hands and claws and legs."

"Oh Rekosh..."

"I know, Ahmya. Know how it feels." Rekosh squeezed her hand over his hearts. "I was small and weak, and they made me feel useless. I followed my father, to hide from other vrix, to flee. But I found...purpose there. Found my use, my skill. Found weaving. Found the first whispers. And as I learned, I knew the others were wrong. I was not like them, but I was not useless. They were more big, more strong, so I made other ways to be better.

"You are not a warrior in body"—he placed one of his hands between her soft breasts, over where her heart beat strong and steady—"but in spirit."

Ahmya's lips parted, and her heart quickened as she leaned into his touch. Her fingers curled, scratching his hide with her blunt nails, and she settled her other hand over his, clutching it to her chest. A content rumble rolled through him.

"But what can I provide to the tribe?" she asked. "What use am I?"

"When I met Urkot and Ketahn and his siblings, I learned something more. We are only threads. Alone, easily cut. Easily broken." He shifted the fingers of both his hands, interlocking them with Ahmya's. "But as a tribe, our threads weave together. Each thread makes the others more strong. A word alone may hold no power, but woven into a story or a bond, it can move vrix to do what cannot be done. A vrix alone—a human alone— may struggle to survive, but in a tribe, they can do anything."

Rekosh moved his hand from the back of her head to her cheek, brushing aside stray strands of her hair and tucking them behind her small, rounded ear. "Each danger you face, each trial you defeat, another thread is added to your weave. You are more strong, and the tribe becomes more strong."

Her lower lip trembled. "I understand your words."

Then her face crumpled. A sob burst from her as she threw herself against Rekosh, wrapping her arms around him, her body heaving with her cries.

Rekosh's chest constricted as he embraced her with all four arms. Her tears wet his hide, undoing the work she'd done to dry him, but they were warm in contrast to the rain. Her soft skin was warm too, and impossible to ignore.

Just as impossible to ignore as her sweet scent.

He clenched his jaw and, still holding her, eased down onto the shelter floor. This closeness made no difference. The feel of her body against his would not pry his focus from what was important. Now was a time to offer her comfort while she was vulnerable, not to succumb to desire and instinct.

He lifted Ahmya and cradled her in his arms. She trembled and cried, and he held her, gently combing his claws through her hair and softly crooning.

Something had hurt his Ahmya. Someone had hurt her. Deep, deep down. Even if he did not know how those invisible scars had been inflicted, he recognized their effects.

Gradually, her cries quieted, and the tremors wracking her faded. Her ragged breaths grew deeper, smoother, calmer.

"You are okay, *kir'ani vi'keishi*," he said. "I am with you. Always."

Ahmya rubbed her cheek against his chest. "Thank you. Thank you for making me feel like I matter."

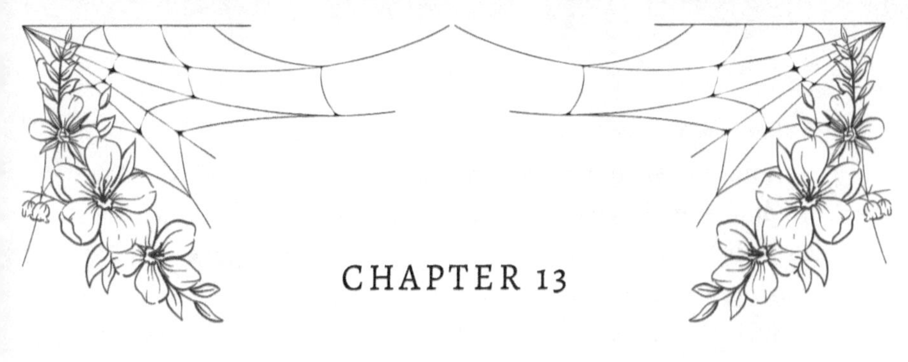

CHAPTER 13

Aʜᴍʏᴀ ᴄʟᴏsᴇᴅ her eyes and tipped her face up toward the morning sun. The sunshine was warm upon her skin, a welcome change from all the rain over the last couple of days. She'd awoken feeling lighter than she could remember. Freer. Sure, she was a bit embarrassed about her breakdown yesterday, but it had been sorely needed.

And Rekosh had held her through it all. He'd petted her, crooned to her, had spoken soothing words in both vrix and English, and when she'd been spent, he'd fed her bluevine fruit and dried meat. After all her worry that he wouldn't have enough to eat, that she was a failure because she'd let the creature get away, she'd discovered that those leaf-wrapped bundles in his bag had been meat.

She'd cried again because of that.

If her father had been around to see her, he would have been disgusted and disappointed. He would've told her to grow up, to get a hold of herself, that the world didn't care about her hurt feelings.

That had been Ahmya's childhood from the age of eight onward—after her mother had died.

But now he's dead too.

Ahmya opened her eyes and stared up at the blue sky. One hundred and sixty-eight years had passed since she'd boarded the *Somnium*. Everyone she'd known on Earth was gone.

Along with almost everyone who was on the ship.

Splashing called her attention to the river, where Rekosh was stepping into the water. They'd found a shallow spot downriver from the waterfall. Here, the current was calm, soft vegetation grew along the bank, and the ground was rocky rather than muddy.

Sunlight shone upon Rekosh, bringing out the red and white strands in his long, loose hair and brightening the crimson markings on his black hide. She ran her gaze over his body. Broad shoulders, lean muscles, a narrow waist. Six long legs and spiderlike hindquarters.

How was it that only months ago, she'd been absolutely terrified of him, and now all she could see was beauty? Because he was beautiful. Monstrous, alien, and beautiful.

Rekosh turned his face toward her. His mandibles lifted into a smile as he raised a hand and beckoned her. "Come, Ahmya."

She chuckled and closed the distance between them, rocks crunching under her boots. But rather than step into the water, she sat on a large boulder near the river's edge.

"Nuh uh. You expect me to get wet again after it finally stopped raining?" She ran her palm over her skirt, which was noticeably shorter after having cut strips of fabric from it. There was also still a hint of dampness in the cloth. "I feel like I've only just gotten mostly dry."

"The sun is warm," he replied, lifting his chin skyward. "You will dry again soon."

Ahmya leaned back, propped herself on her hands, and stretched her legs out, crossing them at the ankle. "You enjoy the water. I'm just going to bask in the sun and hope I don't burn."

"I will clean quickly. I do not want my *vi'keishi* to burn." He walked out a little farther, sank down, and began splashing water on himself, scrubbing the dirt and mud from his hide.

She couldn't help but watch as he ran his hands over his body. He gingerly cleaned around his wounds, all of which had scabbed over, his movements somehow graceful despite the hint of stiffness in them.

And Ahmya didn't look away even when he rubbed his hind legs together and brushed them along his hindquarters in perhaps the most insect-like display she'd seen from him.

What once would have been off-putting to her was now fascinating.

But she was curious about something else.

Her gaze slowly dipped along the rigid, muscular plates of his abdomen, toward his pelvis. His vertical slit, more defined in the light, remained tightly closed, with his claspers tucked against his body.

Ahmya caught her bottom lip between her teeth and chewed on it. What…did his cock look like? Did it resemble a human's at all, or was it wildly different? The only detail Ivy had given away was that Ketahn's cock matched the color of his markings…

So was Rekosh's truly a vibrant red?

Callie's teasing words danced through Ahmya's head.

A red rocket.

Wicked whispers of arousal stirred within her core. Unbidden, she recalled the feel of his tongue dragging through her pussy. Its wet glide had evoked such startling pleasure.

Now, she was haunted by what-ifs. What if she hadn't pushed him away? What if she'd let him continue, what if she'd let him lick her again and again?

That single stroke of his tongue on her clit had felt sublime. How much pleasure would he have given her if she hadn't stopped him?

She squeezed her thighs tighter together as warmth suffused her.

Rekosh's claspers twitched and shifted, crossing firmly over his slit. He chittered, jarring Ahmya from her thoughts. Her wide eyes shot up to his.

He was looking at her, head tilted, mandibles lifted. "You are…keeping watch?"

Quickly sitting up, Ahmya spun on the rock to give Rekosh her back.

I'm certainly keeping watch of something.

Her cheeks blazed. What was wrong with her?

Simple. You're a horny virgin who wants to get fucked.

By Rekosh.

"Uh, yes!" Ahmya called. "Keeping watch. Yep."

Liar.

She heard water sloshing around his legs as he moved toward her. Folding her hands in her lap, she peeked up at him as he moved to her front. His black hide glistened. Though he still favored his left foreleg, he seemed to be able to place more weight upon it than he had yesterday.

"So, um, what's the plan?" she asked in a desperate attempt to focus on anything besides her arousal.

He stopped at his bag, which was propped beside a rock a few feet away, and opened it to retrieve his waterskin. "We must go back to Kaldarak."

Ahmya knew that. She did. It was the obvious answer. But strangely, hearing it dampened her good humor. She didn't understand why. She'd been welcomed there, her friends were there, her new home was there. She was safe there.

But despite all that, she still felt alone in Kaldarak. Alone and lost, with no true direction. She felt as though there were expectations always pressing down on her, but she didn't even know what they were. She was floundering.

And those feelings had been at their worst during those long weeks while Rekosh was gone.

Some part of her recognized that the problem wasn't with Kaldarak or any of the people there. It was a restlessness in her, a sense of…of constant inadequacy.

"I guess I was more curious about how we're going to do that," she said.

"Me too." Rekosh returned to the water's edge, opened the waterskin, and dipped it in.

Ahmya's brow pinched as she turned to face him. "You too?"

He nodded, lifted the waterskin, and closed it before returning it to his bag. She watched water dripping from his hide as he settled down on a carpet of green grass in front of her rock with his injured foreleg stretched out next to her.

"I do not know this ground," Rekosh said as he scanned their surroundings with those intense crimson eyes.

"Couldn't we just follow the river back?"

"The river will lead us back, but we are…down. Must climb." His gaze shifted upriver, in the direction of the waterfall. "But rain has made the ground weak, and the cliff is too dangerous. We must go around."

"And we don't know how far out of the way that will take us, soooo…we're kind of lost."

He chittered as he looked at her. "Yes."

"I think I'd much rather go around the long way than try and climb a steep cliff anyway." Ahmya settled her elbows on her knees, propped her chin in her hands, and grinned. "It can be an adventure. Just the two of us."

Rekosh cocked his head. "I do not know your word. Adventure."

"It means to explore. To find new, exciting things. To have fun."

A thoughtful hum rumbled in his chest, and his gaze raked over her. "What if new things want to eat us?"

The heat between her thighs rekindled, and she dug her toes into her boots. Ahmya couldn't quite tell if he was talking about wild beasts eating her...or himself.

Stop thinking about his tongue!

"Well, that part isn't fun," she said. "But the exploration is. And...the company is good."

He smiled, and the fangs at the ends of his mandibles gleamed.

They should've unsettled her. She'd seen their strength, knew what they were capable of. But all she could think of was the way they'd teased her skin as he'd rubbed his face on her belly, their tips grazing her with the perfect blend of pleasure and pain.

"Yes. The company is best." Rekosh leaned toward her, propping his lower hands on the ground in front of him. "I like to see you, Ahmya. To speak with you."

Ahmya's belly fluttered. "I like seeing and speaking to you too." She had the urge to cover her face and hide so her next words would be easier to say, but she resisted, keeping her eyes locked with his. "I...missed you, Rekosh."

"Ah, *kir'ani vi'keishi*. For many eightdays, I have felt my threads coming undone." He tapped his chest, over his hearts. "I will not be away from you again."

Her skin was flushed, and the fluttering in her belly had increased tenfold. Ahmya smiled and traced her fingers along the ridge of his headcrest and down the side of his face. "I hope not. It was very lonely without you."

He captured her hands with his upper ones, pressed them palm to palm, and laced their fingers together. Hers were so small compared to his, but seeing them like this was so, so right.

"*Kir rayathi kir'ani ikarex elush ul sythal*, Ahmya."

I weave my words into a bond, Ahmya.

Rekosh eased closer. "I will stay with you."

The smoldering intensity in his eyes and the conviction in his voice made Ahmya's breath catch. She curled her fingers, squeezing his hands.

I want to stay with you too.

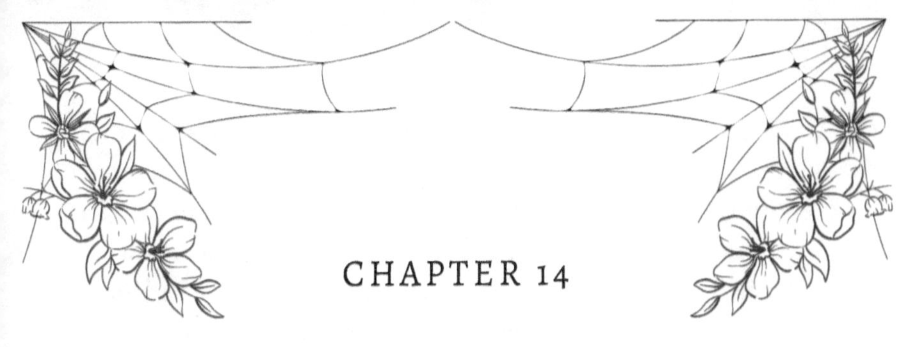

CHAPTER 14

THE JUNGLE only seemed to have two types of weather—cold and rainy or hot and muggy. Today fell into the latter category. Ahmya had appreciated the warm sunshine this morning while they lounged beside the river, but as the day had worn on, the heat had steadily grown unbearable.

She gathered her hair off her neck and pressed it to the back of her head. The air was a balm upon her sweaty skin.

"Leaking again?" Rekosh asked, calling her attention to him. He strode beside her, matching her leisurely pace, with the sharpened stick serving as his spear tucked along his upper right arm.

Ahmya chuckled as she slipped between two trees, using the point of her own spear to check the vegetation in front of her for any lurking beasties—or hidden carnivorous plants. "Be happy that you vrix don't have to worry about sweating."

"I am. The jungle is already wet. I do not know why humans must make themselves more wet."

"We don't exactly have a choice. Sweating is just a natural thing that occurs to help regulate our body temperature. It's how we cool off in the heat."

"We will stop soon, Ahmya. Then you may leak in the shade."

Ahmya laughed. Despite the humidity, it felt good to be out here, felt good to be seeing the Tangle. It felt good to have Rekosh with her. It would've been nice to have reached this point without almost dying several times along the way, but now that they were out here, she was determined to enjoy herself.

And she was. There was no need to rush—no vengeful queens chasing them, no disasters forcing them onward at a breakneck pace. It was just her and Rekosh surrounded by nature in all its beauty.

Their journey had been filled with conversation, though unsurprisingly, he had done most of the talking. And Ahmya had been content to listen. She was eager to learn more about him.

He'd told her about his trip to Takarahl with Urkot and Telok, about how different it was with Ahnset as queen. How peaceful. The vrix who called the city home were no longer hungry because their hunters provided for all rather than being forced to deliver their kills to Zurvashi. The city was flourishing, with broodlings playing in the tunnels and vrix no longer hiding in fear.

Rekosh had also mentioned that Urkot had helped sculpt statues in honor of Ivy and Ella in Takarahl's heart, a chamber called the Den of Spirits.

The thought of those statues brought a smile to Ahmya's face, but it was tinged with sadness.

The cards fate had dealt to Ella had been unfair, and so very cruel. She'd suffered from the moment she'd awoken from cryosleep due to stasis sickness, and her health had deteriorated every day. It'd only been a matter of time before she would've succumbed to her condition. But she'd still lived each day to the fullest, looking upon this alien world with wonder sparkling in her eyes.

As Ahmya and Rekosh had trekked onward through the jungle, he'd answered her questions about the plants, animals, birds, and insects they passed, and even shared vrix myths about some of them. He also went out of his way to point out flowers she might've missed amidst the vegetation. Over the hours they'd been walking, his English had noticeably improved, and she'd picked up more vrix thanks to him so often using his native language and translating it for her afterward.

But for as much as Rekosh spoke, he never said anything about his father, mother, or siblings. He never told other stories from when he was a broodling, or how he and the other vrix in their tribe used to spend their time. Rekosh had offered no details about his past, which was odd for him, as he delighted in storytelling.

She wanted to know those things about him. Wanted to know everything, really. But based on the little he'd told her yesterday, his childhood had not been a happy one. Perhaps he just didn't want to dredge up old, painful memories.

Her heart squeezed at the thought of him being hurt as a child.

Dropping her hair, Ahmya stepped onto a narrow rock formation that ran up the side of a small hill, spreading her arms to the sides to keep her balance with her spear help upright. The stone was worn, cracked, and crumbling, and was being swallowed by dirt and plant growth on one side, but the long, relatively flat tiers seemed decidedly like stairs.

The area the rock steps led up to was fairly level, and though it was shaded by the boughs of towering trees, it felt like a clearing—or rather like it had been a clearing long ago. Like...a glade carved out of the jungle.

Thick roots had pushed up chunks of stone from the

ground, and more rock lay scattered about, much of it overgrown with plants. At the center of it all was a small pool, fed by a spring bubbling from some of those rocks.

Long-stemmed flowers that looked like a cross between peonies and roses grew along the edge of the steps and around the pool. The leafy stems were tall, some of them taller than Ahmya, and were topped with large, lush white and pink blossoms. The air was fragrant with their sweet perfume.

Ahmya stopped, brushing her fingers over the petals of the nearest blossom. They were velvety soft. "What are these?"

"They are called *syth'keishahl*."

"Silkblossom?"

Rekosh trilled. "Yes. It is said they came to be when the Weaver gifted the Rootsinger some of his finest silk. She knew it would not last forever, and that made her hearts heavy with sadness. She wanted to share such beauty with all vrix. So, she planted his silk in the ground, and from it grew these flowers. Now everyone may enjoy the beauty of that silk as she enjoyed it long, long ago."

"That's a lovely story." Ahmya leaned forward and inhaled, drawing in the flower's scent. She hummed appreciatively and continued on. Rekosh kept pace with her as they ascended the steps.

She glanced at him from the corner of her eye. "Rekosh, can I ask you something?"

"Always."

Ahmya stopped on the highest tier and faced him. "Would you tell me more about your childhood? About when you were a broodling?"

Rekosh halted, and his lower hands grasped his sash, adjusting its lay across his chest. His mandibles twitched. "When I was a broodling..."

"You don't have to tell me anything you don't want to," she rushed to say, waving her palms. "I...I don't want to pry. I know you were hurt, that other vrix bullied you. So if you don't want to tell me anything else, that's okay.

"I just…" She drew her spear against her chest and clutched it. "I want to know about you. *All* of you."

His gaze lingered on her briefly before he turned it away, raking it across their surroundings. Afternoon sunlight streamed in through breaks in the canopy, including a rather large one over the rock Ahmya stood upon, making the flowers especially vibrant.

With the spring's gentle trickling combining with the other jungle sounds, this spot was almost serene.

Of course, that didn't mean it was less dangerous than anywhere else.

Rekosh returned his attention to Ahmya, shifted closer, and took her spear from her grasp before plucking her up off her perch. With one arm under her legs and another at her back, he cradled her to his chest.

"What are you doing?" she asked as she looped her arm over his shoulder and placed a hand on his warm chest.

"I will speak," he said, climbing the rock to reach the area at its crest. "But these are not striding words."

"Not striding words?"

"We must sit. The story is…heavy."

She felt some of that weight in that moment; it was apparent both in his voice and in the way he moved, which seemed a little slower, a little more deliberate and measured, than his usual effortless grace.

He walked past the pool and its crystal clear, shimmering water, and brought her to a shady spot nearby. A few taller stone outcroppings, covered in vines and moss, stood there like lopsided pillars flanking a low wall of fallen rocks and boulders. Some of the ground within the natural alcove created by the formation was covered in fine grass and tufts of moss.

Propping the spears against the tall stone, Rekosh slipped

off his bag and set it atop the moss before lowering himself beside it. His folded forelegs created a makeshift seat in front of him, and he placed Ahmya atop them with her back against his chest once he'd settled.

Reaching aside, he opened his bag and took out his water-skin, which he handed to her. "Drink, *vi'keishi*."

"Thank you." Ahmya smiled and uncorked it, taking a long draft of the cool water. He drank too before returning it to his bag.

When she began to shift to face him, Rekosh settled his upper hands on her shoulders, keeping her in place.

Ahmya's brow creased. "Rekosh?"

He slid one of his palms from her shoulder up her neck, where he cupped her throat and gently tipped her head back. His red eyes were solemn as he peered down at her.

Ahmya searched his gaze. "You don't have to tell me anything."

"I want to." He trailed his other hand over her cheek, brushing her skin with the backs of his claws.

A shiver ran through Ahmya at his touch, at his voice, at that gaze so intent upon her. "I will listen."

Rekosh withdrew his hand from her neck and slipped his fingers into her hair. The tips of his claws grazed her scalp as he combed through the strands, but he was so delicate, so reverent, that all she felt was the tingling left in their wake. He simply brushed her hair, remaining quiet for long enough that Ahmya had a feeling it was his way of soothing himself.

Keeping her head tilted back, she closed her eyes and folded her hands in her lap, giving him all the time he needed.

"As I said, I was smallest of my brood," he began, voice low. "My father was a weaver, my mother a Fang. I could not go with her, so I followed him to hide from others. To be safe. He taught me to weave. Taught me many things. Maybe he did not know why I followed him, but it brought him joy. Joy in sharing needle, thread, and loom, joy in teaching and seeing me learn.

"Because I was a small broodling amongst big vrix, I kept my words to myself and listened, and I learned many things. A warrior's fangs and claws have strength, but words have strength also. Knowing is strength. And because I was small, they spoke as though I was not there." His fingers continued their work, parting her hair into sections that he held firm without ever pulling.

"Whispers, vrix say. That is what I learned." Rekosh chittered. "But most are not whispered."

"Our word is gossip," Ahmya said with a smirk.

"Gossip, yes. I sat near my father, and I wove, and I listened. Soon, I learned words could sometimes make me safe. Knowing could be used as a shield and a spear. Knowing the words a vrix wanted to hear was strength. But all I wanted was to be the greatest weaver in Takarahl so my father would see me with all eight eyes, so he would have pride."

A sharp pang struck Ahmya's chest, and her eyes prickled with the threat of tears. She opened them. Drawing in a slow, deep breath, she willed those tears away and settled a hand upon Rekosh's leg. It was harder, more solid, than the rest of him, but its hairs were soft against her palm, and they rose slightly at her touch.

"I understand how that feels," she said. "I wanted the same with my father. He…did not see me no matter how much I sought his approval, no matter how hard I tried."

His chest rumbled with an unhappy hum. "I am sorry, *vi'keishi*. But know that I have seen you always."

Her lower lip quivered, and she couldn't stop the tears from filling her eyes despite her efforts. "I know."

He leaned down and rubbed his hard mouth against her temple. His warm breath flowed over her skin. "No tears, Ahmya. No more rain."

Ahmya released a small laugh. "I'm sorry. I don't usually cry so easily... At least I didn't before waking up in this world."

"I know it is hard. It will get better in time."

She turned her face toward him. Her lips were so close to his mouth, so close to brushing over it, to kissing him. "It has been better with you."

Trilling softly, he lifted his head and set his hands back into motion. "It is better for me too."

"Please continue." She gave his leg a gentle squeeze. "I want to know more."

Again he was quiet, and she could almost feel him gathering his thoughts even as he plaited her hair. He spoke after a deep, slow breath. "I said my mother was a Fang. She served Queen Azunai, who was queen before Zurvashi. She was...big." He chittered softly. "But gentle. Strong but kind. I see her in Ahnset. I did not like when my mother came to our den with hurts, and I always tried to help her. My hurts... They were so small, and hers were so big.

"I tried to hide them from her. But she saw. She knew. Always, she would help, and always so gently. She did not make me feel small, did not make me feel weak. She made me feel... safe. Made me feel worthy.

"I had only seen five years when my mother died in battle against the fireeyes. She was carried back to Takarahl, and I watched my father sew her shroud. I tried to help, wanted to, but he would not let me.

"I did not know why. We two were weavers, and it was the thread that bound us. I was sad. I knew he was sad also, but he was...changed. He strode with a cloud around him, a darkness. I told him stories as we wove, some I had heard from others, some I had made in my mind, hoping to make him chitter. I took better care in weaving so his hearts would smile. But he did not see. He could not.

"My broodbrothers and broodsisters became more kind in

our sadness. We did not have our mother, and our father strode in darkness for a long time. His body was near, but his spirit was far. None of my brood siblings had any want to learn weaving. My sisters wanted to be like our mother, to be Fangs. The only time we saw my sire's fire again was when they told him that. He shouted and growled and told them no, never, they would not follow our mother."

"Oh, Rekosh." Ahmya felt the pain in his words because it was the same as her own—pain that had been buried deep down, that she hadn't been allowed to express. "My mother died when I was eight. I was young, like you. And I felt so very alone. My brother Hirohito is..."

Her heart squeezed as she remembered the passage of time. Hirohito was no longer alive. He'd died on Earth, long ago, while she'd slept aboard the *Somnium*.

"My brother was nine years older than me, so we were never close," she continued. "He was protective and kind, but I was just his baby sister. And when our mother died, our father also changed. He was sad, but also harder too."

Ahmya ran her palm up and down the upper segment of his leg. "Your father was hurting. Grief changes us, and it can blind us to the fact that other people are hurting too."

"I know that now," Rekosh said softly. "But as broodlings, we did not. It was his duty to see. His duty to protect and teach."

The unspoken words hung in the air, as clear as anything Rekosh had said.

His father had failed.

And she couldn't help but wonder if her father had failed her also. She felt horrible even considering it. No one was perfect, and her father had done his best, hadn't he?

Yet she couldn't help but feel like Yutaka Hayashi had failed his duty to his children when they'd needed him most.

Rekosh's arm shifted behind Ahmya, and she heard his fingers tap the hard plate of his chest. "My sisters held their wants close and quiet. They would talk to me in whispers, when the den was dark and our father slept, and tell me of their dreams. They wanted to honor our mother by doing as she had done. By serving the queen and protecting Takarahl.

"My brothers spoke of helping them. Of journeying into the Tangle together to face the enemies of Takarahl, of finding the vrix that killed our mother and slaying them. I did not have the same wants, but I made stories for them. Stories about them— about their journeys as warriors. Loshei's brood, fighting for Takarahl, bringing honor to their mother.

"My stories brought them joy, and their joy was mine. Our sadness faded. If we did not have our father, we had each other.

"But two years after our mother died, sickness came to Takarahl."

Dread filled Ahmya. She remained silent, staring ahead, as she listened.

"It stalked Suncrest Tunnel"—Rekosh extended a hand before her, long fingers splayed, and snapped it into a fist—"and grabbed every vrix it could. Many got sick. It made a smell... I do not have words for it in your language. A smell that would not leave, that went deep into all it touched, that made my insides twist. The sickness came into me first. Then it went into my sisters and brothers.

"I remember the wails echoing along the tunnel. Vrix crying out their agony, some until they had no voice left... They wailed in pain because of their illness, while others wailed in grief as their families and friends died, and long after the sickness passed, I still heard whispers of those wails.

"I remember the hurt all over my body, in my bones, my head, my insides. I was too hot and too cold. My throat was small, almost too small for air, and my thoughts... They drifted away like dead leaves on the wind.

"There were blankets and the green fire of spinewood sap, and my father was there, always with us, offering water and soft words. But it is all in pieces that do not fit. I do not know how many days I was so. Only that when I shed the sickness, I was weaker than ever, and many, many vrix had died. My brothers and sisters…"

Whatever more he'd been about to say caught in his throat, creating a deep, broken sound. His fingers faltered in her hair, and Ahmya felt a shudder course through him. Tears blurred her vision.

"I was the weakest, the smallest. I should not have lived. But the sickness took them. All of them. My father sewed their shrouds, one by one, and I did not try to help. I could not find strength to lift even a needle and thread. When he made the last stitch, he made a vow to the Eight. Never would he weave again. Never would he stitch again. Never would he sew another shroud."

Vrix could not weep, but they were no strangers to sorrow. Rekosh's body trembled with it, his voice overflowed with it, and it swept freely into Ahmya's heart, flooding her chest. All that pain, all that grief, all that distance… To have lost his mother, his brothers and sisters, and then the single profound connection he'd shared with his father must've been devastating. She couldn't imagine how a child would've taken it.

She couldn't bear not seeing him at that moment. Couldn't bear being turned away. Bracing her hand on his leg, she twisted toward him. Her hair briefly went taut in his hold before he released it, and he leaned back slightly, looking at her with eyes brimming with grief.

Ahmya faced him fully on her knees and slipped her arms around his neck, drawing him into the tightest embrace she'd ever given to anyone. She wished she could have done the same for him all those years ago when he was a child.

What tension had been in his hard body melted away against her. All four of his arms banded around her, lifted her, and drew her even closer to him. Without thought, Ahmya wrapped her legs around his waist. Out of all the vrix she'd met, Rekosh was the most charismatic, the most outgoing. But he'd developed those traits to protect himself.

He buried his face in her hair, and his shuddering exhalation teased her scalp. *"Kir'ani vi'keishi..."*

Closing her eyes, she rested her cheek on his chest and twined her fingers in his hair as she cradled his head. Ahmya had no words to soothe the pain, loss, and loneliness he had felt, so instead she let him feel her. Let him know through her embrace that he was not alone, that she was here with him, that she understood and empathized. That she cared about him.

She wasn't sure how long they held each other that way. She knew only that it felt right, despite the circumstances, and that it hadn't been nearly long enough when he finally lifted his head. But he drew back only slightly, ensuring that their arms remained in place.

Ahmya looked up at him, and Rekosh looked down at her.

He trilled softly and retracted one of his upper arms. The backs of his fingers swept over her cheek, spreading tingles across her skin. "I cursed fate for the pain and sadness it gave me. Then, even with every star in the night sky burning between us, our threads crossed. I might have been thankful, but fate has done all it can to keep us apart. I have always spun my own silk, my own words, and now I will also spin my own fate—to ensure it is forever woven with yours."

Ahmya's breath caught, and her eyes flicked between his. Those words had not been spoken lightly, hadn't been meant as simple comfort. They were more. Much, much more. "Rekosh..."

"There is something I must give you, Ahmya." His lower hands guided her legs down, and he set her on her feet in front of him before withdrawing. He retrieved his bag from the ground, opened it, and reached inside.

His hand emerged holding the leather wrapped bundle she'd seen when she set out his belongings to dry.

She recalled what he'd said the morning he'd come to her den with something in his hands.

Ahmya, I must share words with you.

Words from my heartsthread, kir'ani vi'keishi...

Her heart raced, and she pressed a palm against her chest.

Rekosh set his bag down and shifted his forelegs, kneeling on the right while stretching the other out. His eyes met and held hers. "You are my mate, Ahmya. I felt it in my hearts when I first saw you." He passed the bundle to his upper hands, bowed his head, and held the offering out to her atop his upturned palms. "Be mine, my heartsthread, and take me as yours."

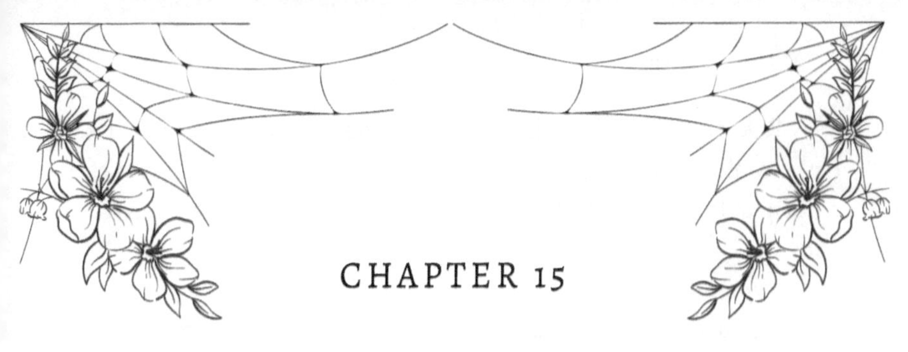

CHAPTER 15

Ahmya stared at the bundle in Rekosh's hands.

He wants me to be his mate.

He wants me to be his mate.

Rekosh had always been attentive to Ahmya and her needs, had always been protective, caring, and patient. He'd spent so much time with her, seeking to learn her language as swiftly as possible so he could communicate with her.

The question had never been *if* Rekosh would declare himself, but *when*.

She'd always known, deep down, that this moment would come. But the trepidation that knowledge had once caused her was nowhere to be found now as she looked upon his bowed head. Rekosh was her friend. He was a kind, fierce protector who would make a loving…

Mate.

He would be my mate. My mate.

My…husband.

A nervous thrill coursed through Ahmya as she reached forward, lifted the bundle from his hands, and drew it close to her chest.

Rekosh released a shaky breath and raised his head. His mandibles ticked up into a vrix smile. Those crimson eyes burned for her, but she did not fear their heat. She yearned for it.

"Open it," he said.

Flooded with eagerness, Ahmya held the gift along one forearm, untied the silk string holding it together, and peeled back the leather wrapping. It revealed another bundle, this one wrapped in silk cloth, which she also opened.

Her breath caught.

Sitting atop a layer of cloth was a pair of shoes—the most beautiful shoes she'd ever seen. They were dainty and elegant, made from white silk with intricate, lacy designs. She ran her fingers over them. They were soft right down to the light brown leather of their soles.

"You made me shoes?" she asked. It was a pointless question; of course he'd made them. But it had been prompted by her surprise. Vrix didn't have feet, and though they sometimes wore adornments on their bodies, they didn't wear clothing like humans did. For him to have made these was so thoughtful.

"Yes. Your boots are too big, and they will not…" Rekosh waved a hand. "Will not look…"

Ahmya chuckled and stuck her foot out, resting her boot on its heel and rocking it back and forth. "Look pretty?"

Rekosh met her gaze. "You are pretty."

Heart fluttering and cheeks warming, she ducked her head and returned her attention to the gift. There was more beneath the shoes. Picking them up, she set them atop a rock before straightening and peeling back the cloth they'd been resting upon. The contrast between that piece of cloth and what was beneath it was like night and day.

Ahmya's lips parted as she ran her fingers over the silk. It was so fine and soft, the softest she'd ever felt, even more so than fluffed silk or the petals of the silkblossom. "Rekosh, is this…"

He carefully grasped the sides of that delicate material with his long, clawed fingers. As he lifted it, the fabric unfurled to reveal a gossamer dress.

She could do nothing but stare in awe as the dress swayed in the gentle breeze, a hint of opalescence playing across its surface.

Ketahn had made Ivy a dress—a wedding dress—after she'd told him about marriage. She'd been wearing it the day she'd awoken Ahmya and the other survivors from cryosleep. It had been strange yet beautiful, with intriguing, weblike designs and fine silk. But this dress…

The sleeveless garment had a low-cut neckline with flower and leaf patterns woven throughout the silk and embroidered lace along the hem. It was embellished not just with fine stitching, but tiny white crystals that sparkled in the sunlight. And the diaphanous material was so sheer that she could see Rekosh clearly through it. The only part of her body it would hide was her breasts, which the fullest patterns would cover.

This wasn't a wedding gown; it was a dress befitting a wedding night.

She set aside the cloth and leather wrapping and brushed her fingertips over the front of the dress. "This is so beautiful, Rekosh."

He trilled, mandibles rising, and held it a little closer to her. "It will only be truly beautiful when you wear it."

Her blush spread, growing ever hotter, and Ahmya couldn't ignore her anticipatory flash of desire for what would come after she put on the dress.

This was it. If she accepted this gift from Rekosh, she would be accepting him as hers. She would be allowing him to *claim* her. It would be…

Well, it would be the same as getting married.

But as she stared at the gown, at craftsmanship beyond anything she'd ever imagined, she grew increasingly aware of the dirty, tattered silk wraps clinging to her. Aware of the sticky sheen of sweat covering her from head to toe, and the smudges of dirt the day's travel had left on her skin.

She couldn't wear that dress in her current state.

Ahmya lowered her hand. "Could I...bathe?"

Rekosh's mandibles fell. He glanced at the dress and back to her. All eight eyes blinked. "Now?"

He thinks you're rejecting him.

She raised her palms and waved them. "Oh! No, no, no. I'm not..." She gestured at herself. "I'm sweaty and filthy."

"You are beautiful, *vi'keishi.*"

Ahmya bit her bottom lip as her heart melted just a little more. There was never a moment when he made her feel anything but beautiful and cherished.

And he is going to be mine.

"For humans, a bride prepares herself to face her groom. Her soon-to-be husband, her...mate." Gathering her resolve, she stepped closer and settled her hands upon his, which still held the dress. "I want to do this for you, Rekosh."

"Ahmya..." He gently tipped his headcrest against her forehead and squeezed his eyes shut. "You accept me as yours? As your mate?"

"I do."

A shudder ran through him. "Your words have made my heartsthread thrum."

She cupped his jaw between her hands and smiled. "You have made mine thrum for a long, long time."

A low, content purr rumbled in his chest. Ahmya dropped her arms as he straightened and stepped back.

Those dexterous hands of his folded the dress with all the grace and precision she'd come to expect of him before he handed it to her. "Bathe, my mate. Prepare as you must. What time you need is yours."

She accepted the dress with a smile, trying to ignore the heat coursing beneath her skin, trying to suppress the excited energy pulsing at her core.

Rekosh remained in place.

Toeing the ground with her boot, Ahmya lifted her eyebrows.

He canted his head.

She held the dress against her belly. "Um, Rekosh…"

"Yes, Ahmya?"

"The preparation is usually done in private."

His mandibles fell again. "Private?"

"Yes. If you could maybe"—keeping hold of the dress with one hand, she raised the other and pointed toward the edge of the clearing—"go over there and turn around for a bit?"

He turned his head to follow her gesture with an unhappy hum. "You wish to be alone? The bathing is not done with your mate?"

"It's not."

"It is not safe."

"I won't be alone-alone. I'll just be by the water and can call for you if I see anything. But I…I need this. I want to do this. For you."

Rekosh searched her face silently before he nodded and rose, plucking up his spear in one hand and his bag in the other. He reached inside the bag and rummaged through for a moment before taking out a little cloth bundle tied with a silk string, which he held out to her. "*Nath'jagol.*"

Cleanleaf.

Ahmya beamed up at him as she took the bundle, touched by his thoughtfulness. "Thank you."

Rekosh grasped her jaw and tipped her face up toward his, keeping his hold gentle but firm. "I will be near, *vi'keishi.*" His gaze dipped to the dress, and another trill emerged from him, this one softer, warmer, and all the more endearing for it. "Call for me if *anything* happens."

"I will. I promise."

He stroked his thumb claw over her cheek, hesitating before he released her, and turned. He strode away, disappearing behind a large rock.

She didn't like it when he was out of sight, when they were separated, but knowing he was close was enough to keep her calm. She'd requested privacy, and he was granting it.

And he wasn't likely to leave her alone for long.

I'm getting married.

Ahmya grinned, clutching the dress and cleanleaf to her middle, and bounced in place. It didn't matter that Rekosh was a vrix. He was going to be her mate.

Crouching, Ahmya gathered the shoes and the cloth and leather that had swaddled the bundle, then made her way to the pool's edge. She surveyed the area for any lurking creatures, and when she was sure there were no predators about to pounce on her, she set everything down, spreading the leather out on a rock and the dress and shoes upon it to keep them protected.

Not wanting to waste time, Ahmya tugged off her clunky boots and undressed. Though she'd been living in the jungle for months, she still hadn't quite shaken her self-consciousness. She always felt like people were watching her even when she knew nobody was around.

It was...silly to hold onto such modesty. Ivy, Callie, and Diego had done away with it, and Cole never had any qualms about stripping and streaking through the village without a care in the world, dick swinging freely. But Ahmya, Lacey, and Will still struggled with it.

Ahmya dropped her dirty silk wrappings on the ground. Her

naked skin prickled as the breeze swept over it, and she fought the urge to cover herself.

I can do this. I will do this.

I want this.

She retrieved a few thick, aloe-like stalks of cleanleaf from the small bundle and walked into the water. Many of the rocks on the bed of the pool were thankfully smooth, but the water, while incredibly clear, was deceptive with its depth. She hadn't stepped in far before it reached her chest. Ahmya smiled. It felt incredible on her heated skin.

Taking a deep breath, she briefly ducked beneath the surface to wet her hair.

As the cool water swirled past, Ahmya broke open the cleanleaf, scooped out the inner flesh, and used it to scrub her hair and body. The substance fizzled on her scalp and skin and made a little hissing sound when it met the water, releasing the strong fragrance of gardenia and lemon into the air. She'd always loved that scent.

Running her hands over her body, she washed away the day's sweat and dirt, relishing the feeling of cleanliness.

The sound of the spring drew her attention. The water ran from a tall rock formation, tumbling down the uneven stone to feed the pool below. Stones of varying shapes rested on the natural ledges and recesses in the formation, and one of them caught her eye—a large stone lying in the path of the water. Erosion had made its surface convex, forming a natural bowl.

Or a cup.

A *sake* cup.

An idea took shape in Ahmya's mind. Even if she was missing a traditional component, she could share a piece of her culture with Rekosh.

She swam toward the small waterfall. Ahmya shifted to the side, squinting against the misty spray, and plucked up the rock.

It was mostly smooth, and the inside had been hollowed out enough that it would work perfectly.

Now to find two more...

Excitement fueled her search. The rock had been a lucky find—a sign to guide her. Though she didn't find any other rocks like the first, she soon discovered an eldernut tree beside the pool with several of its nuts scattered on the ground. Their curved shells, similar to walnuts but the size of her palm, had already been emptied by animals and would suit her needs well enough.

Ahmya carried her finds back to shore, and water ran down her body as she stepped out of the pool. After setting the shells and stone down, she wrung out her hair and picked up the spare silk cloth to use as a towel.

She looked in the direction Rekosh had gone, where he waited for her to call him back.

So they could mate.

Heat spread through her. This was it; she was going to have sex with a vrix.

She was going to have sex with Rekosh.

Ahmya clutched the makeshift towel as arousal flared low in her belly. She wanted him, had wanted him longer than she'd admitted to herself. She wanted to discover how different he was from her, wanted to discover how he would react when she touched him and what would bring him pleasure. She wanted to kiss him.

And she wanted to be pleasured by him in return. Ahmya didn't want to be a virgin any longer. She...she wanted his cock. She wanted to experience the intimacy, the passion, the...*love* that could be shared between two people.

Rekosh had always been gentle with her, but... Would he lose himself to the mating frenzy that she'd witnessed from other vrix in Kaldarak?

Would he lose control with her?

I want him to.

That thought surprised her, but it was true. She wanted Rekosh to let go, to hold nothing of himself back from her. Wanted him to relent to the fierce passion burning inside him.

She wanted all of him.

Ahmya smiled as she picked up the silky, diaphanous dress and held it up.

Soon, you will be mine.

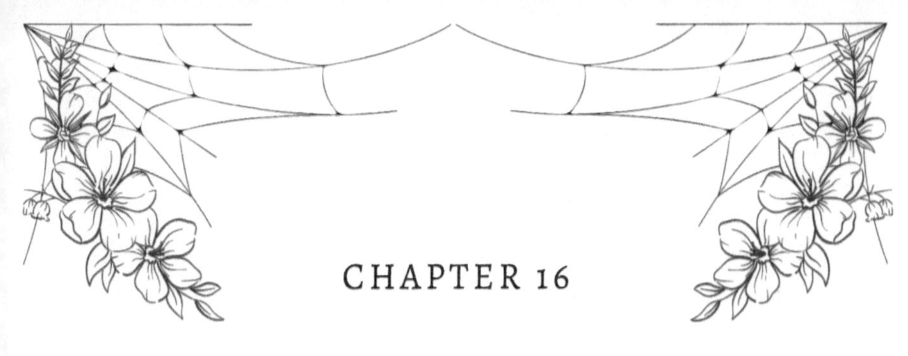

CHAPTER 16

She accepted me.

Rekosh dug his legs into the ground and pressed his shoulder more firmly against the cool, rough stone. That natural barrier was the only thing keeping him in place. He was not so foolish as to think his willpower alone would've provided enough restraint.

His hearts pounded a frantic rhythm, restless energy buzzed through his limbs, and his stem ached against the inside of his slit. Everything within him yearned for the same thing.

Ahmya.

His little flower.

Go to her.

Claim her.

Growling, he squeezed his fists around his bag and spear, making cured hide and wood creak in his grip. He forced his gaze to sweep across the jungle before him.

She'd asked for a little time. He could grant her that much. After many eightdays of waiting, surely his patience could hold out a bit longer.

Rekosh nearly chittered. Patience had twisted into its own sort of torture lately, and his relationship with it had grown ever more tenuous.

A warm breeze flowed across his fine hairs, carrying the jungle's cloying scents. But the only smell he noticed was a faint one, a mere echo, clinging to his hide—Ahmya's fragrance. The Tangle remained calm and quiet, a mocking contrast to everything happening inside him.

The sounds of soft splashes drifted to him from the pool. She was there now, her skin bare and glistening in the sun-dappled clearing, finally free of those inferior, tattered silks. Preparing for him. In his mind, he could nearly see her running her hands over her body, scrubbing away grime and sweat, cleaning, caressing.

He slapped his free hands against the stone and curled his fingers, raking the rock with his claws. His stem pushed outward, parting his slit.

"No," he rasped, drawing his claspers together to pinch his slit shut. He would not succumb to the mating frenzy before even seeing her in the dress. He would not go to Ahmya until she called.

Because this was much more than instinct, more than desire, more than fate. No matter what forces had drawn them together, their bond had become something even stronger and more meaningful—a choice.

A choice to fight through hardships and challenges. A choice to cling to one another in defiance of anyone and anything that stood against them. A choice to be interwoven.

They had chosen each other, and nothing would ruin their joining.

So he trembled against the stone, and he watched, and he listened. Each moment was harder to endure than the last, especially with those sounds from the pool, but he endured them all the same, and he suffered longer when those sounds went silent. What awaited him was worth every struggle he'd undertaken and many more beyond.

"Rekosh?"

Ahmya's voice, sweet and alluring, rose over the jungle's whispered song.

He drew in a deep breath. His chest swelled, brimming with a feeling so vast, so strong, that he did not know whether his body could contain it.

Rekosh pushed away from the rock and strode back into the clearing. Back to his mate.

When Ahmya came into view, Rekosh's hearts stuttered, and he nearly stumbled. She stood before the pool with her hands clasped in front of her, and her long, black hair cascading freely over her shoulders. A single silkblossom was tucked above her ear.

And his creation adorned her lithe body.

The crystal accents sparkled in the daylight, and the white, translucent silk shimmered with subtle colors as it shifted with the breeze. He followed the sheer fabric downward with his gaze, delighting in the skin it scarcely concealed, to the shoes upon her feet.

She was beautiful.

Rekosh slowly moved toward her, dropping his bag and spear without conscious thought. He could not pry his gaze from her. Her legs shifted, and that subtle movement drew his attention to the crux of her thighs, to the dark hair that shielded her slit, clearly visible through the silk.

He'd tasted her there once, had dragged his tongue between her soft folds, where her delicious nectar had gathered like dew. And he thirsted for more.

I will drink from her again.

His spinnerets twitched, and that twitch grew into a shudder that coursed through him completely. Pride, need, and desire crashed together within him, feeding into an instinctual urge to bind her, to restrain her, to claim her.

Mine.

His stem strained against his slit, but he tightened his claspers, refusing to relinquish control. Pain radiated through his core. He would not harm her. He would *never* harm her. If he fell prey to the mating frenzy…

He met her gaze as he neared her. *"Kir'ani vi'keishi…"*

Ahmya's brown eyes held him captive. They had since the moment he'd first looked into them, when they'd been shy, uncertain, and a little fearful. A hint of that shyness remained, but it was accompanied by something brighter—a yearning that matched his own.

Rekosh stopped before Ahmya. She tipped her head back, and her eyes flicked between his. Hands fidgeting, she caught her bottom lip with her teeth, nibbling on it. He longed for it to be his fang nipping that lip, leaving his mark there for all to see.

He'd craved this female for so, so long, and now, she would finally be his.

Yet he was determined to savor this.

"You wear the finest silk ever woven." Raising a hand, he brushed the back of a finger up along the strap of her dress, following it to her slender neck. "Made to echo but a single thread of your beauty."

He caught her chin and carefully used his thumb claw to free her lip from her teeth. Fire blazed deep within him as he smoothed his thumb along that tender, yielding flesh. "And all I want is to tear it from your body."

Ahmya's eyes flared as she drew in a sharp breath. Catching his wrist with one hand, she flattened the other on his chest. "I-I don't want your gift ruined."

Rekosh eased closer, caging her hips between his lower hands, and dropped his head. He pressed his mouth to the place where her neck and shoulder met and inhaled. Her fragrance, so natural and sweet, so wholly her, was accented by a hint of cleanleaf. But there was more.

Her arousal. It was subtle and light, tantalizing and tormenting, and it flooded his senses. He craved more.

"You are my gift, Ahmya." He slowly ran his tongue over her skin as he gathered the fabric of her dress at her hips, drawing up the skirt. His claspers eased at that taste of her, and his slit parted against the pressure of his stem.

Ahmya shivered, her breath quickening. She curled her fingers against his chest, scratching his hide with her blunt claws, and tightened her grip on his wrist. "Rekosh..." She tipped her forehead against the side of his face. "Wait."

He growled and drew in another breath. His muscles tensed as his desire to prolong this moment battled his instinct to rut her *now*. Though the haze was encroaching on the edges of his mind, part of him still knew the dress was important to her. It was also important to him. He could not damage it any more than he could bring himself to harm Ahmya.

"I have waited long," he rasped against her soft flesh. "But I will wait longer if it is your command, *kir'ani vi'keishi*."

"There's...something I want to share with you." She skimmed her lips along his jaw to his mandible before whispering, "Please."

Rekosh shivered. That teasing brush of her lips nearly unraveled him. Somehow, he gathered the frayed strands of his control, wound them tight around himself, and raised his head. He ignored the trail of warmth left behind by her mouth as he lifted his mandibles in a smile. "Anything."

Ahmya smiled wide, flashing her little white teeth, and took a step back, forcing him to relinquish his hold as she withdrew her hands. Rekosh dug the tips of his legs into the ground to resist the urge to follow, to capture her in his embrace. He pressed his claws into his palms. The pain sharpened his focus.

"What is it you would share?" Rekosh asked.

She grasped a thick lock of her hair and ran her fingers through it, turning one of her knees inward in a way that shielded her hair-covered slit. "On Earth, there are all different kinds of wedding traditions that humans take part in when getting married, depending on where they're from or where they live."

Releasing her hair, Ahmya moved past him, stopping to crouch beside his bag. She opened it. "My parents were from Japan. My father immigrated to the United States when he was a little boy and grew up there. As an adult, he joined the *miluh terree*, and he met my mother while he was *stayshund* back in Japan. Even though I was raised in the States like he was, we followed a lot of Japanese traditions."

Ahmya removed Rekosh's waterskin, rose, and walked back to the pool. "And us becoming…mates, well, it's technically like getting married, so I wanted to share a tradition with you that's been performed for many centuries by my people." She waved a hand at a low, flat stone beside the pool.

A bowl-shaped rock with two hollowed out halves of eldernut shells stacked inside had been placed upon it.

Rekosh glanced between the rock and Ahmya, tilting his head.

Ahmya chuckled and clutched the waterskin to her chest. "It's…not quite the same. Not at all really. Normally there would be a beautiful set of *sakazuki*, which are ceremonial cups, but I had to improvise and use whatever I could find. And instead of *sake*, which is *ryce wyne*"—she lifted the waterskin—"we'll be using water. But it's not about what's in our cups. It's about what's in our hearts."

He stepped closer to her and gestured to the stone. "Tell me more, *vi'keishi*. Show me."

She smiled. "This is a binding ritual called *san-san-kudo*, which means three-three-nine times. The couple is supposed to take three sips of *sake* from each cup."

Ahmya grasped the front of her skirt and lifted it as she knelt upon the grassy ground, propping the waterskin against her thigh. Bending forward, she patted the ground in front of Rekosh.

Taking care with his sore foreleg, Rekosh lowered himself onto the ground before her. With less than a segment between them, he could not escape her scent, and heat stirred within him anew, but he held his claspers tight against his slit and settled his lower hands atop his forelegs.

"The number three represents *hehven*, earth, and man," Ahmya said with a smile, "and because nine is three threes, it's very *awspishuss*. Which means that it promises good fortune. Good luck."

"I understand," Rekosh said. "It is a ritual for luck."

"It is, but there's more to it. When a couple goes through *san-san-kudo*, they're forming a deep bond, making an unbreakable commitment to each other. They're swearing to each other that whether in *hehven* or on earth, through life and death, they will never part. They'll endure everything together, good and bad."

Rekosh trilled, his chest tight with emotion, radiating heat. But this was a softer heat. A more soothing heat. He extended a hand and caressed the side of her face. "You wish to share this with me, Ahmya?"

She cupped her hand over his and rubbed her cheek against his palm. "I do. I want to be your wife. I want to be your mate. And I want you to be mine."

Had he let himself lose control, had he let instinct take command, he would not have experienced this. He would not have seen that beguiling look in her eyes, would not have learned the depth of the connection she wanted. Would not have joined with her in the way of her people.

"Share all with me, my heartsthread, so I can finally make you mine."

She smiled, and he felt her heat flare against his palm as her cheeks darkened. Rekosh gritted his teeth as she pulled away, tempted to capture her and draw her back to him. His hand hovered briefly in the air before he returned it to his foreleg. He could not recall a moment in his life, even when working on the most intricate parts of her dress, that had required more patience and control than this one.

Ahmya picked up the top eldernut shell from the stack and held it out to him. "The first cup, the smallest, represents our past."

He accepted it between the fingers of an upper hand, glancing into the empty shell.

She picked up the waterskin and opened it. "We drink this in thanks to our ancestors for giving us life and allowing us to meet despite all odds." Carefully, she poured three small splashes into the shell.

"Take three sips," she gently instructed.

In his mind, vrix emerged from memory. His mother, the details of her face lost to the years save for her vibrant blue eyes. His sire as he'd once stood—tall and proud, with a gleam of joy in his crimson gaze. His brood siblings, so young, so full of life. The weathered faces of his mother's and father's elders, mere shadows from his earliest years.

They'd all taken part in bringing Rekosh to this moment, though no one could ever have foreseen it.

Rekosh stared down at the small shell before tentatively raising it. Opening his mouth, he tilted the shell. Water ran over the edge, falling onto his tongue. He righted it and did it again, and again, draining it on the third drink. Excess water trickled from the corners of his mouth, running down his chin and neck.

He huffed, lowered the shell, and wiped his face with the back of a free hand.

Ahmya giggled. "I guess sipping is difficult when you don't have lips."

"Will it be ruined if I cannot sip?"

Her smile softened, and she shook her head. "No, it won't be ruined. As long as you take three drinks, in whatever way is comfortable to you, it is following tradition."

His mandibles rose in a smile.

She held her hand out and offered him the waterskin. "Now you pour for me."

He traded with her, taking the waterskin in two hands. "Three pours, as you did?"

She held the shell carefully with the fingers of both hands. "Yes."

Using the same care she'd demonstrated, Rekosh filled the shell. Keeping her eyes locked with his, she raised it. He watched, focusing on her mouth as her lips wrapped around the rim. Desire once more stirred in his core.

That human mouth, with its soft, pliable lips, had always fascinated him. Had always tempted him. He longed to feel it on his hide again, to feel the tender press of her kiss.

Ahmya took three small sips before setting the shell down and picking up the next. "This second cup represents our present. It signifies our commitment to each other, and to the long, happy life we are building together. And it is a sign of our two worlds coming together and joining as one, despite all the differences between them."

Like the first, she took the second shell between both hands and nodded to him.

With three measured pours, he added water to the new shell, glancing at her face between each. She was radiant, her eyes sparkling as brightly as the adornments on her dress. She smiled as she drank.

They traded again. After she poured the water into the shell,

Rekosh's mind filled with new images. Not memories now, but hopes, desires—bits of that life of which she'd spoken. A den filled with brightly colored flowers and cloth. Ahmya lying atop him upon a bed of fluffed silk. Shared meals, shared stories, shared smiles and laughter. Shared dreams for the two of them to craft with the same care and determination he'd used to create her dress.

Ahmya gestured to the last of the cups, the smooth, curved stone. Rekosh set down the shell and picked up the stone. The difference in weight was immediately noticeable, as was its solidness.

"The third cup represents our future," she said, pouring water into it. "The harmony and happiness we will share, our willpower to stand united against any challenge in our lives and claim prosperity for ourselves. And…and…"

She looked down and tucked her hair behind her ear, dislodging the flower, which fell.

Rekosh's lower hand darted out, catching the blossom on his palm. He returned it to its place over her ear and caressed her cheek with the backs of his fingers. Capturing her chin, he tipped her face up and forced her eyes back to his. "And what, my Ahmya?"

Pink stained her cheeks. "And the children we will be blessed with."

Something roused deep within Rekosh's chest. Something primal and possessive. His gaze dipped to Ahmya's belly. It would be there that his seed would take root, there that his mate would carry the life they created, there that their broodling would be sheltered as it grew.

But for that to occur, they would need to mate.

And Rekosh intended to claim his lovely little female very, very soon.

He returned his eyes to hers and drank. Her lips parted with a soft, shuddering breath.

No water had ever tasted so pure, so sweet. But nothing would ever compare to the taste of Ahmya.

Only when he had finished did he release her chin and withdraw his hand, presenting her the stone cup. "For our future, *kir'ani vi'keishi.*"

Ahmya stared at him as she took the offered stone, holding it up for him to fill. Swiftly, she brought it to her lips, took her three sips, and set it down upon the boulder, likely harder than she'd intended based on her wince.

Rekosh's mandibles lifted, and he cocked his head. "The ritual is done?"

Ahmya nodded, clutching her hands in her lap and wringing her fingers. "Yes."

"We are mates in your people's way?" He passed the water-skin to his lower hands, closed it, and set it aside.

"There is...one more thing. A tradition from my American heritage."

He flattened his lower palms on the ground and leaned closer. "What is it?"

Clenching her hands, she bounced in place, her gaze flicking everywhere but to him.

"Ahmya?"

Her eyes met Rekosh's an instant before her hands darted out, caught his mandibles, and tugged him closer. Squeezing her eyes shut, she pressed her mouth to his.

Rekosh's eyes flared as her soft, warm lips moved against his hard mouth. Their warmth spread across his face, building and building until it was a wave of fire filling his core.

But she pulled away far too soon.

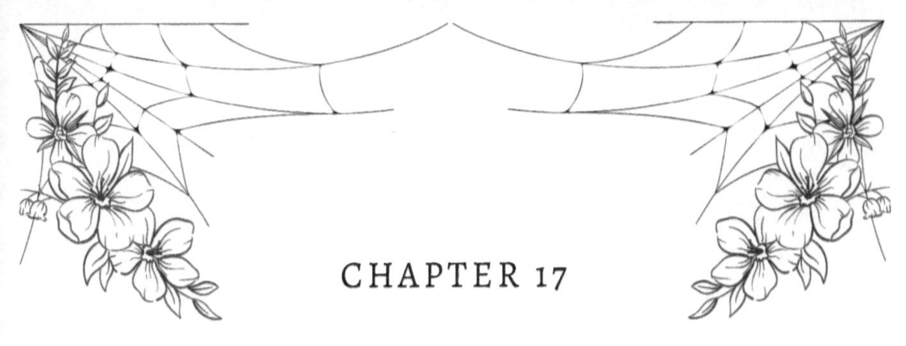

CHAPTER 17

AHMYA'S LIPS tingled as she sat back on her heels, her skin flaming in embarrassment and desire. She curled her fingers against her thighs, bunching the silk of her dress. She'd kissed him. His mouth had been hard and unyielding, but she'd felt the warmth of his hide, the tickle of his breath, and had smelled his spicy scent.

And she wanted more.

With her head bowed, hoping her hair concealed her heated face, she said, "A kiss to seal our bond as mates."

"Kiss me again, *kir'ani vi'keishi*. My *wife*."

Ahmya's breath hitched at that word. She looked up at him. He was staring at her, those red eyes of his blazing.

He lifted a hand, hooked the loose strands of her hair, and swept them behind her ear. "Teach me."

Oh God, oh God, oh God.

She barely knew how to kiss, and now he wanted *her* to teach *him*?

Vrix don't have lips. They don't know what kissing is. If you're horrible at it...well, how is he to know?

That thought didn't make this any easier.

But seeing him like this, with all that passion in his gaze, while she was aflame with desire, Ahmya knew her inexperience didn't matter. Because she wanted this.

And so did he.

Not looking away from Rekosh, Ahmya rose to her feet and stepped closer. He straightened. When he was sitting like this, they were nearly the same height.

You can do this, Ahmya. This is Rekosh. Your friend, your husband, your mate.

My mate.

Warmth spread through her chest, radiating outward.

Ahmya took hold of his thick braid. She brushed her thumb across some of the red and white strands woven into it, which shimmered in the sunlight, before gently tugging on his hair. "Come closer."

Rekosh's lower hands settled on her hips, his long fingers nearly encircling her completely, as he lowered his head with mandibles raised.

She placed her hands upon his shoulders. This close, every breath she took was laced with his scent. "Now press your mouth to—"

He firmly touched his mouth to hers.

And there it remained, unmoving.

Ahmya chuckled, her self-consciousness melting away.

There was nothing to be embarrassed about. They were two people, newlyweds, who would learn from one another. He was just as eager for this as she was.

Closing her eyes, she lightly brushed her lips over his mouth. Back and forth, again and again, learning the feel of him, relishing the delightful tingles sparked by this simple contact. Though his hide was hard, it bore a subtle, suede-like texture that kept him from abrading her. Those brushes turned into light kisses along the crease of his mouth and his faux fangs.

With a trill, Rekosh curled his upper arms around her, and his hands flexed on her hips as he drew her closer. He nudged his mouth more firmly to hers, scraping it against her lips. She felt the pricks of his claws on her skin, unhindered by the delicate silk, and the sensation stirred a wicked desire within her core. A need for more. She wanted his hands all over her body, exploring, teasing, desperate, wanted his fingers in her hair and his claws grazing her skin.

"Kiss me back, Rekosh." Ahmya flicked her tongue over the crease of his mouth.

He drew back with a sharp inhalation. Their eyes met briefly—just long enough for Ahmya to see the firestorm within his gaze.

The intensity of his desire made her heart leap.

Growling, he tightened his grip on Ahmya and pressed his mouth to hers again. This time, his mouth opened, and his long tongue slipped out, sweeping across her lips. Demanding entry.

Ahmya obeyed.

His slick tongue delved into her mouth. Its sensuous strokes sent thrilling shivers through her and coaxed her to open wider, to twine her tongue with his. It banished every thought from her mind, leaving only Rekosh—the feel of him, the smell of him, the taste of him. Sweet and spicy, everything that was wholly him.

How could he taste this good?

Ahmya only wanted more. She closed her lips around his tongue and sucked.

He purred as one of his hands slid up her spine to cradle the back of her head. The sound vibrated into her, making her nipples hard and her clit twitch. A whimper escaped her as she clutched at his shoulders, wanting—needing—him closer.

His tongue did not slow. With every lick, he grew bolder, hungrier, more fervent, and her need sharpened as liquid heat gathered in her core. He left no part of her mouth unexplored, no part untouched.

She felt something else, something long and thin skimming the sides of her calves, curling behind her knees, bunching up the silk of the gown.

His claspers.

Rekosh broke the kiss abruptly, withdrawing his face and curling his fingers into her hair to prevent Ahmya from following. That tongue ran along her jaw and slowly down her neck. She sighed and tilted her head aside. She felt the silkblossom fall again, but it was instantly forgotten. There was no focusing on anything else while his tongue was on her like this.

He licked down to the hollow of her throat before tracing her collarbone to her shoulder. The large, wicked fangs of his mandibles grazed her sensitive skin, leaving tingles in their wake as he trailed his tongue back up.

She clutched his shoulders with a whimper when he licked beneath her ear.

With a satisfied trill, he buried his face against her throat and rubbed his mouth over her skin. She reveled in every rasping swipe, in every teasing scrape of his mandibles, in his every heated exhalation and every flick of his tongue.

He was marking her, and she didn't want him to stop. She wanted to bear his scent from head to toe.

"Ahmya," he rumbled. His mouth opened wider, and she felt his sharp teeth on her neck.

Ahmya gasped, but didn't pull away. Instead, she slipped her fingers into his hair and drew him closer, forcing his teeth to press harder. She'd seen the bite mark Ketahn had left on Ivy's shoulder. She wanted one of her own. Wanted Rekosh's mark for all to see.

But she could not match his strength as he eased his teeth back. Rekosh's lashing tongue soothed away the sting of his fangs, his hunger tempered by reverence.

"Mine. My mate. My *nyleea*." Heat radiated from his hide, and a tremor coursed through his limbs as he released a heavy, harsh breath. His fingers hooked the low neckline of her dress. "Need this off. Now."

"Yes... No, wait!" Ahmya lifted her head and looked at Rekosh, hurriedly placing a hand over his before he could tug too hard. "Please don't tear it."

Hard muscle flexed under her palm, and his claspers twitched around her legs.

"I'll remove it." She brushed her thumb over his knuckles. "But I love it too much to see it ruined."

He released a strained hum. Tension radiated from him, and she knew she wouldn't be able to stop him if he pulled at the fabric. But she also knew that he didn't want to see it damaged any more than she did.

One look at the gown had been enough to tell her how much time and care he'd poured into its creation—how much of himself he'd poured into it. And that made it priceless to her.

Finally, his hold relaxed. He released the dress first, and then he released her, claspers and all, to lean back. The light in his eyes was no less bright as he looked her over.

"Remove it slowly," he ordered. "I want to hear the silk whisper against your skin."

Her belly fluttered at his command. She wanted his hands back on her, wanted his tongue, but more than anything, she wanted to feel him against her flesh with not even this gossamer silk as a barrier between them.

She stepped back.

And froze.

"Oh..."

Red rocket, indeed. One point to Callie.

Rekosh's slit was fully parted, and protruding from it was his crimson cock. It was long, thick, and glistening. The shaft widened at the head before narrowing to a tapered, two-pointed tip with a two-inch slit at its center. There was a pair of bulges near the base of his shaft, one on each side.

Ahmya's pussy clenched—not in fear of his size, but in acute need. She wanted him inside her, filling her, stretching her, wanted to feel his heartbeat thrumming at her core, wanted to be one with him. The proof of her desire was in the pulsing of her clit and the slick wetting her inner thighs. Her body was begging for him.

She gathered the silk of her skirt at her belly and squeezed her thighs together. It did nothing to alleviate the hollow ache in her core. Nothing would...except him.

A breeze swept past her, a balm against her heated skin.

"Ahmya?"

Rekosh's rough, gravelly voice drew her gaze up to his. The open yearning in his red eyes only fanned the flames burning inside her.

"I've never seen a..." Ahmya flicked her eyes down. "I've never seen a vrix cock before."

His gaze dropped to his erection. His claspers drew in tight against his pelvis as he wrapped his fingers around his shaft. The sound he made was half chitter, half hiss. "It is not like human stems."

Ahmya tightened her grip on the silk as she stared at his cock.

No, it most definitely is not.

"Do I scare you, Ahmya?"

"No," she said with a shake of her head before meeting his gaze. "I need you, Rekosh."

He unfolded his right foreleg, extended it toward her, and planted its tip on the ground behind her. The hairs upon his legs stood on end. "Remove the dress, *vi'keishi*."

Whatever inhibitions Ahmya might have had in the past were gone. She didn't care that they were out in the open, that someone could stumble upon them. All that mattered in this moment was him. Was *them*.

She gathered the silk in her palms until the hem of the skirt was above her knees. Rekosh watched, enrapt, as she slipped off the shoes. She curled her toes into the soft grass as a smile lighted upon her lips.

Dropping the skirt, she slowly smoothed her hands up her belly and over her breasts, feeling the embroidered flowers and hard crystals beneath her palms. Her breath hitched as she ran her hands over her beaded nipples. A titillating sensation zipped through her, straight to her clit. But she didn't stop there.

Taking hold of the strap that wrapped around the back of her neck, she lifted it off over her head, her hair teasing her sensitive skin as it tumbled back down over her shoulders and back.

She held Rekosh's gaze as she clutched the dress to her chest.

No more barriers.

Ahmya let the dress go.

The whisper of the fabric against her skin as it fell made her shiver. It was so light, so soft, so sensual, awakening every part of her to a new awareness, a new craving. The silk's caress made her yearn for his touch. For those long, strong fingers, with their rough calluses, to trail along every inch of her, for him to make her feel things of which she'd only dreamed.

All her craving, all her hunger, was echoed in the low growl that rumbled from Rekosh. His eight crimson eyes stared at her, burning, devouring, commanding. Once the gown had pooled at her feet, he shifted his foreleg closer, curling it around her and brushing it along her calf. Its tiny hairs tickled as they glided over her skin.

"The Eight themselves could never have shaped beauty to match yours," he said huskily.

Ahmya smiled, cheeks flushing at his praise.

His foreleg rose to her backside, and Ahmya released a little squeak and settled her hands upon his chest when he drew her closer.

Rekosh smiled. "Ah, my heartsthread."

His hearts hammered beneath her palms, strong, powerful. Alive. She looked down at where she was touching him and traced her fingers over the ridges of his chest, following them to the center of his abdomen. Her hand was so small, her skin in such stark contrast to his black hide. His teak and amber scent was so much more potent now, its notes of lavender even more pronounced; it was intoxicating.

She continued trailing her fingers down, down, down... Rekosh shivered, curling his lower hands around her hips. When she reached just above his slit, just above his cock, he tensed, growling, and his grip tightened before one of his upper hands caught her wrist.

Her eyes snapped to his. "Did I do something wrong?"

"If you touch, I will lose myself," he rasped, head dipping to brush his mouth across her forehead. "I do not want to hurt you."

Ahmya smiled at his kiss. "You'd never hurt me, Rekosh."

"I never want to hurt you, Ahmya, but the mating frenzy..." He exhaled heavily. "I do not know if I will be...me when it takes me."

She closed her eyes and cupped his jaw beneath his mandibles. "Ivy said that when a male calls a female his heartsthread, it is everything. That their spirits and hearts are bound."

Ahmya drew back and met his gaze as she placed a hand once more over his hearts. She stroked his mandible with a thumb. "You are mine, Rekosh. My heartsthread, my mate, my *luveen*. I trust you with everything in me. I *love* you."

Those words flowed from her so naturally. And they were

true. They had been true for so long, buried deep down beneath her uncertainty and trepidation. But she was free from all that. Free to openly and honestly share that love with him.

And she saw those words, saw that love, reflected in his eyes as he stared down at her. She felt it in the delicacy of his touch as he moved an upper hand to her belly and skimmed a finger along the tiny trail of scars.

"You wear the marks of my failure already. I did not protect you," he said in a low, broken voice.

Ahmya's heart squeezed at the pain in his words. She dropped her hand from his chest to cover his, pressing his palm flat against her stomach. "I am alive, Rekosh. The scars are from what I endured, what I lived through. They don't mark your failure. They mark my strength. And I'm here, standing before you now, as your mate, because of you."

She caressed his jaw and mandible. "I'm not helpless, Rekosh…but I need you."

He turned his face to her palm, nuzzling it. "My *nyleea*, my heartsthread… You are my little flower, and you have made my hearts bloom." Lifting his head, he cupped the back of hers, combing his claws through her hair.

Ahmya eased a little closer to him, her scalp tingling.

"We are woven together, hearts and spirits," he continued. "All that remains is our bodies. The final thread to bind us fully. I would learn you first, my Ahmya. Show me what to do."

She pressed her lips to the underside of his jaw, letting the kiss linger before answering. "You can kiss me some more," she said before softening her voice to a whisper. "You can… touch me."

A purr rumbled in his chest. "Show me how, *vi'keishi*."

Easing back, Ahmya took hold of his upper wrists and guided his large hands to her breasts. "Here."

Rekosh dropped his gaze and stared.

Ahmya glanced down as well. His hands covered the

entirety of her chest, and he held them there, unmoving, exactly as she'd placed them.

Why isn't he—

He tilted his head. "Is this…human mating?"

Oh…

Female vrix didn't have breasts. What would Rekosh know about touching them, about caressing a human body to bring pleasure?

Likely just as little as she knew about touching a vrix. About…bringing Rekosh pleasure.

Ahmya chuckled. "It's part of it. Humans call it foreplay. It's when you touch your partner to arouse them. But you don't just hold your hands there. You are supposed to…to…"

Warmth skittered across her skin as she pressed his hands more firmly to her breasts. "You…caress them. Nipples can be very sensitive, and when touched, it…it can bring us pleasure."

"Are yours sensitive, Ahmya?" Rekosh moved his hands over her, the abrasiveness of his palms grazing her nipples and making them harden further. "Does this bring you pleasure?"

Ahmya's breath hitched at the electric current that shot through her body. She tightened her grip on his hands and nodded. "Yes. Very."

A low purr rumbled from his chest, and he curled his fingers, squeezing her breasts. "Your skin is soft, but these… These are softer. So soft."

He cupped the mounds and pushed them up, stroking his thumbs over her beaded nipples. A moan escaped her, and she arched into his touch, needing more.

This was merely skin against skin, yet it was nothing like touching herself. How could it feel so different with him? What did it matter if it was her own hands or Rekosh's?

But it did matter. It was his touch, however light, however brief, that elicited all the pleasurable sensations for which she'd yearned. His touch that brought her body to life.

Rekosh trilled huskily at her response, his crimson eyes narrowing in delight as he gripped her hips with his lower hands, holding her steady. "Such pretty sounds my mate makes when I give her pleasure."

He played with her breasts, molding them, shaping them, and focused on her nipples, coaxing breathy sighs and whimpers from her. With every caress, with every stroke and pinch, the pressure within her core expanded. Slick arousal seeped from her pussy and coated her inner thighs.

She closed her eyes and tipped her head back, sliding her palms along his arms to rest upon his shoulders. Warm prickles of electricity flowed through her, building and building with his touch. Her nipples ached, and her clit pulsed. This…this felt… Oh God, she felt as though she was on the verge of an orgasm from this alone.

"Rekosh," Ahmya begged.

"Your scent…" he rasped, his voice next to her ear. He scraped his mouth over her neck and shoulder before licking the flesh, making her shiver. "Show me, my *nyleea*. Show your *luveen* what you want."

Ahmya lifted her head and opened her eyes to find his gaze fixed upon her, burning bright with yearning, with need, that he'd long contained.

For her.

Rekosh *wanted* her.

There was no reason to be shy, no reason to worry about what he might think, no reason to hold back from him. And she was long past that point anyway.

Because she wanted him too. She wanted *this*.

She dropped a hand from his shoulder and grasped one of his lower hands, guiding it down and slipping it between her thighs.

"Here," she breathed. "Touch me here."

A low growl escaped him. "Ahmya…"

One of his long fingers curled, pressing in along the seam of her pussy, its rough flesh brushing her most sensitive part. Her breath hitched, and she tightened her grip on his hand. She'd never, ever had anyone intimately touch her there before, and now, it took everything inside her to keep from grinding against him.

"So soft, *kir'ani vi'keishi*," he rasped, "and so wet. Is this nectar for your *luveen*?"

"Yes," she whispered. She hesitantly released his hand and returned hers to his shoulder. "Touch me more, Rekosh. Please."

Slowly, he explored her, gliding that finger back and forth through her pussy, tracing the folds of her labia as his upper hands continued fondling her breasts and tweaking her nipples. Ahmya panted, clutching at him, hips wriggling, seeking more, but his grip on her hip held her firm. When he pressed the pad of his finger into her entrance, her core clenched and she groaned.

"The sounds you make are as sweet as your scent." He dragged that crooked finger back through her pussy, as careful of his claws as always, and grazed the swollen nub of her clit.

"Oh God!" Ahmya gasped, bucking her hips as pleasure burst through her. "There! Touch me there!"

Rekosh stilled his finger upon it with a curious hum. "What is this?"

"My clit," Ahmya said in a rush, undulating against his finger. "Please don't stop."

"Clit," Rekosh said, emphasizing the word as he leisurely circled it with the pad of his finger, spreading the moisture he'd gathered.

Breathy, needy moans escaped her, and she rocked in time with the motion of his finger, chasing the promise of release. Arousal trickled down her inner thighs. She was so close to coming, teetering right on the edge.

"Your clit brings much pleasure." He pressed just a little

harder, and that slight change in pressure intensified the sensation tenfold.

Ahmya whimpered and nodded. "Yes. So much. It feels…it feels so good. So, so good."

Rekosh crooned and swept his curled foreleg down the backs of her thighs. The soft hairs brushed against her hypersensitive skin, sending a thrill across it. "Your body does not whisper, it sings, *kir'ani vi'keishi*. And its song is the most beautiful I have ever heard."

He quickened those circular strokes on her clit. Fire licked beneath her skin, and her thighs trembled. Something unfurled inside her, something powerful, something primal.

"But I need more. Must know more of you." He withdrew his hand from between her legs.

"No!" Ahmya cried, legs nearly giving out beneath her, but Rekosh held her fast in place. Her clit throbbed from being abandoned on the cusp of an orgasm. She scraped her nails down his chest. "Rekosh, please don't stop!"

He trilled, but the sound was cut short when a shudder wracked him. The chitter that followed was sultry and rumbling. "Small time, my *nyleea*."

Rekosh raised his hand and shifted his gaze to it. If her skin wasn't already flushed, she was sure it turned bright red at that instant. His fingers glistened with her slick. For a few heartbeats, he stared, turning his hand and watching the rays of sunshine catch upon it.

What is he—

Then his mouth opened, and his long, red tongue slipped out to lick from the heel of his palm to the tips of his fingers.

Ahmya's lips parted with a quick exhalation. The action was shocking and lewd, but it sent a spear of desire straight to her core.

"Your body makes this nectar for me," he purred, mandibles rising. "I would have it make more."

He closed his teeth on the claw of his middle finger and bit off the tip with a dull *snap.*

Ahmya's eyes widened as she caught hold of his wrist. "Your claw! Why would you do that?"

She knew how much care he took with his claws. They were instrumental when it came to his work, essential.

"I would know you inside, *kir'ani vi'keishi.* I would learn you with my touch. I would *feel* you." He flexed his fingers on her hip, pricking her skin. "And I have many claws."

He returned his hand to between her thighs, forcing them wider, and slipped the now clawless finger through her pussy once more, finding her entrance. His gaze held hers. "I would learn you here, my Ahmya."

Rekosh thrust his finger deep inside her.

Ahmya sucked in a sharp breath, body tensing as her sex clamped around the digit. His finger was long and thick, almost as thick as a vibrator she'd once used on Earth, and it stretched her, filled her.

"*Kir'ani vi'keishi,*" he rumbled, drawing his finger back before pushing it in deeper still. "Your body welcomes me. Hungers for me."

His words, combined with the sensation of his finger stroking her within, made her tremble. She ran her palms back up his chest to his shoulders and whispered, "It does."

Tipping his head forward, he nuzzled Ahmya's cheek, then her ear and hair, all while pumping that finger slowly, deliberately, nearly stealing her breath with each firm thrust. "Hot, wet, and soft." He flicked his tongue over the sensitive spot beneath her ear. "What do you call your slit?"

Ahmya whimpered. "My…my pussy."

With a growl, he thrust his finger harder, deeper, making her gasp. "Your *pussy* is mine. *You* are mine, Ahmya, and I will have all of you."

"You have me. You've always had me."

Her every nerve was alight with sensation as he stoked her pleasure higher and higher, and her body responded of its own accord. She rolled her hips, riding his hand, unable to stop her breathy sounds as ecstasy blossomed within her. It was agony; it was bliss.

Ahmya moaned, cupped his jaw, and lifted his head so he met her gaze. "Kiss me, Rekosh."

He released her breasts and cradled her jaw in turn. Then he pressed his mouth to hers, hard and demanding, rubbing against her lips until she opened to him. His long tongue slipped inside, twining with hers.

Ahmya buried her fingers in his hair and pulled him closer. As she bounced upon his finger, she sucked his tongue, flicking her own against his fangs and delighting in their sharpness, and pressed a desperate scattering of kisses along the seam of his jagged mouth. It all felt too good to end.

"Rekosh," she rasped, her pussy quivering.

He broke the kiss with a growl. His breath was harsh, and his body was rigid around her. "Need to kiss you."

Ahmya brushed her lips along his jaw. "Then kiss me."

His red eyes, already burning, flashed somehow hotter and brighter before he abruptly withdrew his hand from her pussy. She immediately mourned the loss of his touch, crying out for it, but he prevented her from following by grasping her hips with his upper hands.

Easing Ahmya back, Rekosh dropped his lower hands to the ground and yanked her forward.

"Need to taste you." He buried his face between her thighs, his tongue spreading her pussy.

Ahmya gasped and clutched Rekosh's hair as pleasure rushed through her. His tongue glided over her, stroking and licking. The sensation was just as strange and overwhelming as when she'd first felt it. Except this time, she didn't push him away. She pulled him closer.

"Rekosh..." she moaned.

He hummed against her, appreciatively, ravenously, and speared her entrance with his tongue, thrusting it deep inside her.

"Ah!" Ahmya's head fell back, and her eyelids fluttered shut. Her nails raked his scalp, and she spread her legs farther, allowing him easier access. Allowing him to push his tongue even deeper. He growled, the sound thrumming into her and making her clit pulse. His long fingers curled, tightening his hold on her and preventing her escape.

Not that escape was on her mind. She wanted to stay like this forever. She was consumed by him. Lost in him. The exhilarating press of his claws, the jagged faux fangs of his mouth on her mons, the sublime feeling of his tongue thrusting in and out of her pussy, his warm breath, and his spicy scent filling her lungs—all of it swirled together to carry her away on waves of ecstasy, erasing the whole universe but for Ahmya and Rekosh.

When Rekosh withdrew his tongue from her channel and twirled it around her clit, Ahmya's pleasure sharpened. She caught her lower lip with her teeth, muffling her growing cries, as he lapped at her greedily, again and again. He squeezed her ass, hard enough to bruise, and the points of his claws dug into her flesh. But she didn't care. Each delicious flick of his tongue pushed her closer to the edge, until somehow, he latched onto her clit and she fell.

Ahmya's body tensed, and her mouth opened in a silent cry. Her world ceased to exist.

She ceased to exist.

And then rapture cleaved through her.

Her cries echoed into the jungle around them as her body convulsed. Her inner walls fluttered, and her core contracted so powerfully it bordered on pain.

And it was followed by a gush of liquid.

Right into Rekosh's face.

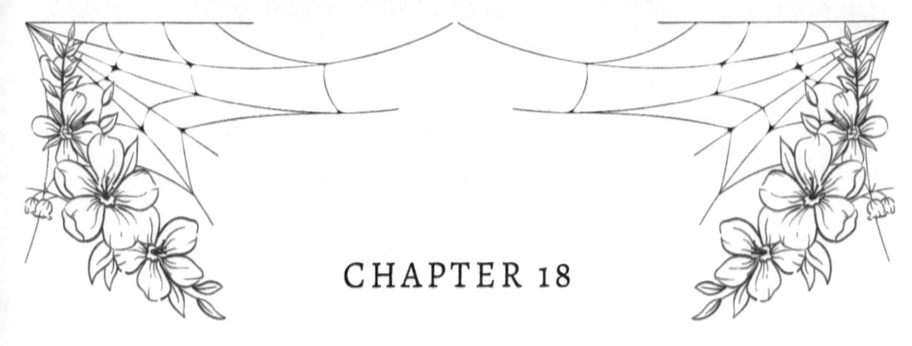

CHAPTER 18

AHMYA'S EYES FLEW OPEN, and all that pleasure was washed away by a wave of mortification.

Reflexively, she braced her hands on his shoulders and pushed.

Rekosh hissed. His claws stung her ass with his tightening grip, and his head snapped up. Glistening liquid—her *cum*—trickled from his mouth and down his chin, and his eyes blazed, wild and hungry. In that instant, he looked like a beast whose meal had just been interrupted.

Their gazes met, and Ahmya slapped a hand over her mouth in shock.

He stared up at her silently, tension radiating from his rigid body. A sharp huff escaped his nostrils before his mouth parted slightly. That long tongue slipped out and slid along the seam of his mouth, licking her cum from his hide.

Ahmya pressed her thighs together. Her arousal coated them and dripped down the insides of her legs.

Oh God... I can't believe I...I...

I just squirted *in his face!*

"I'm so sorry," she said quickly, body aflame.

A low growl rumbled in his chest. Moving stiffly but with obvious care, he lifted his hands from her ass, relieving the pressure that had been on those claws, and stood.

Ahmya's brows pinched as her stomach twisted with anxiety. Had she done something wrong?

You mean besides giving his face a power wash?

Oh, God, Oh God, Oh God!

That had never happened to her when she'd pleasured herself. She'd never felt anything so intense, so uncontrollable. How could something feel so good while being so humiliating?

Ahmya curled her fingers and lowered her fists to her chest, dropping her gaze to the ground. "Rekosh, I...I'm so sorry. I didn't know that would—"

He caught her jaw and tipped her face up, forcing her eyes to meet his. "No."

Her brow furrowed. "No?"

But he only released her and turned away, offering no explanation. His hind legs moved, drawing thick silk from his spinnerets, which he passed to his hands and wound into a growing coil of rope.

"Rekosh? Are you...okay?"

"Need you," he rasped. "All of you."

A thrill coursed through her in response to his words. "Oh..."

He wasn't...disgusted?

Severing the first strand with his claws, he immediately began drawing out another, his movements becoming a little faster, a little less disciplined, with each moment.

"Rekosh, what are you doing?"

"Bindings."

Ahmya's heart leapt. Bindings. For her.

Male vrix bound their females when they were ready to conquer, to...mate.

She wiggled her toes in the soft grass, anticipation mingling with her anxiousness. Her core thrummed with the aftermath of her orgasm, and more than ever, she was aware of the emptiness within her. She'd felt his finger, had felt his tongue, and now...

Now she wanted his cock. Wanted to seal their bond in every way.

Her gaze dipped to his extruded shaft. It shone with its natural oils, which dripped from the tip.

How the heck was that supposed to fit?

Ivy and Ketahn made it work, so it was possible.

I survived a ship crash, wild beasts, a carnivorous plant, a flood, a deadly swamp, a raging river, and a tumble from a waterfall. I will survive spider-alien dick.

And I will enjoy *it.*

After bundling a fourth length of rope, Rekosh strode to the base of a nearby tree. He knelt there, and with practiced speed, tried an end of each rope to the thick, raised roots. Ahmya approached him, wincing at the cool slickness between her thighs.

Rekosh turned to face her. Though his eyes, fervent as ever, met hers, he didn't reach for her. Instead, he lay down on the ground. Rolling onto his back, he grasped one of the ropes, wrapped it around the wrist of his upper arm, and tied it tight and close to the root.

"Rekosh?" Ahmya stepped closer, tilting her head as she watched him take hold of the next strand to repeat the process with the wrist of his lower arm. "I...I don't understand."

"Feel the mating frenzy," he said, his voice low and harsh, tugging the silk tight around his wrist. "Do not want to harm you."

With his left arms bound, he set about securing his upper right arm. With only one hand, he was slower to do so, though not by much. He caught the final rope and held it up. "Need you, *vi'keishi.*"

Ahmya ran her gaze over him, bound and laid out before her, his cock erect in the air. Vulnerable.

He was doing this for her.

She met his gaze again. "You wouldn't hurt me, Rekosh."

"Please, Ahmya." He held the rope toward her. "My need is too big. I will not risk you."

Her heart squeezed at the desperate plea in his eyes and in his words. He truly was terrified of harming her while mating.

She walked to his side, crouched, and took hold of the rope.

"As I taught," he grated.

Ahmya caught his wrist before he could lower it and brought his palm to her cheek. "I'm only doing this because you're asking me to. But in my heart, I know you would *never* hurt me."

"Ah, my heartsthread…" He gently stroked her cheekbone with his thumb. Then, with equal gentleness but irresistible strength, he pulled his hand away and lay his arm on the root. "Fast."

Ahmya looped the silk rope around his wrist and tied a knot that she had practiced under his instruction many times. She tugged on the restraint, making sure it was secure, and looked at him. "It's done."

Rekosh curled all four hands into fists and tested the bindings himself, drawing them taut. Muscles subtly played beneath his dark hide. Then he nodded, settling the fullness of his heated gaze upon Ahmya.

"Claim me, *nyleea*."

Ahmya blinked. He wanted *her* to claim *him*?

Well, what did you expect to happen when he restrained himself?

I didn't think that far ahead!

Biting her lower lip, she ran her gaze down Rekosh's body, over the ridges of his chest and abdomen to the extended claspers twitching at his pelvis, until finally settling it on his straining cock.

He was hers. Hers to take.

Make him yours.

His legs were bent and propped at his sides, the tips digging into the ground. She stepped between them and rested her hand on the rounded underbelly of his hindquarters. It quivered beneath her palm. It was one of the many parts that made him so different from her, one of the many parts that made him so spiderlike. But none of that mattered. Because every part of him, even the most alien, made up who Rekosh was. And all of it was beautiful to her.

She trailed her fingers slowly along his underbelly, down, down, down the slope leading toward his slit.

His legs tensed, forcing their tips deeper into the ground, and he released a ragged breath. "Claim me, female."

That desperate command brought her eyes back to his.

Rekosh was large, strong, and quick, but in this moment...he was at her mercy.

I'm in control.

That realization, that shift in their dynamic, sent a flare of desire to her core and awoke something new within her. It emboldened her.

Ahmya flashed him a coy smile. "Someone seems to be...in a bit of a bind. And I"—her finger traced his slit around his cock—"am now taking my time to learn my mate."

Rekosh trembled with a chitter, the sound rougher than usual, but the brightness in his eyes didn't diminish. His mandibles rose in a vrix smile as he squeezed his fists. "My wicked little mate..."

Her brows rose. "Wicked? When did you learn—"

Cole.

"Never mind," Ahmya laughed and shook her head. "But if you want wicked..."

Ahmya knelt at his side and dipped her fingers into his slit, sliding them through his slick secretions, before wrapping them around the base of his cock. It was hard and hot in her grasp, and she could feel the throbbing of his heart beats through it.

He hissed, and his pelvis twitched upward.

"Climb atop me, Ahmya. *Claim me*," he growled, one of his claspers curling around her arm.

"In a small time," she replied with a chuckle. She lay her free hand atop his clasper, guided it off her arm, and pressed it flat against his abdomen. Then she stroked her fist up over his bulges and along his shaft.

A full shudder wracked his body.

When she reached the flaring head, she caressed the ridge with her thumb and traced the slit at the tip. Rekosh snarled and jerked his arms against the bindings, drawing her attention to him. His eyes blazed crimson, feral and hungry. His reactions stirred her desire anew, making her core clench.

She'd never done anything like this before, had never realized how empowering it could be to have someone's pleasure at her mercy. To have this big, strong, virile male's pleasure at her mercy.

Ahmya watched, attention divided between his face and his cock, as she pumped her fist along his length. Her hard nipples grazed his hide, sending a thrill through her with each movement of her arm, increasing her own need, which was also heightened by his heady aroma.

Rekosh's chest heaved with his harsh breaths, and he bared his clenched fangs as he tilted his head back. "Ahmya…"

His pelvis jerked up, and seed seeped from the tip of his cock. Ahmya paused. The pearlescent white liquid beads stood out starkly against the dark red of his shaft. She swiped a finger over the head, gathering his seed. She stared at it, riveted, until impulse drove her to slip her finger between her lips.

The taste of cinnamon and cloves and something wholly Rekosh flooded her mouth. It was warm, rich, spicy, and sweet. Whatever she might've expected, it certainly hadn't been this.

But *oh*, was he delicious.

"Shaper, unmake me!" Rekosh snarled and pulled on the ropes again.

She snapped her eyes up to his.

"Ahmya," he coaxed, breath ragged, his brilliant eyes locked on her. "Take my stem, *kir'ani vi'keishi*. Let me inside you."

Yes. She wanted him inside her too. She was done teasing him, done prolonging this mutual torment.

Releasing his trapped clasper, she braced her hands on his chest and threw a leg over his waist, straddling his abdomen. His claspers curled possessively around her thighs, urging her closer to his cock at her back.

"*Yessss*. Good female," Rekosh said, voice rough, his English nearly too distorted for her to understand. His eyes roamed over her, staring first at her breasts then shifting down to fix upon her sex, which was spread over him. "Claim your mate. Take my cock into your pussy."

Hearing him say such crude yet delicious words sent a rush of lust through her. Rekosh had always spoken to her so sweetly, but this… This was a side of him she'd never witnessed. And she loved it.

Her hair fell forward as she leaned over him, lifted her backside, and scooted back. She peered between their bodies. The sight was erotic. Her pubic hair was wet with her slick, his claspers were gripping her thighs hard enough that they indented her skin, and most tantalizing of all, Rekosh's glistening cock was poised beneath her spread pussy. Heat flared in her belly, and the empty ache in her core urged her to do what she so desperately wanted to do. What she so desperately needed to do.

Ahmya grasped his hard length. It twitched, and she felt his pulse throbbing through it. Holding it firm, she lined it up with her entrance and lowered herself just enough that the tip pushed inside her before she returned her hand to his chest.

Rekosh hissed, and his claspers tightened around her thighs, tugging her down a bit more. The head of his cock eased deeper inside her, stretching her, and Ahmya gasped at the stinging sensation, digging her fingers into his chest.

She tensed her thighs, halting her descent, and rose back up only as much as his claspers allowed. They abruptly tugged her down again, forcing his head deeper and stretching her further. A whimper spilled past her lips as her pussy clenched.

"Your slit. It is so hot. So tight." Rekosh angled his head back as his legs scraped the ground and his arms strained against the ropes, making silk and wood creak. His mandibles gnashed, and his muscles stood out starkly on his hide. "Ah, my *nyleea*, my heartsthread. Do not stop. Take my stem. Take more."

Gritting her teeth, Ahmya bore down on his cock. The wide head pushed deeper, and the sting sharpened, becoming an agonizing burn. She froze when the pain became unbearable. Her breath sawed in and out of her as tears of frustration welled in her eyes.

Realization came crashing down on her.

He was too big, too thick.

Ahmya bowed her head. Her body trembled with the emotion she struggled to contain. She wanted this, wanted it so badly. But she…she couldn't do it.

At least not on her own.

"Rekosh…" she whispered.

"Take me, Ahmya," he growled, bucking his pelvis and making her breath catch in her lungs as he bounced her upon him. The silk bindings strained, and bark splintered on the roots to which they were anchored. "More of me. All of me!"

"I can't! I…can't…" She lifted her head, her watery eyes meeting his. "I *need* you."

Rekosh went still beneath her. "*Kir'ani vi'keishi…*"

Then he snarled, and his body lurched toward her. The rope caught his arms, and wood and silk alike groaned as he fought the restraints. His chest rumbled with exertion. Ahmya felt the overwhelming tension in him through every point of contact between their bodies, felt the tremors coursing through him, the heat radiating from him, the consuming need.

Wood cracked, the sound as jarring as booming thunder, when the roots securing his lower arms snapped. Bits of bark and dirt sprayed the air. His lower hands were suddenly upon her hips, rough and warm, their claws digging into her skin. His upper arms, still restrained by the bindings, were clenched in tight fists.

Their gazes met an instant before Rekosh slammed Ahmya down upon him while thrusting his pelvis up, sinking his cock deep.

Searing pain tore through Ahmya, stealing her breath and making her vision go white.

When the world came back into focus, she discovered that she had fallen upon Rekosh, and she was now staring down at his chest with her nails curled into his hide. Panting breaths escaped her. There was an immense fullness pulsing between her thighs, accompanied by a burning ache.

Maybe she should have been more frightened of his size, because she'd felt as though she'd been cleaved in half the moment he'd thrust into her. She'd known the first time would be painful, had known that his size would be part of the reason as he breached her untried body, but come on!

Rekosh's chest rose and fell with his own harsh breaths, each of which was punctuated by a growl. His hands held her hips in a viselike grip, and his body quaked beneath her.

"*Vi'keishi?*" His voice was gravelly and bore an undertone of distress.

"I'm okay," she said softly. "I just…need a moment."

"*Ul ahn'vi selyek.* Please."

A very small time.

Ahmya looked up at him and chuckled, unable to ignore the

humor in his impatience. But that chuckle was cut short when she settled farther down upon his shaft and the thicker bulge at its base stretched her pussy yet more.

Rekosh stiffened, fingers flexing as his cock twitched inside her. He made a low, ragged sound that might've been another growl—but it might also have been her name. The sound traveled through him and into her, vibrating against her clit and making her breath hitch.

She felt the pounding of his hearts beneath her palms and their echo in her core, where his cock was buried deep. The pain that had been so acute was fading into the abyss.

Ahmya wiggled experimentally, and when there was no pain, she braced herself up on her hands and lifted her hips, feeling the slow slide of his cock expanding her from within. A shiver of delight flitted through her, and she lowered herself once more. The pain was now all but gone. All that remained was utter, blissful fullness.

"*Axin vux syth*," he rasped as his legs shifted, raking the ground as though to find purchase. He angled his pelvis up and stared at his cock as it disappeared into her body. Rekosh bared his fangs. "Hot as fire, smooth and soft as silk. My flower. My *nyleea*."

He met her gaze and bit out, "*Mine*."

Ahmya stared into his crimson eyes as she continued to slowly ride him, taking him as deep as she could. Each stroke fed that burning desire in her core, that need for more. This was what she had hoped for. What she'd dreamed of. This was not just the sensation, but the closeness—the intimacy—she'd craved for so long.

And she was sharing it with Rekosh.

"Yours," she moaned breathlessly. Her lashes fluttered, but she kept her eyes open, unwilling to look away from him.

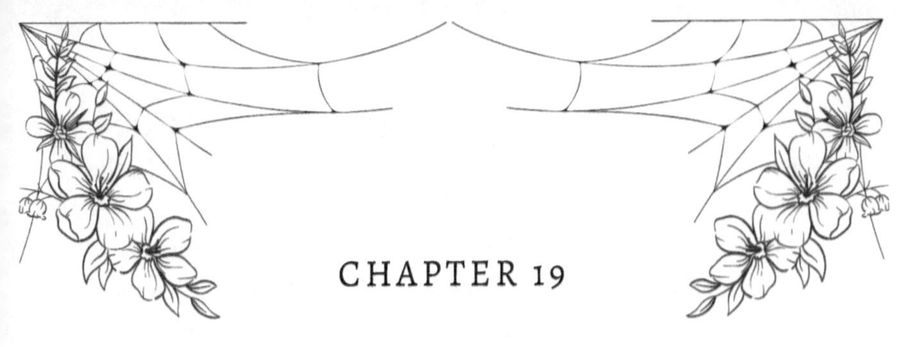

CHAPTER 19

*M*INE.

The word echoed through Rekosh's head like a whisper along one of Takarahl's tunnels, louder and louder with every bounce. It was more than a word—it was a feeling, an instinct, a drive beyond any he'd experienced.

Ahmya was his. Finally, she was his, just as she'd always been, just as she always would be.

Fire blazed through his limbs, making his hide itch and his muscles ache. He needed more, more, more, all of her and then more again. Their bodies were connected now, but he needed their heartsthreads to intertwine, their hearts to beat as one, their spirits to weave together, never again to be separated.

Mine. My beautiful, clever, passionate, gentle mate. My courageous little flower.

Every sensation was heightened. He could feel each blade of grass beneath him, whispering against his hide. Could feel the bite of the silk bindings on his upper wrists, the burn in his muscles as he continued to fight their hold. He could feel her warm skin against his hide, soft and yielding, and the muscles of her thighs flexing, could feel her nails digging into his chest. Even the lingering pain of his wounds somehow added to the thrill.

He could feel her heart beating and her body trembling.

But above all else, he felt the grip of Ahmya's tight, wet slit, hot as molten gold. Felt it clenching, drawing him in, as hungry for this connection as he was. It wept nectar, the taste of which remained upon his tongue, its sweetness beyond compare, beyond words.

Rekosh forced his eyes to hers. He stared into those dark, lustrous pools, stared into the red reflections of his own over-whelming pleasure.

With a shaky breath, Ahmya lifted her hips and lowered herself once more to take him deeper, easing over the bulge at his base.

A shudder wracked him. He tightened his grip on her, drag-ging her down farther.

"Rekosh..." she moaned, eyelids drifting shut. Her head fell back, lips parting as she arched her back and rose over him again, hair swaying with her graceful movements. Tiny droplets of sweat glittered on her sun-dappled skin. Her taut brown nipples beckoned him, but his restraints prevented him from reaching them with his tongue.

He inhaled, filling his lungs with fiery air. If the jungle scents were upon it, he detected none of them—there was only Ahmya's alluring fragrance permeating him, enwrapping him like a cocoon, maddeningly potent with her arousal.

He'd waited so long for this. For her. He'd tried so hard to hold back the mating frenzy, to experience this moment with Ahmya with a clear mind, to relish this time with his delectable little mate. To be gentle, and to give her all possible pleasure.

But what he'd heard, what he'd seen, had not prepared him for the ferocity of the frenzy.

With Ahmya's scent dominating the air, with her body moving atop his, with her pussy gripping his stem, devouring him, he could not resist. His mind was unraveling, the threads coming undone faster and faster with each beat of his hearts.

Rekosh barely felt the ropes biting into his wrists, barely heard the roots cracking behind him as they gave way to his exertion. He barely noticed his bruising grip on her hips, or that he was controlling her movements, quickening her pace. Pleasure crashed through him with each slide of her hot slit along his length, flaring whenever she slammed down on him. And he thrust up to meet her every time, burying himself a little deeper, dragging throaty, ragged gasps from her.

But it wasn't enough. Wasn't deep enough, fast enough, fierce enough. Each wave of sensation only exacerbated his need. He needed to bind her in his silk. Needed to claim her. Needed to rut. He needed to put his mark on her, plant his seed within her, and make himself one with her forever.

"My flower," he rasped.

Ahmya opened her eyes and looked at him.

"Forgive me." The final strands of self-control within Rekosh tore.

With a snarl, he threw all his strength against the remaining ropes. The roots crunched and snapped, finally breaking, and Rekosh's body jerked forward.

He clutched Ahmya tight against him with his claspers and lower arms, tearing gouges in the ground with his legs as he shoved up and flipped their positions so she lay beneath him and he was braced over her.

So she was trapped.

She stared up at him with wide, shocked eyes.

Baring his teeth, he slammed his pelvis forward, thrusting his stem deeper into her.

She cried out and slapped her hands on his chest, her back

arching and legs quivering. The squeeze of her pussy nearly undid him. But his mind was in a haze, stained red by the mating frenzy, consumed by overwhelming pleasure...and instinct would not be denied.

Claim her.

Rut her.

Conquer her.

Rekosh's spinnerets were already working, his rear legs already feeding a silk strand to his waiting hands.

Mine.

Working faster than his eyes could track, his hands deftly guided the rope around her body. He spread her legs wide, bent them so her calves were pressed to her thighs, and bound them, ensuring she could not close herself to him. He looped the strand around her pelvis, securing it with hasty but intricate knots up to her slender waist, over the flat of her belly, and between her small, supple breasts, framing them before he knotted it around her back and shoulders. Finally, he caught her wrists, forced them over her head, and tied them together.

All the while, his cock throbbed, nestled deep in her wet, welcoming heat. All the while, her pussy clenched, assailing him with sensation, thickening the crimson haze that had gripped his mind. All the while, her scent urged him on.

"You belong to me, my *nyleea*," he rumbled, planting his upper hands on the ground to either side of her head. His lower hands grasped her legs, tugging her body snug against his. She let out a soundless, breathy cry, and he growled.

"Forever claimed." Spreading his bent legs to either side, he drew his hips back and stared down into her half-lidded, lustful eyes. "Forever conquered."

Rekosh emphasized those words by driving his hips forward and burying himself in her as deep as he could. Ahmya's pussy wrapped snugly around his bulges.

Her back bowed, her little fingers clawed at the grass, and she sang her pleasure. Rekosh gave her more. And he took everything.

He pumped in and out, his claspers hooking over her thighs to draw her into his every thrust, each of which came faster than the last. Pleasure buzzed through him, an incessant, building hum that eclipsed the jungle around him. There was only him, only her. Only their bond.

Ahmya's moans and cries were the only song he cared about. He added his own sounds to it—grunts, growls, snarls, and hisses as his legs scrabbled for more purchase, as he lifted her backside and angled his pelvis to get more leverage, more depth, more speed.

As he rutted his mate.

"Forever *mine*," he declared.

She writhed beneath him, her dark hair spread wildly around her like the petals of a flower that had blossomed for Rekosh alone. The sounds of her pleasure filled the air. "Rekosh... Please..."

More. Take more. Give more.

She is mine.

She is all, everything.

The fingers of his upper hands curled, burying his claws in the ground. The waves of ecstasy came so fast now that they were as one—an unrelenting stream of sensation that could not be stemmed, could not be denied, could not be diverted.

Not that he wanted to.

This was ecstasy. Even the ache in his injured leg, even the way his ragged breaths tore at his lungs and throat. The pressure building in his stem, already so powerful that it threatened to tear him asunder, was so painful it had become pleasure. The inferno blazing at his core, so hot it would surely reduce him to ash, only made every feeling stronger.

He lifted one of his lower hands to cover her breast, kneading the soft flesh under his palm as he held her down.

"What are you, *vi'keishi*?" Rekosh demanded, catching the hardened bud of her nipple between finger and thumb and pinching, eliciting a gasp from his mate.

"I'm…I'm yours! Yours…forever…" Ahmya's words came short and sharp, escaping between her harsh, panting breaths.

His leg joints sank into the soft ground as he thrust harder, faster. Her tender flesh yielded to his fingers and claws, and her slit clutched at his stem desperately, ravenously, fighting in vain every time he pulled back, drawing him in every time he plunged inside her.

"Your little slit… Feel how it fits? How it takes my cock? Ah, my pretty, pretty mate. See how it needs me?" A ragged snarl escaped him. "How *you* need me?"

Ahmya arched her neck as she rasped, "Yes! I need you so much."

Rekosh's mandibles spread. Her sounds, her scent, her feel, her beauty…he was lost in this, lost in her. But something prodded at his mind. Another instinct, as yet denied. Another need.

Her flesh was so lovely, so smooth and soft. Perfect but for one thing. Missing only one thing.

All will know she is mine.

All will know my claim.

A growl tore from his chest as he bent over her, parted his jaws, and sank his teeth into her shoulder.

Ahmya screamed. Her body went rigid beneath him, and her warm blood trickled into his mouth. It was sweet, with a tang he could not place.

She'll bear my mark.

He sank his teeth deeper.

Mine.

Mine.

Rekosh forced his mouth open. The fire inside him had grown into a scorching blaze, and the pressure in his stem was too immense to comprehend. The slightest twitch of Ahmya's body should've been enough to push him over the edge, to make him burst. Yet somehow, he held himself still long enough to gently lick the blood away from her wound.

"My *nyleea*," he purred. "My precious little flower."

Mine.

"My *luveen*," she said fervently, turning her face toward him. "My husband."

Her words stoked Rekosh's inner flames. He shoved himself up with his upper arms, angling his head to stare down at her. Despite her fluttering lashes, she held his gaze, her dark eyes gleaming with need to match his own.

He pulled back and drove into her hard, again and again, rutting with newfound vigor and passion. Her gasps and moans wove with his growls and grunts after each thrust.

The heat and pressure expanded and intensified.

"Bound to you," he rasped between his breaths. "I...am bound. We are bound. Thread to thread. Hearts...to heart. Spirit to spirit."

"Yes," she whispered.

With a final thrust, Rekosh buried his cock as deep as it could go, until her pussy encased his bulges, sealing him in, and his slit was flush with hers.

That very moment, her sex squeezed him with stunning strength, with staggering need, and all that pressure within him finally burst. A bestial roar clawed out of Rekosh's throat as seed erupted from his stem. He shut his eyes. Pleasure shrouded his vision completely in crimson and silenced his every thought.

There was only all-consuming rapture. It was the thread that bound Rekosh to Ahmya, that wove their heartsthreads, their souls, together fully and finally. Bliss, pure and true.

It was not possible to be this close to anyone. To be this interwoven. To fit together so seamlessly, so perfectly. Not even the Eight themselves could have designed this joining better.

Not even the Eight themselves could have created a creature so beautiful as Rekosh's *nyleea*.

Through that euphoric haze, he was aware of the slit at the end of his stem parting, of his tendrils emerging to stroke his mate from within. His breath shuddered as their fluttering movements sent fresh pulses of ecstasy through him, coaxing forth more of his seed.

But it was Ahmya's reaction that brought him true joy.

She gasped. "What is—"

Her words broke in a cry of pleasure that had her entire body seizing beneath him. Her pussy clenched around his cock so tightly that his breath caught in his lungs, his head seemed to spin, and his limbs nearly gave out.

Liquid heat flooded Ahmya within. Rekosh buried his claws in the ground and growled, riding the currents of pleasure as she came undone around him, as her convulsions and cries drew ever more seed from his stem.

When the frenzy subsided, and the haze lifted from his mind, Rekosh dropped onto his forearms, holding himself aloft over his mate. He bowed his head. His chest and shoulders heaved with his ragged breaths, and his body trembled with the onslaught of pleasure still roiling through him. He was aware of Ahmya beneath him, her warm breath teasing his hide, was aware of his stem buried deep inside her, of her soft inner walls spasming around it, of his tendrils flittering within her.

Ahmya's soft lips brushed across his chest. "Rekosh."

A low purr rumbled in his chest, and he bent closer to her, nuzzling her hair. He drew in her scent, now laced so intricately with his. *Their* scent. With a croon, he shifted his hand from her breast to rest over her heart, which pounded rapidly under his palm.

Alive.

How many times had he nearly lost Ahmya? How many times had her life nearly ended, which would never have allowed them to come to this point? To mate, to bind themselves together so fiercely that Rekosh would challenge the Eight before he let them or anything else take her from him.

Slowly, he moved his hand from her heart to her throat. He curled his fingers around it loosely, again feeling her pulse, and stroked her jaw with his thumb. "My heartsthread, you unmake me."

Ahmya hummed softly and brought her bound wrists to his face, cupping his jaw between her hands. "I love you."

With another purr, he pressed his face into her palms, scraping his mouth over them in a kiss. But he stilled his face as the tremors within him escalated again, bringing new surges of pleasure. His tendrils thrummed, caressing her sex and coaxing her open within, even while building him to a new peak.

She wriggled her body, grinding her slit against his. "Rekosh?"

A harsh breath escaped him as his claspers gripped her firmly, refusing to let her go. He opened his eyes to look at her. "Ahmya…"

Her chest rose and fell in quick succession, and her brows pinched. She arched her back, grinding her pussy harder against him, taking his stem impossibly deeper. "What am I feeling inside? What are you…." She moaned, eyes fluttering shut. "I'm… I'm… Oh God, I'm coming again!"

With a cry, she dropped her bound hands over her head. Her body tensed, and her sex spasmed.

Rekosh snarled as another climax seized him. Their bodies released in unison, more of her slick flowing with his freshly spilled seed, his pleasure mingling with hers, their bodies remaining connected, remaining intertwined.

Rekosh reveled in the sensations. Reveled in this closeness, which was beyond his greatest imaginings, beyond anything he could've hoped for. Together, they rode out the waves of pleasure.

When finally the sensations began to fade, Rekosh chittered. "Ah, *kir'ani vi'keishi*. Would that I could bind us together like this forever, because this is where I belong. With you."

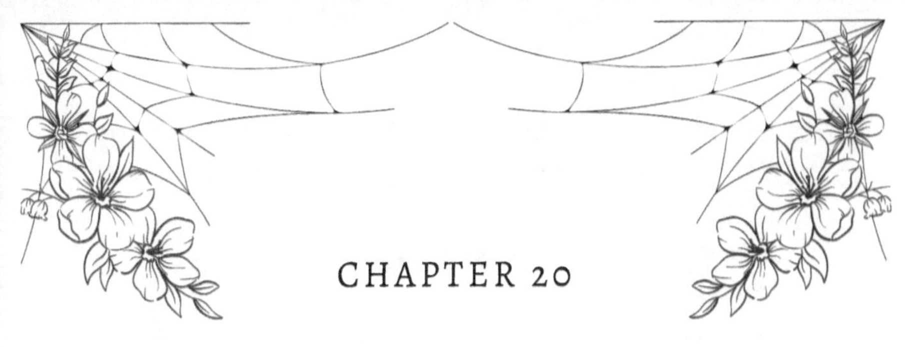

CHAPTER 20

Ahmya lay on her belly atop a blanket spread over a carpet of thick grass. Her arms were folded beneath her head, her eyes were closed, and her lips were curled in a soft smile.

The evening sun was warm upon her damp skin, and the spring burbled soothingly nearby. This spot, here and now, was a little piece of paradise, providing a welcome respite from the hardships of the last couple days. And she never would've envisioned herself in a place like this—relaxing beside a crystal-clear pool in the middle of the jungle, naked, with Rekosh lying on his side next to her.

A delightful shiver coursed through her as Rekosh leisurely brushed a silkblossom along her back. The soft petals followed her spine, dipping into the arch of her lower back before rising over the curve of her ass. The gesture was as loving as it was teasing.

Heat simmered in her belly, and desire burned in her core, but Ahmya was content to simply relish the moment. And as much as she craved to feel Rekosh's cock inside her again, to feel that fullness, that closeness, that connection, she was exhausted from their fierce lovemaking. Her muscles were sore, she had bruises and scratches from his rough, possessive grip, red chafe marks from the silk bindings, and her shoulder stung where Rekosh had bitten her and left his mark.

She had been well and thoroughly fucked.

And she'd loved every bit of it.

Of all her discomforts, it was her pussy that was hardest to ignore. It ached deliciously. Even now, she still felt whispers of his presence there, of his fullness, and each time the sensation passed, it would leave a yearning throb in its wake that almost made her want to ignore the soreness and take Rekosh again.

The flower brushed lightly over the bite mark on her shoulder. Without seeing him, Ahmya knew Rekosh was staring at it. There had been such a covetous gleam in his eyes when he'd cleansed the wound and dressed it with sticky silk.

Ahmya grinned. "Are you preening again?"

The flower stilled. "Preening? I do not know that word."

She opened her eyes and turned her head, resting it back upon her arms as she looked at him.

He reclined on his side with his right elbows atop the blanket and his head propped in his upper hand. His lower left arm was draped over his abdomen, while the upper was extended, holding the flower. He had his right legs curled beneath his hindquarters, with the left ones bent, their tips resting near her legs. His long hair, still damp after bathing, hung loose over his shoulders, its red and white strands especially vibrant in the sunlight. She loved it like this. Loved it when she could run her fingers through his tresses, unhindered by a braid.

Scars were visible on his dark hide—especially the most recent of them, which he'd received while defending her from the kuzahks.

"It means that you're pleased with yourself," she said.

Rekosh trilled, lifting his mandibles. "Then yes. I am preening, *kir'ani vi'keishi*. I have finally claimed my pretty mate."

Ahmya chuckled. "You did. You really, *really* did."

"You are preening also." Rekosh resumed caressing her skin with the silkblossom.

"Mmm… I think a better word would be content." She closed her eyes and drew in a deep breath, releasing it in a happy sigh. "I wish we could stay here, just the two of us, for a little while longer."

He made a thoughtful hum as the petals glided up along her spine. "There is good water, and signs of nearby beasts to hunt. We need only shelter. Kaldarak will wait while this place keeps us."

Ahmya opened her eyes and lifted her head. Wet strands of her hair slid over the back of her shoulder, allowing cool drops of water to run along her arm. "We can stay?"

"A small time, my *nyleea*. So my leg may heal a little more, so you may rest. And…because I wish to add to the memories we have made here."

Happiness burst through her. She rose onto her hands and knees and crawled to Rekosh. Throwing her arms around his neck, she leaned into him and pressed a kiss to his mouth.

Rekosh trilled and wrapped an arm around her, rolling onto his back and dragging Ahmya atop him. She laughed as she straddled his abdomen and propped her forearms on his chest, her hair falling to one side. His crimson eyes shone as he looked up at her. She peppered more kisses over his face.

He chittered and cupped a hand over her ass as he banded another arm around her, holding her securely against him.

Her smile faded. "Won't everyone be worried though? They're probably looking for us."

"Yes. But for many eightdays, I have wanted only to see you." His big hands moved with their usual grace and gentleness as he caught her dangling hair, tucked it behind her ear, and slid the stem of the flower into it. Then he cradled her cheek with his palm. "I would have you to myself a small time longer, my flower."

Warmth flooded her chest, and her heart fluttered. She traced her fingers over his masklike face, so inhuman, so different, so beloved, and smiled once more. "I would have you to myself too."

Ahmya tilted her head as her gaze followed the path of her fingertips around his eyes. Expressive and brilliant, their glow had frightened her all those months ago when they'd first met, but now they were a beacon in the dark that she sought for comfort and safety. They were the eyes of her mate.

Her husband.

Rekosh was silent as he watched her, mandibles relaxed, his own fingers stroking her skin in soothing circles.

In her head, she counted his eyes as her fingertips passed them. Four on each side, eight in total. Eight, a number sacred to the vrix. It was used when they cursed, when they prayed, when they invoked their gods. Their weeks were eight days, and whenever they divided anything into groups, be it vrix or objects, they were inclined to do so into groups of eight.

Ketahn had thought it a sign from the gods when he'd discovered Ivy, the eighth of the survivors aboard the *Somnium*, and the vrix had considered it fortuitous that there'd been eight humans. On top of Ahnset's crushing guilt for Ella's death, the female vrix had believed she'd cursed them all by sundering that sacred number—without Ella, there were only seven humans left.

But they'd overcome the challenges set in their path. They had found a home in Kaldarak. And Ahmya didn't believe they'd made it so far because the vrix fixation on eight was just superstition. No...she believed that there'd been eight humans all along, throughout their harrowing journey, because they'd brought Ella along in their hearts.

"Many Japanese people believe the number eight is lucky," Ahmya said. "It is because of the number's shape."

"Its shape?" His eyes narrowed briefly as though in thought.

"It's different from the numbers we've shown you. This is the symbol in *kanji*." Cradling Rekosh's face, she used her thumbs to draw two lines between his eyes, starting close together and sweeping down and outward. "*Hachi*. Eight. It is lucky because the symbol spreads outward like a fan, opening wide at the bottom, which represents growth and prosperity."

Rekosh moved his lower hands to her hips. With his thumbs resting on either side of her spine, he made the symbol upon her back, slowly trailing his thumbs down and outward to her ass in a way that sent a thrill through her. "*Hachi*."

Ahmya chuckled and nodded.

A purr rumbled in his chest, and Ahmya's breath hitched as the sound stimulated her nipples where her breasts pressed against his hide.

"Teach me more," he said.

Ahmya grinned, hooked her thumbs together, and spread her fingers, wiggling them. "*Kumo*."

He chittered, and an amused light filled his eyes. "I know that shape. *Kumo* is the same as spider?"

"Yes, but it also means cloud."

Rekosh let out a low groan. "So *all* humans use words that mean many things."

Ahmya sighed dramatically and settled her hands upon his shoulders. "We are such confusing creatures."

With a trill, Rekosh caught the back of her neck and lifted his head. "I am happy to be confused, because you are mine."

Once more, he'd set her heart aflutter.

When she'd boarded the *Somnium* to begin a new life on Xolea, Ahmya had expected to enter an impersonal relationship and become a breeder. She'd had no illusions of having a love match with her partner, but she'd at least hoped for mutual respect. Maybe even friendship.

Instead, she'd crashed here. Upon first awakening, this planet had been terrifying, and the situation had felt hopeless. She didn't know what sort of life her and the others would make—if they'd even survive at all.

But there had been Rekosh. He had been her protector, her friend. He'd given her patience, kindness, wisdom, and affection. He'd given her joy.

He'd given her love.

She didn't need to hear those words from him to see it. To feel it. It was in everything he did.

Rekosh made her heart pound whenever he was near, made her body shiver with every touch, made her belly warm with every look.

And Ahmya had felt the overwhelming emotion long before she'd realized it.

Smiling, she tipped her forehead against his headcrest, keeping her eyes locked with his. "Here are some words that aren't confusing. *Anata wa watashi no taisetsu na hito.*"

"*Anata wa...*" he echoed.

Ahmya helped him through the words, until he was able to say the full phrase.

"What does it mean?" he asked.

"It means"—she brushed her lips across his mouth—"you are my *taisetsu na hito*. The person I cherish the most, in this world or any other."

His hands flexed upon her, and his mouth parted, breath mingling with hers. Rekosh slid his fingers into her hair, gaze softening. "Of all the human words I have learned, *kir'ani vi'keishi*, none make my heartsthread sing like these. *Anata wa watashi no taisetsu na hito.*"

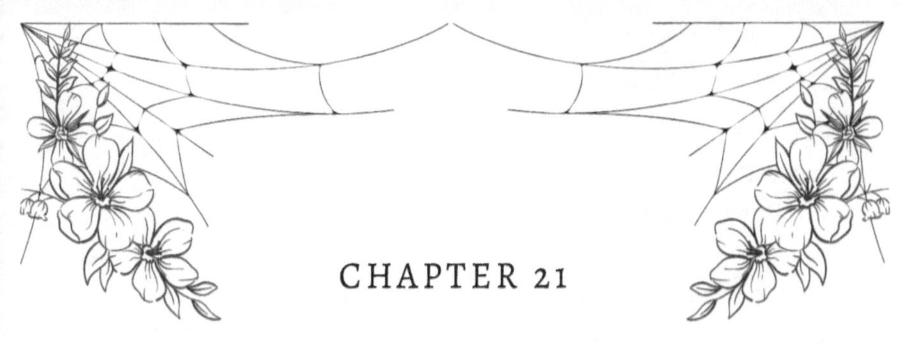

CHAPTER 21

REKOSH KNEW his eyes should've been upon the spitted nurunal roasting over the fire. Between the tantalizing song of sizzling meat and crackling flames and the tempting aroma filling his nose, his stomach was twisting with anticipation. And he was sure his mate was just as hungry.

It had been several eightdays since he'd last cooked, and the task required attention. Most of the humans were comfortable enough with the process that they scarce paid it any heed, almost instinctively tending their meals while engaged in conversations or other tasks. But Rekosh was not so skilled at it yet. He knew only that too little time would result in meat his Ahmya found unappetizing and potentially sickening, while too much would produce a charred, inedible chunk of waste.

And what of his surroundings? They'd found good shelter, but that didn't mean he could neglect keeping watch. They were protected from behind and to one side by rock walls, overgrown with vines and moss. On their other side, a massive, misshapen tree grew at an angle, serving as a wall and roof of their shelter.

Though the entrance to this natural chamber was only a few

segments across, that was more than enough for danger to make its way inside.

But he could not pry his eyes from Ahmya. She sat on a thick branch on the other side of the fire, watching the meat and the dancing flames, oblivious to his struggle.

She was wearing her boots again. He understood why; they were durable and dependable, and kept her feet protected. The boots didn't bother him.

The pink silk coverings she'd put back on very much did.

Those simple garments had been inferior even before the ordeals Rekosh and Ahmya had endured. Now, they were stained and ragged.

And the silk wasn't *his*.

That was the true source of his ire—his mate was wearing silk from another vrix, possibly another male. That was no different than someone else trying to claim her. He would not allow it, would not tolerate it any longer.

His grip on the stick holding the meat aloft strengthened, and the wood creaked in protest.

That fabric did not deserve to touch Ahmya's skin, did not deserve to be anywhere near her.

Only his silk from now on.

He emitted a low growl.

Ahmya looked up at him and arched a brow. "I don't believe that was your stomach rumbling."

Rekosh huffed. "It was not."

The corners of her lips curled into a wide grin, and she tugged on the end of her tattered skirt. "Are you still angry about this?"

His mandible fangs clacked together as he forced his eyes to the meat, folding his lower arms across his chest.

"Rekosh!" Ahmya laughed. "I already explained why I'm wearing this."

Because the dress he'd made for her wasn't appropriate for

traversing the jungle, because she couldn't bear to see it damaged or soiled, because she wanted it in perfect condition to *show off* when they returned to Kaldarak.

None of that changed the fact that she was clad in another vrix's silk instead of his.

With a teasing glint in her eyes, she folded her arms across the tops of her knees and bent forward. "You're cute when you're *powtee*."

"I do not know that word," he bit out.

"Sulky, grouchy, grumpy."

Forcing his mandibles down, he turned the meat over the fire. "I am not *powtee*."

Sitting up, Ahmya stuck out her bottom lip and crossed her arms over her chest with a huff.

He narrowed his eyes. "What is this? What are you doing?"

"Copying exactly what you just did. Pouting."

"Stop."

Ahmya only stuck out her bottom lip again and peered up at him with wide, sad eyes.

Rekosh knew what she was doing. He knew, and yet...that look on her face, in her gaze, seized his heartsthread and pulled on it.

No. No, he would not let her distract him. His mood was justified. And if she did not wish to wear the dress for fear it would be ruined, he would make another, and he would leave her no choice but to don it.

Withdrawing the meat from over the fire, he rose and held the stick toward her. "It is done. Eat."

As soon as she took the stick, Rekosh stepped away, snatched up his bag, and opened it. He reached inside and dug through the contents until he found a clean silk blanket tucked away at the bottom. He tugged it out, followed by his sewing supplies—needles, thread, and a blackrock knife.

"What are you doing?" Ahmya asked.

"Pouting." He unfurled the blanket. "Eat, Ahmya."

Without looking up to see if she obeyed, he began his work. While the blanket wasn't necessarily the fabric he'd have chosen to make into clothing for her, it was woven from his silk, by his hands, and that was all that mattered.

The dress formed in his mind's eye, clear and sure, and he deftly sliced and trimmed the fabric so it would conform to her body. Elegant but practical. That was what his mate needed, and that was what he would provide.

His long fingers manipulated the cloth without need for thought, slipping needles into place to hold the seam together. He checked the form, spreading it open at the waist, envisioning his hands around Ahmya's body. He knew it now. Intimately.

No more guessing. This would fit her perfectly when it was done, he'd ensure it.

After a few slight adjustments, he threaded a needle and began sewing. Though he took care with every stitch, his fingers moved deftly, nimbly, with instinctual confidence and ease. Each time the needle pierced the fabric, he could imagine it more clearly—his silk hugging his mate's lithe body in the form of this new dress.

He could envision patterns running across the fabric, accentuating her natural curves, and his fingers itched with the desire to add those flourishes, but he prevented himself from doing so. Practical. Functional. This wasn't the time for such details.

Every stitch was straight, tight, and precise as he worked along the seam. Though the firelight was erratic, he didn't need it to guide him; he could've done this with his eyes covered, in complete darkness.

As a broodling, how many nights had he lain awake with thoughts, with terrors, with memories tumbling through his mind that could only be silenced through distraction? How many times had he taken up thread in the darkness and focused on its feel, its strength, its delicacy?

When the world seemed so impossibly big, so lonely, so frightening, he'd always had the simplicity of thread to ground him. Because from that simplicity, such wonders could be wrought.

The humans had crafted a massive dwelling of metal, powered by lightning, that had carried them here from distant stars. Even in its ruined state, it had been fascinating. It had been awe-inspiring.

But a cloth skillfully and lovingly woven from tiny threads was no less impressive to him. Silk was everything to the vrix—it could be warmth and privacy, it could be stories and history, it could be community as weavers worked, talked, chittered, and grumbled.

It held everything together. Everyone.

Rekosh was nearing the hem of the dress when a hand appeared in front of his face holding a large chunk of meat.

"Rekosh, eat," Ahmya said.

He started. The needle slipped, pricking his finger, and he reflexively snapped his hand back with a hiss.

Ahmya gasped, her eyes rounding. "I'm so sorry!"

Though he'd neither seen nor heard movement, she'd apparently stood up and walked around the fire to stand beside him.

With a soft chitter, Rekosh turned his finger toward the fire, checking for the telltale glistening of blood. "The pain was small, *vi'keishi*. What do you say? Teenie weenie?" He held up a hand, forefinger and thumb separated by a thread's width of space. "But I do not want to stain the cloth."

"I didn't mean to startle you. It's just…" She looked down, and Rekosh followed her gaze to the stick she held, along with the meat she'd torn from it in her other hand. "Sometimes when you work, you go someplace else, and it's like everything around you disappears. You forget to even take care of yourself."

Something warmed in Rekosh's chest, centered around his hearts. She'd seen. Did that mean that...that she'd been watching him for as long as he'd been watching her? For her to have noticed, to care so deeply, meant more to him than he could express.

And yet, he did not want to worry her. Did not want her to have to fret over him and his wellbeing. As her mate, his duty was to ensure her existence was as carefree as possible.

His mandibles fell, and he lowered the dress slightly. "I do not mean to cause you sadness, Ahmya."

"I'm not sad." She met his gaze and smiled. "I can feed you while you work. You needed to eat far more than I did."

"You would feed me, my *nyleea*?"

Ahmya nodded and held the piece of meat to his mouth.

A gentle trill rolled from Rekosh's chest. He opened his mouth and extended his tongue, drawing the meat in. It had already lost much of its heat, but the flavor was still enjoyable. More so due to how it had been given to him.

"Thank you," he said.

He resumed his work, keeping his attention divided between his stitching and his mate. Now that she'd broken through his haze, he could not help but notice her nearness and her scent, which remained prominent despite the smells of roasted meat and smoke. And every time she offered him another bite, he opened his mouth and accepted it readily.

When he tied off the final stitch, Rekosh cut the thread, removed the needles from the seam, and inverted the dress before holding it up for inspection.

"Were you really angry with me?" Ahmya asked.

Lowering the dress, Rekosh tilted his head and regarded her. "Angry with you?"

She motioned to her clothing. "For wearing this."

It felt like a snare cinched around his hearts and drew taut.

"Ahmya, how could I be angry at you? You are my *vi'keishi*, my *nyleea*. My wife."

She smiled and shyly lowered her gaze, fingers picking at the meat on the stick.

Rekosh placed a finger beneath her chin and tipped her face back up. "I am angry only at that cloth touching you now."

"You know these clothes and the vrix that made them don't mean anything to me, right?"

"It is...instinct." He tenderly stroked her jaw. "Vrix make silk. Even vrix who cannot weave can provide threads, and know that whatever it is woven into, it is from them. It is...a piece of that vrix. So to see you wearing this, it is as though another vrix is touching you, putting his scent upon you. And you are mine, Ahmya. Mine to hold, mine to touch. I would not allow another male to put his hands on you, and I cannot allow this cloth to embrace you."

He felt the warmth of her blush against his fingers as her eyes softened. She leaned her cheek into his hand. "I understand now."

"Good." He set his tools aside, folded the dress over his lower forearm, and gently took the stick from her, placing it upon a nearby rock. "Now..."

Rekosh grasped Ahmya's wrist and tugged her closer. The motion threw her off balance; she gasped, and he righted her by palming her ass, his hand now over the offending cloth.

She laughed. "What are you doing?"

Breathing in her scent, he trilled. This was the last time it would be tainted by the odor of foreign silk.

Rekosh would thoroughly enjoy this.

Releasing her wrist, he hooked the fingers of his upper hands beneath the pink silk of her top and bottom garments.

The sound of the silk tearing as he rent it apart with his claws was amongst the most satisfying he'd ever heard. He ripped the fabric away from her.

Ahmya sucked in a short, sharp breath, hands flying to her body to shield her nakedness. "Rekosh!"

He tossed the tattered pink silks into the fire. The flames leapt and swirled, their light intensifying as the silk ignited. A foul odor, not unlike burned hair, filled the air.

"Not even fit to serve as rags," he said.

That despised silk already forgotten, Rekosh lowered his gaze to drink in his mate's naked form.

He'd been so focused on making the new dress—on her wearing it—that he'd overlooked this part of the process.

Her long black hair hung around her slim shoulders, obscuring the bite mark he'd left, but the rest of his marks were on clear display. Faint bruises and small scratches told the story of his hands on her body, gripping, squeezing, and kneading flesh as they'd mated. His fingers flexed with the yearning to hold her thus again.

He stared at the arm she'd banded across her chest. Even after they had come together so intimately, after she'd taken his stem so deeply, after his hands had explored every bit of her tender form, Ahmya retained her shyness. And he found it endearing.

Rekosh's eyes flicked up to hers. He could not pretend to know all the secrets that dwelt in human minds and hid within their gazes, but he understood the hesitancy that flashed through hers.

Neither of them spoke for the space of a heartbeat, a moment stretched by its weight. A new light sparked in her eyes, strong, steady, determined.

Ahmya took a deep breath, chest and shoulders rising, and lowered her arms to her sides.

"Ah, *kir'ani vi'keishi*," Rekosh purred, his eyes dipping to her small, pert breasts, with their brown nipples. He grazed them with the backs of his fingers. She shivered, and before his eyes, those nipples hardened into little buds, responding swiftly, perfectly, to his touch.

She caught her bottom lip between her flat, white teeth with a whimper.

The finest silk could not rival the feel of her delicate skin, and nothing could match the thrill of watching—of feeling—her body react to him.

Rekosh's hearts thumped a little louder, a little faster, as he trailed his touch outward from her nipples, lightly tracing the soft mounds of her breasts. The heat of her flesh flowed straight into his body and intensified with each beat of his hearts.

"How you have bloomed for me..." He slid his hands down over her belly. He felt it quiver, heard her breath hitch, and something stirred in his core. A sweet, alluring scent danced upon the air, beckoning his fingers lower, lower. One hand shifted toward her hip, while the other continued straight down.

When his touch brushed over the dark curls at the apex of her thighs, Ahmya whispered, "Rekosh..."

That scent, Ahmya's scent, strengthened, growing headier, and Rekosh's stem throbbed, pressing against the inside of his slit. Hunger roared through him, louder than any beast.

He drew his claspers in tight, squeezing his slit closed against that pressure, and stilled his hands. How had he not anticipated this? How could he have expected himself to avoid temptation while she was unclothed before him, while he was touching her, smelling her?

If he allowed this to continue, if he allowed his hand even a thread's width lower, he wouldn't be able to stop himself. He'd plunge into another frenzy.

He'd never known such yearning, such need, as he felt for his Ahmya.

When he'd asked Ketahn what it was like to mate a human, Ketahn had offered only a cryptic response—*Unlike anything*. That conversation had left Rekosh more intrigued than ever, with a thousand new questions and not a single answer. It was a mystery he'd been determined to solve himself.

And now he knew. Now that he'd mated his human, his Ahmya, his *nyleea*, he knew that *unlike anything* was the only response Ketahn could ever have given. He knew there were no words that could ever describe the experience adequately.

Yet as much as he craved to be inside his mate again, to feel her pussy wrapped around his cock, he knew that he'd lost control during their rutting. He'd been rough, and her untried body was sore. Though she'd assured him it was a good hurt, she needed time to rest and recover.

He would set aside his desire and give her that time. He would give her whatever she needed, no matter the discomfort or hardship he'd have to endure to do so.

Rekosh forced his hands off her. He immediately found himself battling the impulse to touch her again, and his hands hesitated in their retreat. In that tumultuous moment, he almost swore Ahmya swayed toward him, as though meaning to follow his hands...

No. It must've been a trick of the flickering light, nothing more.

He snatched his hands back, unfolded the dress, and raised it.

"Arms up, *vi'keishi*," he said.

Ahmya exhaled shakily before lifting her arms over her head.

Willing his hearts to slow and his stem to relent, he slipped the dress on over her arms, trying to ignore the brush of his hide against her skin as he drew it down her body.

She lowered her arms once the dress was in place.

Withdrawing from her took nearly all Rekosh's willpower. Before Ahmya, he'd never realized just how strong—and how conflicting—instincts could be. He was driven to protect her, provide for her, and rut her. He was compelled to clothe her in his silk, yet every time he saw her in it, he was assailed by the overwhelming urge to tear it off her body and claim her again.

That desire was raging now. But he denied it, taking another step back and running his gaze over his mate to survey his work. The dress flowed with the shape of her body, but it was loose enough to easily be donned and removed. The hem hung at the tops of her knees, and the skirt was wide enough that it wouldn't restrict her movement if she walked, ran, or climbed.

"How does it feel?" he asked.

Ahmya smoothed her palms over the fabric toward her thighs. The dress slid down her body, baring the soft flesh of her breasts and exposing her taut nipples.

Rekosh clenched his fists, and the ache in his core intensified.

She caught the top of the dress with a chuckle and tugged it back up as she met his gaze. "It feels good, but I think I need something to hold it in place better."

"Something to hold it in place..." His mandibles sagged as he studied the dress. He'd shaped it for her body, but had left just a little looseness so she wouldn't have to fight her way in and out of it. Of course it wasn't going to cling to her without some means of being secured.

Creating human clothing was new, which made it a thrilling challenge for Rekosh. Despite having spent most of his life weaving and sewing, there was so much he didn't know about the garments humans preferred, so much he had to learn. And he welcomed the process of puzzling it out. He relished the creativity required to do so.

His gaze settled on her bare shoulders. "Ah..."

Rekosh turned away from her, snatched the spare scraps of cloth off the ground, and took up his knife. The solution was so simple, how had he not thought of it before giving her the dress?

With care that belied his excitement, he cut the scraps into thinner strips, which he separated into two sets of three. Holding on to the ends, he quickly and firmly plaited the strips into cords.

When he was done, he closed the distance between himself and Ahmya.

"Be still a moment, *kir'ani vi'keishi.*" Rekosh slipped his fingers under the top of her dress, peeling it slightly away from her skin, and pinned the shorter cords into place over her shoulders. "This is good?"

Smiling, Ahmya ran her fingers over one of the braided straps and nodded. "I love them."

Rekosh trilled. After stitching the straps onto the dress, he trimmed the excess silk and stepped back to look her over.

As the thornskulls might have said... Under moon and stars, his *nyleea* was beautiful. But there was another thing he could do for the dress—something that would adorn it while serving a practical function.

Sinking down, he took up the longest of the cloth scraps and sliced it into more strips, his gaze flicking to his mate as she ran her hands over the dress.

"You're going to spoil me, aren't you?" she asked.

"Spoil you?" Fingers stilling, Rekosh cocked his head, mandibles twitching. "How would you...spoil?"

Ahmya shook her head with a chuckle. "Not spoil like food. Spoil as in *pampurreeng* me. Um...showering me with lots of pretty new clothes and gifts."

Rekosh chittered as he plaited the long strips of silk. "Yes, I will spoil you. I will not rest until I have given you a gift for each star in the sky."

"I'm only kidding, Rekosh! I don't need gifts." She stepped to his side and pressed a kiss to his headcrest. "I only need you."

Soothing warmth coursed along his heartsthread. He caught her jaw in his hand before she could pull away and turned his face toward her. "All you need, all you want. Everything. I will give it to you, Ahmya. You are all I need."

"I'm yours, Rekosh." She trailed her fingers up along his forearm until she clasped his wrist, then slowly guided his hand down her throat to her chest, flattening his palm over her heart. "Until my heart stops beating."

A growl tore from his chest. Setting his work aside, he banded an arm around Ahmya and tugged her against his body, pressing his headcrest to her forehead as his claspers encircled her legs. "You will remain mine even after we draw our last breaths, *kir'ani vi'keishi.*"

Cupping a hand behind her head, he roughly brushed his mouth over her soft lips, determined to mark her in every way.

Rekosh had nearly lost Ahmya more than once. The Eight seemed intent on proving she was not meant for this world. But she was. She was his, and he refused to contemplate a life without her, especially now that he'd finally claimed her. He would do anything necessary to keep her by his side—even if it meant defying the gods.

He pulled back to look at his beautiful mate. Ahmya's eyes blinked open as though she were emerging from a slight daze. Her lips were red from the harsh kiss, and her eyes were dark abysses in the shadows cast by the fire behind her. He'd gladly lose himself in them forever.

Ahmya's fragrance filled his lungs, clung to his fine hairs, permeated him wholly. And his body reacted to its sweetness, to her warmth, to her feel. His aching cock pressed against his slit, which he could feel parting.

Clenching his teeth, Rekosh withdrew from her. The space he put between them felt impossibly vast and cold.

Nothing had changed. She still needed time.

His claspers drew tight against his slit, and he barely held in a growl at the ache in his stem.

"Allow me to finish this," he said, willing his hearts to ease and his body to settle, "so we can rest."

Ahmya chuckled. "Okay."

As he plucked up the partially braided cord, she stepped away. He wanted nothing more than to drag her back against him, lift her dress, and plunge his cock deep inside her hot, wet pussy, to feel her body wrap around him. Instead, he focused on the feel of the silk and the movements of his fingers as they worked, expressing his true desire only through a low, ragged growl.

But no matter how much he tried to concentrate on his task, he was aware of Ahmya's gentle, curious hum, the sound of her boots on the ground as she moved farther away, the whisper of silk against her skin, and the rustling of shifting vegetation.

She drew in a sudden, sharp breath.

The hairs on his legs stood on end and the cord fell from his hands as he rose and spun toward her, seeking the threat.

But there was none. There was only Ahmya, standing next to the stone wall and holding a curtain of vines and moss aloft.

She beckoned him with a hand, eyes alight with excitement. "Rekosh, come look!"

Hearts pounding powerfully enough to rival thunder, he huffed. The strength that had instantly flooded his muscles at what he'd mistaken for a sound of distress made his legs unsteady as he strode to join his mate. Before he'd even crossed half the short distance, his curiosity had moved to the forefront, and anticipation skittered through his chest.

"What is it?" he asked.

"I thought I saw something here. At first, I figured the firelight was playing tricks, but then I saw this." Keeping the vines raised, she shifted aside to allow him to view the wall. "They look like symbols."

Rekosh leaned closer to the wall and brushed his fingers across the surface. He could just feel the tiny grooves in the stone, very shallow but too regular and tightly clustered to have been natural.

"It is writing," he said distractedly as he moved his face even closer to the markings. Though time had worn the symbols down to mere memories of themselves, the shadows cast by the firelight sharpened them enough for Rekosh to recognize the web-like forms and patterns. "Vrix writing."

Backing up, he grasped the vegetation and gently tore the vines and moss away, exposing a wider patch of the stone.

No, not stone, *stones*.

With the plants cleared, the individual stones that comprised the wall were far more apparent, though the space between them had filled with dirt, debris, and moss.

"This wall was made by vrix long, long ago," he said.

"We didn't even notice until now." She pressed her hand to the wall. "I guess the jungle took this place back."

Ahmya glanced over her shoulder, looking in the direction of the spring. "When we first climbed up here, the rock formation reminded me of steps…but maybe it *was* steps."

He twisted to follow her gaze. The fire's glow reduced everything outside their shelter to utter darkness, even for his eyes. But as he thought about it now, he realized that there'd been something very deliberate about the area, about the lay of the various stones and rock formations.

Humming thoughtfully, Rekosh met Ahmya's gaze. Her eyes gleamed with enthusiasm that made his heartsthread sing.

"Help me, *vi'keishi*. Carefully."

Together, they peeled away more of the vegetation. As more of the stone was revealed, so too was something new—images in relief above the writing.

"Those look like vrix," Ahmya said.

"They are vrix. It is like Takarahl, where there are carvings in some of the tunnels that show queens and warriors of old. But these…"

"There are so many." Ahmya stood on her toes to point up at one set of figures. "These ones look like thornskulls."

Rekosh cocked his head. "They do. And these… They look like shadowstalkers."

The vrix depicted here were clustered into several groups, the members of each bearing appearances that were distinct even in these relatively crude, time-damaged reliefs.

"What are the other vrix called?" she asked.

"I know of a few." As he spoke, he gestured to the carvings he believed to correspond to the other vrix kinds, each of which seemed to be represented here. "The fireeyes are from the lands where the sun crests. Winddancers are smaller, and are said to move silently and as swiftly as the wind itself, but no one has seen their kind in many years. I have also read of stonehides, mossweavers, and rainsingers, but little is known of them."

He raked his gaze across the exposed reliefs, watching the shadows dance on them. "But I do not see the spiritstriders. They dwell deep understone, deeper than we shadowstalkers in Takarahl. And they are known to make war on all vrix."

Ahmya peered up at him. "Why?"

"Because they hunger. For food, for flesh, for what other vrix have and they do not." Rekosh folded his lower arms across his chest and drummed his fingers on his biceps. "When I was a broodling, we were warned about spiritstriders. Do not delve too deep, do not wander too far, or you may be snatched by a spiritstrider and be eaten."

"That's…*terrifying.*"

"It is. But it is fear that is meant to protect broodlings. The stories—the histories—written in Takarahl speak of them also. Many past queens battled the spiritstriders, who swarmed from the deepest darkness to attack. Urkot knows more than I do. Delvers must always watch and listen for signs of spiritstriders, and they are taught to do so as broodlings."

"Do they attack often?"

"I have not heard of an attack during my life. But I have heard of vrix going missing in the deep tunnels, never to be seen again. Their fates forever unknown. Every time that happens, there are whispers of spiritstriders, but none can say for certain."

"Why aren't spiritstriders pictured here?" Ahmya asked, looking back at the carvings.

Rekosh brushed his fingers beneath the faded writing on the wall. It wasn't easy to read, and what he could make out was incomplete, but there was enough to make a guess. "I think this was a place of…friendship. Where different vrix came together. Carvings in Takarahl show other vrix only making war, but these are not fighting. They are at peace, as we are with the thornskulls now.

"Spiritstriders do not know peace, do not know friendship. They only know hunger. So they are not here."

Rekosh shifted his gaze to his mate. Her brow was pinched as she ran her fingers over the reliefs, and he could see sadness in her eyes. "What is it, *kir'ani vi'keishi?*"

"These carvings are all nearly eroded away. It was only by chance that I noticed them. Time and nature are erasing what was once here." She glanced around. "This place is a ruin, lost to time, forgotten. I imagine it was once a beautiful, joyful place, where vrix from all over shared stories and traded. But that's all gone."

His mandibles drooped, and he turned his head to again look out at the darkness. It was difficult to imagine what this place might once have been. Impossible to imagine all the different vrix gathered here, when he'd never seen any with his own eyes but shadowstalkers and thornskulls. Yet he felt that sorrow all the same.

Rekosh and his kind had been taught from hatching that other vrix were their enemies. That the only contact between them could be in the form of war, because they feared the shadowstalkers' strength, because they coveted what Rekosh's kind had, because they envied Takarahl's splendor. But despite the bloody past they shared, the thornskulls had welcomed Rekosh's tribe of shadowstalkers into their home and had gladly woven a new friendship with Takarahl.

And that left Rekosh to wonder if it really had been other vrix who'd been making war on the shadowstalkers...or his kind who'd made war on everyone else. If Takarahl's past queens hadn't been quite so noble and honest as the stories claimed.

If Zurvashi hadn't been the exception, but an inevitable progression.

"This place is gone, but it *was*," he said, returning his gaze to Ahmya. "That means those bonds can be woven anew. It has been done before, and it can be done again. The sorrow of this place is also hope, is it not? The threads between Kaldarak and Takarahl have already been mended."

"It is hope," Ahmya agreed, running her fingertips over the sharp points depicted upon a thornskull's headcrest. She chuckled. "The thornskulls aren't quite as scary when they're shown like this. They're actually kind of cute."

He huffed and pounded his fists against his chest. "*I* am cute. They are...prickly."

Ahmya grinned up at him. "You can be prickly too. You're actually quite prickly when you're jealous."

"I am not jealous, Ahmya."

She gave him a droll look. "You just tore off my clothes and burned them because it wasn't your silk. *And* I swear you were about to throw Cole off the tree when you came to visit me the other day."

Rekosh turned his body toward her, cupping her chin in one hand and staring down into her eyes. "I am not jealous. I am possessive. You are mine. Nothing and no one will come between us, my *nyleea*." He chittered. "Even if I must throw them off a tree."

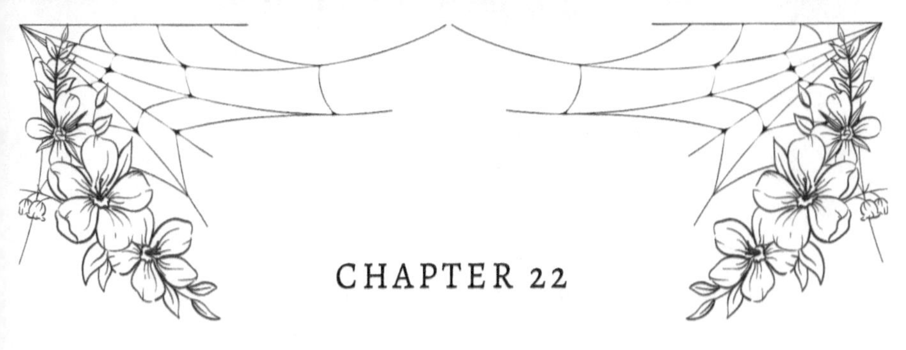

CHAPTER 22

AHMYA'S DREAM faded as her eyes opened. Though the details were already lost, she knew she'd been dreaming of Earth.

Except she wasn't on Earth. She wasn't in a bed with a pillow and a mattress, wasn't curled up in a comfy blanket. She was lying on her side upon a nest of the softest fluffed silk, wrapped in the strong, warm arms of a vrix.

The arms of *her* vrix.

Rekosh held her to his chest with her head tucked beneath his chin and all four of his arms—along with both claspers— banded around her. She smiled, closed her eyes, and breathed in her mate's spicy teak and amber scent. It languidly spread through her, stirring desire in her core.

Ahmya idly brushed her fingers over Rekosh's chest. Even her pallet in her little home in Kaldarak wasn't as cozy as this. The fluffed silk cushioned their bodies, cradling them in the gentlest embrace. It was like lying on a cloud. There'd been no need for a blanket; her mate provided all the warmth she could ever have wanted. She couldn't remember the last time she'd slept so well. Maybe she never had.

She snuggled closer against her vrix.

Something hard dug into her belly.

Ahmya stilled, and her eyes snapped open. Was that… Could it be?

She pressed her body even closer.

Yep, that was definitely a bulge in his pelvis.

Ahmya grinned. She still had so much to learn about her mate, but his cock was the most intriguing mystery to her. She'd seen it, had stroked it from base to tip, had taken it fully inside her, yet she couldn't explain what she'd felt when Rekosh had orgasmed. Something had *fluttered* within her.

You could find out what it was.

Ahmya chewed on her lower lip as temptation flowed through her, causing heat to pool low in her belly. Her finger twitched upon his hide.

He's aroused. You could relieve him, pleasure him.

She recalled the feel of his cock in her hand, the way he'd quivered beneath her touch, the way he'd responded to her. Most of all, she recalled that delicious taste of him.

This time, she wanted more than a taste.

Slowly, Ahmya slid her hand down between their bodies, along the ridges of Rekosh's chest and abdomen, loving the way his hide felt against her palm. Her fingers trailed over the mound at his pelvis, stopping when she reached the top of his slit. It was slightly parted, allowing some of his secretions to seep out and granting her access to the barest amount of inner flesh.

Her breath stuttered. Though she was the one touching Rekosh, the heat in her core flared, filling her with desire, with need.

Ahmya dipped her finger into his slit.

It was hot and wet.

A low, appreciative purr rumbled in Rekosh's chest, and his claspers curled more possessively around her hips. "I have never had so pleasant an awakening, *kir'ani vi'keishi.*"

Warmth suffused her cheeks as she pressed her face against Rekosh's chest and quickly withdrew her hand from his slit.

"Good morning," she squeaked.

One of his hands smoothed along her back. The tips of his claws grazed her skin, sending delightful shivers along her spine. "My mate is bold while I sleep. Should I close my eyes so you may again find your boldness?"

Ahmya chuckled and shook her head. "No."

Chittering softly, Rekosh rubbed his chin atop her head. "I have been awake for some time."

Oh. Well, then...

She teasingly brushed her fingers back and forth across his lower abdomen. "Can I touch you some more?"

A tremor ran through him. His hand continued down, gliding over her ass. "You need never ask."

Ahmya's pussy clenched from his touch and the gravelly tone of his voice. As much as she yearned to guide his hand between her thighs again, to have him stroke her clit and alleviate that ever-growing ache, she wanted to discover what pleasure she could provide him more.

She pulled back, and Rekosh loosened his hold on her enough to allow her to meet his gaze. "Can you lie on your back for me?"

Rekosh's mandibles rose, and a wicked gleam shone in his crimson eyes. "Will I need to draw silk bindings again?"

Excitement washed through her. "Hmm... No, not this time. Hold off as long as you can for me, and then, well..." She pressed a kiss to his mouth. "You can have me any way you want me."

"Ah, my *nyleea*..." The warmth radiating from his body seemed to intensify before he withdrew his arms and rolled onto his back. He spread his arms out to the sides upon the fluffed silk. "I am yours, Ahmya. Touch me as you desire."

Smiling, Ahmya pushed herself up onto her knees and

looked down at Rekosh. Daylight lit up their little haven, granting her full view of her mate. Him being sprawled out like this, with his six legs slightly bent on either side, only showcased how big he truly was. He stared at her, those wicked eyes aglow, mandibles raised in a smile, and his long braid lying on the silk beside him.

She trailed her gaze down his body to his groin. The bulge at his pelvis had grown, and his slit had parted further, revealing the glistening red flesh within. His claspers relaxed against his hide.

Ahmya lightly placed the tip of her middle finger on the edge of his slit and slowly traced it. She felt the flesh quiver, watched as it opened wider, heard the catch in Rekosh's breathing. And then, he groaned low and deep as his long, thick cock extruded, its deep crimson beckoning her.

Settling one hand on the raised curve of his underbelly for support, she leaned closer.

Red should've been a warning. Red should've meant danger. But when it came to Rekosh, all she wanted to do was get closer. All she wanted was to touch.

She curled her fingers around his cock and stroked.

He shuddered and tipped his head back as he clenched fluffed silk in his fists. "Shaper, unmake me… Ah, female, do not stop."

His plea sent a bolt of lust straight to her core.

Keeping a firm grip on his length, Ahmya pumped her hand up and down in a steady rhythm from the bulges at the base to the wide tip. His cock was hot and slippery with his oils, gliding against her palm, and it reminded her of how good it had felt as he'd thrust in and out of her pussy, of how the ridge of his thick head had massaged her inner walls in all the perfect places.

Rekosh tensed and arched his back. His cock twitched and pulsed, keeping its own rapid pace to match that of his thumping hearts. His spicy scent permeated her senses, growing stronger with each passing moment, intensifying the hollow ache in her core.

Ahmya watched him. Watched the way his body moved, the way he fought to restrain himself, watched the way he tried to keep his eyes upon her but was helpless as they drifted closed with pleasure.

He was beautiful, sensual, a creature as deadly as he was seductive.

And he was hers.

My monster. My mate.

She tightened her grip. His oils coated her palm and dripped over her hand. Her clit thrummed, and her core clenched with need. She squeezed her thighs together, but the pressure did nothing to help her discomfort. Even her soft silk dress was unbearable against her sensitive skin—it was restrictive and abrasive, almost painful as it rubbed against her hard nipples.

"I smell...your want, *vi'keishi*," he rasped, opening his eyes to look at her.

Ahmya's lips parted as she stared into his eyes.

God, did she want him. She'd never understood how desire could hurt, how it could make someone burn from within, but it was consuming her now.

Rekosh placed a clawed hand on her thigh and squeezed, letting her feel the pricks of his claws. "Is your pussy wet for me?"

"Yes," Ahmya said breathlessly.

He growled and tugged on her dress. "Let me see you. Let me see my pretty mate."

Ahmya didn't hesitate. Releasing his cock, she raised her ass, gripped the hem of her dress, and tugged it up her body and over her head, eager to be rid of it. The drag of the fabric across her nipples sent a shiver through her.

Trilling, Rekosh brushed the backs of his fingers up her

belly, making her skin quiver. "There you are. So soft, so beautiful…"

Just before his hand could reach her breast, Ahmya caught his wrist and halted its progress. As heavily as she longed for his touch, she knew letting him go further would make it impossible to curtail her desire for him to touch her elsewhere. More than anything right now, she wanted *his* pleasure. She wanted to see him come apart, wanted to unveil the mystery of what she'd felt so deep inside her.

"Not yet," she said.

"Not yet?"

Placing his hand back upon her thigh, Ahmya braced herself over him, once more closing her fingers around the base of his cock.

He drew in a shaky breath, eyes never leaving hers.

She lowered her head until her mouth hovered above the tip of his cock. "I want to taste you first."

Ahmya closed her lips around the head of his cock and sucked.

His legs tensed and dug into the fluffed silk, and his arms went rigid, pushing his torso up as he growled her name. She moaned as his cinnamon and cloves flavor flooded her mouth. The small taste she'd had before couldn't compare to this. He was delicious; he was *divine*. She twirled her tongue around the ridged head of his cock and dipped it into his slit for more.

Rekosh hissed and gripped her thigh tighter, curling his claws into her skin. Their sting only added to her need. She lifted her head off him and panted as she caught her breath. A shudder wracked his body, and his cock twitched in her grasp. She watched avidly as seed seeped from the tip and slid down the shaft.

"Ahmya…" Rekosh rasped in a broken plea.

Dipping her head, she flattened her tongue against his shaft and ran it up. She flicked it over the tip, catching the seed and his oils upon it, gathering as much of his taste as she could before taking the head into her mouth once more.

"Fuck!" Rekosh snarled.

That word—that vulgar, wicked, human word—coming from her mate in reaction to what she was doing was the most arousing thing Ahmya had ever heard. He'd instilled it with such passion, with such unbridled need. Gaze flicking to his face, Ahmya sucked and licked his cock, thirsty and eager for more as she stroked his shaft with her hand to make up for what she couldn't take into her mouth.

"Ah, *kir'ani nyleea, kir'ani vi'keishi.*" The reverence in his voice belied the struggle apparent in his body. His muscles strained, flexing and stretching beneath his hide as his legs dug deeper and deeper, tearing into the fluffed silk while his claws pulled up clumps of it. The possessive hand he had upon her thigh twitched and shifted erratically, moving to her hip, then her back, up toward her hair and back down again after hesitating. Like he didn't know where to place it, didn't know where he wanted to place it.

Finally, he settled his lower hands on her head, his fingers threading through her hair, claws pricking her scalp. He growled as her head bobbed upon him. Her jaw burned from his girth, but Rekosh tasted too good for her to stop.

Cool air whispered over her hot sex, and Ahmya parted her thighs with a groan. Her core clenched, empty and achy, and her pussy wept with arousal.

She needed relief. She needed…

Ahmya slipped her free hand between her thighs and stroked her clit. A whimpering moan escaped her, vibrating into his cock as pleasure sparked in her belly.

"No." Rekosh's voice rumbled like thunder, a sound Ahmya felt more than heard, as he grasped her arm and forced her hand away from her pussy. *"Mine."*

Before she could even vocalize her protest at the sudden halt of her self-pleasure, Rekosh had grabbed hold of her and plucked her up. Ahmya gasped as his big, strong hands clutched her hips, and she clamped hers atop them as he lifted her over his body.

He brought her down so she was straddling his head, facing away from him—looking down his long, powerful, sensual vrix body at the glistening cock she'd had in her mouth only a moment ago.

"Rekosh, what—"

"Need you, *nyleea*," he growled, words clipped and harsh, before he thrust his tongue into her pussy.

Ahmya cried out. His tongue plunged into her again and again, rubbing along her inner walls and another secret place that set her every nerve alight, stoking her pleasure higher and higher. It made her burn with need. And God, she needed Rekosh as much as he needed her. Needed his words, his touch, needed his long, flexible tongue to keep fucking her like this.

She writhed, but he held her firm, allowing no escape, so she clutched him with her hands and thighs. He groaned, and she felt it vibrate into her, amplifying the ecstasy.

One of his lower hands took hold of her calf, further ensuring she could not move away even if she'd wanted to. The other slid down his torso slowly, teasingly, trailing over the armorlike ridges of his chest and abdomen with a nonchalance at odds with the ravenous, frenzied motions of his tongue.

Her eyes widened when his hand curled around the base of his shaft. Ahmya's tongue slipped out without conscious thought, trailing over her lips to lick up his lingering taste. His long fingers encircled his cock fully, stroking up and down, and Ahmya watched, gaze fixated on those motions as Rekosh's tongue delved in and out of her.

Pleasure seared her, spreading through her like wildfire. She panted, gripping his hands, feeling every thrust, twist, and swirl of his tongue. The flames of passion took hold of her, and she yielded to her need. Yielded to him. Her body moved of its own accord, bouncing upon his tongue, craving for it to go deeper, seeking all the pleasure it could give her.

But she did not look away from his cock. Did not look away from that hand stroking it, quickening with his every hot, ragged breath against her wet pussy.

"Rekosh," Ahmya moaned, her hands leaving his to cup her breasts. She pinched her nipples hard. The sharp pain shot through her, straight to her clit, and she gasped, grinding her cleft against his hard mouth. "Don't stop. Please, please don't stop. Please. This feels so good."

Fingers and claws digging into the flesh of her thighs, Rekosh snarled. The vibrations against her clit were all she needed. Ecstasy crashed through her, suffusing her entire being. She writhed atop him, her inner walls contracting as liquid heat flooded her.

Rekosh only tightened his hold, like he never intended to let go. He lapped at her, lavished her, drank from her, his grunts and growls only prolonging the pleasure assailing her. He licked her like a creature dying of a thirst that could not be quenched.

Ahmya's thighs quivered. She fell forward, catching herself with her hands on his chest, but he did not relent as he ravaged her pussy, his tongue flicking her clit. Another wave of heat burst from her.

"Rekosh!" she cried out as she undulated against his mouth, lost in the exquisite torment. "Yes, yes, yes! Mmmph! Oh God, don't stop, my *luveen*, my love."

With a growl, Rekosh tensed, and his back arched, thrusting his pelvis up. Despite the overwhelming, unrelenting pleasure he was giving her, Ahmya didn't let her eyelids shut. She watched as his cock twitched, as it swelled in his fist, as his claspers stretched as though reaching for something, someone, to take hold of.

Then Rekosh groaned low and deep as a great shudder wracked his body. Streams of white cum spurted from his cock, landing on his abdomen, and three tendrils unfurled from its slit, fluttering in the air.

Her eyes widened. Those were what she'd felt inside her, what had brought her so much pleasure. They were long and thin, with featherlike ends that resembled moth antennae. Her core clenched at the memory of them within her and how good they'd felt.

Rekosh's legs scraped at the fluffed silk, and his fingers bit into her flesh. He clutched at his cock as those tendrils continued to rapidly flutter.

"Ahmya," he rasped, his body easing down onto the silk. *"Kir elad rayathi'zak."*

I am unwoven.

He exhaled, his breath hot against her sex, before giving her pussy another long, leisurely lick. "You are so wet for me."

Ahmya's breath hitched, yet she couldn't help but smile. The tenderness of his tongue after such intensity was welcome, providing a different sort of pleasure. It filled her with delight that he'd wanted to eat her out far more than he'd wanted her mouth on his cock.

"You wanted me that badly?" she asked with a soft chuckle.

"Yes. Nothing in all the Tangle is as sweet as you," he purred, lapping at her again, swirling his tongue over her clit. "My beautiful little flower."

She arched back against his mouth with a moan as her fingers curled against his hide.

His body shuddered and tensed once more, and his pelvis gyrated. Those tendrils quickened their motions, drawing her attention back to his cock as more seed jetted from it, running down his shaft and over the hand still clamped around it.

Rekosh's groan pulsed into her.

"Your taste alone could keep me spilling my seed all day, Ahmya. All for you."

Curiously, she reached out and lightly brushed her fingertips over those tendrils. They were firm, but soft, almost like touching the bristles of a feather.

He bucked beneath her, tightening his grip on her hips. "Ahmya!"

They're so sensitive...

The discovery filled her wicked glee.

Leaning forward, Ahmya twirled her tongue around the tendrils.

Rekosh hissed, body going rigid as his cock released another stream of cum, which she eagerly licked up. Snarling, he lifted Ahmya, pulling her away from his cock. Her world spun as he turned her to face him with her legs on either side of his body. Her hands fell on his shoulders, and her wide, shocked eyes met his. There was something feral in his gaze, something predatory. A hint of danger that sent a rush of excitement through her.

Banding an arm around her, Rekosh rolled aside and shoved himself upright, drawing her along with him and keeping their bodies parallel. She felt the jolt as he planted his leg joints on the ground and clamped his lower hands on her ass to hold her up. His claspers hooked around her thighs, and the tip of his cock notched against her entrance, its tendrils stroking her clit.

Ahmya's breath hitched at the pleasurable sensation.

"I will spill no more seed until I am inside you, *kir'ani vi'keishi*." Keeping his eyes locked with hers, he gripped her hips and thrust deep inside her as he brought her down hard.

The stretch was immediate, and Ahmya threw her head back with a silent, breathy cry. The pain was swift, but the sensation that accompanied the fullness and those fluttering tendrils quickly overcame any discomfort. Her pussy clamped around his shaft.

"Rekosh," she whispered, nails digging into the hide of his shoulders as unadulterated pleasure uncoiled within her, spreading through her limbs.

Grasping her hips, he lifted her slightly, withdrawing his cock nearly to the tip, and slammed her back down upon him, stealing her breath again. Before she could recover, he thrust into her again and again, setting a frenzied pace that had his claws digging into her skin and his exhalations coming in ragged growls.

When her head tilted back and her lashes fluttered shut, he caught her jaw and forced her face back toward his.

"*Losak'ven dun,*" he commanded. "Eyes on mine."

Panting, Ahmya did as he commanded. As much as her eyes wanted to roll back in her head in pleasure, as much as her eyelids wanted to close, she held his gaze as he rutted her.

It was raw, untamed, bestial, and all Ahmya could do was wrap her legs around him and hold on as he used her body. His hide scraped her inner thighs, his claws pricked her skin, and he held her so tightly she knew she'd end up with more bruises, but she didn't care. She wanted it all. She wanted Rekosh and everything he had to give her, whether loving or fierce.

She surrendered to him completely.

Ahmya touched her forehead to his headcrest and slid a hand into his braided hair, gripping it. With every pound of his cock inside her body, she uttered his name. His strokes were hard, brutal, and deep, and she only wanted him deeper, deeper, deeper. Wanted to feel the delicious burn and utter fullness from his bulges.

Shivers coursed through her, and those tendrils caressed her from within, a tender contrast to the savagery of his thrusts.

The pleasure coiling in her belly, winding tighter and tighter, sharpened until she felt like she could take no more. Rapture burst through her.

Ahmya wound her arms around Rekosh's neck as her entire body constricted and a scream of pleasure tore from her throat.

"*Ahmya,*" Rekosh rasped, his body trembling as he slammed into her one final time before his cock swelled.

Clutching her tight against him, he roared, and heat bloomed within her core as he filled her with his seed. The movements of those tendrils intensified, stimulating her cervix, sending Ahmya into another release. She moaned and ground her pussy down on his slit, keeping his bulges lodged deep, unwilling to let this moment end.

It seemed Rekosh was just as unwilling, as he kept his hands locked on her hips, ensuring that his cock remained buried in her, sealing his seed inside, while they both shuddered through one orgasm after another, each less potent than the last but no less pleasurable.

When the fluttering of those tendrils finally stopped, Ahmya sagged against him. Her limbs were trembling and weak, and her body was coated in perspiration.

She pressed a kiss to Rekosh's neck. "I love you."

He gently nuzzled the bite mark on her shoulder as he combed his claws through her hair. "You are woven into my spirit, my heartsthread."

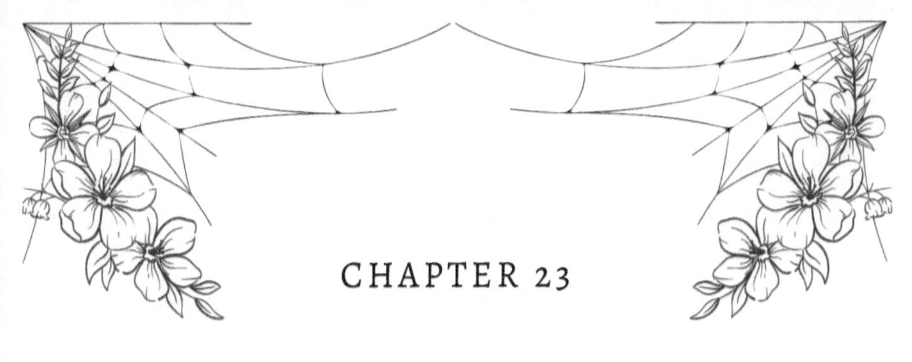

CHAPTER 23

By the light of day, it all seemed so obvious. The signs were everywhere. This had been a settlement—a fairly large one, by all appearances. Much of what Ahmya and Rekosh had mistaken for rock formations or irregularities in the ground were ancient stone walls, caked with dirt and strangled by vines. Despite the trees and cloying vegetation, despite large sections of walls having collapsed or been swallowed by time and the elements, it was easy to visualize the foundations of the structures that once stood here.

It was likely because Ahmya knew what she was looking for now. Her eyes had been opened to the nature of this place, and now she could not unsee it—not that she wanted to. This was fascinating. The vrix were a diverse people, and their history was richer than even Rekosh, with so many stories stashed in his brain, could ever have guessed.

His interest was as piqued as hers as their exploration uncovered more scattered carvings and patches of weblike vrix writing, most of which were too worn for him to decipher. This place represented a part of his culture, his heritage, he'd never known about, and discovering it alongside him made Ahmya's heart swell.

She knew all too well the feeling of being disconnected from one's heritage. Knew all too well the self-doubt that could arise from it, knew the contradictory pull between past, present, and future. Growing up in the United States had left her feeling like an outsider when she'd visited Japan, her parents' homeland. There'd been so much she hadn't known about.

Her mother had taught her as much as she could about their culture, their history, but she'd died while Ahmya was young. And though Ahmya's father had been born in Japan, he'd moved to the States as a boy and spent most of his life there.

Not that he'd been much of a talker, anyway.

Now, she would never have a chance to speak to him again, would never visit Japan again, would never learn more about her heritage.

It would've been the same if you'd made it to Xolea. This is the choice you made.

Yet as much as it saddened her, Ahmya didn't regret that choice. Every step she'd taken had brought her here. It had brought her to Rekosh.

They continued their exploration farther into the scattered ruins, and when they discovered a set of broad, crumbling steps, Ahmya ascended them, her spear tapping the stone as she used it as a walking stick.

Running her fingers along the moss-covered stone wall that ran along one side, she caught hints of faded carvings beneath. "I wish you were able to see this place as it once was. Even as ruins, it's beautiful."

"To see it with you now is enough," Rekosh replied, walking beside with his spear in hand.

"Do you think if we brought the thornskulls here, it could be restored?"

He hummed thoughtfully. "Maybe. But why? We have our home in Kaldarak."

"I know, but"—Ahmya shrugged as she continued up the steps—"shadowstalkers and thornskulls have reunited. Maybe it could happen with the other vrix again. And you could have a place where you all come together as one like they did here."

"We will tell the others about this place, and they will do as they wish. But there is only one I want to come together with, and she is no vrix."

Laughing, she glanced at him to find his mandibles raised in a smile. "I wouldn't mind coming together again."

He brushed a foreleg against her backside with a purr. "My *nyleea* hungers."

Though Ahmya blushed at the open flirting, she couldn't help but respond. "And I would say my *luveen* is quite thirsty."

Rekosh chittered low. "For you, always."

Desire sparked in her core as she recalled just how thirsty he'd been that morning and the feel of his tongue thrusting deep, deep, deep inside her pussy. Walking only seemed to exacerbate the sudden swelling of her clit, and made her aware of how swiftly Rekosh could make her wet.

Jeez, Ahmya. No longer a virgin and now sex is all you can think about?

I can't help it! It just...feels so good.

Rekosh made it feel so good.

He was always so protective of her, always so tender and caring. But she loved that he hadn't treated her like she was made of glass when they had sex. Loved how he'd let instinct take control, loved how he'd fucked her.

Fortunately, before she could dwell on those thoughts any longer, they reached the top of the steps, and Rekosh trilled. The air rushed from Ahmya's lungs at the sight before her.

They'd come to a pond, not much larger than an Olympic swimming pool, backed by a cliffside fraught with roots and vines. Several stone columns stood at the edges of the pond, most of them at least partially collapsed, their details worn beyond recognition. In a large alcove carved into the cliff directly ahead stood a towering piece of stonework.

Like everything else, it was damaged, worn, and covered in moss. But the shape it suggested was clear—a vrix. A female vrix.

She was kneeling, with her forelegs bent on the ground and three broken arms raised. The fourth arm, the only one that was complete, was outstretched over the pond, hand turned and closed in a fist.

The natural break in the jungle canopy created by this rise allowed the sunlight to fall freely upon the pond, bathing it in a warm golden glow that made the water shimmer. Bright suncrest flowers dotted the cliffside, their petals open to the sunshine, but they paled in comparison to the most unique feature of all—the flowers growing from the water.

Bright yellow blossoms with pointed petals stood on thin stalks just above the pond's surface. The tallest of them were less than a foot high, while others were so low their bottom petals were touching the water. Big, spiky, fanlike leaves also grew from the stalks, reminiscent of palm leaves.

They were everywhere, almost entirely covering the pond, their petals so bright they nearly seemed to glow with their own light.

As Ahmya's gaze ran over the blossoms, she was filled with a sense of nostalgia. These flowers reminded her so much of lotuses.

Excitement rushed through her. Ahmya took several steps forward before she abruptly stopped.

No, she'd been down this road before, and she wasn't in any hurry to repeat being attacked by a blood thirsty, carnivorous plant.

She looked at Rekosh. "Is it safe?"

"The flowers, yes," he replied, striding past her to the water's edge. He extended his spear, disturbing the water's surface with the butt end. Gentle ripples spread outward. Some of the plants swayed along with the tiny waves he'd created.

Rekosh stared at the pond for a time, and Ahmya moved up beside him. The water had a slight green tint, but it was relatively clear, allowing her to see the dark shapes of tiny, fishlike creatures flitting around amidst the roots and debris at the bottom.

"Looks safe," he said, withdrawing the spear, "but stay close, *kir'ani vi'keishi.*"

She peered up at him. His body was tense, and she saw the wariness in his narrowed eyes as they swept over the pond and their surroundings. There was no question where his thoughts lay. He remembered when she'd been attacked by the firevine, and he still blamed himself for failing to protect her.

Ahmya settled a hand upon one of his arms. "It's okay."

Grunting, he turned his face toward Ahmya, his eyes holding hers until the tension bled from him. He stroked his foreleg along her calf above her boot. "I know."

Nearly vibrating with giddiness, she lowered herself to her knees at the pond's edge and laid down her spear. Bending forward with one hand planted firmly on the ground, Ahmya reached out and cupped one of the lush yellow flowers, drawing it closer. As she did so, she realized the petals were not as pure a yellow as they'd appeared from a distance, but were painted with splotches of bright red on their tops. That red filled the flowers' centers.

"What are they?" she asked.

"*Aja'ani'nedahl.*" Rekosh knelt beside her and brushed the back of a finger across one of the red-marked petals. "Mother's blood."

"Mother's blood?" She chuckled. "I guess the red spots on the petals do look like drops of blood."

"These flowers are very rare, but where they grow, they grow thick. Pools like this are often made into sacred places." He straightened and gestured across the water to the statue. "It is said that long ago, a terrible sickness came to the vrix. Many died, and all suffered. The Broodmother looked upon her broodlings and was flooded with sadness to see such pain. So, she cut her hand open and let her blood fall as rain. It landed upon these flowers and gave them some of her power.

"Because they are marked by her blood, they are known to heal. They can ease sickness and pain and stop wounds from bleeding. Like mender root, they are rare, but they are sacred too. Vrix dare not take too much for fear that the Broodmother's sacrifice will be wasted."

He hummed and tilted his head. "I am glad Zurvashi did not find this place. She would have destroyed it."

Ahmya frowned as she sat back on her heels and gazed out over the pond. She'd heard the stories of Zurvashi's greed for mender root, wanting it not for its healing properties, but because it made her favorite shade of purple dye. How she'd gone to war against the thornskulls because of it, resulting in so many deaths merely for her vanity. But Ahmya had heard nothing of *aja'ani'nedahl*.

"Why would she have destroyed this place?" she asked.

"Because it is not for her. It does not praise her. And she knew only how to take from others, because she was strong enough to do so."

She looked at the worn, broken statue of the Broodmother. Time and nature had taken its toll on it, but it would remain standing for many years to come. She smiled as her gaze fell upon the flowered-filled pond. "I'm glad she didn't find this place too. It's beautiful."

"It brings you joy, Ahmya. To me, that is true beauty."

Ahmya looked up at Rekosh to find him gazing at her

tenderly. Warmth blossomed within her, sparking a familiar fluttering in her belly.

She caught hold of his long braid and gave it a gentle tug until he bent toward her. Leaning close, she pressed her lips to his hard mouth. "You bring me the most joy."

With a soft trill, he cupped the back of her neck and gently leaned his headcrest against her forehead. "Ah, my *nyleea*, my heartsthread…"

Her heart quickened at this closeness. She loved it when he spoke such endearments, loved how he instilled those simple words with such love and meaning.

Smiling wide, Ahmya twirled his braid around her finger. "Soooo… Can I take some of the Mother's blood?"

He pulled away with a chitter, eyes narrowed with mirth. "I knew you would ask."

Her lips stretched into a wide grin. "So that's a yes? It's not forbidden?"

"Not forbidden. But"—he held up a hand with his forefinger and thumb barely separated—"only a little."

"Yes! I know Diego would love some too. Do you think we could take a couple roots with us to plant in Kaldarak? The thornskulls don't have a place like this as far as I know, but I'm sure they could build something in tribute to the Broodmother."

His mandibles rose. "I think it is a gift they would appreciate."

"Thank you!" Ahmya pecked another kiss on his mouth and rose to her feet. As she began taking off her boots, she asked, "Could I borrow your knife?"

Removing his bag, he set it on the ground and opened it. In short order, he produced the metal, human-made knife, which he presented to her grip-first.

Rather than take it right away, Ahmya slipped the braided

straps off her shoulders and pushed her dress down her body, letting it pool around her feet once it slid past her hips.

"Ahmya," Rekosh rasped.

She looked up to find his gaze fixed on her naked body. Desire whispered through her in response to the blatant hunger in his eyes, and her nipples hardened.

How far she'd come in only a few short days. She would never have undressed so casually in front of others, but with Rekosh? She loved the way he looked at her. Loved the way he responded to her.

Loved the way her own body responded to him.

But right now, she had a task, and she couldn't let herself get distracted. At least...not yet.

Chuckling, Ahmya placed a finger beneath Rekosh's jaw and pushed his mouth closed. "You can look, but you can't touch."

After teasingly trailing that finger down his chest, she took the knife he offered and stepped away to sit at the pond's edge. The water was cool against her heated skin as she lowered her legs into it, making her break out in goosebumps.

Ahmya peeked at her mate over her shoulder with a smile. "Are you going to join me?"

Rekosh growled, and her eyes dipped to see his claspers pressed tight against his slit. She covered her mouth to muffle her giggle.

"Wicked, female. You seek to unravel me." He strode to the pond and stepped in. Within a couple steps, the water was up to his pelvis, covering his claspers and slit. He turned and beckoned her with a curl of his fingers. "Come."

Oh, she would later. She was sure of it.

Ahmya slipped into the water, letting out a slow, shuddering breath at the chill. With her feet on the bottom, the surface came up to her chest, lapping at her nipples. She grasped the stem of the nearest yellow blossom and cut it with the knife.

As she cupped the flower in her hand, staring down at it, she was once more struck by a wave of nostalgia. "There is a flower similar to this on Earth."

"Tell me." Rekosh said.

"It's called a lotus. *Hasu*, in Japanese." Ahmya brushed her fingers over the petals. "It grows in muddy water, but its petals are the purest pink or white. It symbolizes overcoming adversity and reaching enlightenment. They only bloom for a few days."

She set the blossom on the grassy bank and turned back to Rekosh with a smile. "Every summer when I was little, we visited my grandparents in Japan. My grandmother would take me, my brother, and my mom out to harvest lotuses. We'd gather the roots and the seed pods, which are what remain after the petals fall off."

Ahmya cut off another blossom and placed it next to the first. "Often, my brother and I would sneak off and break open a pod to munch on the seeds." She chuckled as she walked farther out into the pond, pushing aside the fan-like leaves. "My grandmother would scold us for not working, but Hirohito would always take the blame."

Rekosh moved alongside her, keeping the spear before him. He chittered. "Ketahn would try to do the same when we were broodlings, but usually I could talk away our trouble when we were caught doing something we should not have done."

She chuckled. "I can believe that. Seeing the way all of you interact, I would guess that you caused most of the trouble?"

"I do not know why you would think that, Ahmya," he said, mandibles ticking up into a wry smile as he cast her a sidelong glance.

She didn't miss the hint of mischief in his eyes.

Ahmya laughed and nudged his arm with her elbow. "So you were the troublemaker!"

"I did not make trouble. I made excitement and fun." He

tapped his chest. "Moonfall Tunnel would have been boring without me."

She cut another flower and held it out to Rekosh. "No wonder Urkot is the voice of reason. He's just trying to protect everyone from your *fun*."

Rekosh took the flower in one of his free hands. "Urkot is not free of blame. None of us are." He cocked his head, regarding the flower. "Maybe Telok is. He was very quiet as a broodling. Almost...timid for a time, though he always fought for us fiercely."

"He's still quiet, and still fierce."

"Very much."

"Why does he keep so much distance from everyone?"

"Telok...carries deep pain in his hearts that weighs upon him, heavier than any stone. I think he believes he must watch, must protect, so he does not have to face that pain again. But that can be a lonely duty."

Sorrow filled Ahmya's heart. She'd seen the lengths to which Telok had gone to protect them all. Maybe he wasn't outwardly friendly most of the time, but he'd accepted Ahmya and the other humans into his tribe. Beneath Telok's rough exterior was a vrix who cared deeply about his family, who would readily put himself in harm's way to keep them safe, who could laugh and find joy amongst his tribemates...but he let his guard down so rarely.

She clipped another flower, which she handed to Rekosh. "I hope he can find some peace now that we're all settling down in Kaldarak. That he lets himself relax and realizes he doesn't have to do all that alone. That he's never been alone."

"I think he knows in his hearts, but it will take time for him to find that peace." He twirled the flower by its stem. "You said you would gather the roots and seeds from lotuses. What did you use them for?"

"Food. We'd take home what we'd harvested and make a dish

called *renkon no kinpira* with the lotus roots." Ahmya smiled at him, though a bit sadly. "The last time that happened was when I was eight, before my mom died."

Rekosh made a low, unhappy buzzing sound as he turned his body toward her. He brushed the backs of his fingers over her cheek before hooking her hair behind her ear. His fingers lingered there, caressing the round shell. "We will make many memories together, *kir'ani vi'keishi*. I will harvest plants with you, cook with you, tend flowers with you. I will teach you to weave and sew if you would learn it. Anything you would do, I would do alongside you."

Ahmya's chest constricted with a powerful wave of emotion that made her eyes sting with tears. Though her father and brother had been alive before she'd left Earth, home had never felt the same after she lost her mother. It had grown cold. And Ahmya had been alone.

Rekosh was offering all the companionship and intimacy she could ever have wished for. Was offering to share not just the moments of passion and heat, but the quiet moments. The mundane moments. And to cherish them all equally, recognizing how valuable each and every one of them were.

She caught his hand and pressed her cheek into his palm, nuzzling it while keeping her gaze locked with his. "I would do it all alongside you too, Rekosh. We will make a home together."

With a soft trill, he leaned down and brushed his mouth atop her hair before drawing in a deep breath. One of his forelegs curled around her legs beneath the water.

After he withdrew, he offered to retrieve some roots for her. She'd been fully prepared to plunge under the surface and feel around for them, but Rekosh didn't even need to hunch down— he used his forelegs to dig up a few of the roots and pass them deftly to his waiting hands.

Once they'd deposited the flowers and roots on the bank, Rekosh lifted Ahmya out of the pond before climbing out himself. Water streamed down her body, and she dipped her feet back in to rinse away the mud sticking to her toes.

"I can't wait to bring these back to Kaldarak and plant them," she said as she wrung out the ends of her hair.

Calloused hands settled on her shoulders, and Ahmya smiled, leaning back against the heat of Rekosh's hard body behind her.

Rekosh purred, the low rumble moving through her, teasing her skin, and stimulating her nipples as he smoothed his palms down her arms and lowered his mouth to her ear. "And I cannot wait to bury my stem deep in my little flower."

Ahmya's breath hitched.

His hands closed around her wrists, their hold firm, and he abruptly spun her to face him. He drew her arms up. His lower hands worked swiftly, lashing a silk strand around her wrists with practiced ease, knotting the rope tight enough to keep her from escaping, but not enough to cut off circulation.

Desire unfurled in her core as he wound the silk around her forearms. "What are you doing?"

His crimson eyes bore into her. "Do not think I have forgotten how you teased me, my wicked female."

"I haven't," she said with a shaky exhalation.

The rope continued down, around her chest and shoulders. "Then you know what I am doing."

She was aware of every brush of his fingers on her skin, and as she stood there, naked with her arms raised and back arched, her pussy swelled with arousal.

When his fingers knotted the silk around her breasts, he pinched one of her taut nipples, producing a sharp gasp from her.

"Rekosh!"

He kicked her feet farther apart, and then those hands were winding the rope around her waist and between her thighs. Ahmya's pussy clenched, and a ragged cry tore from her when he looped the silk between the folds of her sex, placing a knot right over her clit. She squeezed her eyes shut against the sensation. Every subtle shift of her body caused that knot to rub against her, resulting in the most exquisite torture.

An unbidden moan slipped past her lips as she undulated against the rope. Pleasure washed through her.

"Ah, female," Rekosh chittered. He caught her jaw, coaxing her to open her eyes and look at him. "Now it is my turn."

An anticipatory shiver stole through her as he tossed a coil of silk rope high overhead. He didn't look away from her as he pulled down on the other end, drawing her up off her feet, suspending her high enough that she was looking down at him. The rope dug rapturously into her clit.

"Oh God," she rasped, toes curling.

He grasped her legs and draped them over his shoulders. His claws pressed into the sensitive flesh of her ass and thighs as he spread her wide, baring her pussy.

Rekosh drew in a deep breath and released it in a growl. "How your body craves me."

"Rekosh…" Ahmya's breath was quick and shallow as she held his bright, crimson gaze.

He brushed his rough, hard mouth along her inner thigh. "No more words."

Then he thrust his long, thick tongue deep inside her, and Ahmya was lost to bliss.

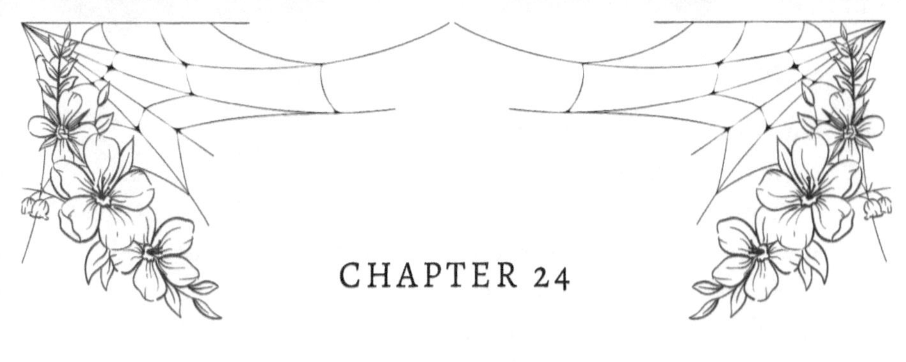

CHAPTER 24

REKOSH'S FINGERS ran through Ahmya's hair, gently combing out all the tangles and knots they encountered.

He offered no mind to the low, orange flames of the crackling fire before them, the jungle's night song, or the deep shadows beyond the fire's glow. Only two things held his attention—the small human female sitting on his folded forelegs, and all the feelings she inspired within him.

Right now, the foremost of those feelings was contentment.

It seemed so new, so fresh, though he knew he'd experienced it before. Happiness...but it was more than that. There was a serenity to it, a sense of satisfaction and fulfillment that was enhanced by his undiminished, ceaseless yearning for his mate.

This was the most content he'd ever been in his life. The happiest he'd ever been.

He separated Ahmya's hair into thick strands as his lower hands flexed upon her hips.

Rekosh might gladly have remained here with her, might've built a home for them and spent the rest of their days together in this quiet place. Just him and his little flower. But neither he nor Ahmya could do that. They could not forsake their tribe, could not cause any more worry.

This would be their final night here. Their final night in this ancient, crumbling ruin, where their love had truly blossomed.

Rekosh filled his lungs with her sweet, alluring scent and began weaving her hair into an intricate braid. Were the Eight ever to take his sight, he'd still be able to find Ahmya. Her fragrance was interlaced with his soul. It was part of him.

The fire popped, drawing his attention briefly to the flames.

He wasn't ready to leave. Wasn't ready to share her time or attention with anyone else. Part of him was actively searching for excuses, for any reason, however small, he could latch onto that would justify remaining here.

But they needed to go back. Not merely because their friends, their family, were in Kaldarak, but because Ahmya was far safer there than she was out here.

As Rekosh gathered the next strand to add into the braid, Ahmya sighed and settled her hands upon his forelegs. Her fingers gently stroked his fine hairs, suffusing them with her scent. A shudder rippled through him, leaving a delightful, anticipatory tingling on his hide. Her palms were warm, adding to the heat her touch stirred within him.

A soft hum rose from Ahmya. Rekosh stilled. It wasn't a thoughtful hum, wasn't a skeptical hum, wasn't one of those brief hums of assent or satisfaction that humans often made. It was flowing, smooth, as though it was drifting upon an ever-changing wind.

It was a song.

And it was the most beautiful sound he'd ever heard.

The hum stopped.

"Are you okay?" Ahmya asked.

Was he okay? Why would she—

Only then did he realize that his hands had ceased moving, holding her hair in a half-finished braid.

"Make that sound again," he said.

Ahmya chuckled and petted his legs. Then she once more produced that song, except this time, her humming led into words. They were soft and lyrical, rising high and sweet, falling low and sultry.

Rekosh had been wrong. *This* was the most beautiful thing he'd ever heard.

Ahmya was singing. He knew it for what it was, though the sounds she produced were nothing like vrix singing.

He forced his fingers back into motion as he listened. Her words were English, and though he knew many of them, he found their meaning more difficult to put together when delivered by song—and somehow, that only added to the beauty of it.

Rekosh closed his eyes. He could gladly listen to her sing through the night and into the next day.

He could happily spend his entire life listening to her lovely voice.

When the song ended, they sat in comfortable silence, which was broken only by the crackling fire and the rustling of leaves outside their shelter.

"Is your father still in Takarahl?" Ahmya asked.

Again, his hands faltered, and his eyes opened. But the weight he should've felt from her question, the weight he'd expected, didn't come. There was only sorrow, a haunting song whispering along his heartsthread.

"He is," Rekosh said.

"Did you visit him when you went back?"

"I did."

She twisted slightly, peering at him from the corner of her eye with her brow creased. "Did something happen?"

Rekosh turned his face away, staring out into the dark jungle. He'd thought he was done with this. Had thought his last encounter with his sire had been the end, that he'd set aside whatever attachment he'd felt. That his goodbye had somehow eliminated his own pain.

What a fool he had been.

Ahmya turned her body to face him, pulling her hair free from his grasp and making the braid come loose. She curled a leg atop his and caught one of his upper hands in hers. Rekosh looked down and stared into the deep, concerned, brown eyes of his mate.

"Remember, you never have to talk about anything if you don't want to." She reached up and cradled his jaw beneath his mandible, stroking her thumb over his hide. "I can tell something happened that made you sad. Just know I'm here for you. To listen, to talk, or to just simply be if all you want to do is hold me."

He tipped his headcrest to her forehead and closed his eyes. Banding an arm around her waist, he held her close.

His heartbeats measured the passing time as he remained that way, soaking in her feel, in her warmth, in the comfort she was offering. Without her, he might've felt that old anger resurging. Without her, he might've been consumed by resentment and bitterness.

Now there was only that sorrow and a pervading weariness not of body, but of spirit.

Rekosh let out a slow, heavy sigh, opened his eyes, and lifted his head, once more meeting her dark, beautiful eyes. "I will tell you, my heartsthread."

She smiled softly before pressing her lips to his mouth. The kiss was light, but the affection and love it conveyed echoed into the deepest recesses of his hearts.

Then, without another word, she turned around again, giving him her back, and took hold of his lower hands. She dragged them onto her lap, lay her palms atop them, and laced her fingers with his.

Warmth bloomed in his chest, pulsing outward in soothing

waves. His mandibles ticked up into a smile. He gently combed his upper claws through her hair, undoing the loosened braid to start over. "My sweet little flower knows me well."

And he wanted her to know him fully. No barriers between them, no secrets, no shame; hearts and souls bared and entwined. With anyone else, such vulnerability would've felt like a weakness. With Ahmya, it was strength. He was neither so prideful nor so foolish as to deny that his mate bolstered him.

But that made it no easier to refine the truth from within his complicated emotions, and to weave that truth into words.

"On our final day in Takarahl, I strode to my father's den. We had not seen each other in many moon cycles. And I cannot say if I truly wanted to see him at all. No, what I really wanted was to show him the dress I made for you. I wanted him to look upon the finest silk ever woven by vrix hands and feel pride in me, in what he had taught me.

"I had the bundle in my hands, and I...did not open it. I did not show him."

"Why not?" Ahmya asked gently.

Rekosh let out a heavy sigh, but he kept his fingers working. "Because he was happy. Happy to see me safe, but more... He was happy in that den, happy in that new life with his mate and their broodlings, who he wanted me to finally meet. And as I looked with all eight eyes, I could see no place for me there. The broodlings' playthings reminded me of my brood siblings, and seeing his goldworker tools...

"What could I do but remind him of the pain and loss he suffered? What could I do but make him remember old hurts?"

She squeezed his hands. "Oh, Rekosh..."

"He took his new mate a few years before Zurvashi made war on the thornskulls. I was already grown, already denning alone, yet I was still angry at him. The life they made is not mine, the family they made is not mine. For so long, I felt...

apart. I felt it most when I was with him this final time. I gave him harsh words before I left."

"And did those words make you feel better?"

Rekosh tilted his head, mandibles twitching. "Should not the question be how my words made him feel?"

"I'm here with you, Rekosh. You are my mate. I want to know what you're thinking, what you're feeling."

A thoughtful hum escaped him. The braid grew more intricate with each passing moment as his fingers continued weaving; they knew their work well, even if his mind was otherwise occupied.

Finding a satisfying answer was difficult. That was a surprise for Rekosh, nearly as much so as the question itself had been.

Ahmya stroked her thumbs over his lower hands, seemingly unbothered by the lengthening silence. She was simply here with him, for him, and he knew she would be regardless of his response—even if he didn't offer one at all.

"My anger has become sorrow," he finally said. "I...I do not regret what I said to him. I spoke the truth of my hearts. But I regret how I spoke. It is as though I threw a stone, when I should have used the softest silk. I made...unnecessary hurt. Do you understand my words?"

She lifted one of his lower hands to her face and pressed a tender kiss to his palm. "I do."

He trilled quietly, lowered his face closer to her hair, and breathed in her scent, seeking solace in it. "He told me he is sorry. For all the hurt he gave me. Even though he could not see it all, even though he could not understand it all, he said he is sorry."

"I believe that he is. He suffered the loss of his mate and children, and in his attempts to protect you, he hurt you too. But I don't think he ever meant to push you away or make you feel unwanted." Ahmya pressed his hand to her cheek. "Why would he have been so happy to see you, so excited for you to meet your siblings, if he didn't want you there? He wants you in his life, Rekosh. You are his family."

An unhappy buzz escaped him. He wanted to argue, to deny what she had said…but he could not. He'd seen his sire's eyes, his posture, had heard the sadness in his voice. Rekosh hadn't expected his sire to take their parting so hard yet so gracefully.

And he hadn't expected to feel it so deeply himself.

Ahmya lowered his hand to her lap. "I know that you're hurt. Rightfully so. I…feel the same when I reflect on my relationship with my father. He never remarried, but after my mom died, he changed. He was harder, more distant. Our relationship growing up was so strained. Looking back, I think it's because he just didn't know how to raise a kid on his own, much less a daughter.

"For most of Hirohito's childhood, our father was *deeploid*, so he was rarely home. When I was little, he retired from the military, but he started working long hours at a new job while my mom took care of us. And after she was gone…I don't think he knew how to process his grief."

Rekosh's mandibles sagged. Whether vrix or human, no one seemed immune to the pain of loss, and no one seemed to bear it quite the same.

"As I grew up," Ahmya continued, "he didn't know how to talk to me, especially when it came to anything girl related. He was always much closer to Hirohito. Like you, I felt unseen. I worked hard in school to get the best *graydz*, I joined *sportz*, volunteered in after school *programz*. My accomplishments seemed to be the only way to get him to acknowledge me. I know a lot of it was because of his upbringing and having spent so much time in the *miluh terree*, but…it hurt. I just wanted him to see me as I was. His daughter."

"*Kir'ani vi'keishi,*" Rekosh whispered, leaning down to brush his mouth across her hair. "Would that I could spare you such hurt. That I could take it from you."

"You can't shield me from every hurt, Rekosh," she replied softly. "I just need you to hold me through it."

He wrapped his lower arms around her. "Always, *my heartsthread*. Always."

"And I'll always be here to do the same for you."

With a trill, he breathed in her scent. His mate was the most precious thing in the world—in all existence—and even if he couldn't protect her from everything, he would forever try to do so.

Rekosh lifted his head. "You seem…at peace with that pain, Ahmya."

"I don't know about peace. But I do know in my heart that my dad loved me, that he did his best, and that sometimes, our best just comes up short. And it's normal for that to make us feel conflicted. To feel love for a person, but also feel hurt by them. It's up to us to decide whether we can set aside the hurt and try to build something meaningful…or if we need to let them go."

She looked down, pulling her hair taut in his grasp. Her voice was thick with emotion when she spoke. "My dad is gone though. I'll never have a chance to talk to him again, to tell him that I appreciate everything he did, that I love him."

Even without seeing her face, Rekosh knew that her dark eyes were glistening with tears, and her pain struck his hearts.

Ahmya hugged his arms tighter around her. "But your father is alive, Rekosh, and so are you. Life is too short and too precious to give up on the opportunity to reconnect with him, if that's what your hearts tell you to do. And maybe…maybe someday I could meet him."

His heartsthread thrummed with emotions he could not yet identify, making his chest feel tight and heavy. Releasing her hair, he took hold of his mate with all four hands and turned her to face him.

Their eyes met. Hers were indeed shimmering with tears. Were vrix able to cry, he had no doubt he would be as well. That sadness…he could not bear to see it in her. Could not fight his need to soothe it away, to draw it into himself so it could no longer harm her.

He wrapped his arms around Ahmya and drew her against his chest. She threw her arms around his neck with fervor, tucking her face against his neck and wetting it with those tears.

Rekosh shifted a hand to the back of her head, cradling it, and smoothed his fingers over her hair. His chest vibrated with soft crooning in an attempt to mimic the song she'd sung.

Even as he comforted his mate, even as he held her, her words repeated in his mind. He could not deny the truth of what she'd said. He'd felt it in his heart even before speaking to her about any of this, but it had been Ahmya's patience and understanding that allowed him to reflect upon it at all. That had pushed him to truly consider his feelings.

What if his parting words with his sire were the last they ever shared? Would they leave a sliver of regret embedded in Rekosh's hearts, forever to cause him pain, preventing him from healing and finding peace? Would Raikarn die believing the only surviving broodling of his first brood despised him?

Because despite all his anger and resentment, Rekosh didn't hate his father. If he hated anything, it was that he'd been denied the relationship they might've had.

He held his mate, and her tears gradually dried, but her embrace did not ease. He brushed his jaw against her hair. Simply holding her was enough. This was where he was meant to be, who he was meant to be with.

Yet he could not help but wonder now…what would it be like to bring Ahmya to Takarahl? To walk her along the tunnels that had seemed so mundane to him, to see them with new awe and excitement through her eyes? What would it be like to bring her to his sire's den, to introduce her to him, to meet his young siblings with her at his side?

She was human, but he hoped those differences wouldn't matter. Hoped that his father would see what Rekosh could see so clearly—that his little mate was strong, intelligent, kind, and selfless. That despite her size, she had carried Rekosh through some of the greatest challenges of his life. That her dedication and tenacity had set an example that served as the core of their new tribe.

And he hoped that after meeting her, Raikarn would know Rekosh had made the right choice. That he'd know Rekosh was truly happy.

Surprisingly, he *wanted* to bring Ahmya to Takarahl. He wanted her to meet his sire, he wanted to show Raikarn and everyone else that his mate was the most remarkable female. That she was his, and his alone.

But he knew the time for such a journey had not yet come. The dangers of travel could be lessened by going in a group—consisting at least of Telok and Urkot, though with Ahmya along, Rekosh would want more companions to ensure her safety. And without a bloodthirsty queen pursuing them, they would have no need to drive on to exhaustion each day.

No, it was Takarahl itself that gave him pause. The city was healing, but its wounds remained fresh. Ahnset needed more time to set things right. More time to set her subjects at ease.

Perhaps when the shadowstalkers of Takarahl were ready to welcome the thornskulls of Kaldarak as friends and honored guests, they would be ready to meet the humans.

But Rekosh would not risk his mate.

He and Ahmya remained like that for a time. Sometimes, she hummed along with his crooning, but both seemed content to allow the crackling flames to fill in the silences between them.

It wasn't until Ahmya stirred against him and yawned that he realized how long they'd remained thus.

"Come, *vi'keishi*," he said as he rose, keeping her cradled against him, "let us rest. Our journey must resume with suncrest."

She murmured a response, and he smiled. That she felt so safe in his arms meant more to him than he could ever say.

Rekosh carried her to their bed of fluffed silk and eased down onto his back, holding Ahmya against his chest. She rested her cheek over his hearts. He could feel her heart beating through his hide, and its steady rhythm coaxed his eyes closed.

"Sleep well, my *nyleea*," he whispered. "I have you."

Forever.

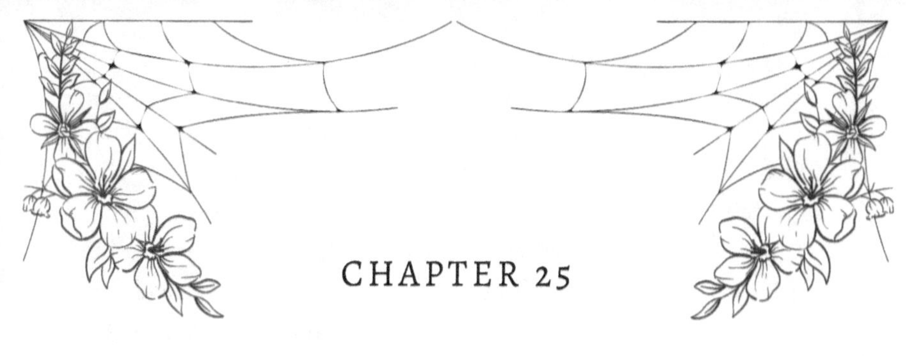

CHAPTER 25

THE SUN SEEMED BRIGHTER, the air fresher, and the Tangle more vibrant than ever as Rekosh and Ahmya journeyed toward Kaldarak.

Though he remained aware of the danger, Rekosh couldn't help but notice the boundless beauty all around. The rich colors, the varied shapes and sizes of the leaves and flowers, the play of sunlight breaking through the canopy and the mesmerizing dance of shadows below.

Yet the sights were only one aspect of that beauty. Sound and smell enhanced it. The song of the wind through the boughs, of animals and insects calling, of branches swaying slowly, gently. The heady, cloying aromas of plants and blossoms, wood and earth.

He could appreciate all of it this fully, this deeply, because of Ahmya. She experienced the world with wonder and curiosity that made him consider everything anew.

They conversed as they traveled, laughing and chittering freely. Ahmya sometimes hummed, sometimes sang, and seemed to dance around Rekosh almost as often as she walked beside him.

He'd never seen her so radiant, so carefree, so alive. Her spirit burned brighter than the sun, and it uplifted him. His steps felt light. Felt effortless.

Rekosh had expected their departure from the ruins to be harder, as both he and Ahmya had been reluctant to leave the place that had become their private sanctuary. He would never forget what he'd shared with her there.

But now that they were on their way back to Kaldarak, Rekosh was glad. With each step, he was increasingly eager to reach their destination and see their friends and family, their tribe, again. But more than anything, he was eager to make his claim upon Ahmya known to all. To show everyone that she was his and his alone.

And then they would finally make a den together. A home.

As midday neared, Rekosh heard the faint sound of running water. It had to be the river, which they'd trekked toward after working their way around the rocky cliffs.

"We need but find a safe crossing and we may reach Kaldarak by sunfall," he said with a trill.

Ahmya stepped into a beam of sunshine ahead of him, tipped her head back, and spun in place. "I wouldn't complain about spending one more night with you under the stars, but it would be nice to have four walls and roof tonight."

"If we must den in the Tangle again, *kir'ani vi'keishi...*" Rekosh closed the distance between them and scooped her up, cocooning her in his embrace.

She laughed, wrapping her arms around his neck and her legs around his waist.

He nuzzled her cheek, breathing her in with a rumbling purr. "I will be your shelter."

As he lifted his head, she moved a hand to his face, brushing his hide with her soft, delicate fingertips. A gleam smoldered in her brown eyes, and pink blossomed on her cheeks. "Mmm... I do love it when you're around me, over me..."

She grazed her lips over the seam of his mouth and said in a low, husky whisper, "*Inside* me."

A shiver passed through Rekosh, and he nearly groaned. Fire slithered along his veins, coalescing in his pelvis. His stem pulsed and pushed against the inside of his slit. He drew his claspers in tight, ensuring it couldn't extrude.

"Ah, female…you tempt me."

Her grin was anything but innocent.

Perhaps they would spend one more night in the jungle after all…

He held her gaze as the heat between them built. His claspers relaxed, and—

The sound of stones clacking together echoed between the trees, dulled by distance but unmistakable.

Rekosh's hearts leapt in his chest, and the fine hairs on his legs stood.

Ahmya's eyes widened as she lifted her head. "Was that…?"

"Yes."

Those sounds had been that of blackrock against blackrock, the manner by which shadowstalkers had long signaled each other out in the Tangle.

The way Rekosh and his friends had signaled each other.

As though she'd anticipated what he would do, Ahmya was already releasing her hold on him and lowering her legs before he set her down. She stepped back the instant she was on the ground and looked in the direction the signal had come from.

Rekosh swung his bag to his front, opened it, and withdrew a pair of blackrock knives from within. He banged their flat sides together, tapping out a response.

As the last clack's echo faded, he held his breath and listened. The Tangle seemed unnaturally quiet in those moments. All the jungle had paused, waiting with him.

When the answering clacks drifted to him, they came on a

hot gust of wind that carried the sickly-sweet smell of wet, rotting vegetation so prevalent in parts of the Tangle.

"Is it the others?" Ahmya asked, turning her excited gaze to Rekosh.

"It must be them," he said, closing the bag and returning it to his back. "Garahk likely sent word back to Kaldarak, and our friends must have come to help find us."

Ahmya stuck out her bottom lip in a pout, but the light in her eyes was playful and teasing. "Aww. Guess we won't have tonight to ourselves under the stars after all."

He growled and caught her wrist with a lower hand, drawing her close. "I will have you to myself one way or another, *nyleea*."

She laughed, stood on her toes, and grasped his braid, which hung over his shoulder and down his chest. With a little tug, she drew him down into a kiss. Much too soon, she pulled away, sliding her arm out of his loose hold. "Now's not the time to keep everyone waiting, my *luveen*."

Chittering, Rekosh strode in the direction from which the signal had come. Ahmya fell into step beside him.

Despite having spent half the day traversing the jungle, their pace was quicker now, urged on by newfound excitement. Occasional signals from ahead guided Rekosh to appropriately alter their course; their path was veering aside, seemingly moving parallel to the river rather than toward it.

Each time the clacking sounded, it was closer, clearer, making Rekosh's anticipation only stronger.

With every step, he and his mate drew nearer to their future. He couldn't guess what it would hold, but under the gazes of the gods' eightfold eyes—and the gaze of anyone else—he would make sure that future was full.

Their path led them gradually uphill, through terrain thick with rocks and vegetation, where visibility was limited from the ground. But the excitement in their strides did not waver.

When the signal came again, it was from no more than a hundred or so segments ahead. Rekosh answered it quickly.

Another series of stone-on-stone clacks came from somewhere behind.

His friends must have split into groups to cover more area in their search, and they were now all converging.

But some instinctual part of Rekosh insisted that he and Ahmya were now surrounded, being enfolded. That two unknown parties were closing in on them like a pair of fanged mandibles ready to land a killing blow.

"We're almost there," Ahmya said, jarring him from his thoughts. "I can't believe our little adventure is about to be over."

Rekosh chittered. "*Little* adventure?"

She scrunched her nose. "Okay, so maybe it wasn't quite so little." Her lips stretched into a smile. "It has been an adventure though, hasn't it? I could have done without the almost dying parts, but everything else… I wouldn't change it for anything."

His mandibles rose as he brushed his foreleg against her calf. "Nor would I, *kir'ani vi'keishi*. Except for almost dying. You are not allowed to be in danger again."

She laughed and lifted a hand, sweeping loose strands of her dark hair behind her ear. Rekosh turned his attention forward again.

They were approaching a huge tree, its base spanning at least ten segments wide. Based on the sound of the last signal, their friends had to be just on the other side.

"Who awaits?" Rekosh called as he and Ahmya rounded the trunk. "The impatient hunter, or the overcautious delver?"

No response came.

Rekosh's fine hairs rose as realization struck him.

None of the blackrock signals had possessed the usual little flourishes he and his friends, especially Telok, added to them. And it was unlike Telok and Urkot to not respond, especially from this close—and especially to such friendly teasing. They should've hurled eightfold as many insults at him in the time it took for his next few steps.

That uneasy feeling reasserted itself. His fingers tightened around the haft of his spear, and his fine hairs remained standing, picking up the various scents on the air.

There was a faint smell of vrix, but it was no vrix with whom he was familiar.

The vegetation to their right shook.

He should have kept Ahmya to his left, shielding her with the tree.

Rekosh's upper right hand darted out to grab hold of her arm, and he yanked her toward him. She released a startled sound as her feet left the ground. Her spear fell from her hand.

A male shadowstalker with dull green markings and gray ash smeared over his face burst from the undergrowth, a coil of silk rope in his hand, green eyes ablaze with fury.

Not Telok. Absolutely not Telok.

Ahmya's momentum carried her straight to Rekosh. He caught her against his side, banded his arms around her, and twisted to draw her away from the lunging vrix. In the same motion, he brought his spear around and thrust it toward the attacker.

The other male dug his legs into the ground and threw his weight backward, pitching his hindquarters into the dirt. The sharpened point of Rekosh's spear passed within a finger's breadth of the male's face.

Ahmya clung to him with arms and legs alike as tightly as she ever had.

Wood cracked overhead. Rekosh braced his left legs against the tree trunk and shoved off, leaping clear of it just before a second male, this one with amber markings, came crashing down on the spot Rekosh had just been standing.

Vegetation thrashed and branches snapped as two huge

females charged around the trunk. Like the males, they had ash on their faces. Both carried long war spears and were clad in dull, dingy, beaten-up adornments and armor pieces—gold that had undoubtedly been weathering the worst of the Tangle's conditions for the last several moon cycles.

They were Queen's Fangs.

Zurvashi's Fangs.

"Capture the traitor!" The lead female commanded in a booming voice.

Rekosh knew her, knew those clear blue eyes. She was Ulkari, sister of Urshar. One of the vrix still loyal to Zurvashi of whom the females in Goldflame Tunnel had spoken.

Rekosh scrambled backward, spear raised and ready, putting precious distance between himself and the attackers. But he knew all too well that the gap could be closed in a heartbeat.

Only as the two males righted themselves did Rekosh see the black furs draped over their shoulders, as dirty and worn as the females' gold.

Zurvashi's Claws.

Ahmya whispered something, but her words were muffled against Rekosh's shoulder. She was trembling, her nails digging into his hide, her heart racing.

And he felt the same fear. Fear for the future that had seemed so close, fear for his little mate with her huge, loving heart. Fear that once again, his entire world was on the verge of destruction, held aloft over some yawning, bottomless pit only by the most frayed of threads.

An ember of fury sparked in his chest, but it was instinct that drove him.

He turned around and ran.

"Coward!" Ulkari roared. "Betrayer!"

The ground rumbled as the ambushers gave chase. Twigs cracked and snapped, leaves rustled, vrix growled and grunted, and Rekosh's hearts pounded like thunder in his chest, pumping sizzling blood through his veins.

He yearned to kill them all. To end Zurvashi's legacy of blood and terror in a final brutal surge, to leave their bodies to the scavengers, to let their flesh rot and their bones be swallowed by the jungle.

But Ahmya was more important than bloodlust, than vengeance, than anything. And no matter the potency of his rage, he knew this was a fight he was not likely to win.

So Rekosh poured all his strength of body and will into his legs, keeping them moving at an impossible pace.

Ahmya bounced against him despite his firm hold. There was simply no way to spare her while maintaining such speed, and he could not allow himself to slow no matter her discomfort.

Ulkari's order hadn't been to kill the traitor, but to capture the traitor. Rekosh wasn't foolish enough to believe that meant these loyalists to the dead queen planned to show mercy.

"Rekosh," Ahmya breathed.

"I have you, *vi'keishi*," he growled. "I have you."

The sounds of pursuit persisted behind him, the ambushers shouting as they ran. Though based on the volume of the noise, he was widening his lead on them, he dared not look back for fear of losing even a shred of his forward momentum.

The river was their only hope. If he and Ahmya could get to the river...

Even if they had to brave being swept along by the churning waters again, he would do so. Their chances were better with the unforgiving river than with these vrix.

Only when movement flickered at the upper edge of his vision did he recall what had so unsettled him moments before —the unknown group that had signaled from somewhere behind Rekosh and Ahmya.

A pair of male vrix were perched atop a thick bough that

crossed above Rekosh's path, with a net stretched between them.

Rekosh's legs skidded along the leaves and detritus atop the jungle floor as he struggled to change direction. The males leapt down.

Ahmya screamed. The males landed on either side of Rekosh, and his momentum carried him straight into their net. The strands closed around him and tangled on his limbs. He desperately attempted to maintain his balance, but his stumbling steps only worsened the net's constriction. His upper body tipped forward.

The males yanked hard on the lower portion of the net.

His hearts leapt, clawing their way into his throat, and paralyzing cold exploded from his core.

Rekosh's legs were swept out from beneath him, and he fell, his body skewing to the right. He tensed and attempted to contort himself to shield Ahmya from the impact, but he could not stop himself from coming down atop her.

He felt her soft form pinned beneath him, felt her nails scraping his hide, felt and heard her breath burst from her lungs. The spear snapped under him, but he barely felt the bite of splintered wood.

"Ahmya," he snarled, fighting the netting to brace his hands on the ground and shove his weight off her.

She writhed beneath him, struggling to draw in a breath, and her near silent gasps were the most alarming and heartbreaking sound he'd ever heard.

"No, no, no, breathe, please." With claws and fangs, he tore at the net, hooking any stands he could. He needed to give her space, needed to be able to see her, to check on her, to tend to her.

He'd harmed her. It made no difference that it had been unintentional.

The males were still tugging on the net. Every pull allowed

Rekosh's claws and fangs to bite deeper into the silk ropes, every pull was like a gust of wind feeding the inferno in his chest.

"Rekosh," she rasped. "I'm... oh..."

One of the ropes broke, slackening the net. He pushed outward on all the strands, seeking further weaknesses. Another rope broke, then another.

"Restrain him!" a female commanded from nearby.

Rekosh growled and pushed harder. He felt more of the ropes fraying, and as they gave way, his rage intensified. This was not how he and his mate would meet their ends. They would not have their future stolen when they'd only just laid claim to it. He would not allow this to happen.

Ahmya's trembling hands found his face, their touch still warm, still soft, despite everything. "I'm...okay... I'm o—"

Something with all the weight and solidness of a boulder slammed into the side of Rekosh's head. The net ripped as the force of the blow knocked him aside, away from his mate, away from her hands, her touch.

"*Rekosh!*" Ahmya screamed.

He tumbled over the uneven ground, over branches, rock, and debris. The Tangle did not cease spinning even when his body came to rest, his hand landing upon the jagged edge of a stone.

A thick, heavy leg came down on his chest, pinning him in place. Rekosh grasped it reflexively. His claws sank into tough hide, which only seemed to draw more weight upon him.

Snarling, he looked up to meet Ulkari's blazing blue eyes.

"Bind this betrayer," she growled, snapping her mandible fangs, "and his creature."

"*No!*" Rekosh's rage flared, hotter than any goldworker's forge, flooding him completely.

No one could touch his mate. *No one.*

A bestial roar erupted from his chest as he grasped the sharp, jagged stone and stabbed it into Ulkari's leg.

Gold adornments clanked as the Fang reared back, snatching her bloody leg away. Rekosh kept his claws latched onto her, dragging himself off the ground and shredding more of her hide in the process.

With a furious cry, Ulkari shook him off. At the edge of his vision, he saw Ahmya crawling out of the net. He would not let them have her. Crimson filled his vision as he lashed out with a wild flurry of claws and kicks. The males who had caught him in the net joined the battle. He sent blows at them too, so quickly and savagely that they had no time to counter.

Do not touch her.

She is mine.

Mine!

Rekosh didn't know whether he only thought those words or shouted them. Hands grabbed at him, yet his claws bit into flesh again and again and again, splattering his hide with warm blood. What pain he felt was distant—like a voice echoing from another world.

Ahmya. Mine.

Must reach her.

Must protect her.

He didn't perceive individuals around him. They were but the limbs of a faceless monster, and he would slay the beast at any cost. Anything between Rekosh and his mate was to be destroyed.

"Enough!" a female vrix yelled.

With another roar, Rekosh lunged toward the female.

A wave of terrible, overwhelming cold crashed into him, forcing him to an abrupt halt when he saw her.

The female, another Fang called Nuriganas, had one hand wrapped around Ahmya's neck from behind, holding her aloft. Ahmya's kicking feet were more than a segment off the ground.

She clutched the Fang's thick fingers with both hands, and her face was already red.

A firestorm clashed with that bone-deep chill. He needed to tear that arm off the female's body, needed to rip out her throat with his mandibles, needed to kill, and kill, and—

"Submit," Ulkari demanded from beside him, "or we will show you what our queen did to the first of these creatures."

Terror and fury swirled within Rekosh, as powerful and violent as the worst storm to have ever battered the Tangle. He met Ahmya's gaze.

Her eyelids were flaring and drooping, and the light in her eyes was fast dulling. But the fear in them remained apparent throughout, tinged with desperation as her struggles continued, a little weaker with each heartbeat. Tears streamed down her cheeks.

All Nuriganas had to do was tighten her grip, and…

And Ahmya would be gone.

A simple contraction of muscle, and Rekosh's mate would be taken from him forever. Before he could say a word, before he could move any closer, before he could so much as blink, she would be gone.

I am sorry, kir'ani vi'keishi.

Ulkari and the two males were already grabbing Rekosh as his legs, suddenly numb, gave out, and he fell onto his leg joints. They pulled off his bag, wrenched his arms back, and lashed them together, claws digging into his hide as they worked.

He knew it didn't matter now, but his hearts stuttered at the thought of losing the dress. Ahmya's gift.

Nuriganas released Rekosh's mate.

Ahmya fell and crumpled forward onto hands and knees. With her head bowed and her hair hanging in disarray, she coughed raggedly and desperately gasped for air.

Rekosh pushed forward, but the males held him fast.

"Ahmya," he rasped, straining toward her.

Ulkari stepped in front of him, grasped his hair, and dragged him upright. "We have caught the weaver. She will be pleased."

"Should have killed him," one of the males growled with a clack of his fangs. "Not worth the trouble."

Rekosh couldn't see his mate, but he still heard her labored breathing, her harsh coughing. His hearts pounded, and his fear and rage remained caught in their maddening storm.

"Have you lost faith, Vuljaz?" Ulkari asked, not looking away from Rekosh.

"No," Vuljaz replied, his tone subdued.

Rekosh's hands curled into fists, and his claws punctured his hide. The pain he should've felt remained beyond his reach.

Just like his mate.

Ulkari jerked Rekosh's head back, forcing him to look up at her ash covered face. "Bind that disgusting little creature. We shall bring them to make an offering to our queen."

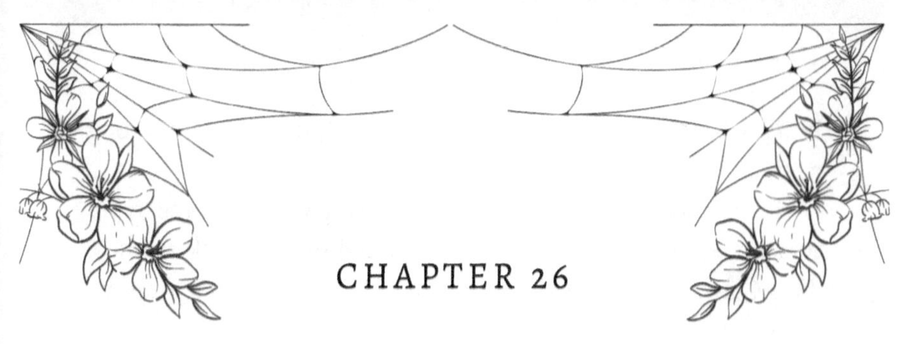

CHAPTER 26

REKOSH WAS GOING to be torn asunder as he marched to the enemy camp behind a pair of Claws.

All his thoughts, feelings, and instincts were in conflict. Fear and fury continued warring in his core. He needed to fight for his mate, to free her, to kill everyone who was threatening her. But if he fought, they would hurt Ahmya.

They would kill her.

To act would hasten her end. To continue onward in submission would only delay the inevitable.

These vrix, still fanatically loyal to Zurvashi, would not spare Rekosh and Ahmya's lives. Whatever choice he made, the ultimate outcome would be the same.

He could not change that…but neither could he accept it. And the last few embers of his hope were struggling to remain alight against reality's relentless deluge.

His internal strife was clawing at his hearts when they reached their destination.

A barrier of branches and brambles ringed the encampment. Rekosh and his friends had sometimes created such barriers to protect their camps, using them to deter overly curious or hungry beasts. But he'd never beheld any quite so tall and long as this.

Standing at the center of that thorn ring was a tall tree, from which a circular platform was suspended by thick silk strands. Two Claws, with barbed spears in hand, gestured from atop the platform.

Ulkari shoved Rekosh into the Camp, hard enough to make him stumble. Heat swept across his back, radiating from the place she'd touched. It was an itch beneath his hide that could not be scratched. A churning in his gut that would not settle.

"Shall I take the lead if you wish me to stride faster?" he grumbled, exerting force on his bindings. The silk creaked and bit into his hide but didn't give by even a threadspan.

"Close your mouth," Ulkari growled, striking the back of his head with the blunt end of her spear.

He stumbled again, the *thunk* of impact echoing through his skull. But the pain, like the many others throughout his body, was distant. Dull. And he was tempted to risk inviting another blow by glancing back to steal a glimpse of Ahmya, who, with her arms tied behind her back and her legs bound together, was being carried over a Fang's shoulder like a beast to slaughter.

Rekosh clenched his jaw and squeezed his fists against a fresh surge of anger. He couldn't do anything with that emotion. Not yet, not until an opportunity presented itself...

Or until one was made.

So, he forced himself to study the camp. There were numerous structures within, shelters crafted of wood, silk rope and cloth, and leaves. Most looked as though they'd been exposed to the weather for at least a few eightdays.

Beneath some of those shelters were racks holding weapons —war spears and barbed spears, blackrock axes, fanged clubs, and hide shields. Though he could not count them all as he moved, there were far more weapons than vrix, even when adding the two lookouts on the platform to the party of eight that had captured him and his mate.

This encampment wasn't merely for survival. Like Needle's Point all those years before, this was a staging place for an attack. This was a war camp.

Yet while Needle's Point had been days of hard striding from Kaldarak, this place was less than a single day's journey from the thornskulls' home.

"You have returned sooner than expected," a female called from ahead in a deep, authoritative voice, drawing Rekosh's attention to her.

The female wore adornments typical of Fangs under Zurvashi—a broad leather belt, a yatin hide gorget with gold bands around her neck, gold arm bands, and jewelry inlaid with sparkling gems. But those trappings were paired with long, flowing white silk wraps reminiscent of a spiritspeaker's garb. Three lines of pale gray ash were smeared down her face, one along the center, between her eyes, the others to either side of them.

Another female, dressed similarly, stood beside and just behind her. They were flanked by a pair of males in tattered, soot-stained silk wraps.

"Prime Speaker Ogahnkai." Ulkari slammed a leg down on Rekosh's hindquarters, driving him down onto his leg joints. "We return bearing unexpected bounty."

A few segments to Rekosh's side, Nuriganas strode forward, bent down, and dropped Ahmya onto the ground. The human hit the dirt with a grunt and curled on her side. Her dark hair was tousled, and her skin was dirty, bruised, and scraped.

"Ahmya!" Rekosh threw himself toward her only to be halted by Ulkari grabbing hold of his arms and forcing more weight down onto his hindquarters. His legs dug into the ground, seeking purchase to thrust him forward, but they only slid and scratched the dirt.

Ogahnkai stepped closer to Ahmya, head tilted and red eyes ablaze.

Ulkari hooked a thick arm around Rekosh's neck as his struggles gained new desperation.

He choked out his mate's name, all his awareness focused on her—and the hulking female approaching her. Ahmya had never looked so small, so helpless, so fragile, not even next to Ahnset or Nalaki.

"One of Ketahn's creatures," Ogahnkai rumbled. She extended a huge foreleg and tentatively touched Ahmya with the tip, prompting a soft, frightened gasp from the human and a roar from Rekosh.

"Not his gold haired mate, but this one still bears a vrix mating scent..." Ogahnkai flicked her gaze to Rekosh, mandibles twitching closer together. "Your mother fought for Takarahl with honor, weaver, and yet you have betrayed all we are to be lured into this *thing's* trap!"

Do not touch her.

She is mine.

Do not touch!

However much he might've wanted to, he could not get those words out through Ulkari's crushing hold on his neck. All that emerged were furious, raged snarls and growls.

Reaching down, Ogahnkai grasped the front of Ahmya's dress and lifted her off the ground. The vrix leaned down, shoulders rising and falling with heavy breaths. Those mandible fangs were much, much too close to Ahmya's head.

Hands clenched behind her back with knuckles gone pale, Ahmya met Ogahnkai's withering gaze and held it.

Rekosh's rear legs sank into the ground. He shoved hard on them, dragging Ulkari forward.

With a bone-shaking growl, Ulkari fell partly atop Rekosh before catching herself. The fanged club at her hip swung down, the sharp shards and teeth biting at his hide. He hissed at the pain.

One of those shards snagged on the rope around his wrists.

Movement to either side marked Ulkari's companions rushing over to help restrain him.

He ensured the rope was hooked firmly as the males grabbed hold of him. It dragged across the shard, and he felt the faint vibrations as threads frayed.

Immediately, he tested the damage, pushing out on his arms, twisting his wrists, putting whatever strain he could on the frayed rope. But it wasn't enough. Not yet.

Ogahnkai chittered and smoothed a palm over Ahmya's hair. "Such spirit. In the weaver's struggles, and in this creature's eyes. Our queen will surely be pleased."

"Your queen is dead," Rekosh growled.

Ulkari caught his hair at the back of his head and shoved the side of his face into the dirt.

Glaring at Rekosh, the Prime Speaker released Ahmya, letting her fall to the ground, and rose slowly, menacingly. "Death holds no sway over one such as our queen. Our queen of ash and bone, god of the Tangle and all within it!"

She spun around and bowed reverently; the three vrix accompanying her did the same, and all repeated those words in a devoted murmur.

Our queen of ash and bone.

Only then did Rekosh see what had been behind the four of them all along.

A towering figure clad in polished gold adornments and vibrant purple silk—a skeletal female vrix. Her arms were outstretched, clawed fingers spread menacingly, and her jaw hung agape, revealing her sharp teeth. The black of her empty eye sockets was impossibly deep, brimming with hunger and malice.

The embodiment of death.

"Oh my God," Ahmya rasped.

Terror's cold hands closed around Rekosh's hearts and squeezed, sinking their claws in to sap all the heat and strength from his body.

Zurvashi.

She was here. Somehow, she was here, and…

He drew in a burning breath as his hearts jolted into a rapid, punishing rhythm.

No, it wasn't Zurvashi. It was Zurvashi's remains. He could see the dark silk string neatly wound around the blackened bones, attaching them to each other and to a framework of sticks and posts rising from the large, flat stones stacked beneath the skeleton.

"She is more now," Ogahnkai declared. "Our queen. *The* Queen. Greater than the Eight, she is the ruler of all vrix, and our paltry offering shall hasten her return to this world of hide and blood."

Ahmya turned her head to meet Rekosh's gaze. Her eyes expressed so much in that fleeting moment. Her fear and uncertainty, yes, but also her love.

That look shattered his hearts and bolstered them at once because it also conveyed a simple but profound understanding.

Rekosh and Ahmya were the offerings.

No.

He could not fail to protect her again, no matter how impossible the situation seemed. He *could not fail.*

As Ogahnkai and her cloth-clad companions straightened, Ulkari pushed herself upright, crushing Rekosh beneath her weight. No sooner was she off him than he was hauled up off the ground by the Claws who'd come to her aid.

He bent his wrists sharply, seeking the damaged rope with his long claws, oblivious to the pain of the angle.

With his head up, he could now see what lay before the skeletal shrine. A square pit, three segments across and two deep, filled with branches and twigs. Beneath the fresh wood was a layer of gray soot, ashen lumber, and charred bones he could only hope had belonged to animals.

The clothed males strode away from the pit to retrieve a large basket filled with dried leaves, grass, and fronds.

"Today, my queen, your will is done," Ogahnkai called, spreading her arms wide. "Two of your enemies face your justice."

Moving in unison, the males threw handfuls of kindling into the pit. Dry as it appeared, it was likely to light quickly.

"Do not do this," Rekosh said, voice steady despite his breaths coming increasingly quick and shallow. "You will regret it."

One of his claws caught the rope and dragged across it.

With a quiet sound of discomfort, Ahmya rolled and rose onto her knees.

"You are in no place to make threats," Ulkari grated from beside Rekosh.

"It is no threat. Only truth."

He heard the clinking of gold as Ulkari shifted, and he braced himself for another blow.

But Ogahnkai twisted to look back at him, making a sharp gesture with one hand. "Allow him to speak. For one who has woven so many words, it is only fitting that his last will be spoken before our queen."

Ulkari growled. No blow came.

Pushing outward to keep the rope taut, Rekosh managed to scrape his claw across it again. A few more threads gave. It seemed so small a thing, but he knew that sometimes all it took was a single thread. A single thread could change everything.

Ahmya sank onto her haunches, placing her hands just above the rope wound tightly around her booted ankles. Her slender little fingers sought the knot.

She couldn't possibly outrun a vrix, but it meant she wasn't defeated yet. She hadn't resigned herself to the fate these vrix had chosen for her.

Swallowing his rage, he said in English, "These will not be my last words, my wife."

His mate looked at him, but he only briefly met her gaze. She took a deep breath, squared her shoulders, and nodded. "These will not be our last moments, my husband."

"You have family in Takarahl, Ulkari," Rekosh continued in vrix even as he carefully worked at the rope with his claw, ignoring the ache in his wrists. "A sister. Urshar. Do you not wish to see her again?"

Ulkari's body bristled with tension and radiated fury. "So now you threaten my—"

"No," Rekosh replied with a snap of his mandible fangs. "Ahnset is queen in Takarahl, and—"

"A false queen," one of the nearby males declared.

Ahmya's littlest finger hooked the knot, which she delicately drew toward her other fingers.

Rekosh made sure not to look at her directly. Right now, the other vrix thought her beneath their notice, and that was the only advantage she had.

"Regardless," he said, "Ahnset controls Takarahl. And your sister thrives there." With no small effort, he swept his gaze across the other vrix. "All of you have family in Takarahl. Brood siblings, mothers and sires, broodlings of your own. They all dwell in peace now. But what you seek to do here will threaten that peace.

"You are warriors." *Cowards.* "I am but a weaver, yet I can see that your battle need not continue. The cloth of Takarahl has been frayed and torn, but it may well be woven anew. It may be made stronger than ever. Lay down this cause and return to Takarahl, to your families, to peace."

Sizzling heat coursed through his veins, flooding his limbs

and making his hide crawl with the need to take action. And thread by thread, he kept up his silent assault on his bindings.

I will kill you all with my bare claws and fangs. I will paint my hide with your blood for harming my mate, for threatening her, for frightening her.

You will pay with your lives.

"But I promise you," he continued, "there will be no peace for any of you should you proceed. You will call the wrath of Takarahl and Kaldarak alike upon you. That need not be. Together, we can make our home whole."

Ulkari snarled, clamping a hand on his shoulder in a crushing grip, but Ogahnkai chittered. The sound was unsettlingly light, airy, and uncaring.

Ahmya tugged on a loop. The knot loosened.

Ogahnkai stared at Rekosh as the silk-clad males returned the basket to its place.

Out of time. We are almost out of time.

"Weakness," Ogahnkai said. "That is all such words have ever been, all they could ever be." She brought her upper fists together with her elbows out, creating a triangle, and mirrored the gesture with her lower arms. The result wasn't the sign of the Eight, but a closed shape with four sides and four points.

Her booming voice echoed over the camp. "Hear me, for I am her Prime Speaker, and I speak with her voice."

No. No, no...

Rekosh dug his legs into the ground, struggling against the holds of Ulkari and the males, his hearts thundering just as loud as the Prime Speaker's voice. The rope around his wrists still held.

The clothed males returned, each carrying a crude clay bowl from which blue-green flames flickered.

By their eightfold eyes, no!

Ulkari grunted as Rekosh advanced by a handspan. The

males behind him wrenched back on his arms, throwing their weight against his.

"The only true strength lies in action!" Ogahnkai shouted. "In nourishing the jungle's roots with blood. The only true might is wielded by conquerors. And the greatest of conquerors is Zurvashi, the one true queen! Our queen of ash and bone, who will rise and conquer these lands once more!"

Another piece of Ahmya's knot loosened, and her ankles separated by a finger's width.

Ogahnkai lunged at the human.

"No!" Everything within Rekosh tightened with cold, devastating pressure.

Ogahnkai's hand closed on Ahmya's dress. She yanked the human off the ground and flung her into the pit.

Ahmya screamed.

Rekosh roared and surged forward, dragging his captors with him. He felt the sound in his chest, in his throat, shredding and clawing, but he could not hear anything over the echoing scream of his heartsthread.

He had to get to his mate. Had to tear through these vrix, no matter how many there were, no matter how much blood he had to spill.

At the edge of the pit, the two males poured their bowls of flaming spinewood sap onto the kindling.

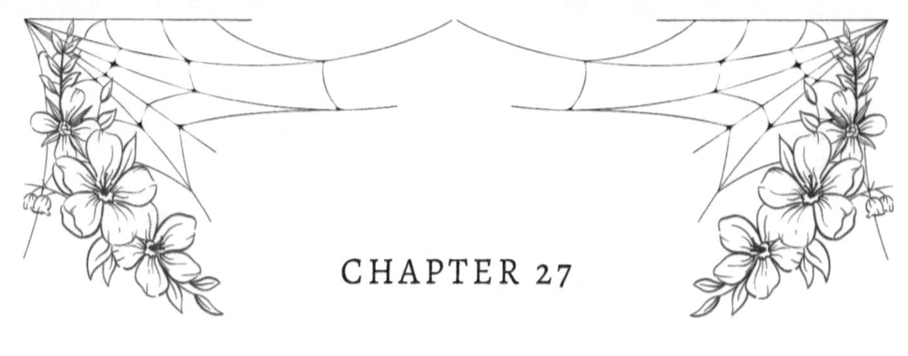

CHAPTER 27

AHMYA GROANED and shifted her shoulders to alleviate the pressure on a particularly pointy stick beneath her. Her landing had seen her poked, scratched, and gouged in many places, but she thankfully hadn't suffered anything worse.

Some of the branches had snapped under her on impact, but many were fresh enough that they'd formed a springy layer that had cushioned her fall. It was a small thing, but she'd take any luck she could get right now.

Rekosh's roars were bestial, fraught with rage, anguish, and fear that penetrated Ahmya to the depths of her soul. Hearing him so raw and ragged broke her heart.

If not for her, he could've fought. Could've run. Could've been free.

She lifted her head, and her eyes widened as icy terror swept through her, colder and more penetrating than the fiercest winter wind.

Smoke curled up from the wood at the pit's far wall, turning the vrix standing at the edge into huge, looming shadow creatures. Demons from the darkest nightmare. The first licks of flame spread upward to some of the kindling, shifting from blue green to orange.

This was the perfect time for swearing. There were so many words she could've uttered just then, so many curses, yet there was only one she could think of.

"Fuck, fuck, fuck, fuck."

Ahmya frantically swung her gaze around. She was near the center of the large pit, which was filled with fuel for the fire. But amidst that fuel, pieces of blackened bone jutted up. The remains of the vrix's prior *offerings*, undoubtedly.

One of those bones was nearby. A rib, perhaps, from some large beast, but it didn't matter what it was or where it had come from. All that mattered was that its end was splintered, leaving a sharp spike sticking straight up. Had she landed just a few feet to the side, that bone would have impaled her.

Ahmya's eyes flicked up to the skeletal shrine standing over the other side of the pit.

She'd been there when Zurvashi had marched on Kaldarak, pursuing Ketahn. She'd watched Ivy, so small, so outmatched in every way, stand against the hulking, terrifying queen. And she'd watched Ivy, against all odds, not just survive the encounter but overcome her foe.

"You don't get to win this time, either," Ahmya whispered, wriggling her feet and spreading her legs. The rope had been tied tightly around her boots, and didn't allow her much movement, even within her footwear, but her efforts on the knot had created some slack.

"Just when I *want* these damn things to come off..."

The smoke thickened, and the flames crept closer.

Her heart raced, but she fought the urge to panic, fought the instinctual drive to kick as wildly as possible. Using her movements to scoot herself toward the jutting bone, she worked the rope deliberately, alternating the motions of her feet and legs.

Finally, the rope loosened enough for her feet to pull free from her boots.

"Yes!" Quickly spreading her legs, she braced her feet as best she could atop the branches, sat up, and bent forward, lifting her arms to blindly seek the jagged bone.

She caught only fleeting glimpses of Rekosh's dark, struggling form through the smoke. His eyes blazed hotter and brighter than the fire, and she could almost feel him moving closer, battling for every inch. At least three vrix were restraining him, including the female called Ulkari.

Pain flared in her hand as the splintered bone cut her palm. Ahmya pressed her lips together, stifling a cry, and adjusted her arms.

Smoke flowed across the pit. It stung her eyes, forcing tears into them, and assailed her throat. She struggled to suppress her coughing; she couldn't have her shoulders shaking. Slitting her eyes, she hooked her wrist bindings over the bone and dragged them up. The point scraped across the rope.

"Damn your eyes, keep him back!" Ulkari shouted.

Pride flared in Ahmya's chest at her mate putting up such a fight, but her pride couldn't help him. Without some sort of distraction, he would be overwhelmed, overpowered.

Killed.

Ahmya's heart quickened, and dread pooled in her belly.

No. I will not let that happen.

Warmth built at her feet and crawled up her legs. The flames were growing, spreading, seeking her out... Icy fear twisted around her heart. Her breaths sawed in and out, each one with a burning itch that threatened a fit of coughing.

But she kept her arms moving as smoothly as possible. Down and up, snagging the strand each time. Despite the crackling flames drawing closer, the *pops* of pockets of sap combusting, and the sharp bite of the bone scraping her skin,

Ahmya pressed on, driven by Rekosh's continued roaring. Little by little, she felt the threads tearing.

No one else is going to make an opportunity for him.

There's no one else who can help.

Fire leapt up near her foot. She cried out and yanked her leg back from the searing heat, and her arms slipped. The bone splinter ripped through the rope and stabbed into her forearm, forcing another agonized cry from her lips.

You don't have time, Ahmya. Neither does Rekosh.

Pressing her lips together and swallowing a scream, she pulled up on her arms. She felt every millimeter of the bone splinter as it slid free of her flesh. Along with the pain came the oddly vivid sensation of her own blood, warm and wet, trickling down her arm.

Gritting her teeth, she pushed her arms to either side, wiggling her wrists to strain the frayed rope.

When the bindings finally gave way and fell from her wrists, Ahmya nearly sagged in relief. She ached everywhere, her eyes were watery, her nose was runny, and her lungs were ablaze. Sweat coated her skin, which was being baked by ever-growing heat. Her head was beginning to swim from the smoke.

It would've been so easy to lie down, close her eyes, and sleep.

Rekosh needs me. And if he can escape to warn the others...

Swinging her arms to her front, Ahmya grabbed her boots. She tore the silk rope away from them before hastily tugging them on and turning away from Rekosh, who remained obscured by the haze.

Though the kindling had been dry, the wood was not, causing it to ignite slower and produce this thick, billowing smoke. Another bit of good luck for Ahmya.

Well, as long as smoke inhalation didn't kill her.

Attempting to walk in the pit would only make her feet sink and potentially get her boots caught in the tangled mass of branches, so she rolled onto her belly and crawled forward, keeping her face low and turned away from the flames.

Twigs scratched at her skin and snagged her dress, but she didn't allow herself to slow. Rekosh needed a chance, and she would find some way to give it to him. That was what drove her on. The loudening flames and blistering heat certainly helped motivate her, however.

She reached the far side of the pit, and only there did she get to her feet, steadying herself with her hands on the dirt wall. Her boots sank in the kindling.

The upper edge of the pit was nearly a foot over her head.

Ahmya jumped, raising her arms. Her fingers caught the edge. She braced a boot against the wall to help pull herself up, arms trembling with exertion, until her foot slipped in the dirt and her arms gave out. She dropped back into the pit, feet sinking a little deeper than before.

"No, no, no!" Ahmya tried to climb again, but her battered body simply couldn't muster the strength to lift itself clear out of the pit, and she couldn't find good footing on the dirt wall. She coughed, the smoke burning her throat and eyes.

New strategy, Ahmya. Quickly.

She turned in place and immediately threw up an arm to shield her face from the heat and brightness of the flames. This pit had become her hell, from which she wasn't meant to escape.

But she wasn't done yet.

Crouching, she grasped handfuls of sticks and heaved them up. More coughs ravaged her throat, embers and disturbed ash swirled in the smoke, and flames leapt as she scoured the detritus for something she could use—for anything.

Ahmya flung branches and brush aside, digging wildly. The fire was close, so, so close, that she could almost feel it licking her skin, and if she didn't get out *now...*

Her hand closed around something hard and thick.

A bone.

She wrenched up on it. Flames rushed closer, fueled by the fresh air flow created by the disturbed kindling. Her flesh stung from the heat. Ahmya closed her eyes and turned her face away from a cloud of scorching embers, pulling on the bone with all her might.

She stumbled backward when it came free, catching herself against the wall.

"*Ahmya!*" Rekosh's tormented call rose over all the other sounds, jolting right through her already shattered heart.

Ahmya spun around, took the bone in both hands, and jabbed it into the wall as hard as she could. It sank deep into the dirt.

Please work.

Holding her breath against the acrid smoke, she jumped and grasped the upper edge of the pit, this time planting her boot on the bone jutting from the wall as she pulled herself up.

She pushed up with her leg. The bone angled slightly down, but it remained in place.

Her fingers dug into the ground, caking dirt under her nails, as she dragged herself out of the pit. Yet even after her boots were clear, she had no time for any relief—and she barely had time to suck in a much-needed breath. From this vantage, she could just make out Rekosh, who continued battling his way toward the pit despite the trio of vrix holding him back.

Ahmya's eyes darted up to Zurvashi's skeleton, which loomed almost directly over her now. Waves of heat from the pit sizzled over her skin. There was a lot of silk on the skeletal shrine, and that wood framework throughout...

Ahmya knew what she had to do.

Without letting herself think, she lay on her belly and reached into the pit, stretching her arm as far as possible to reach for a long stick that had landed standing against the wall.

Flames crackled below her hand, their heat very quickly approaching the unbearable. Her fingertips brushed the stick.

She pushed with the toes of her boots, sliding herself another fraction of an inch forward.

Yes!

Her index finger hooked under the stick, and she tugged it up. Flames danced along its end.

Moving as gingerly as she could, Ahmya crawled back from the edge, eyes fixated on the flickering flame. She felt her heartbeat throughout her body, from head to toe. Keeping the stick as steady as possible, she climbed first onto her knees, then onto her feet.

"The creature!" a vrix shouted. "It is out!"

Ahmya couldn't fight these enemies, couldn't outrun them, but she could give Rekosh the precious time he needed.

In the best vrix she could manage, she called, "Ash and bone are all your queen will ever be!"

On the far side of the pit, vrix faces, still hazy through the smoke, snapped toward her.

Ogahnkai bellowed a command.

Ahmya turned toward the skeleton and held the flame to the voluminous purple cloth around its waist. The instant the fabric ignited, she wedged the end of the stick into one of the joints of the framework. The wood caught fire much more readily than the silk had.

Huge, dark forms raced around the sides of the pit.

Rekosh cried out Ahmya's name again.

Please escape...

She spun and ran deeper into the camp, away from the vrix, away from her mate.

Please, Rekosh. Live.

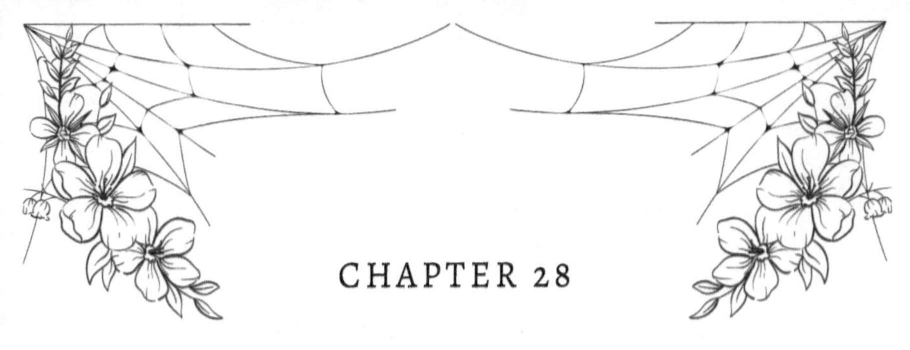

CHAPTER 28

EVERYTHING WITHIN REKOSH went still and silent as he watched Ahmya flee. It was a moment hanging in time, caught and suspended in a huge, complex, chaotic web. And within that moment, there was only him and his mate. No other vrix, no other humans, no heat, no smoke, no fire, no camp. No jungle.

My mate is alive.

By her own strength, cleverness, and determination, she'd escaped the blazing pit. Pride flooded Rekosh, filling him near to bursting.

His hearts thumped. The sound rumbled through him like thunder echoing between the walls of a ravine.

"Tend to our queen," Ogahnkai commanded her companions with a sharp gesture as she reached the other side of the pit. She charged in Ahmya's direction, powerful legs kicking up dirt and leaves.

Fire erupted from Rekosh's core and swept through his body, suffusing him with heat more intense than that of the flames before him.

Ahmya is alive, and she needs me.

Ogahnkai's companions hurried to the burning shrine,

tugged off their silk wraps, and tried to beat out the flames using the cloth.

Ulkari released Rekosh's shoulder and strode closer to the pit. Planting the butt of her war spear in the dirt, she turned to face Rekosh and the vrix around him—the pair of Claws restraining him, along with three more males and two other females.

"Do not stand and stare like fools!" she snarled. "You two, fetch water. The rest of you, ensure that pale worm has no path out of this camp. Now!"

Rekosh was aware of movement around him as the vrix scrambled to obey Ulkari's orders, but he gave them none of his attention. Fury sharpened his focus to a point—a needle, a knife, the head of a spear.

And it was aimed at his first obstacle. His bindings.

He could almost envision the damage he'd done to the rope. It wasn't enough, but it *had* to be. There was no more time.

Live, vi'keishi. *Survive and wait for me.*

Heat gathered in his muscles, buzzing and crackling; a restless, irresistible strength. Clenching his jaw, he forced his arms apart with a growl.

The rope held, but Rekosh did not relent. That heat grew and grew. His arms trembled, his shoulders ached, and his teeth ground against each other.

One thread, he reminded himself. *All it takes is one thread...*

My heartsthread.

The rope bit into his hide in its final act of defiance, and he could almost hear it creaking, could almost feel some greater will behind it, desperate to keep him from the fate he'd chosen.

Desperate to keep him from his mate.

Rekosh's growl swelled into a roar.

The rope snapped, and his arms jerked apart. The males restraining him swayed, and one of them hissed a curse, digging his claws deeper into Rekosh's arms.

Rekosh swept his lower arms backward. His claws raked across hide, and one hand struck something solid dangling from one of the male's waists. A wooden haft. He curled his fingers around it and snatched it free.

He recognized the weapon immediately by its heft—a black-rock axe. His fury nearly sang its approval.

"Kill him!" Ulkari commanded.

The Claws fumbled for their weapons, and in that instant, Rekosh spun toward them and attacked. He lashed out with claw and axe, with kicks and slashes, his limbs moving faster than eyes could perceive, faster than thought.

And the crimson haze in his vision deepened with every drop of blood he spilled.

"Someone approaches!" a lookout called from the platform high overhead. "We are being atta—"

The sentry's words were cut off by a choked cry.

Rekosh hacked through one Claw's throat with the black-rock axe, sending him reeling. The male's barbed spear fell from his hands as he reached up in vain to clutch at the gaping wound, from which crimson flowed in a stream.

Rekosh caught the spear before it could hit the ground. The other Claw staggered back in a panicked retreat.

A black shape crashed down on the retreating male from above. Bones crunched and snapped, and the Claw uttered an agonized, strained cry.

Rekosh blinked. Another male had fallen atop the fleeing Claw—one of the lookouts from the tree platform, who had a spear with familiar feathers adorning it buried in his chest.

That weapon looked like Telok's.

"Defend our camp!" Ulkari shouted from behind Rekosh.

He glanced over his shoulder to see her only a few segments away, war spear raised and pointed toward the camp's entrance. Her eyes flicked to his.

Ulkari began pivoting toward him, moving her legs as

though to advance in his direction. Rekosh spun around and threw his spear hard. The weapon struck the female's abdomen, making her movement falter, but it didn't penetrate deep enough into her thick hide for the barb to catch.

She reached for it.

Before her fingers could close on the wood, Rekosh charged at her. He slammed his palm against the butt of the spear, not allowing himself to slow, using his strength and momentum to drive the weapon deep into Ulkari's belly.

She swung her spear at him in a wide, wild arc. He ducked under it; he both heard and felt her weapon cut the air just above his head. But he grasped his spear with all four hands and pumped his legs, pushing the barbed head deeper still with a savage snarl.

Ulkari stumbled, losing ground to his assault, and made a pained grunt. She sent her spear at his face in an unwieldy backhand thrust. A tilt of his head avoided the strike. He clamped his mandibles on the shaft, breaking the wood apart.

The female's rear legs slid to the edge of the pit, and the ground beneath them crumbled. The female teetered, her eyes going wide, and he gave one more mighty shove.

"No!" Ulkari cried as she fell.

Distantly, from another world, someone called Rekosh's name. A familiar voice, a friendly voice.

Fire and embers leapt high and smoke swirled as Ulkari struck the bottom of the pit.

Rekosh kept hold of the barbed spear as it swung vertical, using it to aid his leap over the pit. Ulkari thrashed and screamed, sending up more fire, and heat lashed Rekosh's legs and underside.

He collided with one of the males beside Zurvashi's bones. The male fell to the ground, and Rekosh came down atop him. Before they'd even come to a full stop, Rekosh struck the male with the axe several times in quick succession.

He felt the weapon's impact jolting through the haft, into his hand, and up his arm, again and again, felt the blood droplets spraying his hide, felt the other male's writhing. But neither the blood nor the male's sounds of agony were enough. Only one thing could satisfy Rekosh's instinctual urge.

Rolling off the male, Rekosh sprang upright and raced in the direction Ahmya and Ogahnkai had gone.

Shouts sounded behind him, adding to a rising cacophony, but he did not look back.

Everything he wanted lay ahead.

His mate, his *nyleea*. His heartsthread.

And she needed him.

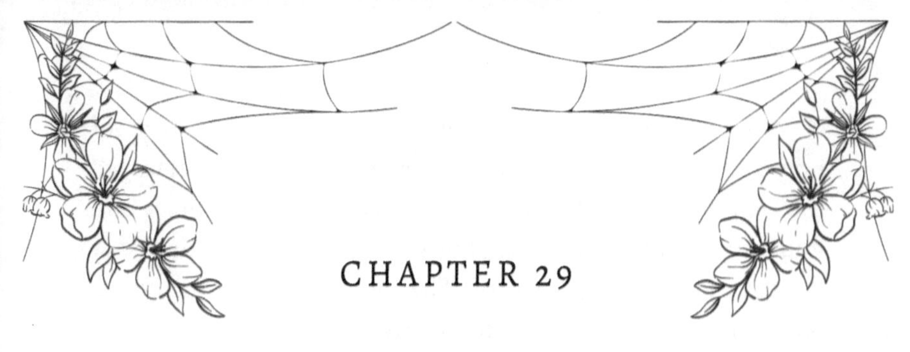

CHAPTER 29

Please be okay, Rekosh. Please, please be okay.

With her breaths like shards of glass in her sore throat, Ahmya threw herself onto her hands and knees before the wall of branches and thorns.

She knew she was being followed, knew that there was no way she could outrun a vrix. It was only a matter of time before they caught her. But all she needed was a little more time. Enough to allow Rekosh to get free, to get help.

She wouldn't find that time while she was trapped in this camp. For Rekosh, she had to go as far as she could, had to last as long as she could.

Ahmya crawled into the narrow gap beneath the wall. Branches and thorns scratched her skin from all sides and snagged her hair and dress, but she had to move forward. Always forward, endlessly forward...until she couldn't.

And she wasn't about to let some sticks stop her.

If Rekosh survived, then her sacrifice would be worth it. She needed him to live. The thought of him being killed...

No. My mate will *live.*

She had to believe he would.

Ahmya wriggled and maneuvered through the maze of branches, breaking off sticks to clear her path. A cry emerged through her gritted teeth as a thorn caught on her dress and dug into the skin of her back, but she didn't stop. She clawed at the ground and dove forward. The thorn cut along her spine, pulling her dress taut before the silk came free with a rip.

As soon as her torso emerged from beneath the wall, she shoved herself up onto her feet and ran.

Behind her, a female vrix growled a curse. Branches snapped, cracked, and rattled.

With her arms pumping at her sides, and her boots pounding the ground, Ahmya glanced over her shoulder. Her blood went cold. She could just make out Ogahnkai's huge, dark figure through the gaps in the wall. The female vrix was tearing a path directly through the branches.

Ahmya's eyes darted around, seeking a place to hide. The trees were too thick and lacked branches low enough for her to climb, and the undergrowth would leave her too exposed.

She halted abruptly, her oversized boots nearly tripping her, as she caught sight of something partially hidden behind the leaves of a fern-like bush.

A fallen, hollowed-out tree.

There was no time for caution. No time to worry about what might've lurked inside. Without hesitation, Ahmya raced to the log and ducked inside it.

Her palms and knees scraped over the rough, damp wood, and she turned, carefully scooting back from the opening.

Thanks to the foliage, her view of the jungle was extremely limited, turning the world around her into a vast unknown.

She struggled to control her breathing, but her heart was racing so fast, so strong, that she couldn't seem to take in enough air. Any louder, and her heartbeat would be echoing along this small natural tunnel.

Sounds drifted to her from outside, oddly muted by the

surrounding wood, which made them seem otherworldly. Shouting, wood cracking and splintering, growls and grunts, and drifting amongst it all like a feather caught on the wind, the whisper of flames.

After brushing off her palm on her dress, Ahmya clasped it over the puncture wound on her forearm.

She had no idea what was going on out there. It sounded like chaos, which was the best she could have hoped for, but was it enough? Had Rekosh been able to—

A faint tremor coursed through the log.

Ahmya froze.

Another tremor followed, then another, and another, each stronger than the last. And each was accompanied by new sounds—the *thump* of heavy legs coming down on the ground and the clanking of gold adornments.

Oh God...

Movement near the log's opening made her breath hitch. Huge, thick vrix legs came into view, along with a dangling length of silk. Ahmya could just make out the tiny hairs on those legs, all standing up.

"I cannot see you, little worm," Ogahnkai said in vrix, her voice vibrating through the log, "but I smell you."

The female lowered herself slowly, menacingly, her body blocking out the opening. With a growl, she thrust a massive arm into the log.

Ahmya covered her mouth, muffling a terrified cry, and kicked her legs to push herself back as the shadowy limb swept around the space within the hollow, seeking blindly. That big, clawed hand slammed into the floor and roof, tearing chunks free and making bits of debris rain onto Ahmya.

Though she was beyond Ogahnkai's reach, everything with Ahmya screamed that this was much, much too close. That she needed to flee, to run and run and run until her legs gave out, and then she needed to crawl. She needed to do everything she could to put as much distance as possible between herself and this monster.

Ogahnkai's claws raked the log's inner walls, splintering the wood with a cracking so loud that the sound threatened to swallow Ahmya up. Beams of light punched through the ceiling as the log fractured against the vrix's onslaught.

Ogahnkai snarled and abruptly withdrew her arm.

Ahmya's ragged breaths burned in her chest; she felt no relief, found no respite from her fear. The female vrix shifted away from the opening, and her heavy steps moved around to the side of the log before falling silent.

Eyes darting from side to side, Ahmya strained to hear any sign of what the female was doing. Dread, icy cold and weighty, pooled in her belly.

Ogahnkai roared. The top of the log exploded inward not two feet from Ahmya, spraying her with wood chips and splinters. One of the vrix's legs hammered down on the bottom of the log, making the whole thing shake.

Ahmya screamed and scrambled back, the toe of her boot actually touching the vrix's limb.

A second leg burst through the top of the log, this one much closer. Ahmya fell back, catching herself on her elbows as the leg came down between her thighs, which had been spread only by sheer luck.

"I will crush you," Ogahnkai growled, tearing her legs out and ripping away more wood in the process. "I will break your soft, disgusting body for our queen!"

As fast as she could, Ahmya retreated, barely aware of the cuts and scrapes she was collecting on her hands, elbows, and legs. Ogahnkai stomped on the log again and again. Each time, Ahmya's heart leapt into her throat, and her insides twisted into a tighter and tighter knot. Each time, more of the log collapsed.

She turned onto her belly and lifted her head. The other

opening was only a few feet away, partially blocked by dirt and debris.

Hope flared in her chest despite her knowing how foolish it was. Even if she made it out, she wasn't fast enough to escape. But she'd never been one to give up, and she wasn't about to start. Not even now.

With the deafening noise of Ogahnkai destroying the log enveloping her, Ahmya dove forward, burying her fingers in the dirt. She frantically raked handfuls of it away from the opening. The log shook violently with the relentless assault, which only seemed to grow more furious with each strike.

Ahmya dragged herself forward. The opening was tight, but the ground was thankfully soft. The instant her legs were clear, she shoved herself onto her feet and began running before she was even fully upright.

Face forward, move as fast as you—

Something heavy struck her leg, knocking it out from beneath her. She fell hard on her side, tumbled, and came to rest on her back. A pained groan rose from her throat.

Ogahnkai loomed over Ahmya, impossibly large and imposing. Her shoulders rose and fell with her heaving breaths, and the lower segments of her forelegs glistened with blood from numerous cuts and splinters on her dark hide.

Ahmya flattened her hands on the ground to push herself up. Her right hand came down on a rough stone jutting from the dirt.

"For the queen!" Ogahnkai snarled.

All the terror Ahmya had felt in her whole life, especially since coming out of cryosleep to find herself in this alien world, should've washed over her at that moment. Those dark, frigid waters should've risen over her head and devoured her. Because...this was it, wasn't it?

But all she could think about was Rekosh. All she could hope for was that he was all right...that he would be all right.

Ahmya pried the stone from the ground and threw it. With a dull *thunk*, it struck Ogahnkai's face. The vrix's head snapped aside, and she staggered back half a step, slapping a hand over her eyes and growling.

Though Ahmya knew those powerful legs would lash out with blind but lethal fury, she struggled to get back onto her feet and keep going. If Ogahnkai remained occupied, it was one fewer fanatical vrix actively trying to harm Rekosh.

The female vrix reared back, raising both forelegs high. She roared, but the sound was drowned out by another roar, far louder, far harsher, far more primal. A roar that both sent a chill into Ahmya's bones and sparked heat in her belly.

However bestial it had sounded, Ahmya knew her mate when she heard him.

Before either female could so much as look toward the source of that roar, before those massive legs could come down on Ahmya, a blur of black and red crashed into Ogahnkai.

With only two legs on the ground, the female vrix fell aside heavily. Rekosh landed atop her.

Ahmya's heart pounded as she watched the frenzied struggle. Ogahnkai had an immense advantage in size, weight, and strength, but Rekosh fought like the embodiment of wildness and rage. He attacked faster than Ahmya's eyes could comprehend, using every limb to inflict damage. Claws, fangs, and an obsidian-headed axe shredded Ogahnkai's hide. She grabbed at him over and over, but she might as well have been grasping at smoke.

And Rekosh snarled repeatedly—not just meaningless, savage sounds, but words.

"Mine. *Mine.* She is mine!"

He shoved Ogahnkai's cheek into the dirt, raised the axe high, and brought it down on her neck. One of her hands finally caught him, claws sinking into his side.

Ahmya's heart skipped a beat.

Unfazed, Rekosh brought the axe down again and again and again, punctuating each brutal blow with a growled *mine*.

Wet, choked sounds burst from Ogahnkai, and her struggles weakened until, finally, she fell still and silent. Between the blood and dirt clinging to the fabric, little white remained on her silk wrappings.

Rekosh grasped the female's wrist and pulled her claws free from his side with a grunt. When he released his hold, Ogahnkai's arm fell away limply. He shoved himself up and stepped back from the body.

Ahmya got to her feet. Her legs were suddenly so weak and unsteady that she couldn't be sure how long they'd support her weight. All the aches and pains the adrenaline had held at bay were starting to make themselves known.

But she forgot all that when he turned to face her. Her chest tightened as she beheld her mate. Blood oozed from countless cuts and puncture wounds on his black hide, which was already darkening further with bruises in several places.

"Oh, Rekosh," she breathed as tears stung her eyes.

He closed the distance between them in an instant and wrapped all four arms around Ahmya, lifting her off her feet to clutch her against his chest. He rasped, *"Kir'ani vi'keishi."*

She clung to him, to his warmth, to his solidness, and for a few moments nothing existed but him. Tears ran down her cheeks as she buried her face against his neck. His teak and amber scent flooded her senses, and she didn't care that it was tainted by the tangs of blood and smoke. Because Rekosh was here, holding her. He was alive.

"I love you," she whispered. "I love you..."

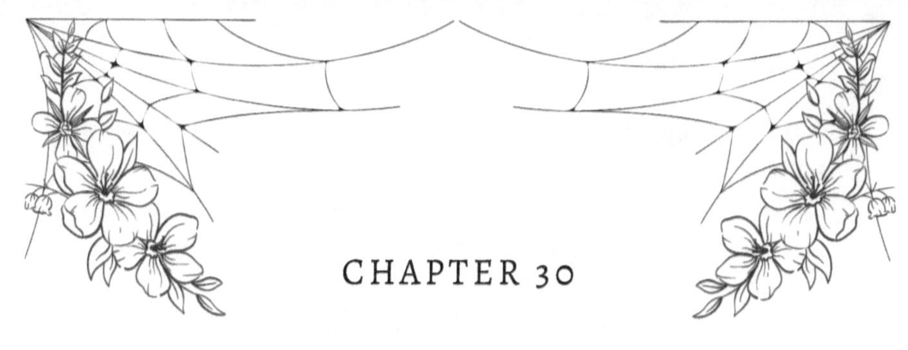

CHAPTER 30

REKOSH CLUTCHED AHMYA TIGHTER. His hearts thundered, their beats echoing through his body all the way to the tips of his fingers and legs. Even with his eyes squeezed shut, the red haze lingered, flashing with each heartbeat.

His mate was warm, soft, and *real*. And he'd never felt closer to her than at that moment.

Gradually, his hearts eased, the haze faded, and the bristling tension in his limbs dissipated. The urge to fight, to kill, to protect, subsided as well. She didn't need a shield now; she needed her shelter.

It felt as though an eternity had passed since he'd last held his mate in his arms. There was no way their joyous, excited journey through the Tangle, finally bound for home, had occurred that very morning. It seemed like a lifetime ago.

"I have you now, *vi'keishi*. I have you," he said hoarsely.

He gently combed his fingers through her tangled hair and breathed in her scent, seeking hints of her sweetness amidst the acrid odor of smoke. She chased away his pains, soothed his rage, balanced his spirit.

Faint tremors pulsed through him as the last of his fury-driven strength vanished. Gods, another moment longer and she might have—

No. She was safe now. He would not follow the chaotic, maddening threads of what might have been. Ahmya was with him now.

But something more than Ahmya's natural fragrance broke through the smoke stench—the cloying smell of her blood. He realized now that he felt it too, on her back, where her dress was wet and sticky.

Opening his eyes, Rekosh drew back from her, holding her up with his lower arms as he looked her over. His hearts shattered at what he saw. Dirt and black soot were smeared across her skin, and she was covered in scratches and cuts, many of which were crusted with blood. Between the dirt, ash, and blood, it was impossible to tell where she was bruised, but he knew that once she cleaned up, there'd be mottled patches of flesh all over her body.

Mandibles hanging limp, he emitted a low, mournful buzz and grasped the strap of her dress with his upper hand, lowering it to check her for any deeper wounds.

Ahmya flatted a palm over his hearts. "I'm okay, Rekosh."

He met her gaze, which glittered with tears. His heartsthread pulled taut, making everything in his chest and throat suddenly, painfully tight. "There is much blood. Too much."

"I'm okay. Just...hold me. Please."

Reverently, he smoothed Ahmya's hair back from her face, unable, unwilling, to look away from those deep, brown eyes. He could feel her trembling against him. Could feel her exhaustion. It was his own.

"Ah, my *nyleea*..." He drew her close and pressed his headcrest to her forehead. "I will hold you until the moons and stars fall dark."

Tears spilled down her cheeks, and she slipped her arms around his neck, embracing him tight.

"Wait." Ahmya abruptly lifted her head, fear creeping into her voice. "There are more of them! We need to go, need to—"

"Rekosh, Ahmya! Thank the Eight."

Both Rekosh and his mate turned their heads toward that familiar voice.

Urkot approached from only a few segments away, mandibles raised in a smile, with Ketahn, Telok, and Garahk just behind him. All four wielded spears and were spattered with blood. At a glance, most of that blood didn't seem to belong to any of them.

Ahmya tensed against Rekosh before sagging in his hold. With a relieved sigh, she said, "Oh, thank God."

Rekosh chittered, drawing her more snugly against his side. "You are late my friends. Did you let old stoneskull lead?"

"Even I could have followed the trail you left, needlelegs," Urkot replied, his blue eyes alight.

"Now I know you did not heed our lessons," said Ketahn with a smile of his own. "You may as well have left a thread in your path for us to follow."

"Exactly as I intended," Rekosh said.

"I am sure it was. Such carelessness could only have been intentional."

Rekosh's amusement faded as his eyes drifted to the camp. He couldn't see anything over the thorn wall but for the smoke billowing from the pit at the camp's center and the now empty tree platform. "Is it done?"

"Yes." Ketahn followed Rekosh's gaze with his own. "A few attempted to flee. We sent them all to join their queen."

Urkot strode closer, grasped the back of Rekosh's head, and dragged him down, pressing their headcrests together.

"I am glad we found you two." The blue-marked vrix's voice was thick and gruff as he momentarily tightened his grip. When he stepped back, his blue eyes met Rekosh's before flicking to Ahmya.

She offered him a smile. "We are glad to be found."

Rekosh nuzzled his mate's hair. "You have taken the words from my throat, *kir'ani vi'keishi*."

"Unfortunately for all of us, your supply is unlimited." Telok strode up to Rekosh and met his gaze. "Yet I am glad to again be deprived of peaceful silence."

He mimicked Urkot's gesture, though he withdrew sooner.

Something warm and full bloomed in Rekosh's chest. "Thank you, my brother."

Ketahn came next to touch headcrests. When he moved back, he raised a lower hand, holding up Rekosh's bag. "And I believe this is yours."

The bag was a little dirtier than before, but intact.

Which meant the dress was unharmed.

Rekosh would've gladly watched a thousand such dresses burn if it kept his mate safe, but he could not deny his relief and gratitude.

"Thank you. But you may soon regret returning this to me, Ketahn," Rekosh said with a chitter, taking the bag and slinging it over his shoulder. Ahmya helped lift his long hair out of the way of the strap.

Once the bag was in place, he tilted his head and looked Ketahn over, from the top of his headcrest to the tips of his legs and back again. "Ketahn, I am glad to see you, but…why are you here?"

"Garahk returned to Kaldarak with Lacey and told us what happened," Ketahn said, eliciting a relieved sigh from Ahmya. "He apologized for losing you."

Ahmya looked at Garahk around the others. "You did not lose us."

The thornskull, his white hide smeared with mud, brought his forearms together in apology. "I was leader of the hunt, and you are mine. Mine to guide, to shield."

"We are alive now because of you, Garahk. Because of all of you." Rekosh tapped a knuckle to his headcrest in respect.

Garahk thumped the ground with a foreleg and chittered. "How many did you give death to, weaver? Four, five? Again, I have missed your *shar'thai*. It must have burned bright as the sun."

"One of those must be counted for Telok. He..." Rekosh's eyes drifted to Ketahn again, and whatever he'd been about to say faded from his mind. His mandibles twitched as he regarded his friend again. "You have not answered my question, Ketahn."

Ketahn bumped a foreleg against Rekosh's. "I could not leave two of my family at the mercy of the Tangle. You would have done the same, would you not?"

"Yes, but you have been inseparable from Ivy and Akalahn. You have been so protective of them that you have seemed ready to attack anyone who so much as looks at them for a moment too long."

Telok grunted in amused agreement.

Garahk pounded his chest with a fist. "They are with my heartsflame and our broodlings. Nalaki watches over them."

Ketahn nodded. "It was no easy choice, but I could not leave the two of you out here alone. I had to join the search. And where safer a place for my mate and broodling than Kaldarak, in the den of the *daiya*?"

Chittering, Rekosh glanced at Urkot and Telok. "You had to drag him away, did you not?"

Both males nodded, their mandibles rising.

"Ivy commanded him to come," Telok said, "and we carried out her command."

Ketahn snorted. "I came of my own will."

Garahk chittered.

"You needed a bit of aid to allow your mate and broodling out of your sight." Mirth dancing in his eyes, Urkot lowered his voice. "And Telok may not want to admit it, but we would not have found your trail in time without Ketahn."

Telok grunted and thumped Urkot's hindquarters with a leg joint.

"Many words to share," said Garahk, "but this is no place to share them. We must make our own wild den for this night. The gods will not favor us if we den where they have been disrespected."

Ketahn moved back, dipping his head to Garahk. "Yes. Let us see to our friends' wounds and hasten from this accursed place."

"I will remain and watch over the area," Telok said. "There may be more of Zurvashi's worms yet to return to their camp."

"Two of Kaldarak's best will keep watch with you," Garahk said. "When the sun crests, they will guide you to our wild den."

"What of the…shrine?" Rekosh asked.

The thornskull pounded the blunt end of his spear on the ground. "Crushed to dust. The Blooddrinker Queen will not rise again while Kaldarak lives. This is true, beneath sun and sky. By my blood and fury."

"Queen of dust," Rekosh said with a snap of his fangs. And that quickly, he dismissed Zurvashi from his thoughts, shifting his attention to his mate. He brushed the long, black strands of her hair from her face and tucked them behind her rounded ear, his fingers lingering to caress it. "I will tend to you, *kir'ani vi'keishi.*"

Ahmya smiled and looped an arm around his head, tugging him down so she could touch her forehead to his headcrest. In a soft voice, she said, "And I will tend to you, my *luveen.*"

Rekosh closed his eyes. He felt every wound he'd suffered over the last few days. Every struggle weighed upon him, every stress clawed at him. But none of it mattered, because his mate was in his arms, alive, and they were going home.

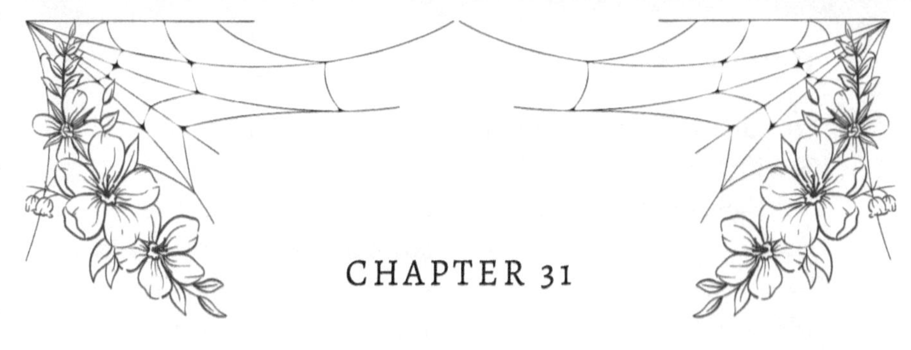

CHAPTER 31

AHMYA LOOKED out over the valley from her perch astride Rekosh's hindquarters.

She remembered the first time she'd seen Kaldarak. It had been wondrous and magical, like a fairytale village with its treehouses and rope bridges, backed by an ancient temple and a shimmering waterfall, where rainbows danced on the mist when the sun hit it just right.

But it had also been terrifying. A new, unknown place, populated by giant, spiky spider-beings who might not have been so accepting of a bunch of shadowstalkers and humans.

The terror had long since passed, but the beauty of Kaldarak had only grown.

Placing her hands on Rekosh's shoulders, Ahmya clenched her thighs on his hindquarters and lifted herself higher to peer past him, ignoring the aches and pains in her body. Despite the distance, she could see the thornskulls gathered on the main platform. She could even make out the humans standing amongst the vrix.

We are home.

She settled back down and smiled as excitement rushed

through her. She couldn't wait for this new beginning, this new life with Rekosh. "Will we be living in your den or mine?"

A thoughtful hum rumbled in Rekosh's chest as he followed Garahk and the other thornskulls down the path into the valley. "Nalaki may offer us a den for a mated pair, as she did for Ketahn and Ivy. But I would rather live in your den than mine, *kir'ani vi'keishi.*"

"Why mine?"

"Because it is made for your comfort and is where you grow your flowers. And because I want to be wrapped in your scent."

Ahmya blushed, but her smile widened. "Will you make us a fluffed silk bed? I don't think you'd fit on my little pallet."

He chittered. "Anything you desire, you shall have. Only the softest silk to cradle you, my *nyleea.*"

Ahmya slipped her arms around his chest and brushed her lips over the back of his shoulder. In a soft voice, she said, "As long as I have you, I don't need anything else."

He purred, settling his lower hands over hers and squeezing them gently. "You will have me always, Ahmya. Always."

"This is still strange," Urkot said from beside them.

"That they are finally mated?" Ketahn asked, turning to look at them from ahead before chittering. "I say it was overdue."

"No, not that. The way he is speaking." Urkot tilted his head as he regarded Rekosh. "He has given so few barbed words since yesterday that I fear he must have taken a blow to the head."

"They must have knocked all those needles right out."

Rekosh chittered and shook his head. "I thought it was fluffed silk in my skull, not needles."

Urkot thumped the ground with a leg. "Who could guess what was lost in that fluff? We will never know, as those needles have been replaced by soft, tender words."

"He sounds like Ketahn," Telok said from behind.

"What?" Ketahn and Rekosh demanded simultaneously.

"It is true!" Urkot swung his gaze to Ketahn before returning it to Rekosh. "Perhaps it is a trait of weavers?"

Rekosh let out an exaggerated huff. "We do not sound alike."

Telok let out a huff of his own. "You speak to Ahmya like Ketahn speaks to Ivy."

"There is nothing wrong with the way I speak to Ivy," said Ketahn.

Ahmya chuckled at their playful banter.

Rekosh's mandibles were raised in a smile, and she could feel the warmth and joy radiating from him. He and Ahmya had been through so much to get to this moment, but they hadn't let themselves be broken. They hadn't relinquished their happiness.

"Do not heed them, Ketahn," Rekosh said. "These two are simply bitter because they have only rocks and trees to speak to."

With a chitter, Urkot bumped a foreleg against Rekosh's. "Sharper, needlelegs, but not enough so to pierce my hide."

"I know of little that could, stoneskull. For now, I shall hold my barbs for my enemies." Rekosh glanced at Ahmya over his shoulder. A loving light gleamed in his crimson eyes. "My time with my *wife* shall be filled with sweet words and smiles."

Warmth spread through Ahmya, and her heart fluttered at the possessive way Rekosh said that human word. She'd never tire of hearing it.

After a brief trek across the valley floor, they reached the wide stairs that wound up and around the trunk of a huge tree, leading to the village.

As they climbed the steps, Ahmya pressed her body against Rekosh's warm back, resting her cheek against his hide, and tightened her embrace. She didn't cling to him due to fear of heights or falling, but in anticipation, in relief, and because finally, they were home. Together, and as mates.

Rekosh stroked her hands with his thumbs.

Thornskulls called out in greeting as the party traversed Kaldarak's bridges and platforms. The air was literally abuzz with excitement, thanks to the countless chattering vrix gathered at the city's heart.

Ahmya again peered around Rekosh as they approached the central platform, where Garahk and his mate denned. It was crowded with colorful thornskulls, a sea of summer and autumn. At the front of the group were several familiar faces.

Nalaki, *daiya* of Kaldarak, stood foremost. Two little white broodlings and a larger reddish brown one were huddled beside her legs, while two more ochre broodlings clung to her back and hindquarters. Ivy stood beside Nalaki, holding Akalahn in her arms, with a huge smile on her face. The other humans were clustered around them, a few of them waving.

When Rekosh strode onto the platform and came to a stop, he crouched and helped Ahmya dismount. She'd barely settled her feet on the ground before she was swept into a tight hug.

"You scared the fuck out of me!" Lacey rasped. "When we heard those things howling, we went back to look for you, but you were just gone, and… I shouldn't have left you. I shouldn't have gone back without you."

Ahmya hugged her friend back. "It's okay. We're okay. Rekosh kept me safe."

Lacey drew back and firmly cupped Ahmya's face. "Don't you *ever* scare me like that again."

There was true fear in Lacey's green eyes, and Ahmya's heart hurt for her.

"I can't make any promises," Ahmya said with a smile. "But I will try."

"I will always be her shield," Rekosh said. "I weave my words into a bond."

She looked at her mate. His crimson eyes bore as much conviction as his words.

"My turn!" Callie announced, slipping past Lacey to steal Ahmya into her own embrace. "You had us all so worried."

She eased back and ran her large brown eyes over Ahmya, frowning. "What *happened?*"

Ahmya knew what Callie was seeing, considering her blanket-turned-dress didn't hide much. Scratches and deep purple bruises covered her skin, and there was a silk bandage wrapped around her forearm where Rekosh had dressed her stab wound.

"It's…a long story," Ahmya said. "But I can say that I helped defeat the Queen of Ash and Bone."

"The what?"

"Let's just say there were some loyalists of Zurvashi who strung up her remains thinking that she would come back after a few…sacrifices."

Callie's eyes widened. "*What?*"

An alarmed murmur swept through the surrounding vrix as the thornskulls picked up on that name—Zurvashi.

Now standing beside his mate Nalaki, Garahk raised his arms, hushing the crowd. In a booming voice, he declared, "The Blooddrinker Queen is no more. We have slain her followers, and made her into dust."

Callie's black brows furrowed as she looked from Garahk to Ahmya. "What'd you do?"

Ahmya grinned. "Set that bitch on fire and sent her back to her grave."

A laugh burst from Callie as she drew Ahmya in for another hug. "Badass."

When Callie stepped back, Ivy stood before Ahmya, eyes brimming with tears. A sob escaped her as, holding Akalahn to her chest, she clutched Ahmya in a tight, one-armed embrace.

"I'm so glad you're okay," Ivy said, voice thick. "After losing Ella… I couldn't stand the thought of losing you too."

Ahmya's chest constricted, and tears burned her eyes. They

were all still mourning the loss of their friend, who'd been taken from them three months ago.

Taken by Zurvashi.

Only Ketahn and his sister, Ahnset, knew what had truly happened, and neither of them had been willing—or able—to describe Ella's death. But having seen Zurvashi in the flesh, Ahmya and the other humans knew the woman's end had been horrific and cruel.

What Ahmya had done to Zurvashi's remains hadn't taken away her sorrow, but it eased her grief a little to know that Ella would be remembered fondly while the reviled Queen of Ash and Bone was slowly forgotten.

"You didn't lose me," Ahmya said softly.

"I'm glad you're both safe and back with us." Ivy sniffled and eased back. She offered Ahmya a smile, then chuckled as she wiped her eyes. "I'm also a hormonal mess right now."

"You just had a baby. There's also nothing wrong with crying." Ahmya grinned and peered down at Akalahn, who was wide awake and alert. His violet eyes were bright against the black of his skin, curiously taking in the world around him.

Ketahn whisked Ivy into his arms, making her yelp, and clutched her to his chest. He leaned his head down and nuzzled her face. "But I do not like when my heartsthread cries."

Ivy laughed and pressed a kiss to his mouth as she curled her arm around his neck. "I missed you."

"And I missed both of you," he said after lifting his head, turning his adoring gaze to Akalahn.

Ahmya watched Ketahn stride away with his mate and broodling until Will and Diego approached her.

Diego shook his head as he looked Ahmya and Rekosh over. "Looks like you two had fun out there."

"Maybe a little," Ahmya said, pinching her finger and thumb close together.

"You'll swing by soon just so I can check everything out, right?"

Ahmya nodded. "I will."

He grinned. "I would have a much less eventful life if everyone knew how to have fun without getting hurt."

"I don't think anything could be more eventful than helping to deliver a human-vrix hybrid baby. I bet *that* was an experience."

Will laughed. "Yeah, that was something." He gently nudged Ahmya's arm with a closed fist. "Good to have you back, Ahmya. You too, Rekosh."

"We are glad to be back," Rekosh replied, tapping his foreleg against Will's calf.

Diego slipped his arm around Will's waist and drew him close.

Cole snickered. "You should have seen how freaked out Telok and Urkot were."

"He is speaking of us?" Telok asked in vrix.

"What is *freaked*?" Urkot asked simultaneously in English.

"It means you were so worried you were acting wildly," Callie said.

After Rekosh translated Callie's explanation, Telok folded his lower arms across his chest. "I was not acting wildly."

Lacey snorted. "Telok was so grumpy. Like far grumpier, bossier, and snappier than normal. And that's saying a lot."

Telok narrowed his eyes on her. "What did she say?"

"That you are sweeter than cloudfruit and more beautiful than the most vibrant suncrest blossom," Rekosh said.

"Why must you spin words from nothing?" Telok demanded with a low growl. "I know that is not what she said of me."

Lacey sauntered forward to stand in front of Telok. The black and green vrix lowered his arms and shifted his spear aside as he looked down at her, an uncharacteristic uncertainty creeping into his stance.

Smiling as sweetly at Telok as she had in Ketahn and Ivy's den all those days ago, Lacey pressed a finger to his chest. "Maybe…" She slowly grazed that finger up, trailing it along his scarred neck, until she turned her hand and held her fingertip beneath his chin. "You should learn my words so you can understand me."

A shudder rippled through Telok, who visibly tensed. He let out a harsh huff, grumbled something that may or may not have been actual words, and withdrew from Lacey abruptly. He strode away without looking back, his posture maintaining that tension until he was out of sight.

Lacey blinked, her hand hovering in the air briefly before she let it fall. "Is it me? Seriously, what is his problem? Everyone else teases him and it's fine, but I do it and he *nopes* right out of here."

"Oh, I have a few ideas," Cole said as he combed his hand through his hair.

Diego hummed. "Probably best not to take it personally, Lacey."

Lacey crossed her arms over her chest and scrunched her nose. "Kind of hard not to."

"Hey big guy," Callie said, poking Urkot's shoulder. She waved in the direction Telok had fled. "What's up with him?"

Urkot glanced at Lacey and chittered. "Telok is Telok."

Callie rolled her eyes. "That's sooooo helpful."

"Anyway!" Cole stepped up to Ahmya, threw his arms around her, and swept her off her feet, causing her to squeak. "Welcome home!"

Ahmya laughed as the world twirled around her. "Cole!"

Their spin halted abruptly when one of Rekosh's hands clamped down on Cole's shoulder.

Eyebrows shooting up, Cole lowered Ahmya onto her feet and retreated, displaying his palms placatingly. "Easy, man. We're just friends."

Rekosh curled an arm around Ahmya's waist and drew her into the shelter of his body. "And she is *mine*."

He wrapped his arms securely around her. Even his claspers brushed her hips possessively. Smiling, Ahmya leaned back against him, folded her arms atop his, and tipped her head back to look up at her mate. Those crimson eyes, once so frightening but now endearing, gazed down at her.

Cole laughed. "It's about fucking time."

"Yes," Rekosh said. "It is."

When he broke eye contact with her, Rekosh looked out at the crowd around them, at all the faces that had become so familiar, and lifted his mandibles in a smile. She felt a soft purr in his chest.

"Kaldarak. My friends, my family," he called in vrix, his voice deep, smooth, powerful, confident. "I, Rekosh tes Loshei'ani Ul'okari, have taken Ahmya Hayashi as my mate. I have conquered her. I have claimed her."

His eyes dipped, meeting hers and holding them. "My little flower, my heartsthread. My *nyleea*. My wife. My everything. And before all, I give myself to her until all the world unravels around us…and even then, I will find some way to keep our spirits stitched together."

A chorus of cheers rang out from the thornskulls.

Tears gathered in Ahmya's eyes as happiness bloomed within her, so radiant and warm. When she'd boarded the *Somnium*, she hadn't dared hope that she would find such happiness. She'd never thought she would have such deep, devoted, fervent love.

But it had found her. Yes, it had come at the bottom of a mucky pit in the rusted wreck of a spacecraft that had crashed on an alien planet, but it had found her nonetheless. And now that she had it, she was never going to let go.

She reached up and cupped the side of his face. He nuzzled her palm without looking away from her.

In slow but clear vrix, she said, "I, Ahmya Hayashi, have taken Rekosh tes Loshei'ani Ul'okari as my mate. I have been conquered. I have been claimed. And I am loved."

With a growl, Rekosh spun her and lifted her into his arms, clutching her close as his hard mouth pressed against hers.

The cheers from the thornskulls swelled, punctuated by them thumping their legs on the platform and making all Kaldarak shake with joy.

All that pounding couldn't match the thrilling thumps of her heart as she returned Rekosh's kiss.

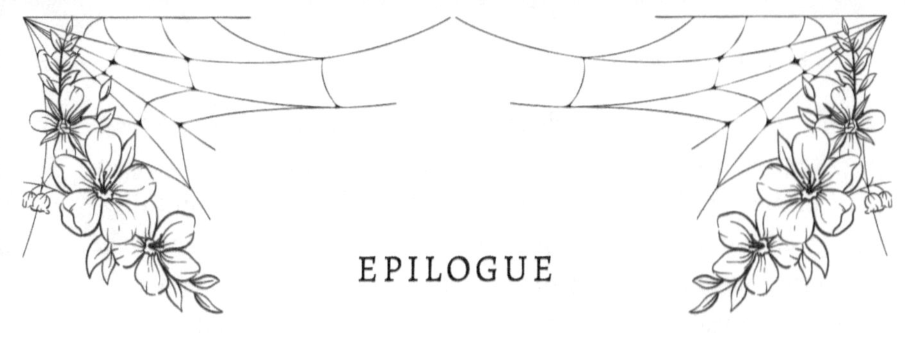

EPILOGUE

Rekosh loved when Ahmya was awake. He loved seeing her smile, seeing her deep brown eyes light up when she laughed, loved when she looked at him with desirous heat in her gaze. He loved the way she touched him, the way she kissed him, the sound of her voice as she spoke to him.

But he couldn't deny that he loved these quiet moments with her too, while she slept.

She lay atop him now, arms snug around his torso and cheek resting upon his chest. Her slow, soft breaths fanned across his hide, and her bare skin was delightfully warm. Even in the dull gray light of the approaching dawn, she was radiant.

Rekosh canted his head and ran his eyes over his mate. He loved seeing her features this relaxed and serene. He loved how her expression would subtly change as she dreamed, and the little moans she sometimes let out that made his stem ache. Loved how she reached for him when he wasn't lying with her and how she clung to him when he was.

He loved her.

Every such moment, every such expression, every emotion —it was all dear to him, all precious.

And it was only made more so by the path that had led them here. All the trials they'd overcome, the dangers they'd survived, all the days he'd spent longing for her, awaiting the right time; it all combined to make everything they shared now all the more meaningful. No one, whether vrix or human, could say Rekosh and Ahmya hadn't earned this happiness together.

Still, he knew their happiness and safety were not certainties, and had vowed to himself to never cease working, to never cease fighting, for them. For Ahmya.

Though the last thing he wanted to do was be apart from his mate, he'd gone out twice in the last moon cycle, along with Telok, Urkot, and groups of thornskull warriors, to seek signs of Zurvashi's followers in the surrounding jungle. They'd found nothing, but they would remain vigilant. He wouldn't allow his mate and the place they called home to be attacked.

Rekosh would face any danger to shield Ahmya from harm.

He found himself resisting the growing urge to trace her delicate features with the pad of a finger, to shift his arms, which enwrapped her securely, so he could caress her body with all four hands.

But he could not yet bring himself to wake her, not while she slept so soundly in his arms.

He barely held back a chitter. He'd crafted a luxurious nest of fluffed silk, the softest possible, to cradle her, just as she'd asked of him. Yet he could not recall a full night thus far during which she hadn't slept atop him.

That filled him with pride and warmth. Rekosh didn't merely tend to his mate's comfort, he *was* her comfort.

With no small amount of difficulty, he shifted his gaze away from her and forced it around their den. He'd studied this place more times than he could count, had arranged most of its contents with his own hands, yet his awe never diminished when he beheld it.

This was *their* den. *Their* home. A place only for Rekosh and Ahmya.

As he'd guessed, Nalaki had offered them a larger den, one that was nearer to Ketahn and Ivy's. This was easily thrice the size of his former dwelling, offering abundant space for a mated pair…with extra to spare.

Rekosh's loom and tools had their place along one wall, and Ahmya's collection of tools and supplies were stored opposite them. The area between was all comfort and color—brightly dyed silks on the walls, dangling from the ceiling, adorning surfaces, and arranged in piles to create sitting places, and flowers, both fresh and dried, filling the air with vibrancy and fragrance from their places on little shelves and dangling from the ceiling. Ahmya's wooden planters hung in the windows, brimming with plants and more flowers.

His gaze settled on the tall structure against the wall near their nest. A wardrobe. Despite his assumption given the name, it was not a box for holding weapons, but rather for clothing. Cole had built it for Ahmya as what the humans called a *housewarming* gift.

Rekosh knew Cole had no intention of trying to steal Ahmya, that his mate and the male human were friends, but his instincts often stirred when Cole was near her. For Ahmya's sake, he stifled those instincts.

And, though he admitted it only to himself—and only begrudgingly—Cole had proven to be both talented in woodcraft and thoughtful in the gifts he made for his friends. This wardrobe had carvings that were surprisingly intricate despite being a bit crude, and its doors opened and closed smoothly thanks to what Cole called *hinges*. It also happened to hold the clothing Rekosh had made for his mate perfectly, letting the silks hang so they didn't wrinkle by being folded.

But Cole wasn't the only one who'd crafted a human object for Ahmya. During one of their long conversations, she'd told

Rekosh about a swing her father's sire had made for her. A simple thing—just a flat wood plank and some rope, suspended from a tall tree. But that simple thing had brought Ahmya boundless joy.

So Rekosh had made a swing for her, right outside their den. The sturdiest braided silk rope and a wood plank that Cole had only *helped* to shape. Rekosh had also made another addition, just for Ahmya—a silk cushion for her comfort.

Her delight upon seeing the gift had warmed his hearts. He loved watching her swing upon it. Loved how brightly she smiled, the way her hair flowed in the air, the way her eyes sparkled. He loved how free she looked, how uninhibited.

When she was swinging, with her feet dangling beneath her and her skirt fluttering behind her, she looked like she was flying.

This was where he spent most of his time, where he wanted to be. Talking with her, basking in the sunlight streaming through the windows with her, sharing meals with her. Telling her stories and listening to hers. Accompanying her as she tended her plants and the garden she had established outside. Weaving new clothing for her and teaching her how to weave.

Sharing his life with her in every way possible.

When he had first left Takarahl all those years ago to fight in Zurvashi's war, Rekosh had learned very quickly, very harshly, that the world was much larger than the city where he'd hatched. He'd learned that there was so much more to life than weaving.

Some part of him had yearned for adventure, for exploration. The war had shown him the brutality that often came with it. He'd gone home afterward feeling...lost. Out of place. Like there was nowhere he truly belonged, nowhere truly for him. He and his friends had proven themselves in battle time and again, but what had that won them? They'd all carried deep scars, both seen and unseen. They'd all returned weighed down by pain. Even the thing he'd loved most, weaving, had become habit, nothing more than the way he'd passed the time.

And then one day, Ketahn had asked Rekosh, Urkot, and Telok to help him with something of which he could not speak. Rekosh would have done anything his friend asked, but he could not deny that the intrigue and mystery had thrilled him.

He never could've guessed what Ketahn would show them. Meeting Ivy had made Rekosh question everything he'd thought he'd known, but when he'd first laid eyes upon Ahmya...

Everything had changed.

Rekosh's mandibles rose as he hooked strands of her hair with a claw and gently brushed them out of her face.

Ahmya had reignited a spark inside him that he'd believed forever extinguished. She had inspired him, driven him, long before he'd confessed any feelings to her. Long before he even understood what he'd been feeling.

As different as she was, he'd seen only beauty in her from the start. Where others might've seen a slight, frail creature, he had seen strength and grace, had seen perceptive intelligence. He'd seen a kindred spirit.

Though he hadn't realized it at the time, he'd seen his mate.

Now, finally, he was where he belonged. He was home. With his mate, his love, his everything. He had found his purpose. Had found himself. He did not envy Telok and Ketahn for the freedom they enjoyed by delving into the Tangle as hunters, because he was no longer trapped.

He was Rekosh. A hunter and warrior when necessary, a weaver at heart...and more than that, mate to the most wondrous female. Husband to the most beautiful wife.

Unable to hold himself back any longer, Rekosh dipped his head and pressed his mouth to her forehead, lightly scraping it back and forth.

Ahmya stirred with a soft, throaty hum that sent a pulse of lust to his stem. "Is it morning?"

"Nearly, *kir'ani vi'keishi.*" He combed his claws through her hair until they reached her back, where he grazed them across her skin, following the gentle, graceful slope of her spine. She shivered. When he reached the small of her back, he teasingly ran them lower, and lower, and lower. He paused, stroking a claw back and forth along the top of her ass.

Ahmya's breath hitched, and her body tensed. She raised her head, and her eyes, dark pools reflecting the red glow of his eyes in the early morning gloom, met his. "Why are you awake so early?"

"I wanted to watch the morning sun fall across your skin and set you aglow," he said, smoothing his lower hands up the backs of her thighs to settle upon her ass. He squeezed the soft flesh, massaging it.

"Oh..."

Though Rekosh could not see her blush, he felt it in the warming of her skin against his hide. He trailed his claws back up along her spine. A shiver coursed through her, and he felt her skin prickle into tiny bumps. He loved how responsive her body was to his touch. He deepened the massage, spreading her ass wide and grinding her sex against his slit.

"Rekosh," Ahmya moaned, curling her fingers against his chest. The bite of her blunt nails on his hide sent another surge to his stem, and anticipation buzzed through him in its wake.

"Ah, my wife... I cannot resist when you say my name like that." He tangled the fingers of an upper hand in her hair and tipped her head back, exposing her throat. She gasped, eyes squeezing shut as his tongue slipped out to lavish that supple flesh. Her salty-sweet taste danced on his tongue, rousing a deep, demanding hunger in him.

Ahmya's nipples hardened against his chest, and her breath

quickened. When Rekosh inhaled, he drew in all the now familiar scents of their den—but her fragrance was foremost, and it already bore more than a hint of her arousal.

"Speak my name again, my *nyleea*," he growled against her neck, again grinding her slick pussy over his parting slit.

"Rekosh…" she rasped, body trembling.

"Yes." He flicked his tongue over her chin, then stroked it along her soft lips. Untangling his fingers from her hair, he moved his hand down to cradle her small breast in his palm, brushing his thumb over the taut nipple before pinching it and eliciting a sharp gasp from her. "Tell your *luveen* how much you need him."

"I need you. I need you so much." Arching into his touch, she tightened her thighs around his sides and undulated her hips, dragging a deep groan from his throat. Her lashes fluttered open, and she met his gaze. "I need you inside me."

By the Eight, he needed the same thing. His throbbing stem was trapped behind his slit, its ache permeating him to his core, strengthening with every beat of his hearts. It needed to be released; he needed release.

Fire roared through his veins, its heat intensified by Ahmya's scent enveloping him, suffusing him, filling his mind with a lustful haze.

Ahmya rocked, gliding her sex back and forth, spreading her nectar over him as soft moans spilled past her lips. "Please," she begged. "I need to feel your cock inside me, my *luveen*."

With a growl, he shifted his hands from her ass to her hips, grasped them firmly, and lifted her. His stem erupted from his slit with a suddenness and power that sent a shudder through him. Its head pressed to her slick slit.

Slowly, Rekosh drew his mate down atop him, pushing his cock into her.

Ahmya bit her bottom lip with a moan as he stretched her,

and though her eyelids lowered, she didn't close her eyes, didn't look away from him. Little by little, he eased deeper. Though he'd been inside his mate countless times, her pussy was still tight around his girth, gripping him in its delicious heat.

And nothing felt as good as this. Nothing came close.

Nothing ever would.

She panted, clawing at his chest, and he felt every quiver of her body as she bore down upon him, taking him deeper, and deeper, and deeper. "Rekosh…"

Hearing his name spoken in so desperate a plea snapped his remaining restraint. Snarling her name, he lifted her off him again and slammed her back down, burying himself in her as deep as he could, lodging his bulges inside her. Ahmya fell upon him with a gasp.

The breath fled his lungs. Her heat surrounded him, clutched at him, devoured him, and he hung suspended in bliss.

At that moment, he existed only in that connection between their bodies. In the raw sensation, the blinding pleasure, the pounding of their hearts, the interwoven threads of their souls.

When the moment passed, he found himself looking up at her face. He brushed her hair away from her cheek, banded his arms around her, and drew her down to press his mouth against hers. She returned the kiss, her soft lips moving over the hardness of his mouth. Their tongues sought each other, stroking, caressing, and entwining. And he savored her sweetness.

When he broke the kiss, he touched his headcrest to her forehead, his breaths ragged. "My heartsthread, my love… You are my home. Our hearts will forever beat as one, and our souls will forever remain tethered."

"I love you," Ahmya whispered, her fingers stroking the sides of his face as she began rolling her hips. "I love you so much."

Pleasure thrummed through him, sharpening with each glide of her wet slit. Pressure built in his stem, and the haze in his mind thickened, but he resisted the frenzy. He would savor this moment with her for as long as he could.

First and foremost, we want to say thank you. Thank you for your support, your patience, your understanding. And thank you for giving our spiders (vrix) a chance from the very beginning. We can't tell you how much it means to us that so many of you love our characters and the stories we write.

This book was a labor of love and so, so many tears. We've struggled with books in the past, but *The Weaver* was the hardest book of all to write. It was discouraging to sit at our desks for hours each day to only achieve 1,000 words (if that), with every one of them being a fight to get onto the page. When I say there were tears...I'm not kidding. We cried. We felt so defeated and depressed, and we were beginning to resent the book as time went by.

That was not something we wanted at all. We love this world and these characters, and we wanted to tell Rekosh and Ahmya's story and give them the happily ever after they deserved. We knew that if we continued down the path we were following, it would bleed into the book, and we didn't want that to happen. We knew we had to step back. So we set the book aside. We know many of you were disappointed and saddened. Hell, we were upset with ourselves and felt like failures. But we knew it was for the best.

After working on something else, we attempted to return to *The Weaver* because we felt like that was what was expected of us. Unfortunately, we ran into the same problem. We received messages, emails, and comments on socials that were not very nice. This did nothing to help our mental health. At that point, we knew that we could not come back to The Weaver until we were ready. We could not and would not force the book.

And we are glad that we waited. Because when we finally felt that burst of inspiration to write Rekosh and Ahmya's story, we enjoyed the journey, and the words came so much easier. That's not to say we still didn't have struggles, because we did, but it was nothing like before. We loved spending time with the two of them as their relationship blossomed, and their scenes together brought smiles to our faces. We are immensely proud and happy to have written this book as it was meant to be.

So again, thank you for sticking with us. We can only hope that you loved *The Weaver* as well.

We also wanted to send out a thank you to our sensitivity readers, Angela McDuffie and Tomomi! Your feedback on Japanese culture and language was incredibly helpful, and your suggestions were absolutely wonderful.

If you're wondering who's next in The Vrix series... It's going to be Urkot and Callie! We already have so many ideas for their book, and we're hyped to begin it.

And if you could, we'd love it if you left a review. Even better would be sharing your love by recommending our books to others. Word of mouth is seriously the best thing you can do for an author.

To stay up to date with what we're working on, our progress, and any other updates we might have, be sure to join our newsletter! Don't worry, we don't spam. We send out a monthly newsletter on the first of each month, and a few others here and there if we have a sale or something to announce. We also have a reader group on Facebook if you'd like to join that as well.

Again, thank you all! We can't thank you enough for your support.

The Delver

The Hunter

<u>THE CURSED ONES</u>

<u>His Darkest Craving</u>

<u>His Darkest Desire</u>

<u>ALIENS AMONG US</u>

<u>Taken by the Alien Next Door</u>

<u>Stalked by the Alien Assassin</u>

<u>Claimed by the Alien Bodyguard</u>

<u>Saved by the Alien Crime Boss</u>

<u>STANDALONE TITLES</u>

<u>Claimed by an Alien Warrior</u>

<u>Dustwalker</u>

<u>Escaping Wonderland</u>

<u>Yearning For Her</u>

<u>The Warlock's Kiss</u>

<u>Ice Bound: Short Story</u>

<u>ISLE OF THE FORGOTTEN</u>

<u>Make Me Burn</u>

<u>Make Me Hunger</u>

<u>Make Me Whole</u>

<u>Make Me Yours</u>

<u>VALOS OF SONHADRA COLLABORATION</u>

<u>Tiffany Roberts - Undying</u>

<u>Tiffany Roberts - Unleashed</u>

ABOUT THE AUTHOR

Tiffany Roberts is the pseudonym for Tiffany and Robert Freund, a husband and wife writing duo. The two have always shared a passion for reading and writing, and it was their dream to combine their mighty powers to create the sorts of books they want to read. They write character driven sci-fi and fantasy romance, creating happily-ever-afters for the alien and unknown.

Sign up for our Newsletter!
Check out our social media sites and more!
http://www.authortiffanyroberts.com